UNBOUND

UNBOUND

A Forbidden Bond Novel

Cat Miller

This is a work of fiction. Names, characters, organizations, places, events, and incidents are either products of the author's imagination or are used fictitiously.

Published by Montlake Romance, Seattle

www.apub.com

ISBN-13: 9781477818329
ISBN-10: 1477818324

Cover design by Eileen Carey

Library of Congress Control Number: 2013919706

Printed in the United States of America

I dedicate this book to the memory of my daddy.

He told me I could do anything, and
he believed that was true.

Griffin sat in a rocking chair, holding his newborn daughter. She was only hours old. He laughed quietly to himself, trying not to wake her mother, Tessa.

He pulled off the little knit cap on her tiny head to stroke her hair. He had always hated the white streaks in his own dark brown hair. His mother had always called them birthmarks. His father had told him they were very rare and were believed to be a sign of great power among their kind. So, when Griffin's daughter emerged into the world with a head full of dark hair with little white streaks, his heart swelled with pride. She was the most beautiful thing he had ever seen.

Her name was Soleil. It meant sun. He chose the name because surely the world would revolve around the perfect child in his arms.

Just then, his pride and joy looked up at him with the palest blue eyes that resembled the lightest of aquamarine jewels. Tessa had smiled and teased him earlier, saying they were the color of Windex. She thought it was funny. Griffin did not. The baby had Tessa's eyes, and staring into them took him back in time to the night he found Tessa walking down a dark, abandoned street.

She was a petite girl with dark blond hair hanging in loose waves down her back, almost to her waist. She wore a dark jacket that was too light for the season and a snug pair of jeans. The sway of her hips drew his eyes to her feminine curves.

As he got closer to his prey, he could feel her warmth and the blood pulsing through her body urging him to feed. It made his mouth water and his pulse quicken.

She turned down a dark alley as he stalked her quietly. Could she make this any easier? Hard to believe no one ever told the little thing to stay away from dark alleys at night.

As he turned the corner, Griffin knew he would catch her before she reached the end of the alley. He was surprised to find her standing there, among the empty bottles and trash blowing in the wind, with both her hands on her hips, smiling.

The streetlight closest to the alley shone on her face, illuminating those pale-blue eyes. They were so clear, he feared she might have the ability to see straight into his soul without all the color of normal eyes to block her view. He felt naked in her stunning gaze.

Being a vampire meant he was a natural hunter, aware of his surroundings and ready for anything at all times. However, at that moment, everything faded into the background. A bomb could have dropped at his feet and he would not have noticed the blast.

"I was wondering when you were going to show up." The little blonde grinned up at him.

Confused, he searched the vacant street behind him. As he scanned and listened for witnesses, he wondered why he felt so off guard. "Are you waiting for someone to meet you?"

"No. I have been waiting for you. You are the man of my dreams, so to speak. Would you like to walk with me?" She cocked her head to the side in a most endearing way, as if they had spoken a thousand times before and she knew just how to lure him away. "I promise I won't bite," she joked, as she started down the alley and turned her back to him.

He could overtake her at any time, but the need to be closer to her was stronger than the hunger for her blood. She piqued his curiosity. What was wrong with him? Humans had never drawn him as she had. His family had taught him from birth that they were cattle to be maintained and respected for the gift they give, but nothing more.

Moreover, how could she possibly have been waiting for him? She must think I'm someone else, *he thought to himself. The thought sent an odd wave of jealousy over him. It didn't matter. Why should he care if she were expecting to meet a human male?*

She strolled down the alley without a care, and he began to follow, as if he were the tide being pulled by her gravity. He felt a sudden surge of anger at her arrogance. She could not lead him, Griffin Vaughn, around by the nose like some weak, human male. He caught up with her in less than a heartbeat and spun her around by her arm so she could see her predator's true face. His fangs extended, and he knew his dark blue irises had darkened to solid black. She needed to develop some respect for the danger he displayed. He would be sure she never acted so foolishly again.

"I don't think I'm the male you were waiting for, little one," he snarled into her face.

"Of course you are. You just don't know it, yet." Her voice wobbled.

"You have no idea what you're dealing with, little one. I'm not one of your timid males." A growl came from deep in his throat.

Why had he done that? He really didn't want to scare her away, and he knew better than to reveal himself to a human. Vampires enthralled their donors and sent them on their way with no memory of the feeding, but she had him so twisted in the space of a minute that he'd exposed himself.

Tessa put both of her fists against his abdomen and pushed with all her might to put space between the two of them. It didn't move Griffin at all, but the motion forced Tessa back against the cold brick wall behind her.

"I'm not afraid of you! If you wanted to hurt me, I'd be dead by now, or at least unconscious from blood loss," she stuttered.

He stepped in closer so they were chest to chest, and she had to crane her neck up to look into his black eyes. The fangs he had on display for her to admire and fear were just inches from her face.

"Are you quite sure about that, little one?" he hissed.

He could hear her suck wind between her glossy, bow-shaped lips, and her heart sped at his touch. She composed herself instantly and laid her head back, turning her face to the side in order to bare her neck to him. Her hair fell down her chest from her shoulder. The smell of vanilla wafted up to him. She was calling his bluff. At that moment, his mouth watered for an entirely different reason.

"Do it, then." There was uncertainty mixed with the challenge in her eyes. "I don't have all night to hang out in a dark alley with you," she said, facing the direction they had come from. Her breath suddenly sounded too rapid.

She stayed motionless for several moments, her neck splayed out before him in what felt like a dare, as he looked down on her in wonder. Humans weren't supposed to know about vampires, but her behavior and lack of shock led him to believe she was fully aware.

"I didn't think so, tough guy," she whispered, as he finally allowed her to push him away. The smug glare she tossed him made his body quicken. So arrogant. So beautiful.

Suddenly, there was a noise on the street. The humans began to filter out of the various watering holes and nightclubs nearby. She stepped around him and started to walk away, expecting him to follow. He did so without pause.

Tessa's weak voice pulled him out of his reverie.

"You know, if you don't put her down, she'll be the most spoiled child either of our worlds has ever known," Tessa teased.

Her weakness concerned him. It had been a long, hard labor for her after nine months of the baby draining her of the blood she also needed to survive. Vampire women would have fed more frequently to replenish the loss, but Tessa didn't have that option. He had arranged for regular transfusions, but it still hadn't been enough. She suffered it all with a smile and joyful expectation of their coming child, and he could do nothing but comfort and try to support her. When Tessa went into labor, he felt absolutely useless. She'd assured him that all women experienced this during childbirth but it wasn't true. Not in today's world of modern medicine, anyway. But there was no such thing as pain medication in a secret home birth. She'd had to endure it with nothing stronger than ibuprofen and some breathing exercises.

He worried about how her body would deal with it all. Carrying and delivering a vampire baby was very different from a human child. She had spent the last three months of her pregnancy in bed. Griffin had never known of a vampire siring a child with a human, but from his research in preparation for the event, he learned that the mothers didn't fare well. They usually died in childbirth, and the babies didn't do much better. In the records he reviewed at the Council Hall library, there had been no known surviving births.

"I fully intend to ensure that is the case. She will be the most pampered little girl in existence. So what does it matter if I hold her all day?" he whispered, as the baby had fallen asleep.

"I love you, Griffin," Tessa told him.

"I will love you always. Why do you sound so sad? Are you in pain? Can I get you anything?" Griffin's heart ached at her weakened state and his inability to do anything for her. If he had been able to stand up to his parents, she would have had the best medical care available to humans, but admitting he was bound to a human wasn't a possibility yet. His parents expected him to bond with the female of their choice, and he'd been ready and willing to do just that, until the night he met a pretty little human in a dark alley.

He felt like he was living on borrowed time because eventually he would be forced to admit his betrayal of the betrothal agreement and his family honor. His odd behavior and frequent absence were already drawing attention to him. Griffin's parents had no love for humans other than as food. Sadly, he just didn't trust them not to have Tessa murdered in an attempt to salvage his honor. Coming clean about his new mate while she was pregnant was a risk he wasn't willing to take. Keeping her hidden was the safest bet until he found a way to deal with his parents.

"No. I'm fine, but I had a terrible dream. I'm afraid this time of joy is about to end for us. We are about to be separated." She shivered and winced with the pain the movement caused her battered body.

Tessa was what humans referred to as psychic. She dreamt of things yet to come and regularly had feelings about people or things that proved amazingly insightful. She usually knew when Griffin needed to leave to meet his parents before suspicions arose. She knew little things, such as a phone that would soon ring, and bigger things, like when he would need to leave her for a time. That prediction was the last thing Griffin wanted to hear. He would not leave his family. The thought nearly broke him. He watched a single tear slide down Tessa's too-pale cheek.

Just then, the door flew open and Griffin jumped to his feet, turning so fast to shield their child that Tessa couldn't even follow his movements. In the doorway stood Mason, Griffin's lifelong best friend. He was the only person who knew about Tessa and their situation. He had helped hide Tessa and had procured a midwife with knowledge of both human and vampire births to assist with the delivery.

"We have a problem. Griffin, you need to come with me now, or they will come looking for you," Mason quickly explained.

"Who will come looking for him?" Tessa demanded.

"The council," Mason replied. "I believe they may know."

"That's not possible! We've been very careful!" Griffin argued.

"I'm afraid the midwife has broken her vow of silence. It seems there's more money to be made by talking to the right people. We have to leave *now*, Griffin," Mason growled. "We will deal with her treachery later."

Stunned by the news, Griffin handed the baby to Tessa after kissing her tiny forehead and gently brushing his hand over the white streaks in her hair. Then he brushed his lips over Tessa's and promised, "I will be back as soon as I can. I love you both more than my own life." He kissed her sweetly one more time and ran out the door, eyes glistening.

Tessa watched Griffin leave, and the nightmare of just moments ago returned to her in a painful rush. She'd dreamt of being ripped away from Griffin, and no matter how she fought, she just couldn't hold on to him. Tessa knew it wasn't just a dream; it was a premonition. Mason was watching her with a remorseful expression. He dropped the small duffel bag he had carried with him onto the end of her bed. He stepped forward and bent to kiss the sleeping babe on the head.

"I'm so very sorry about this, Tessa. I hope this will help. It's the very least I can do for you and my godchild. Please open it quickly and leave as soon as possible. There will be a car waiting for you outside." He left, closing the door softly.

Tessa opened the bag and retrieved a letter placed on top of stacks of cash and a gun. Still in shock, she opened the letter and, as she read it, began to cry.

Several months later . . .

Griffin was losing his grip on sanity. He'd been searching for his missing mate and their baby for months. He'd had a hell of a fight with his parents the day Soleil was born. They wanted the baby, but he didn't know why, since they were adamant that admitting a human into their family was unacceptable. Griffin didn't want to believe they would have his child murdered. They would likely hide his baby girl from the prying eyes of vampire society. They wouldn't want their house name tainted by a half-breed baby. His mate, on the other hand, would likely not fare as well. To buy him some time to move his family, Griffin promised to go get the baby and bring her back for their inspection. The midwife who'd betrayed his trust had disappeared, and he had to relocate his family before his parents found her, because she'd delivered the baby in their home. They had no idea where he and Tessa had been living since their mating. He had a separate property purchased in Mason's name. He'd finally made it home hours after leaving his weak mate to fend for herself with a newborn vampire who was, so far, refusing to suckle her human mother's breast. Griffin feared what he would find in the condo. What he did find was worse than anything he ever could have imagined: Tessa and their baby were gone. They'd just disappeared. Griffin destroyed his condo in a blind rage directed at his meddling parents. He could feel the warm buzz of his mate's soul in the back of his mind, but he could no longer reach her. The connection their bond had created became weaker with distance, but they were in love, so it never mattered to Griffin. Their emotional connection was stronger than blood. But that hadn't helped him find her in the months that had passed since that day. The longer they were apart, the more Griffin questioned Tessa's safety. At times, he felt her and knew she was safe—sad and lonely, but safe. Other times, he feared his heart was playing tricks on his mind.

His mother viewed this time in his life as a youthful rebellion that he would regret when he was older. She had made it her mission to save her son from a life of scorn and embarrassment.

Griffin was at his parents' home in upstate New York. He returned with them from a council meeting instead of going to his own home, at his father's request. His father, Lloyd, a tall, attractive, middle-aged-looking vampire with the same dark hair and steely blue eyes as Griffin, entered the room after wrapping up a business call. He caught Griffin staring out the window onto the perfectly manicured lawn, which somehow remained green even in the winter. His mother would have it no other way.

"Griffin, my boy, it's really past time for you to stop bereaving the loss of your little fling," Lloyd scoffed.

Griffin interrupted. "Father, I don't want to have this conversation with you again. You've made your feelings abundantly clear."

Lloyd shook his head in disgust. "I have been avoiding telling you this, in hopes you would move on willingly, but it seems you will not, until you know the truth." Lloyd paused. "Your mother began to search, against my wishes, after we were made aware of your indiscretions and you returned without the child, as we had requested. She is very resourceful when she wants something," Lloyd huffed.

"I bet she is. She learned from the best," Griffin replied sarcastically.

In a flash, his father crossed the room and dug his nails deep into Griffin's shoulder. Griffin went to his knees with a yelp of pain.

Griffin was strong, but he was still very young. Unlike humans, who became weaker as they aged, vampires became more powerful.

"Listen to me, boy! I have had enough of your disrespect! I am your father and a leader of our race! You would be wise to remember that and act accordingly!" He released Griffin and helped him calmly to his feet, as if he hadn't just nearly snapped his shoulder. "It is time for you to take your rightful position on the council, and you are not nearly ready. My patience grows thin, Griffin."

Carrying a basket of fresh-cut flowers, Griffin's mother, Adele, entered the room through the French doors that led out to the garden and the hothouse. Adele was a tall, statuesque woman with golden-blond hair in a tidy twist at her neck and warm, caramel-brown eyes. Her heels showed no signs of dirt, in spite of her romp through the garden. She always moved as if she were floating rather than walking.

"What seems to be the problem here, darlings?" his mother asked, sounding equal parts concerned and annoyed. She was a lady above all else, and she never tolerated dramatics.

She put down the flowers and removed her gardening gloves. As she moved closer, she eyed the new holes and fresh blood on Griffin's shirt. The wounds had already begun to heal. Her eyes widened as she looked to her husband. Griffin would not allow anyone but his father to attack him without retaliation, and she knew it.

"Adele, love, your timing is perfect. I was just about to inform Griffin of the result of your search," he purred to her. His father knew she would be displeased with him for ruining her son's tailored shirt. His father avoided upsetting his mate at all cost.

"Everything is fine, Mother. We were just doing a little male bonding. Why don't you come tell me about this big secret you and Father have been keeping?" he insisted.

"Well, darling," she stuttered. Her uncharacteristic stumbling sent a chill over Griffin. "Give me a moment to go gather the information I've been collecting." She left the room quickly, and Griffin looked to his father with questioning eyes.

"I think it's best if we wait for your mother to return. Otherwise, I'm sure you won't see the truth."

Adele returned carrying a large, brown envelope and wearing a solemn look on her perfect face. She sat in the chair closest to Griffin and beckoned him to sit across from her, which he did. Griffin's father walked to his side slightly behind him, with a comforting hand on the shoulder he had sunk his talons into just moments before. It was unsettling to Griffin. His parents were not the comforting type. He knew it wasn't a good sign.

Adele began, "The day we found out about your little secret, and you did not retrieve the child as requested, I began to search for her. I couldn't very well have the child raised by your human pet."

"Mother, please!" Griffin shouted. He'd had enough of their prejudices.

"Hush, son, and listen to me! This will be hard enough without your interruptions," Adele barked. She continued without pause. "The girl called a cab to carry her to the human hospital. When the driver was questioned, he revealed that he was uncomfortable driving the girl, given she had no car seat for the child. She pleaded with him, saying she couldn't get the child to nurse. The driver noted the pale and generally weak condition of the girl and thought better of leaving her behind. He helped the girl into the ER and left."

Adele paused, and for the first time in Griffin's memory she looked nervous. She cleared her throat, another thing he'd never heard her do, before she continued. She handed him a stack of papers. "I acquired documentation from a source at the human hospital. Apparently, the girl was hemorrhaging. The delivery had taken the ultimate toll on her body. She succumbed to the injuries she received during birth and died in the ER."

Adele handed Griffin a death certificate for Tessa Lynn Taylor. Tears began to stream down his angry face, and he did not attempt to wipe them away.

Adele continued. "The child lived two more days before she also lost her battle. The cause of death is listed as failure to thrive." She then handed Griffin the birth and death certificates for Soleil Taylor. The documents both listed the father as unknown.

"It's really too bad we didn't find the child sooner. The idiots at the human hospital had no idea she needed blood to survive. The girl's parents died years ago, and she had no other family besides an older stepsister. By the time the authorities were able to locate the stepsister, the bodies had been cremated, as per hospital policy in cases of unclaimed persons. The sister collected the ashes and had them buried in her father's family plot."

Lloyd stepped up, coolly patting Griffin on the back, and said, "Well, now that you know the truth, you can stop all this foolishness."

Griffin's body shook with sobs as his mother went to the window, appearing bored with it all.

His father continued. "We have done all we can to keep this mistake quiet so your name won't be damaged. But people are starting to ask questions about your behavior. It's time for you to move on, son. We have had a binding arranged for you since you were small. Richard Ashburn wants to know if we are going to back out of our agreement. His daughter, Sarah, has waited patiently for too long now. Will you finally do your duty and stop shaming our family name?"

Griffin got up on wobbly legs, still sobbing, and quietly left the room. He clutched the papers to his chest as if they were all he had left in the world. He didn't make a sound as he retreated to the bedroom of his childhood and collapsed onto the small bed. His feet hung way over the footboard.

He wept all night, trying to understand how he could've been unaware of his family's death and why he still felt a connection to Tessa. The only conclusion he could come to was the fact that their bond had not been as strong as he had expected. The emotional bond could not have been stronger, but her humanity had impeded the blood bond.

When morning came, he emerged, red-eyed and defeated. He found his parents in the kitchen, trading sections of the newspaper.

"Mother, Father, I am ready to do my duties as your son and carry on the Vaughn family name with pride. I will disappoint you no longer. Please tell Mr. Ashburn I'll be coming to ask for Sarah's hand today." Without waiting for a response, Griffin left them in the kitchen and set about the business of moving on with his shattered life.

One

Present day

The day Danielle had been dreading since she received her college acceptance letter the previous spring had arrived. She was transferring from community college to an out-of-state school in upstate New York. How was she supposed to leave Lucas there in Perry Hall? How could she say good-bye to the person she had spent almost every day with for two years? Lucas had been her boyfriend and one of her best friends since the first day of college. She thought back to that day and smiled.

Dani could tell the freshmen from everyone else, because they all wandered around, staring at maps of the campus with anxious expressions similar to her own.

She pushed her way through a swarm of plastic-looking girls with cell phones and too much hair product, to get into the science building. She could feel the stares burn through the back of her head. She ignored them and headed off to her first class. She could hear the snickers and comments about her hair as she walked down the corridor.

In high school, nobody even noticed it after a while. They were so used to it that it was no longer mentioned. Dani was going to have to start all over. On the way into class, several jocks shadowed her. They, too, had noticed the white streaks in the front of her dark, chocolate-brown hair. She took a seat at the front of the room and pulled out her map and schedule to find the shortest route to her next class.

One of the jocks snickered, "This place is a zoo. Did you see? They're enrolling zebras now too."

That was when an angel in blue jeans and a Hollister T-shirt came to her rescue. He had entered the classroom just in time to hear the comment and the laughter that followed. He scowled at the jock and quipped, "They've also started letting jackasses on the local football team." Another round of laughter erupted.

"Whatever, Lucas. You'd be on your ass if you stepped out on the field," the jock spat back at him.

Dani's savior brushed her arm on his way to sit with the offending jocks and said, "Ignore him. His mommy forgot his meds this morning."

Lucas was the hottest guy she'd ever laid eyes on. He looked like he belonged in a teen magazine, smiling his perfect smile and breaking hearts. He had flawless suntanned skin, shaggy, honey-blond hair, and steel-blue eyes with gray flecks that made her stomach do strange little cartwheels. Dani thankfully had several classes with him.

That first day she found an empty picnic table in the common area to spread out her lunch. She noticed those steel eyes across the lawn at a table full of mostly older students and other various plastic girls. She found it odd, considering it was the first day of classes. He must be one of those people that naturally draw others to them, she thought. Maybe they'd all gone to the same high school.

He caught her looking, and she wanted to slide under the table. Her face was so hot she knew she couldn't hide her embarrassment as he began to get up and walk her way. Dani stopped breathing.

He sat across from her and leaned over to take a few strands of white hair in his fingers and tuck them behind her ear.

"You do that on purpose? Is that a Goth thing or something?" he prodded with a grin. "Your clothes don't look Goth, and I don't see any black nail polish."

She had to remind herself to breathe, because blue was not her color. Other students started filtering over from the table he'd abandoned. She reached across the table to brush the hair out of his eyes and mocked, "Did you do that on purpose? You look like a Disney Channel reject."

The other students that had come to the table took in the scene and waited for a response from Lucas. He cracked a smile and tilted his head. "I think I'm going to like you. I'm Lucas, by the way." He reached across and stole some grapes from her lunch.

"I'm Dani. The hair's natural. They're birthmarks or a birth defect, depending on your point of view."

"I like it. And I like a girl that doesn't take any shit." He strutted around to her side of the table to get a closer look.

That was all it took. Lucas accepted her immediately, and everyone else followed his gracious lead. Dani was part of the in crowd, and they had been together ever since that day.

Two years and one summer later, they were in the bed of his pickup truck, curled up in the same sleeping bag. The stars were beautiful, but she couldn't take her eyes off Lucas. They had done that a thousand times, but this night was different. She was leaving for school the next morning, and Lucas was staying home. He had also been raised by a single parent, but going to college out of state wasn't an option for him. He planned to continue attending community college and working to help his mom with his two little brothers. Dani wouldn't see him again until Thanksgiving.

He drew little circular patterns all over her face, as if trying to memorize every pore. She placed little wet kisses on his chin and down his neck. He shuddered with anticipation. Chills ran down her spine with every tender stroke of his fingers over her skin.

She wanted to make love again before she went away, but he was still resisting. They'd had sex a few times over the two years, but he never seemed eager after that first night in the back of his truck. Lucas hadn't been a virgin like her. He'd dated a lot and had more experience than she wanted to ponder. Still, it was never very good for her. He did his thing and he always kind of zoned out afterward. They had a great relationship otherwise, and she thought she might even love him. She wanted to love him, but his reluctance to be intimate always made her feel rejected. Tonight she wasn't taking *no* for an answer. She wanted to touch and be touched. She needed to feel a stronger connection to this man before she left in the morning.

Taking the lead, she deepened the kiss and slid her hand down his body and into the front of his running pants. Lucas was rock hard in her hand. He was as hot and ready as she was, and that gave her a little more confidence. Shyly she stroked him up and down and he groaned against her mouth. He never let her touch him like this, so she feared doing it wrong or hurting him. Her shirt and shorts were already gone, and she felt triumphant when he cupped her breasts and began to knead. Her nipples hardened instantly and she arched her back to get closer. She needed more, so much more.

Suddenly he rolled her over and pinned her arms above her head. "I can't do this," he panted. "Not this way. Not in my truck. You deserve better than this, Danielle."

She cleared her throat and fought the tears burning the backs of her eyes. He was doing it again. He always had such a gallant reason for abstaining. "Lucas, all I want is you. Nothing else matters. Please let me love you," she whispered.

"No. Don't you see? It feels too much like good-bye. I want you so bad, but you're trying to prove your love before you leave me and it just isn't necessary."

Feeling embarrassed and rejected, she wrestled to reclaim her arms and push him off. She struggled to unzip the sleeping bag. Mostly naked, she scrambled for her clothes as the tears began to flow.

Why did he always do this? What was so wrong with her that he didn't want to make love to her? There was always an excuse. She wished he would just be honest and say he didn't want her.

"Dani, please stop and talk to me. Don't be angry. I just want the best for you, baby," he begged, but she continued her search for her shoes.

She was pissed. How could he ruin this for them? "Damn it, Lucas!" she cursed. "Did you ever think I might need you to show me your love?" Her heartbeat seemed to pound in her head as she stood topless in the lace panties she'd bought for the occasion and glared at Lucas. She realized distantly that it was the first time he'd seen her quite so bare. The few times they'd been together it had been a hurried affair in the back of his truck, and she'd never actually gotten completely naked. Lucas stared, slack jawed, and something suddenly came over Dani. She didn't care what he thought any longer. She was going to take what she wanted, and she wanted Lucas.

She slid her underwear over her hips and let them fall to her feet. Lucas watched the scrap of black lace as if mesmerized. Dani climbed onto his lap, looking deeply into his eyes.

"Don't you want me, Lucas?"

He didn't answer; still staring at her, his eyes glazed over.

She hungrily kissed him, trying to make him feel her need for him, her love for him, through the kiss. His hands moved hotly over her body while she licked down his neck.

She began to feel strange, as if the world had somehow shifted. Suddenly, her vision was very sharp, and the night seemed brighter. Every beat of his heart was too loud, and the heat pouring off him made her . . . hungry. Dani's head began to spin. It was no longer the sweet, heavy petting and quick awkward sex of their past. It was hot, and the feelings he aroused in her body were overwhelming. She pulled his shirt off, continuing to bathe him with her tongue.

Warmth spread through her body, and, suddenly, odd pictures began to flash through her mind. Were they memories? They weren't her memories, but they were memories of her from the outside. She was so excited and confused, all at once. She saw herself the first day of college, at the Ravens game downtown, reading a book on the beach in Ocean City, and playing in the snow with Lucas's brothers. The images just kept coming. They were Lucas's memories, only that couldn't really be her. The girl in his memories looked just like her, down to the white hair and light eyes, only she looked angelic. She was delicate and graceful. Was that how he saw her? Then she saw the most disturbing memory from just a moment before, when she climbed into his lap. Her pale-blue eyes were black.

She jerked herself up and looked through the rear window of the truck into the rearview mirror in the cab of the truck. Her irises were jet black. She looked down at Lucas for a reaction. He was slumped backward, still looking at her all glassy eyed, as if he was looking through her and not really seeing her. What had she done? She smacked him to get his attention.

He shook his head to clear the cobwebs and said, "What happened?"

"Lucas, I am so sorry! I have to go now, right now. Please forgive me." Dani grabbed her clothes and leapt down from the truck, dressing as she crossed the field where they had always parked, leaving her shoes behind.

"Dani, I'm sorry for whatever I did. Please don't leave this way. Let's talk about this."

He pursued her across the field, but she had to get away from him. His body heat tried to pull her back into his arms, his pulse called her name, and a hunger she didn't comprehend burned her throat. So she ran fast, too fast. In bare feet, she ran through the woods and across the school parking lot. She ran down Ebenezer Road and about ten blocks to her house to curl up on the front porch swing and prayed her mom didn't hear her. She couldn't go into the house. Her mom was still up, and there was no way she was going to be able to act like all was well. She had to calm down and think.

A while later, Lucas's truck pulled up, and he walked past the porch and around to the side of the house where her bedroom was on the second floor. He tossed pebbles at her window and pleaded for her to come outside or answer her phone.

She pulled her cell out of the pocket of her jeans. Good thing it hadn't fallen out in her struggle to wrestle them on while running. She had ten new voice mails. She had turned off the ringer so it wouldn't ruin their magical evening under the stars. What a joke. After a while, he got back in the truck and left. That was for the best, since Dani was too scared to deal with him that night.

In the morning, over breakfast in their little kitchen, her mom eyed her suspiciously over her coffee cup. She was having her standard whole wheat English muffin and coffee, while Dani indulged in her second bowl of cereal with an extra scoop of sugar for good measure.

Her mom still looked mostly the same to her as she had since Dani was little. Her dark blond hair was shorter, hanging to just below her shoulders, but there wasn't a gray hair or a laugh line in sight. Dani wished she had inherited her mother's hair. She looked like her mom, with the same eyes and figure. It was the hair and facial features that stood them apart.

Her mom was her hero. She worked, took care of the house, and did all the things most women would call a man to take care of, and, most of all, she took care of Dani and never once complained or asked for help. Tessa was a photographer, so they had beautiful pictures hanging all around the house.

"*You have to be self-sufficient, Danielle. No one is going to provide for you when you become an adult,*" she would remind Dani over the years if her grades had the nerve to drop below a solid B. "*Your education is the greatest weapon in the battle for independence.*"

Dani never really understood why her mom felt the need to drive that point home. Her mom hadn't gone to college, and she was doing fine. They had everything they needed and most of the things they wanted.

Then Dani remembered the night two years before, when she finally got up the nerve to demand answers. "Mom, why won't you tell me about my father?"

Tessa was making dinner while Dani did homework at their small kitchen table. She'd turned her head slightly in Dani's direction, so Dani knew she'd been heard, though she didn't get an answer right away. Her mother finished plating the meal and brought it to the table as Dani put her books away.

Tessa walked over to stare out the window above the sink in the small kitchen. They didn't need much room. It had always been just the two of them. They had no other family to speak of, and her mom never even dated.

Dani began again. "What am I supposed to tell people who ask about my parents? The immaculate conception thing isn't really working for me anymore. Please don't say I'm too young and it's complicated. I'm old enough for college, so I think I can handle it now."

Her mom still stood there motionless and without turning to look at Dani, she finally started to speak.

"Your father and I were very much in love. I really don't know what to tell you, because, honestly, I don't know much." She choked on the words. "It's difficult for me to talk about." She turned around, still not looking directly at Dani.

The sight of the silent tear running down her mother's ivory cheek was shocking. Dani had never seen her mother cry.

Tessa struggled unsuccessfully to hold it together, while Dani watched in silence. She took a cleansing breath and wiped away her tears. She looked at the wall just above Dani's head, refusing eye contact.

"We came from different," she paused, "worlds. His family was unwilling to accept an outsider."

Her mother's confession floored her. She didn't know what she had expected to hear. Maybe he was dead, or some James-Bond-type undercover agent who couldn't be with them for their safety, never knowing when one of his archenemies might appear to take vengeance by hurting his family. She realized that they were childish imaginings, but it was better than the truth of it.

"So . . . you're telling me that he's out there alive and happy? We just aren't good enough for him and his high-class family?" She wasn't able to keep the shock out of her tone.

"I have no idea how or what he is doing. I haven't seen him since the day you were born, and I'm sure it wasn't you they objected to, baby. *I* was the problem. At least that's what I was told. I never actually met any of them myself." With that statement, her mother went to her room, her untouched plate forgotten.

Dani immediately wished she could take it back. She had caused her mother pain in order to get an answer she no longer wanted.

They just weren't good enough. Dani had a father and a family out there, somewhere, that didn't want her. She finally understood her mother's need to see her strive for the best. She couldn't stand the thought of Dani being below some perceived standard. They never spoke of her father again.

The phone rang and brought Dani back to the present with a jolt. Her mom looked at her expectantly. "Lucas has already called three times this morning. Did you two have a fight?"

"No, everything is fine," she lied and grabbed the cordless off the wall, leaving to take the call in the living room. She didn't want an audience.

"Hello?"

"Danielle, finally! I've been calling your cell all night. I'm so sorry. I don't know what happened. It's all fuzzy, but I'm so sorry. Please, Dani, don't leave me like this. You have to let me come over and say good-bye. Please talk to me," he pleaded, without letting her get a word in.

When he finally paused, she said, "Lucas, you have nothing to apologize for, and I'm just sorry I tried to make you do something you didn't want."

He cut her off. "I want it! I do! I'll come over right now and pick you up! Last night cannot be the way we leave this. . . ." He trailed off.

"You can come over, but not for that. I have to load my car up and get on the road. We won't have much time, but we can talk a little." She tried to soothe him because he was right. They needed to part on better terms.

"I'm on my way. Be there in ten. I'm already in the truck. See you soon." He hung up as if he didn't want to give her a chance to change her mind.

He shouldn't be so worked up, she thought. It's not as if *he'd* turned into some weird, black-eyed freak last night. Obviously he didn't remember that little tidbit. Strange, considering she noticed it first in his memory. And what the hell was that about? People don't see other people's memories!

Dani washed her breakfast dishes and just made it to her bedroom when there was another knock at the front door. She would say good-bye to Lucas, and, afterward, she would have to say good-bye to her mom. Ugh . . .

Lucas tapped on her bedroom door.

She took a deep breath and tried to force a smile, but as soon as the door opened a crack, he barreled through and tackled her onto the bed. Dani shrieked and laughed.

Her mom shouted up the stairs, "All right, you two! Leave that door open!"

"Yes, ma'am." Lucas had to answer because Dani was too busy trying to escape the grasp of the infamous Tickle Monster of Perry Hall. He stopped the monster abruptly after a moment and held her close to him, kissing her softly, in a way that washed away all her hurt feeling from the night before. The kiss said everything they needed to say without the words *I'm sorry.*

After her car was loaded, there was nothing left to do but say good-bye. He kissed her and held her tight for a long minute before walking away wordlessly. Watching Lucus drive away left a lump in her throat. This separation would be tough, but they'd get through it somehow.

Her mom worked so hard to make their little house a home for the two of them. The thought of leaving her alone was causing great tidal waves of guilt. Her mom, on the other hand, was prancing around like the proudest peacock at the zoo, overjoyed at Dani's accomplishments.

Thankfully, there was no tearful parting with her mother, due to her joy at seeing Dani have experiences she hadn't been afforded. She gave Dani some cash, a credit card for emergencies, a big hug, and a little white box. Tessa smiled widely and instructed Dani to open the box later.

Then Dani was off on the long drive to New York State. It was a lot of time alone to think. She pondered the past and dreamt of the future. She worried about Lucas and decided to call him as soon as she got settled. Mostly, she thought of the night before. She remembered the hunger she'd suffered and the shock of seeing her eyes in Lucas's memory. She thought about how insane it sounded to think it possible to see another person's memories. Was she going crazy? She couldn't worry about that yet. First, she had to focus on school. Insanity would have to wait until she had more time to deal with it.

Two

Dani arrived on campus amidst a flurry of incoming students and their parents. There were people everywhere carrying boxes and suitcases to their dorm rooms. Parents were bidding farewell to their aspiring scholars with an equal mix of smiles and tears. She found her building and made her way through the first-floor common room. It was a large room with scattered seating areas and a large wall-mounted flat-screen TV in each corner. Also on that floor were restrooms and a canteen with vending machines, microwaves, and dining tables. The crowded halls were almost impassable, given all the students, parents, and luggage.

Dani ran a gauntlet to reach her assigned room. She pushed open the door to see a petite Hispanic girl staring at the beds. Her dark hair was cut in a short, slanted bob, and her deep, brown, almond-shaped eyes almost lent her features an Asian look. When Dani entered, the girl turned and smiled as if they were already friends and she'd been waiting for her to arrive.

"Well, it's about time. Which bed do you want? I didn't wanna pick one without you. I kinda like the bed by the window. What do you think?" she chirped.

Dani was going to like this girl. Most people wouldn't wait for their roommates to stake their claim.

"I think finders, keepers. The other side of the room looks good to me." She held out her hand in greeting. "I'm Dani. It's nice to meet you."

"Where are my manners?" The girl blushed. "My mom would be ashamed of me. I'm Olivia." She took Dani's hand into both of hers in a nervous greeting.

"I don't know about you, but I'm kind of freaked out." Dani moved her suitcases to the bed farthest from the window.

With that Olivia seemed to sag with relief. "I was afraid it was just me being a sissy about moving away from home. I know I should be excited, and I am, but this is a big deal. I've never been away from my family. Having a roommate will be new for me, also. I have three brothers and no sisters, so I've always had my own room."

"I'm an only child, so I know what you mean." Dani surveyed the rest of the room. It was clean and not what she would call spacious for two people, but the closets were big enough, and there were small desks on either side of the room. She hadn't brought much with her anyway. The door opened again, and several boys who looked like male versions of Olivia carried in boxes, suitcases, and a minirefrigerator.

"Get out of the way, Stripes!" the tallest one barked at Dani. "This thing is heavy!"

"Excuse me." She moved out of the walkway. Here we go again, she thought. She had been on campus for twenty minutes and already she was getting cracked on for her hair. It was a new record.

A brunette woman with ivory skin and an attitude followed the boys. She smacked the boy in the back of the head and said, "Liam, you better apologize before I give you something to be sorry for, boy."

The youngest-looking boy snickered. The woman eyed him harshly. "You will be next, Patrick." Then she turned to the third boy and said, "Reilly, go grab the last box from the truck."

"I'm sorry you were in my way, Stripes," Liam teased as he ran from the room before the woman could catch him. She glanced at Dani apologetically while Olivia stood by the window looking mortified.

"Hello, I'm Olivia's mother, Kelly. Sorry about my boys. They're a little rambunctious, to say the least." She greeted Dani with a motherly hug.

"It's nice to meet you, ma'am. I'm Danielle Vaughn, and, honestly, I've been teased about my hair my whole life, so it's really no big deal." She hoped Olivia's mother wouldn't be too hard on the kid. She looked like she could back up her threats.

"How embarrassing is this?" Olivia moaned from the corner.

"Walk me out, Olivia. We'll go and let you girls get settled." Ms. Kelly put her arm around Olivia, and the look on her face telegraphed the tears that were about to flow.

"I just can't believe I'm leaving my baby girl here to fend for herself. Are you very sure you don't want to go to school closer to home?" She sniffled.

"Please don't cry, Mom. We've had this discussion a hundred times now. Let's go before the boys make this day worse." Olivia wrapped an arm around her mother and ushered her out to the hall, mouthing apologies to Dani on the way out.

So, Dani's roommate was a pleasant Asian-looking Hispanic-Irish girl with three crazy brothers. Cool. Dani hoped her new roommate would be so used to sharing she'd give her some space in the fridge.

Running out to grab another box from the car, Dani remembered the little white gift box from her mom. She jumped in the front seat to open it and found a delicate gold chain with an intricate sunburst charm shimmering in the midday light. Removing it from the box, she noticed the back of the charm had an inscription reading, *"The center of my universe."*

It looked like an antique, and she loved it. Whipping out her cell, she called her mom. Tessa answered on the first ring. "Oh, thank goodness you made it safely. How is it? Did you find your room yet? Did you meet your roommate?" She fired off questions so rapidly Dani couldn't get a word in at all.

"Wow. I'm beginning to think your calm behavior this morning was all a show."

"I knew saying good-bye to Lucas was hard on you, sweetheart. I figured I could take one for the team and keep myself composed," she admitted.

"Thank you for the necklace, Mom. It's beautiful."

"I knew you would like that old thing. It's about time somebody got some use out of it."

"How old is it? Where'd you get it?" Dani was curious.

"You answer my questions first," she said after an oddly long pause.

"Okay. My room is nice but small. My roommate seems friendly. Her family was there, so we didn't really talk, but she did wait for me to pick a bed. I thought that was nice. She has three little brothers, so the room was crowded for a few minutes." She spilled all of the details.

"That all sounds very encouraging. I wish I had come with you. What are you doing now?"

"I'm about to carry in the rest of my stuff. There are so many people here roaming around. It's hard to imagine what it will be like after the parents leave." Dani watched the masses of people crossing the courtyard and parking lot on their way to the dorms.

"Why don't you give me a call later after you're all settled? I'll be working on turning your bedroom into a lounge for all the wild parties I'm going to have now that you're gone," she teased.

"Alright, Mom, you do that while I go hang out at a frat party with some of these hot guys," Dani teased back.

"That is so not funny! That's it. I'm coming to get you. I wonder if I could find a program for college homeschooling." They both laughed aloud.

"I love you, Mom."

"Love you more, Dani. Call me later."

"Oh, wait! You didn't tell me about the necklace," Dani reminded her.

"There isn't much to tell. An old boyfriend gave it to me. I've had it in my jewelry box for so many years I'd forgotten it was there. I just thought you would like it," she explained with a heavy sigh.

"He must have been a serious boyfriend, given the inscription on the back." Her mother never spoke of her past, so this was a revelation.

"I guess so. It didn't last long, though, and he moved on very quickly. Men are fickle that way. You're the whole universe one day and nothing but a memory the next day." There was an uncomfortable silence where Dani wanted to ask for details but she didn't want to push her mom to talk about something painful.

"I have to get going, honey. I have a job today." They said goodbyes and hung up.

Dani clasped the chain around her neck and checked her reflection in the rearview mirror. It was beautiful. The etching in the gold made it shimmer like the sun itself. After grabbing a box from the trunk, Dani crossed the courtyard with an exhilarated rush of hope at this new beginning.

The first week of school went by quickly. Adjusting to the schedules, teachers, and the workload had been kind of tough, not to mention missing her mom and Lucas so much. Dani called them both every night.

Lucas was enjoying his classes too, but he said it just wasn't the same without her. She wanted to tell him everything, but the tension in his voice when she spoke to him about new friends and study groups made her wary. She began to edit some of the information she gave him. Not that she was doing anything wrong, but she didn't see the sense in causing him undue stress. The separation had been hard on them both, and Lucas really regretted their last night together and promised to replace that memory with a happier one over the Thanksgiving holiday. Dani thought Lucas was feeling insecure about their relationship after his rejection of her. It had hurt, but she was over it now.

Dani and Olivia were getting along very well. They had similar schedules, went to the library together, and had made a lot of the same friends. Oddly enough, not many people had commented on Dani's hair. The girls who had mentioned her odd coloring liked it. Maybe her white highlights would start a new trend. Several guys also had admired the combination of her hair and light eyes. She supposed what everyone said about kids being cruel was true. Her new, more mature set of classmates didn't seem to think it was a big deal.

Dani was late for study group. She rushed down the stairs of her dorm heading across campus to meet Olivia and the rest of her study group at the library.

It was really beautiful walking through the trees that seemed to bend over the walkway to meet each other and hold hands. They created a natural, arching tunnel of green, backlit by evenly spaced lamps that cast a warm glow all over campus. She imagined the effect would be lost when the leaves turned colors and fell, but for the moment, it was breathtaking.

It seemed more like a social hour than a study group in the overly full library, and the people at her table were making plans for the next evening without a single open book in sight.

"Are you coming out with us tomorrow night, Dani?" asked Steve and Jared. They were roommates, and both of them were juniors. Jared reminded Dani a little of Lucas with his shaggy blond hair and all-American good looks, but he had a more mature air about him. He exuded a confidence that belied his age and had the girls on campus clamoring for his attention. His light-green eyes reached out and grabbed attention, and drew her into conversation. Steve was the best-looking redhead she'd ever seen. Even his freckles were cute. His look leaned more toward a skater boy, and his frisky personality could win a girl over without effort.

"Of course she's coming," answered Olivia as she put an arm around Dani's shoulder and raised an eyebrow in question. "Aren't you, Dani?"

"Where are we going?" A table full of expectant eyes peered back at her.

"We're going to a club downtown called Thirst. You're gonna love it." Olivia squealed.

"I don't know." Did she really want to explain this to Lucas?

"Come on, D! It'll be fun!" Jared pressed. "What else are you gonna do?"

She thought about that for a moment. Dani had only recently turned twenty-one. She'd imagined her first trip to a club would be with Lucas, but they hadn't gotten around to it yet. What would she do while her friends went on an adventure without her? She would likely mope and wish she had gone.

"Alright, I'll go with you." The table erupted into cheers. The whole group was going, and hopefully there would be strength in numbers. She couldn't spend her whole college career hiding in her room. She could have saved her mom a lot of money and gone to community college if that was her goal. Her mom always told her to enjoy herself, but to also think of the consequences of her actions and be herself. Tessa believed that new experiences were a huge part of college and growing as a person. So here was Dani's first chance to jump in and start expanding that limited horizon.

The next morning, the girls slept in until noon. It felt so good to rest on a Saturday, just like at home. Dani woke to the sound of her cell phone chirping. It was a text from Lucas.

"I miss you, Dani," it said.

She missed him so much. It had been almost a week since he'd kissed her good-bye and left her standing on the sidewalk in front of her home. She texted him back, *"I miss you so much."*

He immediately replied, *"I'm going to work. I'll call you later. XOXO"*

After a shower, she went to the library to get the work done that she hadn't finished the night before during social hour. It was quiet and oodles of people were actually working in small groups and individually. She didn't want to worry about homework the next day after staying out late. Dani was a little nervous about the evening's outing. She'd never been to a club and had nothing to wear, but all those thoughts could wait, because for the moment she needed to focus on her schoolwork.

A couple of hours later, she started to doze off but woke when someone pulled out the chair on the other side of the table. She opened her eyes to find Lucas gazing down at her. Dani's mouth fell open. The library was empty. The only light was from a few scattered desk lamps. How long had she been sleeping? Without saying a word, Lucas came around to her side of the table and easily lifted her onto the table. He stepped forward to stand between her thighs. His eyes smoldered as he cupped the back of her head and took her mouth hungrily. His lips were strong, and his tongue delicious sliding against hers. He began alternately kissing and biting her jawline down to her neck while simultaneously unbuttoning her shirt and slowly pushing it down her arms. His breath on her neck made gooseflesh rise and had her eyes closing with pleasure. It was way better than waiting for her next trip home.

Lucas whispered against her ear, "Now, baby. I want you, now." He stepped back.

She watched him rip his shirt off, and the sight of his perfect six-pack and lean hips caused her to shudder. Now was good, and she was ready to move before he changed his mind, but he was already pushing her back to undo the snap of her jeans and slide down the zipper.

Lucas pulled off her jeans by inches, staring at her body with a wicked grin on his kiss-swollen lips. He unbuttoned his pants, climbed up on the table, and pulled her around to straddle his lap.

She wrapped her legs around him. One hot hand burned the skin of her thigh, while the other traveled up her body to caress her breasts, causing them to peak and ache in anticipation of an unknown pleasure. Her breath came in ragged pants as she began to nibble down his neck and prayed he wouldn't make her stop.

As he slid farther back onto the table, Dani leaned over him, continuing on her path down his neck, until he was on his back in the center of the long, wooden table. She could feel his pulse with her whole body, and it pulled her into him. She needed him, all of him. He tugged at her panties while she licked at the delicious skin above the pulse at his throat. She needed to taste that steady thud with her tongue and feel it running down her throat. Dani rubbed herself against his denim-clad erection. The contrast of her bare thighs against the stiff fabric brought another unexpected layer of sensation to her overly sensitive skin.

"Damn, that hurt, baby." Lucas took a sharp breath and tightened his grip on her hips with a whimper.

Dani's head jerked up, but she was no longer looking down at Lucas. She was peering back up at herself through Lucas's eyes. Her irises were black as midnight, and blood ran down her chin from red-stained lips. What had she done to him? Blood trickled down his neck in two small streams. The look of hurt and betrayal on his sweet face singed her.

Then, she woke up with her face stuck to a book. The library was still full of students, who glared at her when she jumped up and her chair tipped over, crashing to the floor and shattering the silence.

Olivia was in her closet tossing clothes over her head and onto the bed when Dani reached the dorm. Olivia mumbled in agitation under her breath.

Dani watched a few minutes before interrupting her. "What are you doing in there?"

"I was in your closet already. You don't have anything to wear that will do for a night out. So, I'm trying to find you something of mine to wear. But you're bustier than me. I'll be right back. Maybe Lindsay has something that will fit you," she called over her shoulder on the way out the door.

Dani knew she didn't have anything to wear out. Everything she owned said "comfy night in the dorm" not "paint the town red." She was digging for shoes when someone knocked on the door. To her surprise there was a deliveryman in the hall. He held an electronic clipboard, and a big box sat at his feet.

"Delivery for Danielle Vaughn," he said and held out the stylus pen. She signed and thanked the man, who nodded and promptly jogged off down the hall. Dani dragged the box in and opened it. Inside she found shopping bags of clothes from several trendy stores and a note from her mom.

> *I thought a few new things would brighten your day. I love you. Mommy*

She smiled broadly to herself. These clothes were just what she needed. She grabbed her cell and speed-dialed home. He mother answered on the first ring. "Hey there, baby girl."

"Thanks for the clothes, Mom. They did indeed brighten my day." Her mom was so good to her.

"They had some great sales at the mall. I seemed to have gone a little overboard. I hope you don't mind." Dani could hear the smile in her mother's voice. She had this odd way of knowing when Dani would need help. She always knew when Dani missed the bus home from school as a kid and would be there waiting to pick her up. Her mom always knew when she was getting sick and never failed to be ready with the appropriate remedy. She always knew when Dani was sad, no matter how hard Dani tried to hide it. Dani knew it had something to do with her mother's dreams that were more like premonitions. So she shouldn't have been surprised when the clothes she wanted showed up right on time.

"I miss you, Mom. Thank you so much, for everything you do for me."

There was a pause before her mom answered. "You know I love you, and there isn't anything we can't get through together? I realize at your age you aren't always going to want me in your business, but I hope you'll confide in me anyway. If you needed help, I could get it. No matter how out of the ordinary the problem may be, I can help you, baby."

Dani was a little frightened by this serious change in conversation. She wondered what kind of dream had brought this about, but she knew better than to ask. She didn't really know what to say in return.

"I have to go. I'm glad you liked the clothes. Be careful and stay with your friends if you're going out. There's safety in numbers," her mom advised.

"Okay, I will. Thanks again for the clothes. I love you."

Olivia arrived then to help her paw through her new duds and get them hung in the closet, leaving out an outfit for Dani to wear to the club. "Your mom has great taste. Mine would never have gotten me clothes like these."

Danielle agreed with Olivia. Her mom had sent some very stylish clothes that would nicely mix and match. Olivia had picked out a pair of dark, low-cut skinny jeans, a tight, cream-colored sweater that hung off the shoulders, and a pair of black, high-heeled, leather boots.

The girls took turns showering and primping to get their hair and makeup just right. Dani was beginning to get excited about the outing. There was one last thing to do before they'd be ready to go. She had to call Lucas and hope her going out wouldn't upset him. She wasn't going to lie about it, so she dialed his number and was a little surprised to hear loud music and laughter in the background when he answered.

"Hey, babe, are you there? Can you hear me?" he yelled over the music.

"I'm here. Where are you? It's really loud," Dani shouted back, hoping he could hear.

"I'm at this club in town with some guys from school."

"That sounds like fun—" she tried to answer, but he cut her off.

"I can't hear you!" he shouted louder. "Call me tomorrow, okay? Are you still there?" She supposed he couldn't hear her reply, because the phone disconnected.

He wouldn't have a problem with her going out if he was going to do it, and without the courtesy of talking to her about it first. She had been worried for nothing. They both had to learn to move in their separate circles. Maybe he could ride up one weekend and they could go out together.

There was a knock at the door. "Are you girls ready?" Lindsay opened the door. "The guys are waiting downstairs. Jared is going to drive the four of us, and the others are riding with Steve." She chattered on in her usual cheerful way. "You guys are hot. Damn, I gotta go change this shirt." Lindsay cursed, giving Olivia and Dani an appraising look before turning on her heel to go revamp her outfit.

Catcalls and whistles from Jared, Steve, and a few other random boys met the girls when they reached the common room. Jared put his arm around Dani's shoulder and told the others in a dry, matter-of-fact tone, "Sorry. I changed my mind. I'll be taking Dani. The rest of you can walk." Olivia smacked the back of his head. "I'm just kidding." He ducked.

Lindsay reappeared in a silver sequined halter top, skinny jeans, and silver strappy stilettos. Smiling, she winked at Dani. "You're not the only girl with a bag of tricks."

The catcalls continued as they crossed the courtyard to the cars, and they almost lost Olivia to a guy in a Porsche. It was a short ride to the club in the back seat of Jared's Mustang. Lindsay was talking at high speed about the ladies' night she went to on Wednesday, and Olivia was in the front with Jared, arguing over the radio station. When they arrived, Dani told herself to relax on her first real night on the town.

She could feel the thumping of the bass from inside the club. There was a long line to get in. A doorman checked IDs and placed wristbands on the people old enough to be served at the bar. Some people were forgoing the line and heading straight to the bouncer, who let them in quickly. She became self-conscious when she realized the people she watched skirt the line were staring right back at her as they passed. She wondered if her choice of outfit had been off the mark. Then she realized the problem was her hair. It figured that just as she began to forget about it, everyone else started to notice.

When they finally made it to the large, muscle-bound doorman, he reached out his heavily tattooed python of an arm to check her ID. He looked her up and down in a way that made Dani feel dirty.

"Princess, you didn't need to stand in this line. The next time you're here, come straight to the front. Vince will hook you up, baby girl." He referred to himself in the third person as he placed a wristband on her arm. He escorted the group inside, refusing to accept their cover charge.

"You come see Vince if you need anything else, baby girl." Eyeing her again, he said in a low, rolling timbre, "Anything at all." He retreated to his station while speaking into the earpiece she hadn't noticed before.

The rest of the group cheered Dani and patted her on the back as they shuffled into the club. They all had a little extra cash in their pockets now.

The first thing that hit her when she entered the dark club was the loud, pounding bass of chest-vibrating music, followed quickly by flashing lights that seemed to match the rhythm of music and bodies on the floor. Combined with the smell of beer and cologne, she felt a bit of sensory overload as they began to weave through the crowds of dancers to find a table. She'd been stopped at least ten times crossing the floor by guys asking for a dance. Jared and Steve seemed annoyed by this holdup in the action but quickly forgave her when a waitress approached.

"Your VIP table is ready. Please follow me." Dani looked at her, confused. The waitress pointed to the front door, where Vince waved at her and winked. "Vince requests that you save him a dance."

Dani smiled and nodded in agreement, and her friends cheered again. She knew it was silly, but the attention was very flattering. The group was led to a comfy section in the corner that overlooked the dance floor. It was equipped with its own bar and big, semicircular sofas with low, round tables.

Olivia smiled widely at Dani and asked, "Do you plan on making use of that wristband?"

She didn't answer. After settling into a table, she ordered a soda from the waitress and went to join the throngs of dancers. Everyone else ordered drinks, but she wasn't ready for that, not tonight. She wanted to keep a clear head.

They danced for what seemed like hours. The strobe lights mixed with the swaying crowd were dizzying. She began to feel dehydrated and leaned back against a railing on the edge of the floor to catch her breath. Before she knew it, her friends were nowhere in sight. *Shit.*

A deep voice rumbled right next to her ear, "Hello. Would you like to dance?"

She turned to find a guy who looked like he belonged on the cover of *GQ* eyeing her. He was at least six feet two inches of sculpted perfection that was visible through his tight shirt. He towered over her as she stood in his shadow. Dani stared, mesmerized by blue-green eyes and rich coffee-brown hair.

"I'm Chase, and you are?" He held out a hand and waited for an answer, while Dani gathered her scattered wits.

She smiled and accepted his hand. He turned them toward a less crowded corner to dance. Finally, her brain located her mouth. "My name is Dani." Getting closer to him, she was overwhelmed by the essence of summer. It made no sense at all, but he smelled like line-dried linen and sunshine instead of the heavy cologne she'd expected. It was heavenly.

They danced in silence for a bit, until he leaned down and questioned, "Do I know you? Lovely as you are, I'm sure I would have remembered you."

His speech seemed a bit too formal for someone their age, so she figured he must be an uptown boy. Maybe she was hearing the polish of a private school. "No. I just started school at the university last week. Do you go to school here?"

He blinked rapidly, as if she had missed something. "My family lives in the area, but I have friends at the college, so I frequent the grounds."

They were interrupted when Vince grabbed Chase by the shoulder and barked, "Hey, man. Thanks for entertaining my girl. Now take a hike."

Chase turned slowly toward Vince with one eyebrow raised in agitation. The shock on Vince's face when Chase knocked his hand off was astonishing. Vince was a huge, muscle-bound monster, yet he flinched at the sight of Chase's face.

"Chase! I didn't realize it was you, man. I'm sorry." Vince scampered away as if afraid for his life, or maybe just his job.

When he turned back toward her, Chase's eyes darkened and his brow creased in anger, a stark contrast to the beautiful face she had been admiring a moment before. There was no hint of that stunning greenish-blue color in his eyes that she was sure had been there a moment ago. He quickly put his face back together.

"I'm sorry about that, Lovely. Vince can be quite crude," he apologized, pulling her closer.

Something about the way Vince reacted to him, and the way Chase looked when he turned around, made Dani want to get away from him quickly. He loosened his hold on her.

"Thanks for the dance. I gotta get back to my friends. Maybe I'll see you around campus," she told him politely. She tried to pull away, but he caught her arm.

He leaned in close, looking deeply into her eyes, and tried to persuade her. "Don't you want to stay with me, Lovely? I'd really like you to stay."

She cocked her head to the side, showing the confusion she felt. Suddenly she did want to be with him, and a look of pure triumph crossed Chase's face.

Dani heard her mother's voice in her head saying, *Stay with your friends. There's strength in numbers.*

He leaned into her again and was clearly not ready for her reaction when she said, "No. I actually would rather be with my friends. Catch you later, maybe." She quickly returned to the VIP area to drink her watered-down soda and tried to shake the urge she felt to go running back to Chase. She settled for watching him cross the floor to his table, wanting nothing more than to follow. But something had frightened her in that moment out on the floor.

Olivia smirked at her and said, "You're my hero. You just left that fine-ass man standing there with his jaw on the floor. Girl, if you don't want him, I'll go keep him company. He's yummy."

Dani smiled wryly. "Go get 'em, tiger. I have a boyfriend."

Olivia was off like a shot.

Dani spent the rest of the evening in the VIP area, dancing with Jared and Steve. Olivia got her up on the sofa to shake it with her, until the waitress started shooting them dirty looks. They didn't want to lose their big, comfy couch privileges for the next visit, so they were climbing down when Jared came to help Dani. She fell happily into his arms. He spun her around once, like a little kid, before setting her feet on the ground. With his arms still around her, Jared began to dance slowly, swaying back and forth, in stark contrast to the fast pounding of the music.

She felt so comfortable with his warm body against hers. So comfortable, she wanted to lay her head on his shoulder and take the scent of him into her lungs. He smelled of mint and rain. Suddenly she was hungry. When she looked up, he smiled, and the spell was broken.

He spun her out in a silly move and pulled her back into a more appropriate dance pace.

On the way out of the club, they passed Chase, sitting at a corner booth with a bevy of girls fawning over him and another guy. Dani made eye contact, just as a half-nude blonde rubbed against Chase's side and took his hand. Why did that annoy her? Seeing that really pissed her off.

He jerked his hand away and stood, staring at Dani intensely, as Jared wound an arm around her waist. She didn't know why, but she leaned against Jared and rested her head on his shoulder. Her eyes still locked with Chase's, and she saw the flash of anger he couldn't hide. Good, at least she wasn't the only one who looked pissed.

At the door, Vince wouldn't make eye contact with Dani, but reminded her to come straight to the front of the line on their next visit. He apologized for interrupting the dance with Chase and said again, "Come back anytime, and Vince will hook you up."

Earlier that evening Chase Deidrick had parked his Mercedes in front of Thirst and tossed his keys to Vince, the new head of security. "I don't know how long I'll be staying, so keep it close."

Vince nodded and opened the door for Chase to enter.

Chase's father had bought the nightclub for a very practical purpose. It was a good front for a feeding ground. With a college down the road, the students flocked to the club nightly. Instead of stalking their prey, they just sat back while students filed in the door and paid nicely to be there.

All the young vamps for miles around came to feed, and as long as they followed the rules, they were all welcome. There was no feeding allowed in the building, due to the risk of witnesses. It was no problem for vampires to enthrall humans into following them. No one killed or injured the humans, ever. Last but not least, the humans were not to remember anything. This was also no problem, once they were enthralled. Keeping their kind a secret was the utmost priority.

Chase occasionally broke the "no blood in the building" rule, but he had a private room in the back at his disposal. No witnesses in there. Those who violated the rules faced the judgment of the ruling Council for North America. Chase's family, the Deidricks, was one of the three ruling houses that made up the council. Everyone who entered Thirst carefully obeyed the rules. It was, after all, a House of Deidrick, and nobody wanted to cross the council.

Chase glided through the door past the line of humans waiting to enter the club. The crowd parted for him as he made his way to his regular table. The need to feed was an itch under his skin, nagging him for attention. He surveyed the room for potential donors. On a Saturday night, business was good, and there were plenty of suitable ladies from which to choose.

While he scanned the floor, an odd scent caught his attention—sweet, yet floral, like vanilla and lavender. He wondered where that delicious smell originated. It was another vampire, for sure, but was nothing like anyone he'd ever met before. Chase moved to search for the owner of the lovely aroma. Vampires were naturally attractive to their human prey, which made searching the crowd difficult, because every girl he passed wanted to dance and talk with him.

In the middle of the dance floor, he saw her. She was a living goddess, dancing among her worshipers. Every other woman, vampire and human alike, suddenly wilted in his eyes. She was perfection. A beautiful dark mahogany mane with unusual white streaks and eyes so pale, they reflected the light like mirrors. He had only ever seen hair like that on one other vampire. She was petite, yet perfectly curvy at the same time.

Chase could do nothing but stand and gawk at her for a time, worshipping the sight of her, along with her followers. He returned to his table to observe the goddess from a better vantage point. His friend, Kayden, arrived and put a hand on Chase's shoulder, making him jump. The rest of the club had seemingly disappeared while he watched her dance and smile.

"Chase, you alright, man? You look lost." Kayden stepped into Chase's line of vision.

"Do you know that girl, Kayden?" He cocked his head toward the dance floor.

"Which girl do you mean? The house is full of ladies tonight." Kayden flashed a bright white, wolfish smile.

"You're not catching that?" He inhaled deeply. "The scent is absolutely unique."

Kayden turned to find the object of Chase's current obsession. "I'd remember if we'd ever crossed her path. Her scent is off somehow, but still altogether intoxicating." Kayden sniffed the air. "I assume you don't know her?"

"Not yet, my friend, but I'm about to correct that injustice." They both hit the dance floor.

He found her leaning against a railing, looking rather winded. Chase stopped and watched a little longer. What was this? Vampires didn't get winded easily. He inhaled again. She was definitely a vampire. Kayden was getting a little too close to her, and his proximity was pissing Chase off. Stepping up to the railing next to the goddess, he leaned down.

"Hello. Would you like to dance?" She turned her eyes on him, and Chase was caught momentarily in the web of her scent and the beauty of her eyes. Gathering himself, Chase tried again, "I'm Chase, and you are?"

She extended her delicate hand to him, and the combination of her touch and scent was a shock to his system. She didn't answer until he'd guided her to the nearest corner, noticing how her eyes searched the floor along the way. Maybe she wasn't alone. He hadn't seen another male, but he hadn't looked for one, either. A flash of jealousy had him searching the floor as well, but he didn't see any competition. When they reached their destination, she looked up. "My name is Dani."

Dani wasn't a suitable name for a goddess, at all. He'd have to come up with a nickname. As they danced, his head swam with unusual and frankly unsettling urges. He wanted to taste her. He wanted to hold her. He had to know her. Chase preferred to keep a safe emotional distance from females. But at the moment, even the very short space between them felt like way too much distance.

"Do I know you? Lovely as you are, I'm sure I would have remembered you."

"No. I just started school at the university last week. Do you go to school here?"

Chase blinked stupidly. Did she really not know who he was in his own house? "My family lives in the area, but I have friends at the college. I frequent the grounds regularly."

Just then, Chase had to deal with a rude interruption by an employee. When he returned his attention to his dance partner, her body tensed, and she began to pull back.

"Thanks for the dance. I gotta get back to my friends. Maybe I'll see you around sometime."

She had dismissed him. Stunned, he grabbed her arm, leaned in, and tried to persuade her. "Don't you want to stay with me, Lovely? I really want you to stay."

She began to lean in toward him again, and he smiled victoriously. She stopped cold with her lovely face slightly tilted. "No, I actually would rather be with my friends. Catch you later, maybe." She stalked away, leaving icy confusion in her wake.

Chase had never been rejected in his life. He stood with his mouth agape as waves of disbelief and fury washed over him.

"I never thought I'd see the day Chase Deidrick got shot down. Man, I'm glad I came out tonight. Tough break, Chase, but now that she seems to be available, I think I'll go take a stab at her myself." Kayden was clearly amused by Chase's expression as he started toward the girl and her friends.

Chase stepped in front of Kayden. His vision sharpened and Chase knew his eyes had blackened with anger. It was the second time that night he'd lost his temper needlessly, but he couldn't hold it back when he growled through his teeth, "Don't touch her, if you want to keep all your fingers."

Kayden just chuckled. "Dude, would you relax? Alright, I'll leave the girl alone, but it's a shame to let her get away. I just thought she might like me." Kayden raised his hands in defeat.

Chase returned to his table and sat, brooding. He was annoyed by his own behavior when he'd snarled at Kayden.

Kayden made his way back with several girls on his arms and hailed a waitress. Vampires couldn't get drunk by drinking themselves, but if their hosts were drunk, it had the same effect. For that reason, Kayden liked to treat the girls to a few drinks before he led them away.

One of Chase's regular girls had been trying in vain to get his attention, but he only had eyes for the lovely creature who'd rejected him. She stood on a sofa with a human girl as they danced suggestively together. Chase couldn't help smiling at her playfulness, but his smile disappeared when she climbed down from the sofa and into the arms of a tall blond human. His veins burned with pent-up agitation while he watched the boy's hand, placed way too low on her back.

What is wrong with me?

He went out the front door to get some air. Walking around the side of the building, he punched the brick wall, causing the brick to shatter into red sand that blew down the alley.

Vince followed him into the alley. "Vince is really sorry about that earlier, Boss. He was admiring your lady friend when she entered. He had no idea she was with you."

"That is the problem, Vince. She isn't with me. Have you ever seen her before?" Chase asked through his teeth.

"No, sir, I never met her before tonight. Would you like Vince to see if he can get some information? I have friends all over. I'll make some calls. Given her name I'm surprised you're not familiar with her."

"You know her name?" Chase raised an eyebrow.

"I'm on the door tonight. It's my job to check IDs," he defended. "Her name is Danielle Vaughn. I assumed she was a friend of your family. I set her and her human entourage up in VIP."

Chase staggered back a step. The Vaughn family was another of the three ruling houses on the council. The council consisted of senior members of the Deidrick, Vaughn, and Stafford families. "You did well, Vince. I want you to keep this to yourself until I sort out a few things and try to get information through my own channels. When she leaves, try to assure she understands she's welcome to return." Vince nodded obediently as Chase passed him to reenter the club.

He decided to make the best of the rest of the evening. He really did need to feed that night, so he settled on the girl who'd been working so hard for his attention all evening. She reached out and took his hand, and he leaned toward her.

Just then, he saw the goddess coming in his direction. Jerking his hand back, Chase stood to greet his little lovely. That was her name . . . Lovely.

The loathed blond human boy wrapped his arm around her hip. She eyed Chase with an intensely angry heat. His blood burned again as she laid her head on the boy's shoulder and allowed him to pull her away, not breaking eye contact until she was out of sight.

Was Lovely pissed about the human girl touching him? That made no sense. He had to feed. They all had to feed.

Back at their dorm room, Dani fell onto the bed. She pulled off her boots and dragged the blanket over herself.

Olivia chastised her, "You better get that makeup off your face. Do you like clogged pores and pimples?"

She pulled the blanket over her head to block the light and informed Olivia, "I've never had a pimple in my life."

Olivia made a disgusted noise. Dani could hear her humming and washing her face as she drifted off to sleep.

A loud bang at the door woke her, and she begged Olivia to get it. The knocking came again. Dani sat up in bed. Olivia wasn't in the room. She must have locked herself out. To her surprise, it was Jared at the door looking upset. "What's wrong?" she asked, rubbing her eyes.

"We need to talk, D." He stepped around her and into the room.

"Sure, come on in," she said a bit sarcastically, since he hadn't waited for an invitation. "Is everything alright? Have you seen Olivia? I didn't even hear her leave." She crawled up on her bed and Jared sat nervously at her feet. "Jared, what's wrong?"

"I want you to have me, D," he said with his face in shadows.

"Have you?" She blinked the sleep away.

Jared stood and turned out her lamp, but she could still see him in the light streaming from the bathroom. He was shaking when he pulled off his shirt and climbed into the bed next to her.

Remembering how easy it had been to let him hold her made Dani shake a little, too. "Jared, I really like you, but I have a boyfriend. I'm sorry if I gave you the wrong impression earlier. We were only dancing."

"I have what you need," he insisted, only inches from her face. "I want you to take it." He leaned over and brushed her bottom lip with his, a simple act that sent a shot of warmth straight to her core. His green eyes begged her not to reject his offering.

Dani tried to get out of the bed, but was pulled in by his heat when she attempted to crawl over his body to escape. The smell of his skin made her mouth water. He was just so sweet and warm, like mint and summer rain. She draped herself over him, trying to absorb the warmth with her face pressed into his neck. One of his arms wrapped around her waist. The other brushed gently through her hair.

"That's right; take whatever you need. Take it all." He tilted his head to give her better access to his neck.

"I don't know. I can't." She whimpered against his neck. She could hear his pulse pounding in her head, beating against her lips. Her teeth ached. She wanted it. . . .

Her cell phone rang and woke her up. It was just another damn dream. She saw Lucas's name on the screen of her phone. She answered, trying to convince herself she was actually awake. "Hello?"

"I've called you five times. What's wrong? Are you pissed because I went out?" he huffed.

"I just woke up, Lucas." The room around her was still dark. The clock read 4 a.m. "Why are you calling me at four in the morning with an attitude? I didn't get to bed until two o'clock myself."

"What do you mean by that? What the hell are you doing out at two in the morning? Don't you have a curfew or something?" he slurred.

"Are you drunk?"

"Don't change the subject! I asked you a question! Where were you?" He was yelling at her.

"I refuse to argue with a drunk." She said each word slowly. "You can call me later, when you locate your common sense." She hung up on him. He called right back, so she turned the phone off. She was too pissed to sleep by that point, so she quietly slid on her tennis shoes. Still fully dressed, she whipped her hair up into a messy bun and left for a walk.

Surprisingly enough, she was not the only one out wandering. It seemed as though several people had finally started drifting back to campus. She turned the cell back on to find eight new voice mails and erased them all without listening to them.

Dani walked down the old cobblestone sidewalk that circled her favorite patch of arching trees and found herself a bench in a clearing a few yards back into the trees. People passing could be seen, but they wouldn't see her, unless they looked in her direction as they passed. She watched all the partygoers stagger back to campus and was highly entertained observing all of them, except for the guy who puked in the bushes. That she could have happily missed.

Lying on the bench, she stared up at the sky and remembered all the nights Lucas and she had spent in the back of his pickup, gazing at the stars and making out. As the sun began to rise over the trees, the peacefulness around her began to sink in. She continued to watch as the sky turned from black to dark blue and the stars began to fade. In the quiet, she allowed her mind to wander over the thoughts she'd been avoiding. She feared she was going crazy and was sure something was wrong with her. First, she wanted to do God knows what to Lucas, and her eyes went black as she invaded his mind. She'd had a great dream about making love to Lucas that turned into a nightmare when she bit him. The vivid dreams had then turned on her friends. And to top it all off, she couldn't stop thinking about the beautiful blue-green eyes belonging to a hot stranger, and Lucas suddenly becoming a drunk.

It wasn't like she could talk to anyone about that stuff. She'd always been able to tell her mom anything, but how would one go about bringing that up? *Hey, Mom, guess what? I attacked Lucas, read his mind, and I dream of biting people. How's your day?* Maybe she would talk to her over the holiday break if it didn't stop, or maybe not.

She'd slept most of Sunday away, ignoring Lucas's phone calls until about the fifth time he tried to reach her, before she sent him a text saying, "*I'm still upset with you. I'm not ready to talk yet.*"

Apparently, he had no memory of speaking to her, which led her to ask Lucas what else he might have done that he didn't remember.

On the way to class on Monday, Dani stopped at the coffee shop for her usual nonfat mocha with extra whipped cream. While waiting for her necessary caffeine fix, Dani thought she heard someone call her name in the faintest whisper. She turned to see who'd said it, but no one looked her way. She shrugged it off, grabbed the heavenly brew, and headed for the exit.

Then, she saw him at a corner table. Chase was drinking an espresso and typing on his laptop. He looked up and smiled, then nodded toward the seat on the other side of his table. Knowing it was the wrong thing to do didn't stop her. She'd been thinking about him since Saturday night, so she was happy to see him—a little too happy. She sat across from him and waited, until he smiled and raised one finger in a request that she give him a moment. He finished typing and closed the laptop.

Looking at him in the light of day made her feel at ease. She'd been having so many odd dreams that it was easy to convince herself the man she met at the club wasn't real. He couldn't have been as striking as she remembered. But he was. Chase was a beautiful man. He was sexy as hell with dark hair in perfect disorder, and his blue-green eyes still stunned her.

"You're just as lovely in the daylight," he flattered her with a soul-melting smile.

Funny, she'd been thinking the very same thing about him. Dani struggled to choke out a reply. "You're not so bad either. What brings you to campus this morning?"

"This is the best coffee shop in town. They have a great baker also. You should try the scones."

"So you're a morning person?" she inquired curiously, eager for insight.

"I'm not usually, but I have a meeting with my father in an hour, and the espresso helps get my brain going." He wrinkled his nose, as if the idea of being up before noon actually had a bad smell.

"Oh. Well, I'll get going so you can get back to work." Feeling like she'd interrupted, she got up from the table and tried to leave before her pout became embarrassingly evident.

"May I walk you to your next class?" Chase grasped her hand, and the warmth of his touch burned straight through her body.

"Sure, if it won't make you late." She was way too elated at the offer and glad for the chance to talk with him a bit longer. Maybe he would be an idiot or a total jerk, and she would stop thinking about him.

Together, they left the coffee shop. He insisted on carrying Dani's bag, and as he held the door for her, she could feel his eyes making a circuit of her body. Her outfit was only slightly better than pajamas, and it clung to her in all the best places. The tank was low cut and too short to reach the top of her yoga pants. He said nothing as they meandered slowly across campus.

After a few moments, Dani nervously peeked up to find him staring at her. "What?" It came out sharper than she had intended.

"I apologize, Lovely. I was just admiring your hair. It's unique." The half smile he gave her was genuine, not sarcastic as she'd grown to expect, and it melted her a little more. He should have to register that smile and be licensed to carry it, like a weapon.

"I guess *unique* is one word for it. I was born this way, and it's been the source of many a tear-soaked pillowcase in my life," she admitted. "Have you forgotten my name already? Lovely isn't it, you know?" she teased to change the subject.

"Of course I know your name. Your nickname is what I don't care for, Danielle. You are far too lovely to be called by a boy's name. Therefore, I chose to call you Lovely. Does it offend you?"

"It might offend my mother, but I guess I don't mind." Arriving at her destination, Dani pointed at the building and smiled. "This is it."

He suddenly looked disgruntled. "You know you hurt my feelings the other night? Rejection isn't something I'm used to dealing with, Lovely."

"That's funny, because you didn't look hurt to me. You actually looked quite cozy." The memory of the sleazy blonde made her tone sharp again.

"I can assure you, I was quite wounded. You should come out with me on Wednesday and make it up to me." He took her hand and placed a kiss in the center of her palm. It was surprisingly sensual and caused her to pull back and think about Lucas.

"To be honest with you, Chase, I have a boyfriend at home, and I don't think an evening with you would be healthy for that relationship," she confessed, but everything inside her was screaming to accept his invitation.

He put a hand over his heart and whispered, as he handed back the bag, "She wounds me again." In a clearer voice he said, "Perhaps you will save me a dance the next time you visit the club?"

Not wanting to make any promises, she answered, "Perhaps."

He nodded and walked away swiftly, disappearing into the crowd.

Four

Chase was on the way home after meeting with his father. He'd been enlisted to help organize the upcoming gala, and he knew he should be focused on those details as well as his other various house responsibilities, but he was distracted. The gala was a big deal for the council. It was an annual event that the three ruling houses rotated hosting, and it was their turn.

Pulling up to the building that housed his penthouse condo, Chase could only think about Danielle's rejection of him. She had told him she had a boyfriend at home. The thought of that caused a burning knot at his core. If she was a Vaughn, he should be able to get some intel on her quickly. Where exactly was home for her? He would be able to size up his competition if he just did some digging. He was running the list of potential suspects through his mind. It would have to be someone with good breeding and physical attributes to even be worthy of her attention. He couldn't come up with anyone who wasn't already dating or bonded to another.

He exited the Mercedes, tossed the keys to the valet, and dug out his cell to call Vince. Vince answered on the second ring.

"Good evening, Chase. Should Vince have your regular table ready for you?" Vince said in greeting.

"No. I have more pressing matters I need your assistance with, Vince." Chase was in no mood to go out tonight. "I need you to contact your people and see what information we can get on Danielle Vaughn. I need you to use the utmost discretion. I don't want her to know I'm checking up on her. The last Vaughn I tangled with caused me nothing but trouble. I don't want my reputation to precede me. Do you understand?"

"Sure thing, boss. Vince is on it. I'll call you as soon as I know anything."

"I need to know about her boyfriend also," he said, feeling awkward. This was new for him. He had never had to try to get a girl he wanted before her. Normally all the girls, human and vampire alike, flocked to him and gave him whatever he wanted without question, but not Danielle.

"Do you have a name for the boyfriend?"

"That's what I need you to find out," he snapped. Chase's face burned with the indignation of needing help to get what he wanted.

"Vince will get back to you as soon as he has any information." Vince disconnected.

In the elevator, he continued to mull over the situation. He was so distracted when he entered his condo, he didn't notice the red high heels by the door. He decided to go jump in the spa to relax his nerves. After changing into trunks and grabbing a towel, he was startled to find the spa out on his rooftop patio was not empty. He cursed when he noticed the long, platinum-blond curls hanging over the side of the bubbling spa.

"Samantha, what are you doing here?" he barked.

"Now, is that any way to greet a guest in your home?" She batted her eyes at him and stood to reveal her barely-there bikini. Samantha was the girlfriend who just wouldn't quit.

"Generally speaking, a guest is invited. You're more of an intruder. How did you get in, Samantha?" He really didn't have the patience for her theatrics.

"I used a key, of course." She smiled at him wryly.

"I took your keys back." He was annoyed and not charmed by the way she tried to look so innocent while bending over to display her thong.

"But not before I had copies made. Now, hop in with me. You look like you could use a soak. I'd be glad to rub your shoulders." She tried to distract him.

Samantha was a pain in the ass but he could handle her. She didn't do anything without a reason. He'd find out what she wanted and send her on her way. The soothing heat of the water was calling to his tense muscles. He hopped in and moved to the opposite side of the tub. "You just stay over there, and I won't have to put you out."

Samantha and Chase had started dating during his senior year of high school. Never exclusively, but it was the most serious and long-standing relationship either of them had ever had. The whole thing was a secret, due to their age difference and the tension between their families. Neither of their parents would have approved. The council families would never bond to each other. That would shift the balance of power between the houses, creating an alliance between two families and leaving the third at odds.

Samantha was a couple years younger, but she and her twin sister were advanced in school. They both graduated two years early without even trying. She didn't act like it, but Samantha had more than just great hair and a hot body going for her. She was very intelligent but preferred to receive attention for her bombshell beauty rather than her brains.

When Chase turned eighteen, his parents had gifted him with his condo. Vampire society had vast differences from the human society. By eighteen years of age, vampires had already been hunting on their own for years, and males roamed freely. A tighter leash was kept on females, because upper-class families didn't want their girls bonding to someone beneath themselves. Vampire bonding, or what humans would call marriage, was often arranged by the parents in powerful houses.

Samantha and Chase had a lot in common, both coming from ruling houses. They understood each other's limitations and obligations to their houses. They never knew when they'd have time to meet up, so Samantha had a key for convenience. She would come over when she could, and he never knew if he would be out hunting or home for the night. They would often not see or speak to each other for weeks. They broke up when Chase brought another female home with him and Samantha had been there waiting. She had made an awful mess that day. Apparently, the fact that they had never been exclusive didn't matter. She always assumed she was the only girl allowed in his home. That was their private sanctuary, in her mind. After her temper tantrum was over, Chase reclaimed her keys, and they parted ways. Not long after, she came back to make amends, but Chase was tired of running around in shadows. Something in the past had caused a rift between their families, and the Vaughns would not welcome his poaching of their daughter.

"So, to what do I owe this visit? I assume you have a reason." He was curious after the silence stretched a little too long.

"I was wondering if you were going to ask me to the gala." She smiled brightly.

He sat up straight and tried to laugh, but it came out as more of a choking sound. "Are you crazy?"

"Actually, I have some great news for us," she said with a bitter edge. "Your parents have been visiting with my parents. I overheard them talking about how it's time for our houses to put the past behind them, and maybe if they bonded you to one of us girls, it would start the process. They would share grandchildren. It would bind our houses. They said something about a sighted ancestor of mine and a vision. I didn't get much of that part."

Chase stared at Samantha in disbelief. All the color drained from his face, and he felt sick. He knew exactly what vision she spoke of. His father had told him the story without mentioning that Chase was the focus of the tale. Many people in his family were blessed, but he had no extrasensorial ability like his father and uncle. Given the stories he had been told of past generations of gifted Deidricks, Chase hoped his children would be very powerful.

"I'm assuming, of course, that you would prefer to bond with me rather than my sister, so I need you to show some interest, or your parents may choose Brandi. She does look better on paper," Samantha continued.

Chase had to use all his strength to pull himself out of the spa. He felt as though his bones had melted. Samantha scurried out of the spa as well and hurried to follow him inside. Maybe that was why his father had recently insisted Chase take part in house business and help with council affairs. He was being groomed for a bonding.

As Chase entered his bedroom, Samantha took advantage of his weakness and tackled him, knocking him onto the bed. "Aren't you excited?" she giggled. "We can be together and not hide it anymore!" Samantha beamed with joy and anticipation of the future.

"We're not together and I'm not ready to be bonded." He dumped her onto the floor and went to dig for some clothes. He'd changed his mind. He would go to the club and get one of his girls really drunk. He was ready to be numb. This was the worst day ever. First Danielle rejected him, then his father scolded him for being lazy and loose before forcing him to help with the gala, and then Samantha had ruined his hopes for a future with Danielle. He hadn't realized he was looking to the future until Sam informed him that his was already mapped out for him. His chest ached at the thought of not having Danielle as his bonded mate. He had never wanted to be mated, never permanently tied to a female, but for the first time, he was crushed by the need for it. A painful pull in his chest was dragging his soul toward a girl he had only just met and just found out he could never have.

"I'm not ready, either. It'll probably be another two years before they start forcing the issue. The point is, our relationship will be accepted. The council is completely in agreement with bonding. The Staffords are also eager to fulfill this mystery vision. We can start over, try again," she explained.

Chase had his back to her, walking into a closet large enough to be another bedroom. He returned to find her in nothing but her thong.

"That's it!" he shouted. "Get dressed and make sure you leave the keys on the way out! I'm not in the mood for your shit! The last time we spoke, I made it clear how I felt about things! I care about you, but this is not a relationship!" Calming down, he looked her in the eyes. "Sam, I need some time to absorb this, okay?"

Samantha crossed the room and grabbed her purse, digging out a set of keys. She tossed them onto the bed and left the room wordlessly. Chase sat on the end of the bed with his head hung, listening to the click of heels coming back toward him. Her top was still on the floor. He lifted his head to find Samantha's usual perfection in nothing but the thong, red heels, and a black trench coat. Her hands on her hips and a wide smile on her recently glossed lips.

"You do what you need to do. I will let you be. But it's going to happen, and you know it. We'll be bonded, and this relationship will be forever. We'll be happy together, and our families will prosper." She retreated again. The front door slammed behind her as she left the condo.

A few weeks had passed since school started, and Dani concentrated on her studies. Olivia and the rest of the group had been going to Thirst twice a week. Olivia was annoyed with Dani for not going, but Dani had been avoiding Chase. She thought about him too much and had dreams about him that left her frustrated and wanting the real thing. Dani feared she wouldn't be able to resist touching him if she ran into him again. Now it was Friday, and after two weeks of work and no play, Jared had talked her into attending her first frat party.

Lucas called twice a day, every day. He was still trying to make up for the fight and his drinking. She'd already forgiven him, of course. After all, she'd been no angel herself that night. She hadn't done anything wrong, but the thought was there, and guilt over it assailed her. She hung up with Lucas before entering her first class of the day. He seemed agitated when she mentioned going to a party, but Dani wouldn't be holding back anymore. She told him everything, because they both had to get used to living apart. He went out with his friends, and she was learning to deal with it. Besides, she didn't drink the way he did, so he had no reason to worry.

The rest of the day dragged. She tried to think of an excuse not to go out, but she knew Olivia would be pissed if she canceled.

The fall air was crisp and clean smelling after her last class. Autumn had always been her favorite season. She stopped on a bench to enjoy the weather and admire the scenery. Her favorite area of campus, where the arching trees held hands, was starting to change colors. The leaves fluttered in the light breeze, and Dani was content just taking it all in, until she was interrupted by a voice she couldn't believe she heard. Dani snapped her head around when he said, "There you are, stranger."

"Lucas!" There he stood, looking like home. His steel-blue eyes made her heart skip.

She squeaked when he dragged her over the back of the bench and into his arms. He spun her around in circles and kissed her hard. It felt so good to be in his arms again. He whispered, "I love you," between every kiss he placed from her forehead all the way down her neck.

"What are you doing here? I can't believe you're really here," she murmured, still attached to his neck, afraid that if she let go he would disappear. She prayed it wasn't another crazy dream.

"I couldn't be away from you any longer. I had to hold you," Lucas cooed against her temple. When he finally released her, they walked hand in hand to the dorm.

A bunch of Dani's friends were there, watching TV in the common room. Olivia caught sight of them first. She jumped up and ran toward them, getting the attention of the others. All the introductions were made, with the exception of one. Jared had been there when Dani came in, but he was gone before Olivia finished squealing. Then Dani and Olivia led Lucas up to their room.

"You are still coming tonight, aren't you?" Olivia pouted.

"She'll be there with a date tonight," Lucas assured her with a smile.

"I thought you might want to be alone." Olivia winked at the couple.

"I don't want to interrupt Dani's evening. I just want to spend it with her." Lucas absently brushed his hand through her hair. He'd propped himself up against her headboard as she rested against his chest. Dani knew if they were alone, he would have her naked by now. That had been all she'd wanted for so long, but at the moment, she was hedging a bit.

"I'll tell you what. After the party, I'll go stay with Lindsay. You guys can have the room to yourselves. We just have to figure out how to sneak you in the building."

"Are you sure, O?" She felt bad about putting Olivia out of her own room, and Dani could tell by Lucas's possessive handling that there would be no going back if they had the room to themselves.

"Just call me cupid." Olivia smiled devilishly. "How long can you stay?" she asked Lucas.

"I have to leave tomorrow evening. I can't miss work on Sunday," he informed them with a frown and a shake of his beautiful blond head.

"I think we will hit the party early and get back here so we can chill alone." Dani waggled her eyebrows, and Lucas laughed at the silly gesture.

As they crossed campus in the dark, Dani gave Lucas a tour, pointing out which buildings she had classes in and anything else that was familiar to her on the way. The music from the party could be heard a block away. Earlier, she'd wanted to stay behind, but now she was excited to share the experience with Lucas.

They entered the frat house and it was exactly what she'd expected. There were people everywhere, dancing and swaying to the music, just like at the club. Every corner and hall was full of people. There were speakers in every room piping in loud, thumping hip-hop.

Lucas looked around, and his expression settled halfway between joy and concern. He clearly liked the party, but not the idea of her attending them without him. It might have been a bad idea after all to bring him. He smiled and held out his hand to her for a dance. They danced, laughed, and talked as much as possible over the music. Lucas wrapped his arms around her for a slower dance, and his body was warm and familiar against hers.

"Maybe we can find something to drink," he suggested and grabbed her hand to tow her down the hall.

Dani felt a pang of jealousy as every girl they passed looked at Lucas like fresh meat.

In the kitchen, there were several kegs on tap and a large basin of some kind of punch being ladled into cups. It was an odd purple color. A guy walked up and added a bottle of grape juice and a whole bottle of clear liquor to the mix.

"What is that?" Lucas wondered aloud.

The guy smiled at them and spoke slowly, as if he were speaking to children. "It's called Purple Jesus. Everybody brings a bottle of liquor and dumps it in. Then we add enough grape juice to make it purple." He poured a ladle full into a cup and handed it to Lucas, who took a big swig.

"Jesus!" Lucas coughed and sputtered while the guy laughed.

"And that's why it's called Purple Jesus. That's what everybody says the first time they try it." Laughing again, he walked away.

Lucas held the cup out for her to take a drink. "I don't drink." Dani wrinkled her nose.

"It's alright if you're with me. I won't let you go overboard." He gave her a chiding look and all but forced the cup into her hand. She'd missed him so much and wanted to make him happy. Peer pressure was a bitch. She took a big gulp from the cup. Coughing and gasping, she handed it back. He laughed as he put his arm around her waist and led the way to one of the kegs.

"Maybe you should start with something less potent." He handed her a cup of beer and watched expectantly. She took a drink at his coaxing. It wasn't pleasant, but not nearly as bad as the other stuff.

He chugged his cup and refilled it with beer.

Lindsay and Olivia came down the hall with their eyebrows drawn together at the sight of her holding a cup of beer. Dani shrugged and inclined her head toward Lucas. One of the guys hanging out in the kitchen had struck up a conversation with Lucas, and they stood several feet away.

Dani spoke to Lindsay as Lucas continued to drink and talk with a group of students. The students made Dani uncomfortable, taking turns staring at her and Lindsay. She could hear them talking about her hair and complimenting Lucas on his taste in women. Occasionally he would come and refill her cup or insist she have a drink of his purple punch. Numbness was setting in.

"Maybe you should take it easy. It's not like you to cave this way," Lindsay chastised her for giving into Lucas's wishes.

"I've missed him so much, and he has to leave tomorrow. I don't want to upset him. I want him to be happy," she slurred, leaning against Lindsay. "I gotta pee." Dani realized it was unusual for her to announce her need for a ladies' room, as she staggered down the hall.

She saw a guy she recognized, and she couldn't seem to stop herself from being social. He was on his cell looking confused. She patted him on the shoulder.

"Don't I know you?" she asked, realizing too late that this sounded like a pickup line. "I mean, really. I have seen you somewhere before, haven't I?" That close, it was hard to miss how large and absolutely yummy the guy was. He looked like a bodybuilder with the face of a very tough angel.

"Yes, I'm sure it's her," he said into the receiver while looking at her. "Dani, how are you?" He looked at the phone and rolled his eyes. "I mean Danielle. How are you, Danielle?"

"I'm sorry. I didn't mean to disturb you." She stumbled past him, and he steadied her before she fell against the wall.

"I'm Kayden, a friend of Chase's. You probably recognized me from the club. I haven't seen you since that first time," he said with the phone still to his ear. That was odd, but Dani was too numb to care. "Are you here alone?" he asked.

"I'm here with some friends and my boyfriend." There were so many people passing in the hall, she'd been pushed a bit uncomfortably against Kayden.

"Your boyfriend is here? Do I know him?" he asked. Then he jerked the phone away from his ear. The person on the phone was yelling. He turned away from her to prevent her from overhearing and said, "I'm trying, but she's drunk. Why don't you get your ass over here?"

"I really gotta find the ladies room." She took off before she could pee on his feet, and tripped twice on the way up the stairs. She realized she was drunk when she had to lean against the wall to stop the room from spinning while she relieved herself.

The trip back down the stairs was slow going. She pushed through the crowd back to the kitchen, but Lucas and his new friends were gone. That was bad. Dani wanted to leave and didn't think she would make it alone.

Lindsay suddenly appeared from a door Dani had assumed was a pantry, but it led to the basement. "Lindsay, have you seen Lucas? I'm ready to go back to the dorm," she slurred, leaning against the wall.

"I just saw him downstairs with the jock squad. He's trashed. You don't look so good either." She looked Dani up and down disapprovingly.

"I'll see you tomorrow." Dani headed down the steps, ignoring Lindsay's critique of her appearance. She needed to find Lucas and get out of there.

She found him at the bottom of the stairs with his new friends, laughing at someone vomiting in the corner. "Lucas, I'm ready to go now," she yelled over the music.

He turned to look at her, annoyed. "Don't be such a bitch. It's still early," he snapped.

A bunch of girls she hadn't noticed laughed from behind her. The leader of the jock squad patted Lucas on the back and said, "That's right, man, you can't let a bitch ruin your fun." He stepped closer to her. He picked up a lock of hair from her shoulder and sniffed it. "If you want, I can distract her awhile."

Dani smacked his hand away, and the effort knocked her off balance. She stumbled against the railing, hurt that Lucas would speak to her that way and more hurt that he would allow that jerk to speak to her the way he had. She glared at Lucas as he laughed with the others and went back to partying. Anger and embarrassment carried her up the stairs. She lurched for the door to find her way home before passing out. On the porch, she literally ran into Kayden. He once again saved her from a spill. She looked up to find his amused face. Suddenly all her muscles felt limp.

"I don't think I can walk home." She paused. "Hey, has anyone ever told you how beautiful you are? Damn, boy. You are beautiful." It sounded like her voice, but she didn't remember deciding to say the words, true as they were.

"Don't worry, Dani. I'll give you a ride. To answer your question, I have been called handsome or attractive many times, but I don't believe *beautiful* is one I've heard." He scooped her up into his arms and smiled down with something like satisfaction in his hazel eyes.

Chase pulled up to the address Kayden had given him to find Danielle being loaded into Kayden's car. "What happened to her?"

He pushed Kayden out of the way and snatched her up, trying not to jostle her too much. He leaned her limp body against the side of the car. He supported her head while he checked her for injuries. Chase's heart sped while he looked her over. He used his lower body to pin her against the car in an effort to hold her up, and the contact was torture.

"She fell into me, literally, and said she couldn't make it home alone. She passed out. I was going to take her to the dorms and try to track her scent to her room." Kayden was clearly annoyed. "You should talk to her about not feeding on people who are overintoxicated. The practice is dangerous and a bit unethical." Kayden filled Chase in.

Dani half opened her eyes and mumbled, "I'm nobody's bitch!"

Chase wondered what had brought about that comment. "Where's her boyfriend? He should be protecting her!"

"Dude, I never saw him. The only vampires I scented were we two. I think he may have left her here. Nobody inside is even looking for her. I would have left her to her own devices, had I known you'd be treating me like the bad guy. *Shit*," Kayden said indignantly.

Feeling like a heel, Chase apologized. "Look, I'm sorry, man. Thanks for calling me. She looks like she needed both of us tonight."

Chase lifted her luscious body into his arms and carried her to his car. He fastened her seatbelt as she breathed his name. "Chase?"

He pulled back, thinking she was awake, but her eyes were still shut. "Yes, Lovely, I'm here." She sighed, reaching up to his face, and pulled him closer. His heart was pounding as she brushed her lips across his cheek to just below his ear and inhaled deeply. Her hand fell, and she turned her head to rest against the seat. After leaning against the car for a few minutes to calm down and put his thoughts back together, Chase drove to the dorm area.

When he carried her into the dorm, he had to enthrall a group of females so he wouldn't be seen. No males were permitted in the dorms at night. Her room number was on the key he'd fished out of her pocket. Once inside her room he saw a note on her bed. Chase laid her down and picked up the note.

BE SAFE! I'll be back tomorrow afternoon.

He spied a box of condoms on the bed, and his blood boiled. She was being left alone to have sex with a guy who didn't even care enough to see her home safely. Be safe? What a joke! Chase struggled to understand why he felt so possessive and protective of Danielle. She made him crazed. He'd never been territorial like he was around her, and she wasn't even his friend, much less a girlfriend.

He decided to leave her there and do his best to move on. He'd done his good deed for the year and it was time to go. She must have loved the guy who'd left her that night. He shook his head and went for the door.

She stirred on the bed. "I'm too hot," she whispered and began to disrobe. Before he knew it, she had her shirt off and was in the process of shimmying out of her jeans. She sniffed the air. "Chase, where'd you go?"

"I'm here, Lovely." Maybe he could just stay a little while to be sure she was well. Yeah, that was it. He wasn't making an excuse to stay near her. No, he was just staying until he was sure she wasn't going to be sick. He shut the door and locked it.

A sliver of moonlight spilled from the window across her body, revealing the perfect peaches-and-cream skin of her abdomen and her black panties. She weakly patted the bed next to her in an irresistible invitation.

Chase climbed in next to the delicious heat he'd been craving for weeks. She nuzzled in closer to his chest, and he wrapped his arm around the sweet curve of her hip. He brushed the hair out of her face and took the opportunity to freely absorb her perfect features. This was the face that haunted his dreams.

She opened her eyes and leveled him with the full force of her ice-blue gaze, combined with her skin against him, and the scent of vanilla and lavender. She turned her head, brushing his cheek with her soft lips, and told him, "I can smell you. You smell like happiness and sunshine."

The smile that crossed his face threatened to crack it. She was perfection, and knowing the attraction was mutual made him feel a little less insane. Chase didn't moon over females. He got what he needed, whether that was blood, sex, or a combination of the two, and he moved on. He didn't obsess and he *never* begged. He didn't have to, but something about this female made the blood drain from his head and gather in his rod every time he thought of her. Her rejection still stung, but at least he knew she was thinking of him as well.

"Why did you do that?" she spoke with her lips near his ear, sending chills over his skin.

"What did I do, Lovely?" He tensed, hoping he hadn't somehow offended her. She'd invited him into her bed, after all. Christ, if this little contact offended her, she'd be horrified by what he really wanted to do to her.

"You make me think of you, dream of you. Why?" she asked with a furrow in her lovely brow. It seemed her drunken mind wanted to speak a sober tongue, as the saying went.

"I've been dreaming of you also, my Lovely. Every minute of every day, since the first night I found you," he admitted. He couldn't take it anymore. He turned his face to find her lips, soft as petals. She kissed him back so sweetly, stroking him with her little pink tongue. He feared he would lose his heart right there in her arms. He ran the back of his hand down the bare skin of her side and further down past her lace panties. The waves of goose bumps rising and falling on her tender flesh made him want to follow them with his mouth.

"Do you want me, Chase?" she whispered around wet kisses.

Chase's mind swam with the thought of having all of her, but he wouldn't do that tonight. She was drunk, and he couldn't violate her trust that way. He'd taken too much from her that night. He already invaded her private thoughts, and she likely wouldn't remember it. "I do, Danielle, but I don't think this is the best night."

She giggled and threw her leg up over his hip.

"What's so funny?" he asked.

She was quiet for a moment. "I like hearing you say my name." She sobered. "You're not the first to turn me down."

"What is that supposed to mean?" He wasn't turning her down. He just needed to wait for her to be there with him mentally before he crossed that line. Who in his right mind had turned her down?

She rolled the rest of the way to straddle him and laid her face against his neck. It was not in a sexual way, but affectionate. "Lucas never wanted me either. I thought boys were supposed to be horny. Two years together, he never wanted me, not really. I feel like such an idiot for begging him to show me love." She sighed deeply and slurred, "There must be something wrong with me. Something is definitely wrong with me."

Chase's breath caught in his throat. The most alluring creature he'd ever laid eyes on had to beg for attention? How could the other male not want her every minute of every day?

"There's absolutely nothing wrong with you, Lovely, nothing at all." She snorted disbelievingly. He didn't argue the point. She drifted off to sleep, and he held her all night. He watched her breathe and played with the streaks in her hair. He daydreamed about what they could have together. He inhaled her seductive scent and eventually relaxed enough to fall asleep himself.

Chase woke in the morning to the sound of the door slamming. He jumped up to find Danielle's friend scowling at him.

"What did you do to her?" Olivia shouted.

"What? Where is she?" Chase was confused, and his Lovely was nowhere in sight.

"I don't know. She called me crying and said she had to go away for a few days. That I shouldn't worry about her. She said I should ask you to leave, before Lucas comes looking for her."

"How long ago was that?" Chase jumped up and picked his shirt up off the floor.

"Fifteen minutes ago, maybe," Olivia snapped.

Chase took off out of the room and ran smack into a large, blond wall at the door.

Olivia called from behind him, "Lucas, what happened to you last night?"

Chase realized he was eye to eye with the competition, and shock floored him. This was the male she'd referred to not wanting her the night before. Lucas was the reason she'd rejected him. He was the boyfriend waiting for her at home . . . and he was human.

Lucas moved first, having no idea Chase had spent the evening with Danielle. Stepping around the offending human, Chase followed Danielle's scent down the stairs and out the front door, wishing he could move at full speed, but there were too many witnesses. Her scent led him to the other end of the courtyard and into another dorm. She'd entered a male dorm building. He stalked up the stairs, still following the vanilla trail, until he reached the door where she had entered.

He could hear her crying inside as a male voice consoled her. Then she gasped and whispered, "He's here, Jared. Tell him I'm not here." She retreated into the bathroom.

"Who is here? What are you talking about?" Jared asked through the bathroom door.

"I can smell him. Tell him I'm not here," she whispered.

"Smell him?" Jared was confused.

"Just open the damn door," she hissed.

Chase stood there, trying to decide if he should force his way in or obey her wishes. The door opened to yet another blond human male. It was beginning to piss him off.

"I want to speak to Danielle," Chase told Jared, and he put a touch of mental compulsion behind the request.

Jared stepped out of the way in a daze.

Chase entered the room and grabbed a pen and paper from the desk to scribble on. He entered the bathroom and found Danielle curled up in the dry bathtub, crying. He leaned over to kiss her forehead.

"Please call me when you're ready to talk. I'm sorry if I offended you. Nothing happened between us last night, Lovely. I swear. Please don't be angry with me. I just wanted to protect you." Then he walked away, leaving his cell number behind. He wanted to scoop her up and carry her home with him. He wanted to be the guy she turned down other males for, but she didn't want to see him and his pride wouldn't allow him to stay.

Tessa slept restlessly on the sofa after dozing off while watching TV. She sat up with a jolt and let out a little gasp. Tessa snatched the phone from its cradle and called Danielle, but it went to voice mail. She paused to calm her voice before leaving a message.

"Dani, give me a call as soon as you can. I was thinking that maybe you could come home one weekend soon. Love you." She hung up and ran upstairs to dig for a box hidden in the back of her closet. She sat on her closet floor, holding the old shoebox on her crossed legs. She closed her eyes and sat there taking deep breaths. "Just relax," she told herself. "Don't jump to conclusions." Once she crossed that line, there would be no turning back. She would hold off as long as she could before making that phone call, but she dug out the number she needed and programmed it into her cell phone.

She returned the box to its hiding place. Then she jumped when the phone rang. It was Danielle returning her call. "Hello, sweetheart, how are you doing?" Anxiety laced through her tone.

Danielle's voice was shaking. "I'm on the way home, Mommy. I'll be there in an hour." She hung up.

Tessa sat back down on the floor of her closet. She stared at the wall and waited. The time had come.

Five

When Dani got home that night, she found her mother sitting on the floor of her walk-in closet with her head in her hands and her cell phone in her lap. They didn't talk about what had brought her home or what had caused Tessa to hole up in the closet. Dani helped her up off the floor, and they stood holding each other. They crawled into Tessa's bed wordlessly. Her mother held her all night, just like she had when Dani was a child.

The next morning Tessa made a big breakfast and they ate in silence. Each waited for the other to start. Dani really didn't know why she'd come home. She only knew that her mother would help sort out the confusion. So why couldn't she get the words out? The phone rang and Tessa went to answer it.

"Hello?" Tessa turned to look at Dani and mouthed, "Lucas."

Dani shook her head vigorously and mouthed, "I'm not here."

"No, Lucas, she's not home," Tessa lied and listened to Lucas's response. "I know her car is here, but she isn't. Can I give her a message?"

"I'll tell her. Good-bye." She hung up the phone and returned to the table. "Lucas said he is very sorry and to please give him a call," Tessa relayed the message. "And I will wait until you're ready to tell me what's going on, sweetheart." Then she went back to eating her breakfast.

They did the dishes—Tessa washing and Dani drying—as they

always had. Dani was thinking about how simple life had been just a month before, and she couldn't shake the feeling that it would never be that way again. Sadness began to well up in her chest, and she became consumed by the events of the recent weeks. The tears spilled down her cheeks, and she sat on the floor, leaning against the cabinets. Sobs began to shake her body, and she became swamped by all the fear that had been building up in her heart.

Something was wrong with her. She was somehow different, and it was terrifying. She'd felt this way ever since her fight with Lucas before she left for school. She'd thought she was going crazy then. Since then it had only gotten worse. How could she explain something to her mother that she herself couldn't understand? All she knew for sure was that she was somehow changing.

Tessa sat on the floor, taking Dani's hand in hers. She turned to face her daughter and was startled by her eyes. Her irises had gone jet black with no visible trace of her usual beautiful ice blue. Her eyes looked just like her father's eyes when he was emotional. His eyes had also turned when he fed or when they made love. Extreme emotions and need were his triggers. Tessa said nothing to alert Dani to the difference.

"Mom, I don't know what to do. I don't know what's wrong with me. I don't know why I can't get my head on straight, and I don't know what I think you're supposed to do about it, but I need help." She sobbed the words through bouts of hiccupping tears.

"I need you to be more specific for me. What does this have to do with Lucas? How did he know you were home?" Tessa tried to sort out what was going on with Dani without giving away anything Dani didn't need to know yet. Dani gave her a blow-by-blow description of the situation with Chase and Lucas.

Tessa was actually a little relieved. Dani's rant sounded mostly like the problem was the stress that transferring colleges had put on her relationship with Lucas. Tessa could deal with those kinds of problems. But the state of Dani's eyes was another situation altogether, and for that she would need backup.

"Sweetheart, this really is to be expected. You and Lucas were joined at the hip for two years. Now that there's a little distance between you, you'll both have to figure out who you are individually. Boys aren't as mature as we are, so they have more difficulty. That's no excuse for his behavior, but that likely has more to do with the people he is filling his free time with now that you're gone. Do you think you're going to be able to get past what happened yesterday?" Tessa watched Dani mull that over.

"I don't know. He was so mean, and I really don't know what happened. Maybe he doesn't want to be with me anymore. Maybe the distance is too far to maintain a relationship." Dani sighed.

"Do you want to find out what happened? I can tell you, judging by the conversation I had with him, that he still wants to be with you. He's made some mistakes, and you're going to have to deal with him either way." Tessa hoped that wouldn't happen until Dani got her emotions under control, because those eyes were enough to freak anybody out.

"I guess, but it might take me a while to get over it, and I feel like that will just make the situation worse. If he can't handle the distance between us now, how will he deal with me needing more space to get past this hurt?"

"Tell me more about Chase," Tessa pried.

"Chase is beautiful. Being near him makes me crazy, because I want to touch him, and I can't do that. Being away from him makes me crazy, because I want to touch him and I can't. And he smells like sunshine and happiness," Dani blurted.

"He smells like what?" Tessa raised one questioning eyebrow.

"I know. I know it's crazy, but I swear he smells like sunshine, and I can smell him before I see him. He came to find me yesterday, and I knew he was on the other side of the door," Dani admitted sheepishly. "I think I'm going crazy, Mom." She hung her head again.

"I see. That actually isn't crazy. Your father had quite a sense of smell. He always said I smelled like vanilla." She looked away from Dani, already knowing the answer and fearing the consequences of keeping her daughter in the dark for so long. "Does anybody else smell strongly?"

"I have been able to smell a lot of odd stuff lately. Everybody has a smell, but some people smell like food and some people are more like plants and flowers." Dani leaned into her mother and smiled. "You do smell like vanilla."

An odd look crossed Dani's face, and Tessa knew she was surprised to hear her speak of her father. "I guess I did inherit some stuff from him."

"You got a lot from your father. You have his hair, and some of your expressions are totally his. You look very much like him, actually. You just got stuck with my eyes and height." Tessa stared off into the distance, as if she could see him standing on the other side of the kitchen table.

"You never told me that," Dani whispered and ran her hand through her hair.

"I fear there are a lot of things I haven't told you, but now is not the time to start my confessions."

"Why not tell me now?" Dani scoffed.

"Because Lucas is about to knock on the door, and I think you should talk to him." Tessa pointed toward the large mirror above the table in the foyer. From where they sat on the kitchen floor, they could see that Lucas was pacing on the porch.

"I'm not going to tell you who you should choose, but I'd be interested to see what might happen with Mr. Sunshine. Those were some powerful feelings you were talking about, and it has to be hard to ignore feelings that strong. Just be honest with both of them, no matter what you decide."

Tessa took one more look at Dani to see if her eyes had returned to normal. Everything was in order, except for the obvious tracks of tears. Tessa went to the door to let Lucas in, directing him toward the kitchen, and then went to her room to give them some privacy.

Dani listened to Lucas slowly sulk into the kitchen with his shoes dragging on the hardwood floor. Dani faced away from the door, still sitting on the floor against the cabinet. He sat in the spot her mother had just vacated and laid a hand on her shoulder, but Dani jerked away.

"What do you want?" she asked without inflection.

"I want to talk to you. I want to apologize. I want things to be like they used to be between us," he pleaded. "It kills me to see you huddled on the floor crying because of me."

She shook her head. "I haven't changed, Lucas. Not toward you."

"Yes, you have. You have new friends, a new home, and practically a whole new life that I don't have a place in anymore," he spat out.

"You seem to have made some new friends too. I'm not complaining about that. What did you think was going to happen? Was I supposed to go to school, sit in my room and cry over your picture, while you hit the clubs and partied with your new friends? I can't believe you're sitting there trying to make me feel bad about having goals and wanting to go to school." She was crying again. Damn it!

"Dani, will you please turn around and look at me?" Lucas put his hand on her back. "I want you to tell me what happened Friday night."

She kept her back to him. Looking at his face would wash away her anger, and she needed to be angry. She wanted the truth. Her vision went blurry with the rage that burned at the memory of that night. She focused on getting the truth.

Lucas was quiet at first. He was thinking, trying to decide how much to tell her of what he could remember. She didn't realize, at first, that he wasn't speaking out loud, until the pictures started to flash in her mind. Then she knew she was in his head, just like that night in the back of his pickup. She decided to relax and close her eyes. Everything that was running through Lucas's mind flashed behind her eyelids.

She saw the entire evening from his perspective. The football players thought she was the hottest thing at the party, and they told him so. He didn't like the fact that he would be going home and she would be staying there with all those guys. The more they drank, the more comments the guys made about her.

He saw her leave the kitchen area and followed her to the hall, where he watched her speak to Chase's friend Kayden. It was fuel to his jealous fire after listening to the jocks all evening. He went back to the kitchen, where the guys were then joined by a bevy of girls. He stood and watched the group, imagining her with all the ballplayers who wanted her more than any of the other girls. The crowd headed down the stairs to the game room, and he followed. Looking around the room, he noticed the girls were checking him out. "That's right," he thought to himself. "She's not the only one who can find someone else."

One of the girls stepped forward. He smiled slyly at the girl and said suggestively, "What can I do for you?"

The girl raised her eyebrows in disgust. "You can get your shit together and go find your girlfriend. You got her all drunk and left her alone, asshole!" She stomped up the stairs. It was Lindsay. Dani was mortified. One of the jocks saw the conversation and patted him on the shoulder. "You're screwed, man. You might as well have fun while you can. Bitches stick together."

After that he only had flashes of memories of rolling around making out with some chick. He was trying to screw her, because it'd been so long since he had any ass, but he was so wasted he couldn't get it up. So he got her off with his hand. Everything else was blank until he woke up. He was lying on the floor of a bedroom he'd never seen before with a half-naked girl sleeping in his arms. He ran back to Dani's dorm and the door opened before he could knock. He collided with another guy who he assumed was with Olivia, but it was Chase just leaving Dani's room after spending the night with her.

Lucas let Chase pass. He was more worried about finding Dani but she was already gone. He sat on her bed with his head in his hands. He couldn't even call her. His cell phone was missing. He had ruined everything, again.

Dani jumped up, and when his hand left her back, the images stopped. She was so focused on finding the truth that somehow she'd been sucked into his memory and absorbed by it. She turned to Lucas, but he was staring off into space, the same way he did that night in the back of his truck. She wasn't sure what she'd done, but she was glad he wasn't going to follow her. A hiss escaped her lips. She was so angry and hurt by her look into his mind.

Dani ran up the stairs and into her room. She was forcing a few things into an old duffel bag to go back to school when her mom entered the room. Dani was furious. So furious she wanted to hurt someone, break something.

Apparently her mother knew, because she said, "I can feel the waves of tension in the air around you. It's just like the angry static your father used to emit at times. Danielle, I need you to calm down. Where is Lucas?" She put a hand on Dani's wrist, but Dani yanked it away. Tessa grabbed her by the shoulders and turned her around, flinching slightly when she looked into her eyes.

"Please, let me go. I need to get back to school. I can't deal with his crap. I just want to leave. He's in the kitchen. Don't wake him until I'm gone." Dani pulled out of her mother's grasp and headed for the stairs. She needed to leave and leave immediately. Whatever was wrong with her was getting worse, and she just wanted to run from it.

"You aren't leaving until we talk! What happened with Lucas? Why are you so angry? We can get through this together. I can get help." Tessa chased her down the stairs.

"Oh, now you wanna talk? Twenty-one years of silence, and now you wanna talk!" By the time she reached the foyer table to grab her purse and keys, not only were her eyes black, but her canine teeth were also slightly elongated. She froze at the sight of herself in the mirror and stared for a moment before squeezing her eyes shut and taking deep breaths to calm herself. When she opened her eyes, they were ice blue again, and her teeth were normal. Tessa stood behind her taking ragged breaths. Tears fell from her chin, making dark spots on her pink shirt.

"I love you, Mom," Dani told Tessa's reflection in the mirror. "I'll text you when I get to school. Tell Lucas I need some space. It seems boys are the least of my worries right now." She tilted her head in the direction of the kitchen. Dani didn't want to see Lucas sitting there, dazed. She was stunned by what she'd just seen, and what she'd done to Lucas. Her mind raced, and the only explanation that came to her was one she couldn't yet accept. This was all about her father. Her mother had implied it just a moment ago. This was happening to her because of who, or what, her father was. It was a crazy thought. She didn't want to believe it, but the proof had just been staring back at her in the mirror.

Tessa stepped forward and wrapped her arms around Dani. "I love you too, baby. I think it's time we get some help."

"This has something to do with my father, doesn't it?" She still watched Tessa in the mirror.

"Yes, it has everything to do with your father," Tessa finally admitted.

Dani hung her head and shut her eyes. "I'm not ready, Mom. I thought I wanted all the answers but I was wrong. I'm not ready." She gathered her things and left.

Tessa sat at the kitchen table. Lucas slowly began to come around. She recognized the absent look in his eyes. She'd seen it before on the faces of people who had been lulled into giving a little blood or information. Vampires enthralled their donors before feeding so they didn't remember the experience, and it was actually very pleasurable for the human. Something about the saliva messed with the pleasure centers in the human brain. Tessa knew so from personal experience. She bent to look at Lucas, turning his head from side to side. There were no signs of a recent bite. That meant Dani was able to enter his mind to retrieve the information she wanted. She picked her cell off the counter and found the newly programmed number. She no longer had a choice. She had to get help for her daughter.

Dani looked around the empty parking lot at Thirst and sighed. She'd been sitting on the sidewalk, propped up against the brick building with her hoodie pulled over her head, for an hour. On the long ride back to school she began to understand people who said they needed a drink after a stressful day. The blissful numbness that came with getting a good drunk on sounded like just the thing she needed.

Her life up to this point had been drama free. Now she had more issues than anyone she'd ever known. She wanted to be alone and she was tired of driving. If she went to the dorm she would have to face Olivia and Lindsay. Dani was too mortified by the things her friend had seen to face them just yet. So Dani went to the club for some solitude and a dose of liquid courage. It was too early for the club to be open, but she expected the staff to be rolling in soon. Vince was the head of security, so she hoped he would be in early and ready to live up to his promises to "hook her up." She'd nearly fallen asleep waiting.

"Can Vince help you?" Vince's baritone asked gruffly as he passed her. "We aren't hiring any waitresses right now if you're looking for a job, and I can't let you squat here, so move along."

Dani hopped to her feet and hurried after him. "You said I should come to you if I needed anything." Vince turned and a wide smile cracked the harsh planes of his face when he recognized her. His eyes ran down her body with interest.

Danielle cocked her head to the side and tried to be cute. She stepped a little too close for comfort. She saw a flash of something hot in his eyes before he shook his head and took a step back. His expression changed from heated interest to concern. He brushed her cheek with the back of his hand. "Vince would be glad to help you get whatever you need. As much as Vince would like to be the male to take your mind off of whatever ails you, I can't risk my job. Your boy Chase would have my ass handed to me right after he canned it." Dani blushed and frowned. Did he have to bring up Chase?

"Princess, are you alright? You look sad," he asked with true concern.

"I'm fine, Vince. All I need is some privacy and a few drinks. You think you could let me in until the club opens? I would prefer to drink alone today." Tears began to form in her eyes. "And don't call Chase, please. I know he's a friend of yours, but we're friends too, right? And I do still owe you a dance. If you get the music going, I'd be happy to pay up."

Vince let out a hearty chuckle. "Bad day, princess? Come on in, and Vince'll hook you up." He put an arm around her shoulders and led her into the club.

Once inside she settled herself onto a sofa in the VIP section. Vince got the music on, but not too loud. A very attractive man came to take her drink order. "What can I get for you?"

"I'll be honest. I'm not a drinker, so you can surprise me. Maybe something sweet would be good," she politely suggested.

"Of course you're not a drinker." He smiled at Dani playfully and went to get her drink. As he walked away, she took in his broad shoulders and the tight jeans that showed off his assets and wondered what he meant by that. Did she look so young that she obviously wouldn't be a drinker? Vince gave her a wave from the other side of the club and disappeared.

The bartender returned, shirtless, with a tray of drinks and shots. Holy smoke, but he was hot. He had dark hair and smoky eyes to match, his body honed to perfection. He handed her a drink and took a shot for himself. They clinked their glasses together, and he downed his shot. Not to be outdone she gulped hers as he took another shot. He took her empty glass and handed her another. They were good. It didn't taste anything like the nasty Purple Jesus or the beer she'd choked on. She drank it quickly, and he took a third shot.

Holding out his hand to her he asked, "Would you like to dance?"

She smiled and took his hand, feeling a little torn. She was second-guessing the wisdom of being alone with a guy. This wasn't what she'd come for. She only wanted time alone to think about everything that was happening in her life and to her body. Then the memory of Lucas nearly having sex with some strange girl came back to her like a kick in the gut. "I'd love to dance." She held out her hand to the handsome bartender.

And so they did. He led her out to the floor, and they danced. She could actually see the beautiful hardwood floor that had been obscured by so many people the last time she'd been there. The lights flashed as they moved together to the beat of the music. He left her on the floor once to go fetch another drink. She was already pretty buzzed, but that was what she'd come for, right? To achieve the same numbness she'd experienced the other night. She wanted to forget for a while, and so far, she had done a good job. Dani threw back one more drink, and her companion, whose name she hadn't bothered to learn, drank his shot. He looked buzzed too. They laughed and danced and spun around the floor, until she was so dizzy she could hardly stand. Thankfully, a slower song came on, and he gathered her up in his strong arms and held her close to his chest. She smelled him then. He smelled spicy, like hot cinnamon candy. His essence was so sweet and hot, she wanted to taste it. The urge became overwhelming, and her vision went all weird. Memories of her own jet-black eyes gave her pause. That had to be how she looked. What would the bartender do if he noticed? He looked down and smiled at her with smoldering expectation. Good thing it was dark, and she was too drunk to care.

"That's right, beautiful, you're ready, aren't you? You want me right now, don't you?" He scooped Dani up and carried her back to the sofa. He positioned her so that she straddled his lap and pulled her mouth down to his. Dani froze at first, but his body was so damn hot, and she could hear his heartbeat. It pounded out her name, over and over. His sex was stiff, and he rubbed himself against her. She kissed him back, until he turned his face and guided her to his neck. God, the smell of him was so delicious, and his pulse beat wildly against her lips.

"Take it. Take me now. Please, I want to feel you," he whispered huskily.

She felt pressure in her mouth. Her teeth ached. The need was overwhelming. She was so thirsty, or was it hunger? His pulse pounded in her ears, and the spicy, sweet smell permeated her mind. Instinctively, Dani found a spot below his ear and bit down on his neck. He writhed under her and panted, "Yes. Please, yes." The flow of hot, sweet liquid running down her throat was intoxicating and delicious. She felt strong and sensual, and she hungered for more.

Mason and his mate, Deborah, were having dinner with Griffin and his mate, Sarah. It had been so long since they had done this. Mason missed Griffin's companionship and hoped to make it a regular event.

Mason had witnessed Griffin's greatest heartbreak, and seeing Mason sometimes brought those painful memories back to him. So, over the last few years, Griffin had withdrawn from him. They spoke frequently at council meetings but almost always kept it to council-related issues.

The waiter brought their selections, refilled their wine glasses, and retreated to the kitchen. The women ate and planned a shopping trip to select new dresses for the gala. They also made plans to have a girls' night out on the town.

Mason looked at Griffin. "So how are you these days?" Mason didn't expect an honest reply, at least not when Sarah was present.

"I'm still here. Business is good, and the kids are growing and healthy. That's all you can ask for, right?" Griffin mumbled around a bite of steak.

"I'm going to the range to hit some balls on Saturday. You should come with me," Mason said, when his phone jingled in his jacket pocket and interrupted him. "Excuse me," he said as he pulled it out.

Deborah shot him a dirty look from across the table. She hated it when he took calls at the table.

He didn't recognize the number. Normally, he'd let it go to voice mail, but he was compelled to answer.

"Mason. It's me. I need your help," a voice whispered on the other end of the line.

"I'm sorry. Who did you say this is?" Not recognizing the caller's voice, he shrugged and smiled at Griffin, who watched intently.

Sarah said loudly from across the table, "Griffin, dear, please don't dump so much salt on your vegetables."

"Shit! He's with you!" the voice on the other end exclaimed. "You should call me later, when you're alone. It doesn't matter what time."

Now Mason was dumbstruck. "Who did you say this was again?" Everyone at the table was looking at him now.

"It's Tessa Vaughn. You promised that if your goddaughter ever needed anything, I could count on you. Well, now's the time, Mason. She's turning and I have no idea what to do. Please, help me," she pleaded in a trembling voice.

The shock of hearing the voice of a woman whose secret he had kept for over two decades nearly felled him before the words began to sink in. He couldn't react, and he needed to diffuse the situation in front of him. He had the attention of the table. As casually as he could manage, he replied, "I'm sorry, but you have the wrong number." He paused a moment and then continued, "No problem, good-bye." Looking back at everyone, he shrugged again and went back to the talk of a golf outing.

Six

Chase slumped on the sofa of his usual table at the club. He looked out over the crowd where Kayden was busy showing off his dance moves. But Chase wasn't really seeing anything at all. He was far too busy replaying the evening he'd spent with Danielle over and over in his mind. The unforgettable smell of Danielle had clung to him the whole next day, making Chase crazy with desire. Once it wore off, the fact that he could no longer smell her drove him insane.

When he'd entered the club, he actually thought she was there. He was sure her scent lingered all over the dance floor, but a search turned up nothing and left him disappointed. That sweet vanilla with just a hint of lavender haunted him. He closed his eyes and remembered the feel of her skin on the back of his hand as he caressed her, the silk of her hair as he brushed it with his fingers and it poured over his shoulder, the weight of her body lying on him as she breathed deeply against his neck. God, her lips on his neck as she admitted she couldn't stop thinking of him, dreaming of him. The thoughts did nothing but make him hot and eager.

He hadn't fed in two days. Not since just before he had picked her up that night. He couldn't do it. His stomach had been in knots since he'd left her curled up in another male's bathtub. He'd left her there, vulnerable and crying. His need was intense and clouding his thoughts. He swore he could hear her calling his name. In the back of his mind, he heard a whisper.

Help me, Chase. I'm afraid. Please, help me.

The voice brought to life the protective instinct Chase had for Danielle. He needed to feed worse than he realized if he was hearing voices.

Idly he thought, *Where are you, Lovely?* and was shocked up off the sofa when he got an answer in the form of a picture in his mind. It was dark, but he could see light shining under a door, illuminating the bottoms of shelves and boxes. He could hear the very same music that was playing in the club. She was there, and she was calling him! Or maybe he was actually going crazy.

Just then, Vince came in his direction from the door. Seeing the alarm on Chase's face, he scanned the floor. "What's up, man? You got trouble?"

"Have you seen Danielle? I think she is here somewhere."

Vince looked away and shook his head before returning to answer, "Well, she was here a few hours before we opened. Maybe you're just catching an old scent."

"What do you mean she was here? Why didn't you call me? Why didn't you tell me?" Chase growled right up in Vince's face. "When did she leave?"

"Vince didn't see her leave. He gave her the privacy she asked for, and when he came back downstairs, she was gone. She was sitting outside crying when Vince got here. She asked him not to call you and asked to drink in private. He provided her with Nathan and left them alone," Vince defended with his hands up in surrender. "It seemed like a good opportunity. You know we've been coming up blank on her, so I figured if I befriended her she might give some info directly."

"Nathan was her host?" Maybe he would know where she went.

"Yeah, but he left not feeling well before his shift started. Vince had to call in another guy and figured she must have gone a little overboard and left the poor guy weak. He was looking pretty drunk, eyes all dilated and unfocused." Vince smirked at the thought of Dani draining the human to exhaustion.

Chase heard it again. *I need you, Chase.* So weak and quiet, the voice almost wasn't audible.

"Check every square inch of this building now! She's here!" Chase shouted and took off to look for her himself.

After a thorough search, Chase started to doubt his sanity again. Vince appeared at the stairs and waved him over. Vince turned and headed back down the steps. Chase stalked down to the storage level of the building to find Vince.

Danielle was in the back, laid out on the floor with her face toward the rear door, recreating the exact image portrayed in Chase's mind. Vince tried to rouse her while Chase stood for a moment in shock. He snapped to attention and began to growl at Vince.

"I think you've done enough already; get out of my way! Go bring my car around and have Kayden meet me out front now!" Scooping the lifeless-looking beauty up onto his lap, he sat on the floor trying to get a response out of her.

"Lovely, can you hear me?" She didn't answer. He held her face by the chin and opened an eyelid with his thumb. Her pupils were entirely black, her fangs extended, and her breath was very shallow.

Chase rose to his feet in one smooth motion and carried her out the back door and around the front to avoid pushing through the crowd upstairs. He told himself over and over like a mantra, "She will be fine. She will be fine."

When he got outside, Kayden was leaning against the door of his waiting car, looking annoyed. Kayden's eyes flew open when he caught sight of Chase running at him. "Open the door and help me get in the back." Kayden obeyed, and Chase climbed in, still holding Danielle. He laid her on his lap and began to look her over more closely for injuries. "Drive to my place quickly. I don't care if you have to run every light. Can you get Doc Stevens to meet us there?"

Doc Stevens was a vampire with a medical degree, who made house calls for vampires. It wasn't as if they could go to the hospital for care. His expertise was needed if someone was severely injured, and he usually attended all the vampire births in the area. Being a doctor gave him the perfect opportunity to feed. His busy practice brought human patients to him daily.

Chase knew something was very wrong with Danielle. He tried uselessly to wake her, and her eyes were all wrong. A vampire's eye only reacted like this to extreme emotion or intense need like stress, anger, hunger, or passion. It wasn't simple drunkenness if Nathan had been able to walk out on his own motor. He'd have been dead from alcohol poisoning for her to have been laid so low.

"Doc will be there shortly. He's finishing up with a patient in the area. We really need to get this girl help. She doesn't know when to say when." Kayden shook his head in shame for the girl.

"Something is wrong with her!" Chase raged. "The person she fed from left on his own two feet after speaking to Vince. That means I'm gonna have to find him, because she didn't make it to the basement on her own." He ran his hands through her hair and whispered to her when they arrived at his building.

Chase handed Danielle over to Kayden so he could climb out of the backseat. As he emerged, he saw the last person he wanted to see sitting on a bench in the vestibule. Samantha was not going to like this, but he couldn't deal with her now. Retrieving Danielle from Kayden's arms, he took off for the elevator. "Kayden, deal with her, and then come help me."

"Aw, man!" Kayden drawled. "Give her back to me, and you deal with that nightmare."

Chase ignored this suggestion. He didn't like seeing Kayden touching his Lovely. She looked so fragile, and she smelled weird. She smelled like someone sedated. The smell of it was overwhelming her usual delicious scent.

Samantha jumped to her feet when he entered the building and asked, "Who the hell is that? Please tell me you're not killing your prey these days."

The elevator opened and Chase jumped in, hitting the penthouse button without responding or so much as looking in Samantha's direction. Again he told himself, "She's going to be fine. She's going to be fine."

Mason was taken off guard when the call had come in from Tessa. He knew something was terribly wrong. The last time he'd seen her was the day he told her of Griffin's engagement to Sarah. That had been a difficult day for both of them. Tessa had lost her mate and the father of her newborn to another female, and Mason was feeling guilt and responsibility for the separation of his best friend from his new family.

Tessa was very lucky that the baby was able to accept human breast milk. It took several frustrating tries, but once she was hungry enough, the babe sucked it down greedily. Tessa was able to care for the baby without vampire intervention.

The day Tessa gave birth to Griffin's child, the midwife broke her vow of silence and reported it to his parents. Lloyd and Adele Vaughn were the heads of the House of Vaughn, and her information was very valuable. A human would not be tolerated. Mason knew Griffin would be followed when he returned after meeting with his parents. His mother wanted him to bring her the child and to get rid of the mother. If Griffin wouldn't do it, they would wait until he left her again and take care of the situation themselves. So Mason hid her and the baby without Griffin's knowledge. Tessa and the newborn were already long gone when Griffin returned to his condo to retrieve them after the confrontation with his parents.

Griffin searched high and low for his mate and the baby, using every resource at his disposal without tipping off his parents. Unfortunately his parents were also hunting for them. At that point it seemed to Mason that the bond between Griffin and Tessa had to be weaker than Griffin wanted to admit. If they'd had a true vampire blood bond, Griffin would have been able to feel her presence clearly. He would have known for sure that Tessa was safe, but Griffin lost hope with every day that passed.

Mason had planted fake medical records to make them believe neither mother nor child had survived. Mason had felt like the worst friend ever for not reassuring Griffin that his family was under Mason's protection, but he couldn't risk their lives. Mason had to wait for the records to be discovered before he could take Griffin to their hiding place. If he told Griffin they were safe before that, it would all be for nothing. He would rush to Tessa's side and give them away.

The information was found within a couple months, but his family had waited another month to tell Griffin. Mason was afraid they hadn't taken the bait and were still searching, so he waited for Griffin to come to him with the sad news of their deaths. That had been Mason's mistake. He believed his best friend would call him immediately in need of comfort, but Griffin didn't call Mason until days after he had proposed to Sarah. Then they were in a pickle. Griffin was already bonded to Tessa. Mason thought Griffin was insane for bonding with a human, but his love for Tessa was plain to see. Mason had wondered if it would work like a normal bonding for that reason, and it did work, but as far as he could tell the bond was weaker than a true vampire bonding . . .

Vampire bonding was a strong connection. Vampires would always be aware of their mates and their mates' emotions. Vampires could feel their mates' fears, joy, and sometimes pain or pleasure. That was why vampires didn't share blood unless they were bonding, or in extreme emergencies to save another's life. The connection was soul deep and so strong that even if the vampire weren't in love with his or her betrothed before the ceremony, it would be different afterward. Being without that person would be unthinkable. There was no divorce in the vampire world. The only separation was in death, and that would be crushing for the one left behind.

The day he went to break the news about Griffin's engagement, Tessa was out of her mind. Griffin was supposed to meet Mason later that day, and Mason intended to bring him back to Tessa. They would have to figure out how to break his engagement without starting a family feud. Griffin and Sarah were to be bonded in only a week.

Tessa raged, and Mason began to think that Griffin had given her too much of his blood. Maybe she was becoming a vampire after all. Her heart broke at the news that Griffin had consented to bond with another woman less than twelve hours after he learned of her supposed death.

After she managed to break every dish in the house and several pieces of furniture, she calmed a bit. Her next request was against Mason's best wishes for his friend, but Tessa had a right to protect her child, and she felt betrayed by her mate. She asked Mason not to tell Griffin she was alive. She reasoned that if they broke the engagement, Griffin's parents would suspect foul play. They would follow him and come for the baby. Losing her baby was not an option, and Griffin hadn't even mourned their loss.

Mason had no idea how Griffin's new bonding would affect her. It had never been done, to his knowledge, unless the first mate was actually dead. He left her that day, and when he returned to see how she was doing after Griffin's bonding, she was gone.

Mason felt the weight of blame for not trusting Griffin to do the right thing to protect his mate and child. If he'd at least given Griffin some hint that Tessa was waiting for him with their child, everything would have been different. With a heavy heart he'd returned Tessa's call the previous night and was surprised to hear her account of the recent events in Soleil's life. She'd made it to twenty-one years old before her father's genes made themselves known. Mason was on his way to meet Tessa. They had to decide the best way to help Soleil make the transition.

As he pulled up to the restaurant, Tessa was crossing the parking lot. She was still absolutely perfect, slight and curvy in all the right places. Her hair was shorter, but the same glossy dark blond. She didn't look to be any more than three years older than the last time he saw her, much less her actual forty-one years. The vampire blood she'd ingested years ago was responsible for her agelessness. Griffin had chosen his first mate well, Mason had to admit.

As he entered the dining room, she saw him and came to wrap him in an embrace. Her sorrow immediately overwhelmed him. Mason was blessed—or cursed, depending on the point of view—with an extrasensorial gift. All vampires had certain abilities, like strength, speed, mind control of humans, and incredible eyesight and hearing, but a few had extra abilities. Some were able to read minds or predict the future, or, in Griffin's case, had telekinesis. Mason was empathic. He could read the emotions or manner of a person or vampire with a touch. If a person was a cold-blooded killer, he could feel his or her evil and anger with a touch. If he were a humanitarian, Mason could feel his love of others and his giving nature, as well as his current emotions. It was very difficult to lie to Mason.

When he touched Tessa, he realized that she'd been in mourning all those years, and his heart felt the anguish of her daily struggle. He pulled back and looked her in the eyes. He thought he would cry at the pain and the rawness of it, as if no time had passed since the day he'd told her of Griffin's engagement.

She smiled weakly and said, "Oh now, don't you do that. I'm fine, Mason. It's been a long time, and I've learned to deal with it just fine."

"My God, Tessa, how do you breathe? It's stifling." He was suddenly angry at Griffin and regretted going along with the plan so many years ago.

"I said I'm fine. And that's not what I've dragged you out here for. I'm very sorry about having to involve you in this situation." She tried not to show her pain and apparently had become a pro at it. As they took their seats, she handed him the most recent picture of Danielle she had. It was from the day she'd left for college. She was leaning against her car, wearing a university T-shirt. He stared at the picture appraisingly.

"She looks so much like Griffin with that hair. It's unreal. She has your eyes and figure, and the rest is all him. It's actually surprising this hasn't happened sooner, given the resemblance. She is a breathtaking beauty."

"Thank you. Does she look anything like her siblings?" She looked at the table.

"Yes, she looks like her little brother. J. R. is also the spitting image of his father." Mason looked at her cautiously. "How did you know she has siblings?"

"I know heirs were very important to his house, but I also felt his joy when his kids were born. It was the same as when Danielle was born. Overwhelming pride and adoration is the only way I can describe it. I believe one child was born slightly more than a year after Danielle and another maybe ten years ago." She still couldn't look at him.

"You can still feel him?" The thought made his stomach sick.

"I feel him every day," she whispered.

"You are correct. He had twin girls a couple of months after your daughter's first birthday and a son who is now ten." Pausing, Mason thought about the fact that Tessa didn't call the girl Soleil. "You called her Danielle?" Mason had noticed twice she'd used the new name.

"Her name was changed. I thought leaving her with the unusual name her father gave her would make it easier to find her, but we both kept his last name," she explained.

"You never remarried?"

"I'm still bonded, Mason. When he broke his bond to me, it

didn't change mine to him. I still feel him, even if he doesn't feel me. I can't even look at another man. I'm sure if you considered leaving Deborah for another woman, you'd see what I mean. I'm still his mate." Tears began to well in her eyes. "Even if I forced myself to move on, it wouldn't sever our bond. Humans don't bond the way vampires do. Humans don't share blood, and there is no soul connection. I suppose if I bonded to another vampire it might break my bond to Griffin, but there aren't many vampires who are willing to do more than feed on my kind. I'll be honest, even if I found a willing vampire, I don't think I could do it again."

"I see your point. Has Soleil . . . I mean Danielle, ever asked any questions? How much does she know already?"

"She's been asking questions about her father since she was old enough to understand she should have one. I never gave her any answers until a couple of years ago, and even then I didn't tell her anything other than his family didn't approve of me, and that he had married someone else. She asked me yesterday if her condition had anything to do with her dad. I told her it had everything to do with him, and then she ran out."

"Do you know if she has fed yet?" Mason pondered Danielle's state of mind, and if she had bitten someone while having no idea what was happening to her. He also believed she would need to feed soon; and once she did, her abilities would make themselves known. The poor kid probably did believe she was going crazy.

"No, I don't think so. I haven't been able to reach her since she left yesterday."

Mason stared at Danielle's picture. "Is this the school she attends?" he asked, pointing at her shirt.

"Yes, she transferred there this year."

"That university is no more than forty-five minutes from my home. It shouldn't be too difficult to keep an eye on her, but we're going to have to figure out how to break this news to her. She'll likely need a little Vampire 101. We can't have her out there breaking laws she isn't aware of yet. The sooner, the better, I think." Mason hesitated before asking, "Do you want Griffin to know?"

"Not if he doesn't need to know. I'm afraid of what his family's opinion will do to her. I can just imagine the slurs other vampires will fling at her. Not to mention the displeasure he will have with you if he discovers your part in our disappearance." Tessa spoke with her head in her hands. She lifted it when the waiter came to the table, and she ordered a martini and a salad.

"No wonder you're still so thin." Mason smiled and ordered the same martini and a steak with potatoes.

"When can you talk to her?" Tessa asked as she pulled out her cell.

"Can you get her home on Saturday? I think we should do it as soon as possible. Tell her to call you if she has any trouble. I'll go get her sooner if necessary."

Tessa nodded in acknowledgment and placed the call, but it went straight to voice mail. She made another call to Danielle's roommate and was informed that Danielle hadn't returned to her dorm. Tessa's hands shook when she disconnected the call and laid her phone on the table.

"She should have been there no later than four o'clock yesterday afternoon." Tessa downed the martini the waiter had just set in front of her and asked for another. "I shouldn't have let her go."

Brandi Vaughn was visiting her grandparents with her brother, J. R., when a disturbing call came in. Several young vampires had gone missing over the last few weeks, and one of them had been found dead of complete consumption. Brandi listened intently from the dining room while her grandparents spoke with other members of the council over the speakerphone in the study.

"We can't let this happen again, Lloyd. We need to find these kids and their captor," the speaker argued.

"We don't know that this situation has anything to do with what happened in the past, Alexander," Grandpa replied, sounding agitated.

"Adele, will you please reason with him? This cannot be a coincidence," a female voice said. "The Davis boy was gifted, and so was one of the other missing youths. The fact that he was found completely drained should be a clear sign."

"I realize this is a sensitive subject for your family, but we can't let this situation get out of hand. I'm going to go examine the body to see if I can get a scent. I wish you would come with me," Alexander pleaded.

Brandi stepped into the kitchen, holding her stomach as if she would be sick. She was a friend of Shane Davis's at school and knew he had been missing. To hear of his death made her heartsick. He had the extrasensory ability of being able to sense the gifts of other vampires. He didn't like it, because when babies were born, their parents would call his parents to have him come see the newborn. They just couldn't wait until they were older to see if their child was gifted.

After gathering herself and calling Samantha to inform her of Shane's tragic death, she went to see if she could ascertain anything else from the meeting. But it was over, and Grandpa was already heading out the door with her father.

Brandi entered the study, where her grandma still sat at the desk in deep concentration. "What's wrong, Gran? Can I help you with anything? Grandpa looked upset."

"Don't worry about anything, sweetling. Everything is fine. Grandpa had some business to attend."

"Does it have to do with the missing kids? I know two of them. I would be glad to help search." Brandi was digging. She knew she wouldn't get far with her grandmother but tried anyway.

"I do think there is something you can do to help. I don't want you or your sister going anywhere alone until we find the missing children. You girls need to watch each other's backs and keep your eyes open for danger. Don't be surprised if your father gives you a curfew until this is all straightened out. I know you're too old for a curfew, but he has good reason to worry, and it's in your best interest to obey your father's wishes." Adele turned and raised one eyebrow at Brandi. "Did you overhear our conversation?"

Brandi couldn't hold back the tears. She nodded as her lower lip trembled. "Shane was my friend. We went to school together, and I can't imagine why anyone would want to hurt such a nice guy." Gran stood and came to put her arms around Brandi. It was a little weird because she'd never been the comforting sort, but Brandi was glad for the affection and support.

"I'm sure you and your siblings will be safe, given none of you has an extra ability, but I still want you to stick together for the time being."

Brandi didn't understand her statement until the phone rang again. Her father called to inform Gran of the recovery of another child. Melinda Prince was the other kid Brandi and her sister knew that was missing. She had been found drugged but still alive on her parents' lawn. Doc Stevens was on the way to examine her and assess her injuries. Her dad was hopeful they'd be able to get some information from the girl once she was well enough to speak to them.

Suddenly things made a little more sense to Brandi. Melinda was an athlete, but she didn't have an extrasensory ability. Shane, on the other hand, had a special touch. Melinda came home, but Shane didn't make it back alive. Someone was hunting for gifted young vampires. Brandi was going to be sick. She sat down heavily on the leather sofa and shut her eyes as her stomach churned. Everyone was at risk whether they were gifted or not, and the thought of how many friends she could lose was horrifying.

Chase paced nervously up and down the hall leading to the closed door of his bedroom. Doc Stevens had come back to examine Danielle again. He'd been there earlier to have a look at her but had to leave for an emergency once he was sure she was stable. Chase sat bedside and watched for any movement the whole time Doc was gone. It'd been four hours since he laid her in his bed, and she hadn't moved a muscle. Chase stared at her beautiful face and all that gorgeous, mahogany hair spilling over his pillows. Her peaches-and-cream skin, so soft and pale against the slate gray of his satin sheets, made his fingers itch to touch her. He could imagine her there every night for the rest of his existence. She looked like she belonged there with him. It took all of his willpower to keep his hands to himself. He decided that he wanted her to remember the next time they touched that way, so he wasn't about to crawl in bed with her. It was a good thing Doc came back when he did, because Chase's resolve had begun to thin.

Kayden watched from the sofa down the hall while Chase wore a hole in the carpet. "Dude, you look like you're waiting for that chick to have your baby or something. What's the deal with you?"

"Shut up or leave, Kayden." Chase glared at him.

"I'm not leaving you here like this, man. You look like you might need me to fetch you something sweet to feed on. How long has it been, anyway? You aren't gonna be any good to sleeping beauty in there if you go under."

Kayden had a point. It was very early on Monday morning, and Chase hadn't fed since Friday night. He felt weak, and confusion was setting in. "Fine. I need to feed, but I'm not leaving. Maybe you can get one of the regular girls to come over." Crickets could have filled the silence that followed his request.

"Wait a minute. Did you just agree to feed in your house? I can call a couple girls over?" Kayden was clearly astonished.

Chase didn't respond, except to nod in defeat. Bringing girls home was a big no-no for Chase. This was his private space, not to be invaded or tainted by outsiders. His home was his temple.

Extracting his cell from his jacket, Kayden quickly had two girls on the way.

Changing the subject, Chase asked, "How did it go with Samantha earlier?"

"She was pissed I wouldn't tell her who you were carrying in with you. I acted like I didn't know and was just the driver. She went off on a tear about how I'm a bad influence on you, and in the future, things will be different. Until her phone rang. Whoever was on the line had her upset, and she left before finishing her tirade. Dude, does she think you guys are gonna be together, like bonded together? That'd really suck for both of us."

Doc came out, looking annoyed, before Chase could answer. "I need to know the exact circumstances that led you to this girl and how she got so polluted and bruised. I believe she has a few broken ribs, and her back looks as though she's been kicked or beaten. I've taken a blood sample to run some tests, but I'm sure she has been drugged. You can smell it, but it's nothing I'm familiar with. There was another girl found earlier tonight in the same condition. Actually, the other girl was in better condition because she wasn't beaten, just drugged." Doc slumped into a chair at the dining table, pinched the bridge of his nose, and continued. "I may need to move her to my office for X-rays and observation. She isn't healing as quickly as she should, and her breathing is too shallow for my liking. When I get these results, I'll return to check on her again. Now, one of you needs to fill me in."

Anger seeped through Chase's blood while Doc explained the extent of his Lovely's injuries. Chase relayed the story of finding Danielle at the club and all the details Vince had given him. Doc Stevens listened to him incredulously until the story was finished.

"So she reached out to you telepathically in her condition? Asked for help, and when you responded, she 'showed' you where she was? Astonishing! What is the child's name? I'm sure her parents will be looking for her."

Chase hesitated and then lied, "I only know her first name is Danielle." Chase didn't want Danielle taken away from him just yet, unless it was in the best interest of her health. So he played dumb in order to keep her with him. That annoying protective instinct was on high alert after finding her the way he had.

"While I'm gone I want you to try to reach her again. It's obvious she has a connection to you if she picked you out of all the people in the club and called to you by name. Try to speak to her telepathically and verbally. The gifts of some vampires are stronger with skin contact. If you're not opposed to touching her, it might help. If you can get through to her, I need you to try to get some details about what brought her to this end. I'll call shortly to let you know when I'll be back."

"Do you think this is connected to the other girl? What happened to her, exactly?" Chase pondered the Doc's earlier comment.

"You haven't heard? I think that may be something you need to speak to your father about, Chase. You know I do my best to stay out of council business. I'm going to go now." Doc picked up his conventional black doctor's bag and retreated.

Chase was going to have to put some feelers out to get information about the other girl. The last thing he wanted to do was involve his matchmaking father. His first priority was to follow Doc's advice and try to help Danielle. When he returned to the bedroom with Kayden on his heels, Chase realized the Doc had stripped her of all but her underwear.

"Damn, Chase, it must be your birthday, 'cause that is a sweet little present right there. I bet touching her is gonna be a nightmare for you," Kayden drawled sarcastically. Chase immediately pushed Kayden out into the hall and shut the door.

Laughing, Kayden said through the door, "Let me know if you get tired, man. I can come and relieve you for a while. I'd hate to see you do all the hard work." Kayden's voice faded down the hall. "I'll let you know when dinner arrives."

Chase stood by the bed, doing his best to think about things like football, cars, and his grandmother, as he covered the nearly nude beauty up and tucked the sheet under her arms, careful not to disturb her bandaged ribs. After going out on the patio for some fresh air to wash away the cloud of lusty thoughts, he returned to the bed. He pulled off his shirt to get some skin contact and climbed into the bed with Danielle, focusing on doing what Doc asked of him, not on his awakening desire.

As he snuggled in closer, he noticed something different about her. The white streak in Danielle's hair suddenly had red strands running through it. He was sure it hadn't always been that way. He held her tucked against him back to chest with one arm. Her chest rose and fell with steady, even breaths that reassured him that she was alive despite her unconscious state. With his other hand he brushed her hair back away from her face before resting his hand on her forehead. Taking a deep breath, he cleared his head again and reached out to her with his mind and voice, resolved to bring her around before Doc returned. "Come on, Lovely. It's time to wake and talk to me."

It felt as if she were under water. She could hear a muffled voice from very far away. Her limbs were too heavy to lift, and her eyes wouldn't budge. Dani struggled against the weight and pushed for conscious thought, wishing she could remember where she was and how she'd gotten there. She should have stayed home with her mom, but she'd needed to get away from Lucas.

Fear set in as she began to recall the evening. Going to Thirst had been a huge mistake. That's where he had tried to hurt her. Why had she bitten the bartender? He'd wanted her to do it, and it tasted so good. It *felt* so good, until he bucked her onto the floor and kicked her repeatedly. The memories flooded back in and she was reliving the nightmare over again.

The pain had exploded in her chest, but she'd been too weak to defend herself. She couldn't move.

He stood over her, amused, and mocked, "How does it feel to be the one hunted, you little bitch!" Then he kicked her again, and she heard the crunch of bone.

The bartender dragged her down the stairs, cursing the whole time. Telling her his "master" would be pleased with such a gift, and would reward him handsomely. Oh God. He was taking her away, and she couldn't move, couldn't fight back. Her self-defense training had taught Dani not to allow someone to take her to another location.

He dragged her down to the lower level by her feet. The back of her head hit every step, rattling her teeth and her brain. Pain and anger filled Dani. She clearly remembered wanting to see his head smack against the door they were approaching. She wished he would feel the same pain he was inflicting on her.

He released her leg suddenly and flew across the room to strike the door with force. The metal door made a loud, ringing sound when he crashed into it. She'd watched him rise from his sprawl on the floor and shake off the cobwebs. He came at her again. Dani felt panic rise. She had done that to him. She had no idea how she'd done it, but she knew that somehow she had made his sick, twisted head hit the door. She concentrated on slamming him back against the door and with a fearful thought he flew backward and was planted against the door again with a sickening thud. He cursed and staggered away, promising to come back for her very soon.

Chase only left her for a few minutes to feed. Feeling refreshed and energized, he went to her and began pleading again, focused on trying to reach her. "Please tell me what happened to you, Lovely." The shock pulled him up short when images began pouring from Danielle's mind into his. He was sickened to see the events as Danielle had in the moment. He felt the sorrow and confusion that brought her to the club, but not the reason for her sadness. He tried to dig for it, to no avail. He felt every kick to her torso and every step against the back of her head as she was dragged down the stairs that led to the club's storeroom.

He pulled her closer, turning her in his arms to bring them chest to chest, and he listened to her memories. She'd been telepathically aware of him at the club before he'd heard her voice in his mind. She'd heard all of his thoughts about her and reached out, hoping if she could hear him that he could hear her as well.

She lay motionless, begging for his help, and he'd heard her. He was a bit embarrassed to hear himself ache for her, knowing that she was fully aware of his feelings. This connection with his Lovely was an incredible gift. He didn't understand how it had happened but he couldn't regret it, no matter how exposed he felt at the moment. He asked her again to open her eyes.

It's too deep. I can't break the surface. Don't leave me. Please, she murmured the plea to his mind.

She could hear Chase talking to her. He'd come when she called, and he'd saved her. Dani begged him not to leave her alone again. She didn't know where she was, and she was so afraid that man would come back before she could fight.

"Can you hear me, Lovely?" Chase called to her.

God yes, she heard him and smelled him. He begged her to open her eyes. Over and over he pleaded with her to open her eyes and speak to him. She tried to reach him, but the water was so deep. She kept trying to swim up to find him, but her body wouldn't work.

Where am I? she sent to him through the depths.

He answered her using the connection that had allowed her to call him for help when she'd heard his thoughts in the club. She didn't understand it, but it felt like a blessing. Chase was there with her. Through Chase's mind's eye she could see a king-size bed, smoky-gray sheets, and big puffy pillows. She could see French doors that looked like they led outside. She saw herself snuggled up close to a warm chest and wrapped in a protective pair of arms. It must be his bedroom. This new telepathic ability was crazy, and it had to be yet another contribution from her father.

"You're safe at home with me, Lovely," he reassured. "Do you know why Nathan wanted to take you?"

She said *No*, but he didn't seem to hear it, because he asked again. It was quiet for a while, and Dani took in his warm, sunshine scent. He chuckled. *Shit.* Guess he heard that one. She was embarrassed. She helplessly mooned over his very presence, and he was listening. How pathetic was that? She enjoyed being able to hear his tender thoughts about her but wanted to keep her own private. She recognized the double standard for what it was but still wished she could control the outward flow of thoughts.

"I could smell what you smelled just then. How do you do that?"

She had no idea. Dani didn't even know who she was anymore, much less how she communicated with him.

As time passed, the pain of her injuries crept up her side, and she remembered being kicked. Sensation returned to her body. Unfortunately, her body was in bad shape. Chase's sharp intake of air made her realize she'd caused him pain, too. She tried to pull away from his mind, but he wouldn't allow it.

"Don't you dare leave me now, Danielle!" he barked sharply. He must have been pissed, if he used her actual name. "I need you here with me. Please stay," he pleaded in a gentler tone.

"Distract me. I feel like my chest is caving in. It hurts," she begged through the depths, as her breathing became shallower and shallower.

He must have gotten the message, because a movie clip began to play in her head, complete with sounds and smells. He showed her the night of the party. The night he spent in her bed. Holy hell! She'd looked like shit when he'd taken her out of Kayden's car. Chase had brought her to her room and tried to leave, but she asked him to stay. He showed her everything from that night, and she was mortified by her behavior. He had been so good to her that night when she really needed it. Now he was caring for her again.

Time passed slowly. Eventually, she was able to open her eyes. She was wrapped in Chase's arms, his face in her hair. His hot breath on her neck sent chills down the entire right side of her body, and she moaned a low, hoarse sound of contentment. His head snapped up and his eyes, the perfect blue-green color of summer, popped open. Relief washed over his expression, and he kissed her gently, but with heat. Delicious, wet heat that was a far more potent drug than the one she was recovering from. The delicate brushing of lips became a deeper, needier tangling of tongues that went on until they were both panting, but this wasn't the time for more than that. Dani could feel Chase's need to protect and cherish her and that meant more to her than she could express, but somehow, without her saying the words aloud, she knew he felt it and understood her gratitude.

"You scared me to death. I thought I was losing you, Lovely. Please don't do that to me again."

She felt so safe and protected in the haven of his arms, as he held on tightly and told her of the affection he held deep in his heart. She had already known, after hearing his mind chatter earlier, but hearing him say the words to her face was enough to make her heart explode. Chase wanted her to know, before they separated again, that he wanted her to be his. He wanted her to be his Lovely alone, with no others between them.

"I will protect you and care for you always, if you'll agree to be mine. I know you have a boyfriend, and I'll give you time to take care of that unfortunate issue." A flash of anger crossed his face when he spoke of Lucas. "I swear, I'll make you so happy you'll never miss the guy who left you alone and made you cry. I'll never hurt you, my Lovely."

They laid there for hours, talking about nothing at all and everything they wanted from life. They were still very young at twenty-one and twenty-four years old, but conversation eventually turned to the future. They both wanted several kids, having both been only children. Neither of them wanted that for their kids. He wanted a huge house on plenty of property with security for the kids to run and play without worry of outsiders harming them. The word *outsiders* echoed around her mind. Her mother was considered an outsider to her father's family. Dani pushed those thoughts away. She didn't want to return to reality yet. She just wanted to be there with Chase for as long as she could and forget all of the unanswered questions swimming in the back of her mind.

They held each other in silence, touching and being touched, kissing and inhaling each other. It felt like they were imprinting themselves on the fabric of the other's being. A connection forged in those peaceful moments of loving and being loved as never before.

The illusion of being the only two people in the world was shattered by the sound of arguing from somewhere beyond the closed bedroom door. Everything was still a bit cloudy when she lifted her head, but there was definitely a girl yelling profanities in the hall.

"Don't tell me I can't see him! You're the one who needs to get out, asshole!" the voice screeched.

A deep male voice replied, "I'm telling you that you don't want to go in there, Sam. He's gonna be pissed you're even here, and somebody's head is gonna roll for letting you in."

Chase cursed under his breath. "Just relax, Lovely. I'll handle this. There's no need for you to be disturbed. Just rest." He made no move to leave the bed. Instead, he snuggled in closer. The door flew open.

"Don't call me Sam, you prick!" A beautiful platinum blonde in heels and a dress so short it was more like a long shirt burst into the room, and Chase's friend followed, trying to get a handle on her. "What the hell are you doing?" the blonde bellowed from the doorway.

The noise hurt Dani's head and made her nauseous. She turned her face into Chase's chest and tried to cover her ears.

"What are you doing in our bed? Get your filthy hands off my mate!" she hissed at Dani.

That cleared all the clouds from her mind. Dani looked at Chase with a wide-eyed question, but his attention was on the blonde intruder.

"This is not your bed," he remarked dryly.

"She's your mate? What does that mean?" Dani was confused, but Chase just pulled her back to his chest and kissed her forehead.

"She's not my—"

"That means he's mine, you idiot! We're going to be mated!" the blonde hissed at Dani, cutting Chase off.

"Chase, are you engaged to her?" Dani felt betrayed. He didn't deny anything; instead he turned an angry scowl on the blonde.

That was all Dani needed to see! She was getting out of that domestic dispute. Slowly, painfully, she got herself to a sitting position as Chase tried to stop her progress.

"That's right, you little slut, get your shit and go!" the blonde insulted.

Kayden tried to hold her back from the bed.

"Kayden, get her out of here now," Chase ordered while pushing Dani back onto the bed. "You need to rest. Please stay in bed."

"Oh, I'm not going any damn place until that bitch is gone! You can count on that!" the blonde barked. "And what the hell is up with her hair? You're into freaks now, Chase?"

Just then Kayden lost his grip on Sam, and Chase leapt from the bed to stop her.

Dani got a good look at Sam then. Her irises were jet black, and she sported thin, curved fangs. Oddly familiar looking, she thought. Dani obviously wasn't the only black-eyed freak around. She was a vampire, just like the nightmare in high heels. The pieces of the puzzle were coming together for her now.

Neither Chase nor Kayden were frightened or even seemed surprised by the woman with fangs and black eyes. It stood to reason that both of the men were also vampires. Christ, was the town full of them? This development made her VIP treatment at the club make a hell of a lot more sense as well. It was also possible that all vampires had telepathic ability like she and Chase had shared. She just didn't know. But now wasn't the time to figure it all out. She and her mother were going to have a long talk.

Stiffly rising from the bed, Dani was mortified to be standing in nothing but her panties with bandages wrapped around her ribs, as three other people in the room argued. The blonde was trying to get around Chase and Kayden to reach her. Her pants and shirt were cut into shreds on the floor. She supposed they'd been cut off out of necessity to treat her injuries.

The blonde was really pissing her off with all the shouting, and Dani's head was splitting. Her vision sharpened, and she figured at that moment she probably resembled the blonde a bit. Frustrated, she screamed, "Shut up!"

The struggling, yippy blonde instantly fell silent and still. She just stood there with a blank expression on her face.

Chase and Kayden looked at the girl, then at Dani, and then at each other. Chase snapped his fingers in front of Sam's face, but she didn't flinch.

"How did you do that?" Chase gaped.

"Cool trick! Can you teach me?" Kayden asked excitedly.

"Get me some clothes? Mine are cut into pieces," she asked Chase, before turning her attention to Kayden. "Could you get Nightmare Barbie out of here while I get dressed, please?"

Kayden guided the silent and dazed-looking girl out of the room and shut the door. Chase stood and stared at her in amazement.

"How did you do that?" he insisted.

"Fine, I'll get some clothes myself. But don't worry; I won't take your fiancée's clothes." She tossed the statement over her shoulder and entered the huge walk-in closet that actually did have some girl's clothing.

He followed and located a T-shirt and a pair of running pants she could cinch up around her waist.

"You don't understand. She's supposed to be bonded to me. It's an arrangement between our parents. I didn't ask her to be my mate," he tried to explain as she pulled on the clothes with him looking on.

Her head swam. What a strange way to put it. Mate? Bonded? She guessed these were vampire terms she would need to assimilate.

Leaving the closet to search for shoes, she asked, "Are you, or are you not, going to marry that girl?" She cut straight to the quick, because she didn't want to hear any excuses.

Chase sputtered, "I . . . but, I . . . and they—" He growled. "Don't you understand?"

"Is that a cowardly *yes*? What were you going to do, play with me until the big day comes? I feel so unreasonably connected to you, and I was sure when I woke in your arms that we had something. I actually believed that crap you were spouting about wanting a family and forever with me. She was right. I am an idiot!"

"Don't you understand? I have family obligations. I was going to try to get out of it. What else am I supposed to do, Lovely? I want you, not her," he tried to explain.

Pinning him with black eyes, she spat, "Don't you ever call me that again! In fact, I don't want you speaking my name at all!" She drew nearer to him, and using the same method of projection she'd used earlier—without knowing how she did it—she sent a quick succession of mental clips, starting with Lucas holding her and saying he loved her, then Lucas's memory of calling her names at the party and kissing another girl he held in his arms. She followed with clips of Chase holding her, kissing her, and the shared words of affection and forever and her imagined image of him marrying the blonde. She punctuated it with a verbal and mental slap: "You're all the same."

She dug her cell and car keys out of the destroyed jeans and tried to leave the room. Chase stepped into her path and wrapped his arms around her waist, hauling her up against his chest. He begged her to stay with those beautiful blue-green eyes. She couldn't resist taking one last deep breath of the sunshine and happiness she couldn't have, and pressed her lips to his before detangling herself and pushing past him. She felt Chase watch her walk past the still-muted beauty in the living room and out of his home. His soon-to-be wife's home, Dani reminded herself.

Kayden followed Dani to the elevator, in awe of the power she'd just displayed. It was unheard of for a vampire to control another vampire. "Are you going to release Sam?"

She looked at the door, and Samantha's screaming could be heard from inside the condo again, just as if it'd never stopped.

"Thanks, I think." Kayden grinned and took the phone from her limp hand and programmed in his cell number. "Call me if you need anything. I'm not hitting on you. You just look like you could you use a friend, and I have a strong shoulder if you need someone to lean on. Chase is my best friend, but I can keep a secret if you don't want him to know we're amigos." He found himself genuinely hoping she would give him a call.

Dani smiled and, to his surprise, she allowed herself to fall into his arms for a moment. Tears streaked down her cheeks, making him want to beat his friend to a pulp. Kayden supported her, stroking her beautiful hair, rocking slightly, until she pulled herself together and backed up into the open elevator. The anguish in her eyes tore at Kayden. There was more to the situation than just a little heartache.

"I'm not what you guys think I am. I'm not like you. Trust me. I'm nothing but bad news for you and your friend." The elevator doors slid closed on her misery.

Kayden stood in awe of the emotions the girl provoked in him. Holy shit, but she was powerful, smart, and, he believed, capable of wrapping any man around her little finger. He even had trouble not following her, and if it weren't for his best friend in the apartment behind him, Kayden would have.

"There she is, Master!" Nathan eagerly pointed at a girl with flowing dark hair and distinguishing streaks of white and some new red that he hadn't noticed before. She walked right past their limousine. Nathan had been livid with the bitch when he left the club. He'd informed the master he'd be bringing him a gift.

Earlier, he'd ingested the drug given to him for the purpose of immobilizing vampires. When the vamp fed from him, it had taken her down, but she had still been able to use her mental powers to defend herself. The other three vamps he'd taken hadn't fought him after the drug took over, so she had surprised him. He'd had to call the master to inform him of the mishap. The master was displeased and sent him back to the club. The girl had to be something special in order to fight the drugs, and he wanted her for testing.

He'd gotten back to the club just in time to see the owner's son carrying her out the back door. He followed them and called the master to inform him of the girl's location.

The rogue vampire who was his master sat across from him in the limousine laughing darkly with no humor in his voice. He was frightening and cold behind the dark shades he always wore in public.

"She looks just like someone I used to know. This will be much to my advantage. I'm quite sure I know exactly who this girl belongs to, and I can't wait to watch his dismay at her reappearance. How disgraced he will be." Another low rumble of laughter made Nathan's skin crawl.

Nathan never saw it coming when the brutal vamp grabbed him by the neck and glared at him with black eyes and fangs an inch from his face. "You are very fortunate the girl survived your reckless attack." Without another word, Nathan was launched out onto the street.

The rogue curled his lip in distrust at the human male sprawled on the pavement. "I'd hide if I were you. The girl is well connected. I'll bet there's already a reward for your sorry hide." He ordered his driver to follow the cab the girl hailed. It took her to a parking lot, where he watched the girl hop into another vehicle, before following her to the nearby university.

What a turn of events. He'd acquired a telepathic, telekinetic beauty with who knew what other talents. Withstanding the effect of Hypnovam was very impressive. He thought of all the possibilities as he directed the driver to take him back to the nest. He hoped she might consider joining him. It would be a shame to waste such pretty wrapping to get at the gifts inside.

Chase had to threaten Samantha to get her to finally leave, saying he would choose to bond with Brandi. She ranted and raved about how this shit was going to end, and he would be a faithful mate to her once they were bonded. He had to watch what was said in front of Sam, not wanting to give her any information that would lead to his Lovely.

After she left, he placed a call to Vince, informing him of the vampire slayer in their midst who had chosen the wrong girl to slay. Danielle had stopped the attack, but she was badly injured, and it had Chase on the edge of a meltdown. She was hurting and weakened, so if attacked again, it might not end the same way. Vince was directed to locate Nathan at any cost and bring him to the council for questioning and judgment. They needed to know whom Nathan was working for and why they wanted Danielle.

Chase had made sure to lift her cell number from her phone while she slept earlier and had tried to reach her several times since she left, but she wouldn't answer. He couldn't leave a message because her mailbox was full. That made him wonder about how many people were leaving her messages. Jealousy crept into his mind at the thought of all the guys who would love to fill her in-box.

Holding her while she struggled for consciousness and later while they talked had made Chase feel for the first time like the world didn't revolve around him. He now had direction and goals. Chase wanted to be worthy of a female like Danielle. With her he easily expressed his feelings in a way that he never had been able to in the past. Chase believed that it was easy and natural because it was right and meant to be. The best hours of his life were spent in Danielle's arms, before Sam showed up and ruined it.

When Danielle had left his apartment, she believed him to be cut from the same cloth as a guy who had publicly embarrassed her. If he were to be honest with himself, he had to admit that he'd behaved less than honorably. His father knew he didn't want to be bonded to either of the Vaughn girls, but without a solid reason for rejecting them his pleas had fallen on deaf ears. The future of their house outweighed Chase's personal wishes.

He'd tried to win Danielle's heart, knowing he would have to leave her before he was bonded. Of course, his intentions were to try getting out of the bonding, but if he couldn't, he had the solace of knowing he wouldn't hurt for long. She wouldn't be so lucky.

Why did the grudges of his grandparents and the words of dead people have to derail his life? Why should he have to pay for his family's past with his future?

At the home of Melinda Prince, the girl who'd been recovered earlier that day, Griffin and his father attempted to gather as much information as possible, once she was conscious and Doc Stevens had pronounced her to be on the mend. The girl couldn't remember anything useful. The last thing she remembered was feeding, and then everything was blank until she woke up at home, surrounded by her parents and the doctor.

His phone rang, and he wasn't surprised to be getting a call from Doc. He was, however, surprised to hear what Doc had to tell him. It was their biggest lead up to that point, and his father was going to have to accept that the past was, indeed, repeating itself. A lot of old wounds would be reopened by this news.

The Prince girl had been drugged by whomever she'd fed from after leaving the nightclub. Doc had treated another girl who was found in the club's basement, beaten and unconscious. The two girls had the same drug in their systems. The newest victim also ingested it during a feeding. Fortunately for the patient he treated earlier, she was a talented child with telekinetic and telepathic abilities. According to the boy who found her, she was able to call him telepathically for help.

"That's incredible; but how did she get away? Did her rescuer see the assailant?" Griffin questioned. "We are going to need to visit this girl. If she was aware enough to call for help, she may have some useful information."

"That is going to prove difficult. I went back to check on the girl, and she was gone. Chase was caring for her, and he did have some information he acquired from her, but not much. When she woke in a strange place, confused and frightened, she bolted. All Chase could tell me is her first name."

"Do you mean Chase Deidrick?"

"Yes, sir. He found her in the basement of the club his father owns. He took her to his condo downtown. He had Kayden Paris call me while he was still en route. I arrived shortly after him. It was fast thinking of him to get her out of there before anyone noticed a problem. I'm thankful he immediately called for help, because all we have to connect these kidnappings is the drug I found in their blood. If I hadn't seen the girl before she took off, we wouldn't have a clear link. I have samples of the Davis boy's tissues being analyzed, but that'll take a little longer to process. There was no blood left, and tissue analysis is more time consuming," Doc explained.

"That doesn't explain how she got away from her attacker. Did she tell Chase how she escaped?"

"He said she *showed* him how she got away." Doc sounded disbelieving.

"I don't understand."

"I think you should speak to Chase about that. The girl is telekinetic, as well as telepathic." Doc relayed this information with a skeptical tone.

Griffin had never heard of another vampire with telepathic and telekinetic abilities, and judging by the silence on the other end of the phone, neither had Doc. "I believe you are correct. I'm going to visit the young Mr. Deidrick. Thank you for the information. I want you to call me as soon as you get results back on the Davis boy." Griffin hung up and began to rub his temples.

He followed his father home and took his parents into the study to present his case for aggressive action. Then he called Chase. Griffin needed to sit down with Chase and Kayden in order to glean every bit of information he could.

Eight

Dani knew her friends at school were pretty pissed at for her disappearing from school, especially after her mom called and Olivia realized she was completely off the grid. No one had a clue where she was, and she was sure they would really want to know what she'd been doing if she decided to tell them.

Olivia tackled her when she entered the dorm on Monday afternoon. She said she was just about to start making "Have you seen this girl?" posters and stapling them all over town. After her jubilant reception, Olivia wanted answers that Dani wasn't about to give. Olivia was mad for a couple of days, but she soon came around.

She only missed one day of school, so catching up wasn't too difficult. Dealing with the injuries still plaguing her body was another thing entirely. It had been tricky hiding the bruises from Olivia and trying to move around slowly to avoid wincing in pain from her cracked ribs, especially since Olivia was watching her like a hawk.

She spoke to her mother without giving much detail and promised to drive back home on Friday. Her mother would be interested to hear what happened the other day; not that Dani thought she would be surprised. Dani went all black-eyed freak and her mom hadn't reacted at all. She couldn't wait to see how she took the news that Dani was also a blood-sucking freak. That's right, a black-eyed, red-and-white-striped, blood-sucking freak. Wasn't that what all parents dreamed their children would grow up to be?

Tessa had someone coming to help explain her heritage to her. Dani thought *heritage* was a ridiculous understatement. The first and most obvious thing Dani noticed was her hair. Several of the white steaks in the front of her head now had thin red highlights running through them, and she actually liked it. The new highlights had also been a source of constant jabs from her friends in the past few days. Jared had chosen to believe her absence was due to her attending a Goth spa to get her hair tricked out. Of course, Jared knew she'd left because of boy drama, but he was too much of a gentleman to tell.

Dani had all-new nifty abilities, like being able to turn the lights on and off without getting out of bed, and picking things up from the other side of the room and floating them around. The first time it happened had scared the shit out of her. She'd been thinking that it would be nice if her laptop would come to her since she was so comfy in bed. Imagine her surprise when it lifted from the desk, drifted across the room, and landed on her lap. It was handy when she left her cell at her desk and was too lazy to get up when it rang. Just the day before, she was studying on her bed when Jared knocked on the door. She knew who it was by his distinct smell. Jared smelled like mint and rain, not something intangible like happiness—as if happiness had a smell. She willed the door to open and the look on his face when he entered and found no one behind the door was hysterical, but he didn't ask who had opened it. Her senses of smell and sight were off the charts. She could tell what the specials of the day at the cafeteria were from a block away, or who had illicit drugs in their rooms when she walked down the hall.

The most difficult part had been trying to learn to control her telepathic senses. She didn't like unintentionally eavesdropping on the thoughts of others. It was just rude. Plus, the fact that she didn't normally hear words but actually caught pictures made it even more intimate and embarrassing. When she was trying to concentrate on her professor and the professor was imagining the things she'd like to do to the cute guy in the front row, it put a nasty spin on her day. Twice while drifting off to sleep she'd thought about Chase and she somehow breached the distance between them. He felt her there in his mind. He tried to talk to her and apologize both times, but Dani quickly retreated. The belief in her ability to do all of those things was enough to get a girl committed. But as she had seen at Chase's place, she wasn't the only black-eyed freak in town. These things had to be vampire traits. Her daddy's legacy lived on.

Dani and Jared were growing very close. They studied, ate dinner, and hung out together every day. Not that Dani was ready for a relationship. But if she were, Jared would be the kind of guy she wanted. He was good-looking, smart, and not engaged or dating anyone. She knew Jared was aware that there was something strange about her, but he didn't seem to care. He pretended as if he didn't notice when she accidentally commented on his thoughts or opened the door without getting up.

There were two problems with dating Jared. First was that she couldn't stop thinking about Chase, and second was that as time passed, she found herself thinking about feeding more often. She hadn't done it again since the first disastrous time, but she knew eventually she'd have to give into the need. She would have to deal with both of these problems if she were going to move on with her life. Chase wasn't an option for her, and Dani was afraid feeding would become something she couldn't avoid forever.

It was Thursday, and the gang decided to head to the club. Of course they wanted her to go, but the club didn't bring back happy memories for her anymore. Jared agreed to stay behind with her, but she knew he really wanted to go. After giving it some thought, she decided that she wasn't going to let her fear, or the possible presence of Chase, stop her from living. She had two long years to live in that town, and she wouldn't spend it cowering in her room. So when Jared showed up to study, she answered the door in a shimmering black minidress she'd borrowed from Lindsay, a black belt that accentuated her small waist, and a pair of black strappy heels.

Jared took a long, slow stroll around her, checking out everything from the loose updo of her hair to the red polish on her toenails. She meant to be sexy that night, and it seemed to have worked. She didn't at all mind standing there while Jared looked her over and gathered his thoughts.

"Is this the new study hall dress code? If so, I'm going to need a change." His smile was blinding.

"I had a different subject in mind tonight. I thought maybe you'd want to study chemistry." She tilted her head, flirting. "Do you like my chemistry experiment?"

Jared reached out and ran his fingers down her arm. "I'm definitely experiencing a chemical reaction. I think your experiment is a success."

"Would you like to take me out tonight? We could continue the experiment, if you don't mind being my test subject." Dani offered him a shy smile. Jared took her hand and began to drag her out the door. "Where are we going?" she said and laughed.

"I need to change and I'm not letting you out of my sight. You'll disappear in a hurry looking like that." He chuckled. With a huge grin, he led her across the courtyard to his dorm. Neither of them missed the stares and comments of every guy they passed.

"See what I mean? I'm going to have to stay very close to you all night . . . for your safety, of course."

"Well, thank you for agreeing to be my bodyguard on such short notice." Dani's eyes were full of fake innocence when he opened the door to his room. She sat on his bed while his roommate, Steve, eyed her with interest.

Jared went to take a quick shower and change in the bathroom. Before he walked away, he shot Steve a look that clearly said, *Don't even think about it.*

Just out of curiosity, and for practice, Dani decided to see if she could catch what was running through Steve's mind. He sat with his back to her at the computer. She focused on words only, not wanting to see anything graphic, and she was shocked at what she heard. It was something along the lines of, *Don't even look at her. Jared has had the hots for her since that first night at the club. He will kill you, so don't look at her, no matter how badly you want to.*

Dani was surprised at this insight. She hadn't realized Jared was that interested. They were good friends, but he had never crossed the line. Maybe this was what she needed, someone normal to date. Maybe it was a bad idea, given the fact that she and Lucas had just broken up very recently. And, she couldn't stop thinking about Chase.

Everything that she'd learned about herself recently made getting involved with anyone a bad idea. After drinking the blood of the bartender, her earlier suspicions had been verified. She was a vampire, or at least half vampire. Then she learned from her visit to Chase's condo that she wasn't alone. The funny thing was that they knew she was one of them all along, and she'd had no idea. Dani was sure she would have a huge reality check about vampire life during her upcoming visit with her mom. There had to be some good reasons for her mom to keep this life-changing knowledge from her, and Dani needed to understand those reasons. But for the night, she just wanted to have a good time and relax.

Jared stepped out of the bathroom looking every bit the honey, and his wonderful mint aroma poured out with the steam. His shaggy, blond hair was neatly slicked back. He wore black slacks and a dark gray button-down. Yes, he was exactly what she needed. That kind of distraction would do nicely.

"Well, shit! Now I am going to have to guard my bodyguard. I must remember to send a thank-you letter to my high school chemistry teacher."

Jared sat next to her on the bed and bent to put his shoes on. She lifted his chin gently with two fingers and placed a sweet little kiss on his lower lip. Jared stared back at her as if mesmerized. He licked his lips and leaned in for more, but the moment was shattered when Steve fell off his chair and papers went flying.

"I'm gonna wait for you in the lobby. I have to make a call before we head out," she told Jared with her lips still very close to his.

His only response was, "Uh-huh."

She giggled and left the room. She had gone about ten feet down the hall when Jared and Steve erupted into a chorus of hoots that startled people walking by their room.

In the car on the way to the club, Dani was staring out the window when Jared put his hand on her leg and then looked at her to make sure it was okay. She smiled and placed her hand over his in a gesture of acceptance. At the club, Dani decided to use her vampire all-access pass. She led her group to the front of the line, where Vince snapped to attention at first sight of her.

"Princess, Vince is so glad to see you all in one piece. The last time he saw you, well, it was not your best day. He hopes you can forgive him for the mistake he made," Vince apologized sincerely and bent to kiss Dani's hand.

Jared looked from the huge, muscle-bound man and back to Dani in confusion. Then he stepped up and took her other hand possessively. She smiled at him and grasped his hand tighter.

"Vince, there's nothing to forgive. I am not sure what happened but it is over, and I do not want to think about it tonight. Could you get me a table, please?"

"Sure thing, Princess. Vince will seat you himself." Vince held the door for her party to enter. Once inside, he parted the dance floor like the Red Sea as he led them to the VIP section. They sat at the usual spot, and Vince went to the bar. He returned with a waitress who was carrying a bottle of top-shelf champagne and six flutes. Vince winked at Dani before heading back to his post. It was a nice gesture, but there was no way in hell after her first two experiences with alcohol that she was drinking anything. She'd let her friends enjoy the bubbly. Her nerves were off the chart. Just being there at the same table where her life had changed forever was overwhelming.

Jared and the others had heard every word of the conversation with Vince and clearly had no idea what to make of it. Dani was very glad of that, because an explanation was out of the question.

She got up to hit the dance floor and, after scanning the crowd, realized that Chase was indeed there and watching her intently. No matter. That was his fiancée's problem, not hers. She put her hand out for Jared, and he was up and at her side. Dani was sick and tired of worrying. She was going to dance and have fun with someone she knew and trusted.

As she started for the floor, she did her best to pretend she wasn't being watched, ignoring the telepathic plea she was receiving from Chase. It was hard because he was persistent, but she'd learned how to block it. She'd tell herself to listen to a different channel or turn off the radio of her mind, and off it went.

She danced and spun around the floor with Jared. The whole crew was full of smiles and laughter as they performed their own little dance-off in the center of the floor. Jared and Steve danced as a team against Dani and Olivia. The crowd made room for them to dance. They yelled and shouted for their favorite dancers. Vince came over at one point to check out the commotion. He just smiled and shook his head as he walked away. Olivia and Dani won the contest when they broke into an old-school move, hooking their feet and spinning around in a circle. The crowd roared, and the girls were named the victors.

Jared swept Dani up in a congratulatory hug and returned her sweet kiss from earlier. He continued to kiss her softly, caressing her lips gently. He coaxed a response from her with teasing nibbles and warm strokes of his tongue as the music slowed, and they swayed to the rhythm. It was a perfect evening, until Chase tried to cut in. Dani felt Jared stiffen under her lips. She opened her eyes and turned to see Chase behind them.

"May I cut in?" Chase practically snarled at Jared. It was phrased as a question, but he clearly had no intention of taking *no* for an answer.

"No, you may not." Dani stepped forward, putting space between him and Jared.

"I need to speak with you, Love . . . Danielle. It's important. We need to get some information about your attacker. You're not the only one. Another girl is still missing." Chase reached out to take Danielle's hand, but she jerked it away.

"You were attacked? When? Why didn't you tell me? Were you hurt?" Jared showed his shock at the news she hadn't been able to share with him.

"I'm fine. I just have some cracked ribs and bruises. It's nothing that's kept me from dancing the night away." Dani rubbed Jared's chest, trying to soothe him, and turned back to Chase.

"I'm on a date. I don't want to talk to you now, or later, for that matter. I'll call Kayden. He can get me in touch with whoever would like to speak to me," Dani snapped.

"I'm sorry. Did you say your ribs are still cracked? You should have healed the day you left me." Chase stepped closer. He reached out and began to probe her rib cage with gentle fingers. Jared moved in and pushed Chase's hands away. Chase growled a low curse, and Dani heard the mental command he sent to Jared to get him away from her. Chase told Jared to go find another dance partner.

Jared's eyes glazed over and he began to comply with the mental push, but Dani grabbed him by the arm and spun him around for a kiss. This stopped Jared in his tracks. Danielle was able to override Chase's mind games. Chase stood there fuming. She scowled at him while angry color rose from the collar of his shirt and crept over his face.

"Can you give me one moment to speak with Chase? I'll only be a minute; I promise." Dani didn't want to upset Jared, but the conversation wasn't going to go well, and she had a feeling Jared would get hurt if it came to a fight. "Just go get us another drink or maybe order something to eat, my treat. I'll be right over." She smiled and gave him a quick kiss.

"Alright, but don't be long, okay? We didn't get to finish our slow dance." He smiled back at her and caressed her cheek before striding away.

Dani turned back toward Chase, and, thankfully, it was dark in the club, because he was pissed and his black-eyed freak was showing. His eyes were dark as night and the tips of his pearly fangs were just barely visible.

"Let's go somewhere we can talk privately." Chase pointed the way and gave Jared an angry growl as he stomped past.

He led her to what seemed to be a private suite in the back of the club. It was like a studio apartment, with a king-size bed, a private bathroom with a shower, a seating area with a wall-mounted TV, and a tiny kitchen. Dani tried to contain her nerves as she entered the space. If she screamed, no one would hear her over the music.

"Do you really believe I would hurt you?" He cocked his head and gave her a look of utter disbelief.

"I'm really gonna have to learn to control that, because it is very annoying when you can hear me all the time. Please make an effort to stay out of my head," Dani scolded.

"I'm not doing that, Dani. I can't read others. You're projecting onto me. I'm not trying to listen. Okay, maybe I have tried a few times." He seemed embarrassed by that admission. He moved farther into the surprisingly large room. "Please, let me see your injuries. Doc came back to see you after you left my place. He's called me every day since. It would be nice if I had something to tell him. You were really sick when he came to care for you," Chase explained.

"I'd have to get undressed for that, Chase. Why can't I just make an appointment with the doctor?" Dani didn't want to tempt him, or herself, by removing her clothes.

"Oh for Christ's sake, Danielle, I've been in bed with you practically naked twice and managed to control myself both times. Would you give me a little credit and let me see your damn injuries?"

"Fine," she said with acid in her voice. She turned away from him and undid the belt she wore, dropping it to the floor. Then she pulled the dress up over her head and dropped it on the nearby coffee table. She heard Chase's breath catch when he caught sight of her black-and-blue back. The bruises spread all the way down to the cleft of her ass that was barely covered by the black lace thong she wore. She hadn't worn a bra because it hurt her back. Besides, she didn't really need one. Her breasts stood up like proud soldiers all on their own. She covered her breasts with her hands and pivoted so Chase could see the bruising that reached all the way around her torso and met in the front.

Chase approached her slowly, in wordless astonishment. The sight of her, so battered and fragile, made him want to rip that female-beating piece of shit apart all over again. He wanted to sweep her up and rush her back to his home, where he could protect her the way she deserved to be. He was instantly hard from the sight of her beautiful body wearing nothing but a scrap of cloth and high heels, but the bruises that marred her skin made him irate.

"I don't understand. You should be healed." Chase went to his knees in front of her to get a closer look. It still looked pretty painful.

"Yeah, well, I'm not. It's not as bad as it was a couple of days ago. Several ribs were broken, but they're mending." She backed away from him. "Ask your questions so I can leave."

"Why do think you're not healing? Is it the drug that guy gave you?"

"Don't you have any more important questions? I thought you needed to know about the attack." She rolled her eyes at him. Chase just watched patiently, waiting for an answer.

"I told Kayden that I'm not what you think I am. Do you have any other questions?"

"He relayed that message, but I have no idea what that means or why it should matter. I want you, no matter what, Lovely." Chase stepped closer to her and touched her face. Just that small contact sent ripples of heat over his body. "Why don't you sit with me and explain?"

She chuckled. "I don't know what it means either. I'm still trying to wake up from this nightmare. If you don't have any pertinent questions, I'll contact Kayden tomorrow."

That had his hackles up. "Why are you always in a hurry to run to some damn human when you can have anyone you want? And what the hell is this shit about Kayden, because I will kill him!"

Dani just shook her head. A few things fell into place for her. She was willing to bet her father's vampire family would have said the word *human* with just as much distain. They wouldn't have accepted her human mother and the half-breed child. This must be why her father was completely absent from their lives. It explained her mother's story about being an outsider to his family. That had been a clever choice of words. It wasn't about her social or financial standing, but her breed.

"I'm not what you think I am," she whispered. He was still on his knees in front of her. She sat on the edge of the coffee table. As hard as it was, she looked him in the eye so he could see her anguish. She reached for her dress but Chase moved in closer, and she was distracted by his nearness. She wanted to press her breasts against his firm chest. She shook her head to clear those lascivious thoughts.

"I was raised with humans. They are my kind. They are all I've ever known. I need Jared's comfort and friendship to help me stay away from you. I have wanted you since the first night we met. I can't get you out of my head. I would give anything to have that morning in your bed back for just a little while. To hear you say those words again and believe you meant them."

"I did mean them, Lovely. Please believe me. I want you more than anything. It kills me to see that guy out there touch you, kiss you." He gripped her jaw so she couldn't turn away from the pain she caused him.

"Those are *my* kisses you're giving away. Knowing you're purposely blocking me out of the connection we share burns me, Lovely." Chase moved closer to her, spreading her thighs, and granting her wish to be pressed against his firm chest. He tipped her head back with a finger so she was looking into his black eyes. She wanted to give in and take the kiss he offered. His hot breath blew over her face and his chest rose and fell, causing sweet friction to tease her nipples. She fought the need to take everything he wanted to give her. She weakly raised her hand and placed her fingers against his lips, but he easily moved her fingers and moved in to taste her. He licked and nibbled her lips until she gave in with a groan and opened her mouth to him. His tongue explored and toyed with hers until need spread through her blood like fire. They held on to each other and made love with their mouths for several moments before she pulled back. It was hard to remember he belonged to someone else when he was touching and tasting her.

"Don't push me away yet. Not yet." He nuzzled her neck. "Let me have just a taste, please." She didn't struggle when he rose to his feet and lifted her into his arms. The scrape of his shirt against her hardened nipples made her shiver.

"Are you cold?" he asked as he laid her out on the big bed. She answered with a shake of her head. He removed his shirt and shoes while she watched. Chase was tall and broad shouldered. The lines of his tailored clothing hid the rippling muscles that played beneath them. He was perfectly formed, a god, an Adonis. For the moment, if she let go of her racing thoughts and forgot the world on the other side of that door, he could be hers. If only for tonight, he was hers.

He crawled in beside her and pulled her body against his. He lifted her leg up to rest on his hip, opening her to him. The heat of his solid length burned through his pants and warmed her belly. She wanted him. Every cell in her body screamed for her to accept him, to hold him like this forever.

Chase licked at her mouth, begging entrance, and she opened for him. It was like swallowing a mouthful of summer. Chase's flavor was like the taste of saltwater taffy by the ocean, sweet and warm on her tongue. His fingers burned a slow trail from her collarbone all the way down the center of her body. She was so absorbed by his drugging kisses that she jumped when he slid his hand into her panties and cupped her mound. He hummed into her mouth and fondled her teasingly, barely moving for a bit. She gasped when he slid his middle finger between her damp folds and began lightly brushing small circles over and over her clit. Another finger followed, and the tension built with the added pressure he applied. She climbed higher, trying to follow the sensation. She felt the edge of something she wanted desperately.

She rocked her hips against his hand. He pulled away from the kiss and panted in her ear, "You're so hot, so wet for me, Lovely." He moved those fingers slowly into her slick core, circling and exploring her secrets. The oxygen left the room and she struggled to breathe. This was nothing like her past experience. This was intense and consuming. Chase was focused solely on her. He moved unhurriedly, stroking her until the pleasure passed into something hotter, greedier. He used his thumb to continue the assault on her clit. She wheezed and writhed against him. "Look at me," he said, palming the side of her cheek. "I want to watch you come." She looked into his beautiful black eyes and couldn't look away.

He whispered praises and told her how hot she made him. He played with her breasts and nipped at her lips, kissing her hard and fast so he could pull back and watch her eyes while he brought her to a crushing climax. The world imploded around her, and she knew her eyes were as black as his. The pressure of elongating fangs made her mouth feel full. She closed her mouth and shut her eyes. She wanted him, needed him, but she knew it would only be this one time. "Please, don't stop."

Chase took a cleansing breath and prayed for control. His tether to sanity was stretched thin. She asked him not to stop and for that he was grateful, because he wasn't sure how he would have walked away if she'd said *no more*. Everything in him knew she was his mate. He needed to feel her wrapped around him, now. She helped him undo his pants and shuck them while they continued to kiss and touch and rub their bodies against each other wherever they could reach. This hunger was like nothing he'd ever experienced. He'd had a lot of females, but he'd never been sure he would die if he couldn't get inside of them. He suckled one rosy nipple, pulling hard on the tight little peak. She thrashed beneath him.

"Please, Chase. Please." The needy purr in her voice reached across the small space between them to stroke his senses. She smelled like warm and floral honey.

He rolled her onto her back and spread her thighs wide with his knees. She looked up at him and his chest tightened. She was so beautiful, and her heart was there in her eyes. She needed him too, wanted a future just as much as he did. As gently and slowly as his hungry body was capable, he stroked his length against her damp heat until he was coated and she was panting. When her hips began moving to meet him, he couldn't wait any longer. He wanted to make it last, but lust for his female consumed him. In one long stroke, he pushed into her tight channel. Danielle gasped at that initial penetration and whimpered. Damn it, he would never last.

"I'm sorry, baby." He tried to soothe her and spent several long moments going as slowly as he was able, placing kisses on her cheeks, her eyelids, and her lips, to allow her body time to adjust to his size. He knew she had limited experience, and for that he was heartily grateful. Slowly, he withdrew and returned, withdrew and returned. She made a strangled sound of surprised pleasure and need. His control broke, and all thoughts of a slow loving were replaced with steady thrusts into her tight body.

Dani wrapped her legs around Chase's waist and lifted to meet his deep strokes. His thick shaft pushed and pulled on her core, strumming every nerve in her body. The intense mindless pleasure had her moaning for more. Chase slid his hands under her ass and lifted her for a deeper angle. The position took him to a hidden place deep in her core. He began to pound out a rhythm that stole her ability to think. He rode her hard and fast into a scattering climax. Pulsing, gasping, gripping at him, she begged him not to stop. She never wanted to come back to earth, back to where reality would claim her again. Chase shouted and bucked wildly above her. She watched him find his completion, trying to absorb and retain every moment of this unparalleled experience.

He fell against her and peppered her face and neck with feather kisses. She held on tight to the man she could never have and prayed for a miracle. She prayed that he would choose her over his betrothed, no matter the consequences. But that would be his choice to make, and she would do nothing to sway him either way.

"Stay with me," he said and kissed her before she could deny him. He rolled to his side and pulled her to him. "Let me take you home. Let me make love to you in my bed all night long. We'll figure this all out later. I know you feel the same way I do. I can feel you inside me." He flattened his hand over his chest. "Here." He tapped his temple. "And here."

She really hated knowing he was in her head. He'd meant it to be romantic, but it only reminded her of how much she had to learn about this new life she'd fallen into. She felt suddenly very vulnerable and exposed. She wondered if he was only telling her what he knew she needed to hear.

She rolled from the bed and got to her feet. He tried to pull her back down, but she pushed him away and went to find her dress. Chase jumped up and pulled on his pants.

"Shit. I can feel you pulling away, Lovely. Please don't do this." He wrapped her in his arms from behind and tugged on her belt, preventing her from putting it on. "Did you feel what we just did over there? Baby, I don't know about you, but I think I'm ruined for other females." He kissed her neck. He was charming and handsome and he'd just given her two soul-crashing orgasms. Did she want to do as he suggested and stay in his bed until morning? Yes. But when the time came to "figure it all out," nothing would have changed. He was still engaged, and if his father didn't agree to help him get out of the agreement, Chase would have a new mate in the near future.

"I didn't know about the bonding until after I saw you that day at the coffee shop. I couldn't do anything but think of you. I was there on campus that morning hoping you'd happen by or even stop in for a coffee, just so I could get a glimpse of you." He sounded so sincere, but it didn't change anything. He still belonged to someone else.

She stepped out of his arms and finished dressing. "It seemed to me that you and Nightmare Barbie were very familiar with each other, and I didn't see you standing up to her. I didn't see you pronounce your love for me to her," she countered.

"She's an ex-girlfriend, and what she thinks doesn't matter. I didn't need to explain anything to her. I have just as big a chance of being bonded to her twin sister as I do to her. Our parents will make the final decision. I didn't purposely deceive you. I just couldn't give you up once I had you in my arms. Seeing you hurt and vulnerable made me look at everything in a different light. I just wanted you to be mine for as long as I could have you."

"Wow. That's exactly what my dad did to my mom when they met. They were in love, but his family wouldn't have approved of her. The day I was born, he left her and never came back. He married his parents' choice, and my mother has spent her life mourning his loss. I won't let you do that to me, Chase. I would rather be truly loved by a human than humiliated by the likes of you." Tears ran down her cheeks.

He stood there naked, looking like a sullen god, the god of heartbreak. Dani continued. "Tell Kayden I'll be calling him tomorrow.

I'd be glad to help in any way I can to locate the missing girl. I hope that he can put me in contact with the proper authorities. I'm leaving now. Please thank your doctor for his care and concern on my behalf. And please stay out of my head."

Dani returned to her friends after a quick trip to the restroom, but she didn't want to be at the club any longer. She had to get as far away from Chase as was possible. If not, she would run back to his arms and do her best to forget the impossibility of a future with him. If she didn't leave, he would convince her to go home with him. She wanted to spend the night—hell, the rest of her life—in his arms, but she couldn't forgive his manipulation and the lies he'd told her. She knew very well he didn't consider what he did to be lying. But in her mind, omission was just as big a crime as an outright falsehood.

The ride home was silent. Dani said nothing to her friends. Jared watched her anxiously from the corner of his eye. Finally, he reached out to stroke her cheek, measuring her reaction. She smiled weakly at his worried face. She took his hand from her cheek and twined her fingers with his, resting them on her leg. This would be it for her and Jared. One date was all they would have. She felt intense shame wash over her as she looked down at their entwined fingers. It was their first real date and it had been a lot of fun. All the way up until she'd wandered off and had sex—amazing, mind-bending, life-changing sex—with Chase. No. She couldn't be with Jared. He deserved far better than she was capable of giving him. She only hoped their friendship would survive.

Dani would need to tell him now that this relationship was over before it started. He was a good friend and she wouldn't lead him on, even to save his feelings. It would be easier to end it now. Still holding hands, they walked down the path to the dorms. She leaned her head against his arm as they neared his dorm.

"You ready for me to walk you to your dorm, or would you prefer a walk around the park first?" Jared asked.

"I would love to get out of these heels, but I'm not ready to go home yet. Maybe we could go to your room for a while and talk," she suggested.

"I'd be glad to remove your slippers, Cinderella," he teased. "But I'd hate for you to wake in the morning and see a pumpkin instead of the prince you're really after." His tone was serious. He obviously already knew this wasn't going to work out.

She stepped in front of him before they passed his dorm. "I believe you are the only prince I have ever met, Jared. I'm not going to take advantage of you. Your virtue is entirely safe with me." She winked. "I promise." Jared laughed and hugged her to his chest a bit too tightly.

"Alright, let's go get you out of those shoes." He took her hand and led her up the front steps of his dorm.

When they reached the room he shared with Steve, Dani suddenly felt sick. If she could go back in time she would start the whole evening differently. She would never have flirted or kissed Jared. Again guilt made her cheeks burn. She'd wanted to forget her troubles and she'd used Jared to help accomplish that goal. It was shameful.

Jared flicked on the light and scooped up the dirty laundry that was scattered across the floor. She sat nervously on Steve's bed and he grinned at her. "Let me make this easier for you, D. You care about me and I'm a lot of fun, *but*—and this is where it gets uncomfortable—you don't want to be with me. Am I getting close?" He turned to dig around in the minifridge in the corner and came out with two bottles of beer. He opened one and handed it to her. Dani took a healthy swig. She was in need of liquid courage, but it would take a hell of a lot more than this beer to give her that. Sitting across from her on his own bed, Jared smiled sadly and rolled his unopened beer between his hands.

"I'm sorry." She set the beer down on Steve's nightstand. She rested her arms on her thighs and hung her head. "I didn't mean for this to happen. You're honestly the perfect guy. Unfortunately, I'm an extremely flawed girl. I hope you can forgive me."

"It's the guy from the club, Chase, right? At first I thought you were trying to get over Lucas. Then I saw you with Chase tonight. He's the one you're trying to forget, isn't he?"

"Am I that obvious?" She was horrified. "Wait . . . you knew?" She looked up to find him smiling.

"Yes. As much as I would enjoy exploring a relationship with you, I knew you weren't ready. It was only a matter of time before you figured that out. Sadly for me, it didn't take long at all." He was still smiling. Dani's heart lifted a bit. He wasn't angry or truly hurt. "Why don't we just take a step back here, huh? I care about you a lot, and I don't want to lose a great friend over one night."

Jared turned the twist top of his beer and winced. "Damn! That was sharp." He rose from the bed and went into the bathroom. Blood dripped on the floor from his hand as he walked away. The scent of rich red blood cells hit Dani's senses. She gripped the bedding to keep from going after him. She was suddenly starving, and the need to feed crashed around her brain and shattered all other thoughts. She tried to breathe through it, but that only made it worse. Her fangs dropped to fill her mouth and her vision sharpened suddenly. *Shit!* The black-eyed freak was out in full force. She sat there shaking and praying for the strength to get up and leave before he saw her condition. The water came on in the bathroom sink.

"Ouch! That stings. It's just a tiny slice, but it burns like hell," he told her though the open doorway.

"I, uh . . . I gotta go. Okay? I'll see you tomorrow." She hopped up and leaped for the door. Jared stepped out of the bathroom to block her path.

"Hey, don't go yet. I want to be sure we're okay before you leave." He ran his arm up her arm and held his injured hand away. Dani looked at the floor so he wouldn't see her eyes. Fat drops of blood spattered the floor between her feet. She tried to get around him but he held onto her arm. "What's wrong? Does blood freak you out? It's just a few drops. I'll clean it up."

The heat of his body, the thrumming of his heart, pulled her into him. The scent of his blood in the air made her want to taste him. He grabbed her arms with both hands then, smearing his blood on her.

"I have to go. We need to talk, but not tonight. I have to . . . leave." Dani's gums throbbed. Her belly cramped painfully and she nearly hit the floor. Jared grabbed her before she collapsed.

"Easy now, D, there's no reason for you to run off. We have all night to talk." He dragged her over to his bed and pushed her back onto it. He propped himself up against the headboard, carrying her along and depositing her on his lap. He took her in his arms, but there was a different quality to the feel of his embrace now. He was once again her supportive friend, instead of a potential love interest. It wasn't a sensual hold but a reassuring one. She couldn't hear his thoughts, but she felt the concern and genuine love of a close friend flowing from him. Jared tried to look into her eyes, but she turned away. The warmth of his body under her and the steady beating of his heart were a torment. Her instinct took over. She had to feed. She would die if she didn't. Her head spun and she leaned into him, nuzzling his neck. He stiffened.

"Hey, I thought we decided we couldn't do this." His voice wavered. She panted and licked the pulse in his neck. Oh god! She couldn't stop. She was going to bite him.

"I'm sorry. Please, forgive me." There was no turning back. Unable to hold off any longer, she sank her fangs into his flesh. He stiffened, and his fear blew through her like a cold wind. She didn't know how to soothe him or make him forget what she was doing to him. So Danielle concentrated on showing him what she had become. She knew she could pick up memories and emotions from others, and she hoped for the ability to make it work in reverse. He needed to truly see her.

She wanted him to feel the urge she had to taste him. He watched her story in his mind. She showed him all her recent experiences with fangs and black eyes, Lucas's betrayal, and her attack. She allowed him to feel her fear and sense of rejection. It was very likely he would run screaming from the room when she finished. Her only hope was to help him understand her and know that she would never hurt him.

Jared had bucked at first when she broke his skin, but the strike was fast, and she immediately pulled her fangs from his neck and began to suck and lap at the hot sweet liquid. His fear abated quickly as her memories were broadcast from her mind into his. After only a moment he was groaning and writhing under her. She drank him in, swallowing mouthful after mouthful of his blood. They clung to each other and rode out the storm of hunger and need. Jared tensed beneath her and thrust his hips up against her bottom and climaxed. Feeding was a very pleasurable thing for the human involved, Dani knew from her experience with the bartender at the club. The bartender had reacted the same way when she'd bitten him. Instinctively, Danielle brushed her tongue over the wounds on his neck when she'd had enough, and the small puncture wholes began to close. Dani and Jared sat like that for long moments, while his breathing returned to normal and he absorbed what had just happened.

Finally, he whispered, "This is what you've been hiding from me?" He raised his fingers to her lips, which she parted slightly to reveal her shiny, white fangs. His eyes widened, not in fear but fascination, when he brushed the sharp points of her fangs with his thumb.

"Let me see your eyes, Danielle," he demanded, tipping her chin up. She opened them to reveal the cold black of a hunter. "I knew you were different, honey, just not exactly how." His eyes looked wild and confused. "Damn, but that shit was freaky. It was like I was you for a minute. I should have checked out your boobs while I had a chance." He joked to break the tense mood but Dani couldn't laugh. Her mind was clearing, her heart calming, and the burning ache in her belly had ceased. She could tell from the change in her vision that her eyes had just faded to blue, but she still felt like a monster. She'd just attacked her friend. Her body was returning to normal.

"I saw and . . . felt your need. I saw . . . everything. I'll admit to being a little freaked out, but I know I can trust you not to hurt me. I would rather you came to me than take a chance at getting hurt again. So, vampires . . . are real. We can deal with this. Now, if you were a zombie, then I'd have to shoot you in the head, but a vampire I can deal with." He chuckled. She was so relieved he hadn't run screaming, she hugged him tight. She'd shared every memory, and he was still right there by her side.

He lay back on the bed and pulled her down with him. They cuddled with tangled legs and arms until he was snoring softly. It was a contented, peaceful sound that made Danielle's heart swell. This was what she had been searching for—total acceptance. And after her behavior in the club with Chase, she didn't deserve it.

Hours later, she slowly slipped out of bed, not wanting to wake Jared. She recalled the dream she'd had the night they went to the club that first time. Jared had come to her and told her to take what she needed from him. He wanted her to have it. It was a premonition. She knew, even back then, that Jared would be there for her.

People were stirring in the hall. Jared was still sleeping, and she didn't want to get him in trouble for having a girl in the dorm. Unable to find her shoes in the dark, she crept barefoot into the hall and quickly exited the boys' dorm. She found crossing campus barefoot that early in the morning an experience she would like to have missed. It was too early to go into her room without waking Olivia and Lindsay, so Danielle turned on a TV in the common room and promptly dozed off. All the things she should be thinking about could wait. For now, she just needed some sleep.

Nine

The rogue looked out over the park beneath the window of his downtown penthouse. He watched the humans milling about, moving through their lives with no idea of the powerful and dangerous breed of predators living among them. His people had become cowards, hiding in plain sight from the humans. He was sick and tired of living that way, and he was fed up with the council's rules. He was getting closer to the power needed to breach their ranks and live his life as it was meant to be, without fear of retribution from that panel of weaklings and power junkies. He would rip them apart, turn them against each other, and bring about a new era of leadership.

He had almost done it all those years ago. He'd been gathering power by absorbing the lifeblood of the local vampire youth and, along with it, their abilities. That was a unique talent handed down to him from his grandmother. She could see they shared the trait, and she taught him never to use his horrible gift. But he had grown sick of that restriction. He didn't believe he'd been given the talent by mistake, or that it should not be used.

Leann Vaughn had ruined all his plans. David Deidrick had died by his own hand to protect his family and his mate, Leann. It was a valiant deed. David was to be the bait to lure his mate out into the open. The fact that the couple had been mated was a secret, and David's capture alone hadn't been enough to get Leann out in the open. Her family was doggedly protecting her and her ability.

The rogue had been certain the news of David's death would bring her out to attend his memorial. Instead, it had crushed his plans entirely. Leann Vaughn-Deidrick had ended her own life when she learned of David's death.

He'd wanted the Vaughn girl's precognitive abilities. She was a talented beauty with the sight. He hoped he could convince her to join him. Then he could keep her for himself and not have to kill her to take advantage of her sight. The problem was the unforeseen complication the bond between them caused. It had been the undoing of his plan, because the girl so loved her mate that she followed him to the grave.

"What a waste," he scoffed. He'd had to retreat into the shadows and wait for an opportunity to present itself again. The memory of hiding, of being thwarted by a love-struck girl, made his stomach turn. How romantic, how pathetic, that the bad guy's evil plan had been foiled by true love. It sounded like the plot from a bad made-for-TV movie.

Recently, he had acquired a handy tool in his search for the perfect abilities. The Davis boy's talent would move things along. Instead of resorting to snatching kids off the street and testing them for extrasensory abilities, he could now discover their abilities with just a touch. With the power he absorbed from the Davis boy and the lucky find of the mystery girl at the club, he could put his plan into motion.

Smiling in anticipation, he stepped over the body he'd just drained. Sending the kids back alive had proven to be too big a risk. The council had been drilling the Prince girl since she awoke from her drug-induced haze. It hadn't done them any good, but he wouldn't continue to take that chance. He still had one hostage—the son of a council member and a wonderful bargaining chip, not to be wasted. The young male had no extraordinary power, so there was nothing to be gained. He would detain the kid until he was ready to cash in the chip.

Kayden sat in the lobby waiting for Chase to come down from his penthouse. Chase had discovered the convenience of having his "meals" delivered to his home after he was forced to try it when Danielle was under his care. After that, he enjoyed it. At the moment, he was finishing up with a sweet little redhead.

They were going to lunch with Griffin Vaughn that day, so Chase needed to get a move on before the limo arrived. Mr. Vaughn needed all the information they could give regarding Danielle and her attacker. Kayden's mind began to wander over the events of that night when he was startled by a voice that sent chills down his spine. Her voice was like fingernails on a blackboard.

"Are you boys ready? Daddy is waiting in the car." Samantha peered at him over her designer sunglasses. How could such an annoying creature come in such a pretty package?

"I didn't realize you were coming, Sam. Chase hasn't come down yet. I'll call him again." Kayden went for his cell.

"No, wait. I'm kind of glad to find you alone. I think we should talk. And could you please stop calling me Sam?" She put her hand on Kayden's arm to stop him from retrieving his cell.

"What could you possibly want to talk to me about, Sam?" He enjoyed watching her grimace at the use of her childhood nickname. She tried so hard to be a grown-up but she was just barely eighteen, and to him she was still the little girl who would run and cry to her mom because he and Chase wouldn't play tea party with her. Some things never changed. She was still pissed because they wouldn't play her games; only recently, she wanted to play adult games.

"You see, Kayden, I believe we have a common interest. I am interested in keeping this new toy of Chase's away from him. She's all shiny and new to him now, so he's obsessed and doesn't want to play with anything else. He thinks he loves her, but he'll grow tired of her, just like he does with the rest of his playthings." Samantha waved her hand in a dismissive gesture, as if to wave her competition away.

Kayden's brow creased in annoyance. "What's your point, Sam? This has nothing to do with me."

"The point is that I didn't miss the way you looked at the half-naked tramp when we were in Chase's room the other day. I also didn't miss the lost-puppy expression on that sweet face of yours when you came back in from chasing her down. Neither did I miss the dreamy way you described her collapsing sadly into your arms in the hall. I can't believe Chase hasn't seen it yet, but I see it clearly. You want that girl too; don't you, Kayden?" Sam raised a perfectly shaped eyebrow at Kayden, daring him to deny the truth. He kept looking at the elevator, hoping Chase would hurry. Kayden wanted nothing to do with Sam's conniving ways.

"I don't need an answer because it's all over your face, Kayden. Why should Chase always get what he wants? He has tons of girls, and he is going to be bonded in the near future. Why can't you date her if he can't be with her anyway? She walked out on him, right? I mean, who could blame the girl? He did lie to her to get her into bed." Samantha was encouraging him to see things her way and planting the image of Chase in bed with a girl Kayden so clearly wanted. A muscle in Kayden's jaw began to work, and he could feel his eyes flash to black.

"He did not sleep with her! We were helping her. He was doing what Doc said. That's all, Sam." Kayden didn't want to think of what Chase might have done with Dani if Sam hadn't shown up. He'd never been so happy to see Sam as he was that day. She had busted up Chase's little love nest right on time. Kayden was doing his best to pretend he had no interest in Dani until Chase lost interest. Chase always lost interest after a while.

The night they met her, Kayden had hoped it wouldn't take too long, due to the way Dani dissed Chase. He'd made the mistake of calling Chase the night he came across her drunk and in need of a hand at a party. He should have just moved in on her then, but he knew Chase would have caused trouble for him if he weren't done pursuing her. Kayden always deferred to Chase's wishes. It was just how it had always been. Then Danielle told him he was beautiful. She thought the rough-edged, arrogant guy who did all he could do to exude angry vibes of aggression to keep others away was beautiful. The words and the soft, honest expression on her face had stunned him. He'd decided to take her home with him and let Chase sniff around in circles all night. Then Chase had shown up and snatched Dani right out of his car. *Damn it!*

"Touchy much? Don't get your shorts in a twist, big boy. I don't blame you. I guess she is pretty in a freaky punk sort of way, if that's what you like. You sure he hasn't hit it yet? They looked awfully familiar with each other when we walked in to find him all wrapped around her in bed." Samantha knew she had him, and she was stoking the flames of jealously and encouraging Kayden's imagination to run with that memory.

He turned to look at her. "Get to the damn point, Sam. I'm not gonna stand around and listen to someone of your 'experience' tear her down, and her hair is natural, by the way. I'd like to see you tell your father his hair is freaky." He hesitated a moment. "You should really watch your step, Sam. She's more talented than you can imagine."

"Are you really that stupid? You want her, and I want him. I don't care what she can do. I just don't want her sharing her 'talents' with Chase. You need to find a way to get closer to her, while

I keep him tied up with Daddy and council business. I'm going to be cochairing the gala committee with him, and that'll mean a lot of time together in the next several weeks. Daddy will be talking to him about the schedule today. It's expected that he will ask me to the gala. That would be the perfect time to let Chase see how she prefers you. That is, if you can convince her to attend the gala with you. You can be the one to introduce the new girl to our society. I bet if we play our cards right, you could be bonded before too long yourself.

"If you can't handle it, let me know and I'll find another male to distract her. I'm sure I can find another guy who would love to try her on for size, if you know what I mean."

Kayden's head snapped up, and he glared at Samantha.

"I'll keep her busy. You keep your bloodhounds away from her. I'll be pursuing her, but only because I like her and I wanna get to know her better. Don't blame me if you can't keep Chase away, because he is not going to give up easily. He won't wanna be with you until he's forced to by a blood bond." Sam looked at him as if he had just slapped her. "The truth may hurt, Sam, but that doesn't make it any less true."

Just then, Chase came off the elevator with a sleepy-looking redhead under his arm. He froze when Samantha came into view. He whispered something to the girl, and she left on wobbly legs. "What are you doing here, Sam?"

"Hello, darling. I'm here for our lunch date. Daddy has been waiting, so we should get a move on." She turned and wagged her ass all the way out to the car.

"What is she up to, Kayden?"

"Looks like you two are going to be spending some quality time together planning the gala. Congrats!" Kayden slapped him on the back in sympathy on the way to the car.

Chase was in a foul mood when they arrived at the country club. Sam was getting on his last damn nerve with her constant chatter about the gala. Griffin had to make the rounds at the bar, socializing and rubbing elbows before taking his seat. He insisted Chase go with him to watch and learn. It gave Samantha more time to drive home the fact that Chase was being groomed for the council and prepared for bonding.

Over lunch, they continued to discuss arrangements for the gala and planned for Chase to come over and meet with Samantha frequently for the next several weeks in preparation. They would be attending several meetings with vendors to assure a smooth-running event. Chase knew it was an attempt by Samantha and their respective parents to kindle a romance between them. He thought Brandi was looking better and better every day.

Chase was grateful when Samantha's father dismissed her after lunch so the men could talk. Griffin wanted a full accounting of their experience with Danielle. He and Kayden relayed everything they knew about Danielle and the attempted kidnapping.

"We haven't found Nathan yet, but Vince won't give up. He feels responsible. He does all the hiring, and this guy made it past him." Chase decided not to reveal her last name. He found it odd that Griffin would not know a member of his family was attending college so close to his home. There couldn't be any relation, but sitting across the table from Griffin, the resemblance between him and Danielle was striking. It was hard to dismiss it when they even had the same hair, the same chestnut color, and the same streaks that looked like purposely placed snow-colored highlights.

"I think I should meet this girl. If she's all you boys say she is, we may need to contact her family and place her under our protection until we get this mess sorted out. If her talents were to fall into the wrong hands, it would be disastrous." Both the boys stiffened at this comment. "Do either of you have a number for her? Kayden, maybe you can go pick her up and bring her over? I'll be home all evening."

Chase spoke up quickly. "No. I will go get her, Mr. Vaughn. She's a friend of mine."

"Really? I was given the impression by Samantha the girl wasn't speaking to you, and that I should go through Kayden to reach her." Griffin turned to Kayden. "Are you friends with the girl also, Kayden?"

"Yes, sir, I know just where to find her. I would be more than happy to speak with her, Mr. Vaughn. I'm sure she'll cooperate," Kayden assured Griffin.

Chase banked on the fact that once Griffin met Danielle, he would want her protected.

"Mr. Vaughn, I live five minutes from the university. I would be glad to put her up in my spare bedroom if she needs protection. It would be convenient for her to get to school. I have the space, and security in the lobby of my building. You still live at home, about thirty minutes from the university, right, Kayden?"

"Yes, that's correct." Kayden tried to control his scowl as he answered.

Griffin leaned back. "I will speak with the girl and decide if protection is in order. We'll speak again after I decide where she will be safest, if protection is called for."

Chase and Kayden didn't speak to each other directly the rest of the afternoon. There was a new tension, a distance between them that neither of them seemed willing to cross.

Kayden didn't bother to say good-bye to Chase when they were dropped off in front of his building. When the driver opened the door for him, Kayden bowed his head respectfully to Mr. Vaughn and exited the vehicle in search of a fight. His size alone made most people stay out of his way. He was six-and-a-half feet of hewn muscle that screamed *menace*, but he could always find someone willing to rumble among the warriors.

Kayden Paris came from a long line of warrior-class vampires. They were the strongest of their species and took great honor in protecting their community and families. So Kayden had an inborn temper and an aggressive streak that just wouldn't quit. His father, Gage Paris, the commander of the warrior class, reported directly to the council. By all rights, Kayden should have been well on his way to following in his father's footsteps.

Until that moment, he'd had no interest in becoming a warrior. This was a source of disappointment for his father. Of course, Kayden had plenty of training. He'd been wrestling and sparring with his father pretty much since birth. He was deadly with a gun and as accurate as any warrior with a blade, but hand-to-hand combat gave him the most pleasure. He enjoyed challenging others with his strength.

He was pissed off and ready to break someone's face. Stalking off to his car, he decided to pay his father a visit. Maybe he could work out some aggression at the compound. Samantha should have left him alone. He was used to the way things were. Chase was from a ruling house, and Kayden never had a problem dealing with his dominant nature. It had always been that way. They'd grown up together. Gage, Griffin, and Chase's father were good friends, so their families mingled often. Kayden was comfortable with his lower-class status. It never mattered, as long as Kayden wasn't eyeing something or someone Chase wanted.

But all he could think of was Danielle. He realized that Sam had played a head game with him in order to secure her own happiness, but she'd made some valid points. There was no reason he shouldn't be able to pursue Danielle. Chase would do nothing but break her heart in the end. She would be nothing but a memory once he was bound to Sam. The one good thing about being lower class was he would bond to someone for love, not out of obligation or duty to his house.

His father was in a meeting when he arrived, so Kayden went to the locker room and changed. As there was no shortage of warriors willing to spar, Kayden made himself busy getting bloody knuckles and working out his pent-up anger. He'd need to be calm when he went to see Danielle.

His father's look of pride when he left the ring was worth the world to Kayden. He didn't like disappointing his father, and that day marked the end of his resistance. Kayden would join the warriors and make his father proud. Taking his place among his people felt like a good thing now, instead of the duty he'd always dreaded. The thought of having purpose made him feel oddly settled. His life would be about more than just the next party or night out on the town. Kayden would make himself worthy of his family name. He would be worthy of Danielle, and he'd make it his job to protect her. He would use his father's authority to be assigned to her detail and personally ensure her safety. Chase would use his father's influence to get Dani under his roof. Kayden had to use his father's sway to make sure he would be right there beside her, no matter where she ended up.

"Dad, we need to talk. I've been doing a lot of soul-searching lately. I need to start thinking about the future and what I'm going to do with my life. I'm ready to join your ranks, if you'll still have me. I hope you can forgive me for my hesitation in the past, but I wanted to be sure I was ready for the commitment. I am now, Dad. It would be an honor to serve you and our people." Kayden spoke to his father from the heart. Every warrior in sight stopped and watched father and son staring at each other.

Gage's always-stern face never changed during Kayden's brief speech. He seemed to be measuring his son's sincerity. Finally, after several long moments, the smile that cracked his face stunned the crowd of onlookers.

"Welcome to your new family, son. I'm sure I speak for everyone when I say it's about damn time." Gage wrapped his son in a manly embrace and pounded on his back. The other warriors broke the silence with hoots of approval.

Chase knew Griffin would want his Lovely protected after he met her and observed her talents for himself. If the stories were to be believed, it was dangerous for Danielle to be out there alone. Someone was on the hunt for powerful young vamps, and Danielle had spelled out some of her abilities for the hunter. Chase couldn't stand the thought of her coming to such a brutal end. He'd protect her at all cost.

The problem was going to be Samantha. Would Griffin place Danielle in his care if Samantha protested the arrangement? Chase needed to speak with his father again about the situation. He didn't want to be with Samantha and didn't want his life ruled as if he were already bonded to her. There had to be another way.

He continued to prepare the spacious spare bedroom in his condo, refusing to accept any possibility of Dani not staying with him. He'd ordered new linens and towels, along with a plush bathrobe. He wanted her to be comfortable, and his taste tended to run toward a manlier, darker color scheme. He selected the new bedding with the image of her soft skin laid against it. The deep peach and ivory would be warming against her alabaster shade of heaven.

With his eyes closed, he could clearly imagine the soft curves of her body sleeping peacefully, wrapped in the warmth of his protection. He imagined her scent filling his home the way it had filled his bedroom when she had slept there. He still couldn't enter his studio at the club without being overwhelmed by her aroma. He went hard just thinking about having her under him again.

She was angry with him for the moment, but once she spent some time with him, she would realize how much he cared for her. She would see how sincere his intentions had been from the beginning. Chase would do whatever it took to get her in his arms again.

Ten

Danielle woke to find the smiling face of Kayden Paris looking down at her. She was disoriented for a moment, until she remembered where she was and how she'd come to be there. She had a kink in her neck from sleeping on a sofa in the dorm's common room.

"Hey there, Sleeping Beauty." Kayden's grin grew even wider when he surveyed her outfit. "I'm sorry to disturb your rest, but your help is desperately needed. I'm told Chase informed you that we needed to talk to you about your attack."

"Yeah, he did mention that to me. Thank you for coming to talk to me. I can't handle Chase right now." She blushed because she knew Kayden was well aware of why she didn't want to see Chase. He'd been there to witness her embarrassment at Chase's condo.

"Actually, it isn't me who wants to speak with you. Not that I don't want to talk to you," he rushed on. "It's the council, you know, our governing body, that needs to hear your story." At her look of confusion Kayden sat next to her and quietly, so as not to be heard by the others in the room, educated her on the vampire executive branch. He explained that the ruling houses of North America consisted of the three families who originally settled in America. Three members for each of the three houses made up a committee that created and enforced their laws, protected their secrecy, and maintained their historical records. The continent was split into regions that were governed by principals who report to the council.

"I'm to take you to meet one of the councilmen at his home today. He'll report his findings back to the rest of the council. Thank you for coming with me today. We have two missing people at the moment. It's possible you could remember something that will help us find them," he finished.

After a quick shower, Dani packed an overnight bag for her trip home while Kayden waited in the common room. When she returned from her room she found Kayden seemingly absorbed in watching sports highlights on the news, while girls gathered in the common room looked at him and drooled. As soon as she entered the room, he was on his feet and ushering her toward the door and out to the parking lot, which made her believe he wasn't as oblivious to his surroundings as he appeared to be. They drove separately. Dani followed him across town and parked her car behind Kayden's in front of a huge house. Well, *house* wasn't really the correct word. It was a mansion on an estate with a guarded gate at the entrance.

Her phone startled her when it rang in her jacket pocket. It was her mom.

"Hey, Mom, what's up?" she answered.

"Danielle, where are you? Please tell me you're not where I think you are!" She sounded panicked and out of breath.

"I have an appointment." She hesitated. "It's kind of a long story that I planned on telling you tonight. Why are you so upset?" Dani didn't like the way her mother's voice was shaking.

"Are you at the home of Griffin Vaughn? Was there a big 'V' on the front gate?"

"Yes. There was a 'V' on the gate, but I don't know whose home it is. Should I leave? Who is Griffin Vaughn?" Dani began to feel sick.

"Oh my God, I'm going to vomit!" Tessa wailed.

"What's going on? Did you have a dream; should I leave? Who is Griffin Vaughn?" Dani jumped when Kayden tapped on her window. She put up her finger to ask for one more minute.

"No, it's too late to leave, and yes, I had a dream. They will follow you and ask way too many questions if you run now. I don't have time to explain this properly. I was going to do it tonight, but you need to know right now. You are at your father's home."

Dani felt like she'd just had the air knocked out of her. Her head spun while she listened to her mother's hurried account. "He believes that you and I both died not long after you were born. You look so much like him, I'm afraid he'll guess who you are, so you need to lie. I want you to give him a false last name; using your first name is fine. Tell him whatever you have to, but don't mention me. Can you do that and call me as soon as you're out of there?"

Dani sat in stunned silence. She was about to come face-to-face with her father. "Alright, I have to go. They're waiting."

"I love you, baby. I'm sorry. I was only trying to protect you. Are you wearing the necklace I gave you?"

"Yes. I'll take it off. I guess it came from him . . . my father?" She could hardly speak.

"I promise to explain everything later. Just call me as soon as you're out of there," Tessa prompted, before she hung up.

Dani opened the car door and practically fell out. Her knees were weak, and her stomach was on fire. Kayden steadied her with one large, muscular arm.

"Are you alright? Chase said you were still injured." Genuine concern showed in his eyes.

"I'm not feeling well. Let's get this over with, so I can get home." She fought back nausea.

As they walked, she could tell by the way Kayden kept opening his mouth and shutting it before any sound could escape that he had something to say. Finally, he seemed to find his voice and stopped walking halfway to the door.

"I was wondering—" He paused, running his fingers through his hair and looking down at her. "I don't know why this is so hard. I'm never this nervous."

He tripped over his words, suddenly unable to look her in the eye. He took a deep breath, reached out to take her hand, and asked, "I was wondering if you would consider going to the gala with me. I know you've never been before. It's a stuffy, formal, vampire-only affair, but it may be tolerable if I have the most beautiful female on my arm."

Dani's head was too busy preparing a believable lie to tell the man she was about to meet to really absorb Kayden's invitation. She smiled absently, mindlessly.

"Sure, Kayden, that sounds like fun." She pulled her hand away and continued toward the house.

From behind her, she heard Kayden exclaim under his breath, "Yes!"

They reached the ornate double doors, and Kayden rang the doorbell. Dani realized she hadn't removed the necklace. She cursed and pulled it off, stuffing it into her front pocket. A string of complaints could be heard from the other side of the door. It seemed the butler was nowhere to be found and the lady of the house was displeased about answering the door herself. A tall, elegant woman with an air of superiority answered the door and invited them into the foyer. The twist in her pale blond hair was as tight as the stick that seemed to be lodged in her ass. Dani looked around the big entry, with its white marble floors and a crystal chandelier hanging from the high ceiling between two staircases. The woman spoke to Kayden and hadn't even acknowledged Dani.

"Griffin is waiting for you in his study. We've received more bad news. Christopher Stafford is missing." Then the woman noticed Danielle, and she stopped in her tracks. She stared for a moment, until Kayden introduced them.

"Mrs. Vaughn this is Danielle . . . Umm. I'm sorry. I don't know her last name." Kayden seemed a little embarrassed.

Dani stepped up and extended her hand in greeting to the woman who had stolen her father.

"My name is Danielle Scott." She had chosen to use Jared's last name without a thought. He would get a kick out of that. "It's a pleasure to meet you." She smiled politely, but imagined bashing the woman's blond head into the lovely etched mirror on the wall between the staircases.

"I'm Sarah Vaughn. Kayden will take you to see my mate." She looked confused and stared intensely at Dani's hair.

As Dani and Kayden walked away, a boy about nine or ten years old came running up to Sarah. Dani was struck by his resemblance to her. The boy looked just like Dani, minus the streaks, and his eyes were a deep sapphire blue. Dani followed Kayden down the hall with her head reeling over the fact that she had a little brother, she wondered if she had any other siblings.

The door to the office was open, but Kayden still knocked before he entered.

"Come." A smooth and commanding voice rang from within. She was sure she'd be sick. That was her father's voice. She hesitated on the threshold, but Kayden snagged her arm and dragged her into a masculine room with dark wood furniture and an oversize sofa by the fireplace. At the other end of the room near the bar was one of those things for practicing your golf putt.

At first Kayden blocked her view, and she wished he would stay there, so she didn't have to look at the face of the man who had broken her mother's heart. Then Kayden stepped to the side and she saw him. He stood with his back to them, looking at some paperwork on a sideboard. He was tall with dark hair and broad shoulders. He wore an expensive-looking suit Dani was sure cost more than her whole wardrobe. When he finally turned to face them, she saw the streaks. *Dear God.* She was like his damn clone. He hadn't looked up at her, and that was good, because her jaw was on the floor with her stomach. She shut her mouth with a click when Kayden began to speak.

"Mr. Vaughn, I'd like to introduce you to Danielle Scott."

Griffin didn't raise his eyes from the paper he read as he crossed the room, until they were within a few feet of a handshake. Then he froze, his eyes locked on hers, and the breath that caught in his throat was audible. He stood there with his hand half extended, staring at her.

She smiled and took his hand. "It's nice to meet you, Mr. Vaughn. I hope I can be of some service in your search for the missing people." She decided to stay calm and pretend that she couldn't see the obvious. She would be polite and play her part so she could get the hell out of there.

"It's a pleasure to make your acquaintance. Thank you for meeting me on such short notice," he stuttered, trying to pull his gaze from her eyes. She imagined he saw her mother's eyes, and she hoped it hurt him to remember those unique, icy gems.

"Please come have a seat so we can talk. I've heard some amazing claims about your abilities." He pointed her toward a chair in front of his large desk.

"Kayden, you can go make yourself at home in the kitchen until we're done here. I'm sure you're hungry," Griffin suggested.

Kayden rubbed his washboard abs. "I'm always ready to eat. See you later. I'd hate to be late for lunch." He left, closing the door on the way out.

Griffin went to the other side of the desk and sat in his high-backed leather chair. For several moments, he said nothing. He just looked at her, until she interrupted the awkward silence. "What have you heard about me, sir?"

He seemed to shake himself back to attention. "I've heard you have multiple talents, from telekinesis to telepathy. Is that true?" He sounded like it was an incredible claim.

"Is that unusual?" she countered.

"I've never met anyone with multiple extrasensory abilities. Have you? What about your family? Are there other multitalented individuals in your house?"

"I have no family left. My parents died when I was little. I was raised by a servant, who died just after I turned eighteen. She was a bit of a recluse. She never talked about others like me, and I received only the most basic training, because my guardian was human. I know nothing about your people, or of what is normal for them. I'd never even met another vampire, until I started school at the university and went to the club with my friends." That was quick thinking. Sticking as closely to the truth as possible would help her keep the lie straight. She hadn't figured out her lie, until asked about her family. She couldn't have him asking questions about her mom.

"How are you paying for college?" he wanted to know.

"With the proceeds I received from the sale of my parents' house. I also applied for financial aid, so that helped." She needed to redirect the conversation away from her past. "That's enough about me, Mr. Vaughn. I should tell you about my attack, so you can get on with your search. Better yet, I'd like to try to show you, if you don't mind. It'll be much easier for you to understand. Please keep in mind that my abilities are new to me, so I have to hope they work on command."

"It's normal for extrasensory ability not to be apparent until you come of age. How old are you?" Griffin asked.

"I'm twenty-one," she replied, walking around to his side of the table. "I think I can do it without touching you, but it seems to be clearer and easier for me if I can touch you. Is that alright?" She stood right beside him.

He took a long, slow breath and held it, before blowing it out through his nose. "You smell like vanilla and something else, lavender, maybe. It's the most beautiful scent." Shaking his head as if trying to free himself from a memory, he asked, "How do you intend to show me?"

"Like this." Dani rested her hand on his and asked him to close his eyes. He jumped when she began to project her memory into him. She showed him everything from when she was thrown onto the floor, up to when the guy, walking away, promised to catch up with her later. Then she raised her hand and went back to her chair. He didn't open his eyes for several moments. She figured he was reviewing the scene in his mind. "That was better than a description, wasn't it? You would probably recognize that guy if you saw him on the street."

"Let me see what else you can do, Ms. Scott." He made an admirable effort to hide his astonishment.

"I can do what I just did to you, in reverse. Not like I can find what I want in your mind or anything, but I can see what you're remembering. It comes back to me in pictures just like I showed you, but it's more like a slide show with clips of audio."

"Tell me what I did yesterday at noon," he challenged her.

She reached across the table for his hand and stretched her mind, trying to find what he was thinking about. Her eyes darkened as she said, "You were at the cemetery visiting the graves of your first wife and daughter." She tilted her head as if reading something. "They've been gone a long time."

He was again unable to mask his shock. "Do you have anything else to show me?"

Danielle concentrated on the cell phone resting on the corner of the desk. It slowly rose a few inches and floated over to hover in front of Mr. Vaughn. "I can do that, too." He smiled.

Danielle felt her chair rise off the floor, and she lost her concentration, causing Griffin's phone to clatter against his desk. She jumped up. "I'm so sorry, Mr. Vaughn. I told you, I'm new at this."

But he laughed, quite amused. "There can't possibly be anything else for you to show me," he said, still laughing and shaking his head.

"I can make people do what I want them to do."

"Yes, we can all control human minds. That's normal." He rolled his eyes.

"I can do it to vampires. Or at least I did once," she added.

One of his dark eyebrows rose, and he hit an intercom button to page Kayden back to his office.

"What do you want me to tell him to do?"

"What did you do before?"

"I made this girl who was running her mouth shut up. I actually froze her there, until I left the apartment, and I released her from the hall. She kept on yapping like it never happened."

"That's good. I'll get him talking and you can stop him," he suggested. "Come in," he called when Kayden knocked. "What did you have for lunch?"

Kayden started, "Your cook made me and J. R. this huge—"

That was all he got out before Dani said, "Stop," and he did. She said, "Turn," and with a blank stare he turned around. She said, "Sit," and Kayden plopped down cross-legged like a little kid.

Griffin rose from his chair in disbelief. He strode around to Kayden and lifted his face. He called his name and gently slapped him to get his attention. It didn't work. "Release him, please," Griffin requested politely.

Kayden then continued, as if he had never stopped, "Italian

cold cut sub with chips and cream soda. Hey, how did I get on the floor?" He jumped up, embarrassed.

Ignoring Kayden, Griffin watched in bemusement. "Is there anything else you would like to share?"

Without moving her lips, she spoke to him telepathically, "Is this normal? I have the most trouble with answering people's thoughts and unintentionally letting them hear mine. It kind of comes and goes, but mostly I get pictures instead of words."

Shaking his head in astonishment, he replied verbally, "It's more common than your other abilities. To block your thoughts, you should imagine building a wall around your mind, or maybe locking your thoughts behind a door. It will take practice, but it will help."

Kayden looked back and forth between her and Griffin. "What am I missing here?"

Griffin continued to ignore him. "I wish I had more information about your family. These things are usually hereditary."

The conversation was heading in a direction she wasn't going to go. "Is there anything else I can do for you, Mr. Vaughn? I have an appointment this evening, and it takes me several hours to get there, so I need to get going." Dani went for the door, when it shut, untouched, in front of her. She turned and eyed Griffin.

"There's a problem we need to discuss, Ms. Scott. You are a very talented young lady, who has already been identified by whomever is kidnapping our youth. We have already lost a talented young male. Two females were abused and returned, and we are now missing two others. It's not safe for you to be roaming around alone. Particularly since your attacker promised to return for you."

"I'm not a member of your youth and will not be hiding in a corner from anyone. As I'm sure you've noticed, I was completely capable of defending myself."

Griffin came quickly toward her, his hand out as if he might grab her. "A young lady of your talents in the wrong hands—"

"Stop!" Danielle halted him with one word and a frantic need to escape his attempt to control her.

Both Griffin and Kayden froze, and she left the room quickly, hoping she would be able to hold them long enough for her to get off the property. She had no idea how far she could go before her ability gave way. On the way out, she passed the boy, J. R., as Kayden had called him. They smiled at each other, and he followed her to the door, working a handheld video game. He smiled and waved as she jumped in her car. Even in her hurry, she couldn't help waving back at the boy's sweet face and dark-blue eyes peering at her from under long, dark lashes. He was her brother. There was no questioning the resemblance, and she felt a connection to the boy.

Dani shook herself. She had to get out of there. Her heart hammered when she pulled up to the security gate. She smiled at the guard who had admitted her and Kayden earlier. He gave a flirty wink and opened the gate for her to exit. She was safely a few blocks away before she thought to release her hold on the men she'd frozen. She didn't even know if it was still in effect from that distance.

Dani drove a few miles in the wrong direction, nervously checking her rearview mirror to be sure Kayden or the security guard weren't following her before she finally hopped on the freeway and headed toward home. She extracted her cell from deep in her jacket to call her mom, who had a lot of explaining to do.

Eleven

Griffin snapped out of Danielle's trance, confused at first and then pissed off. He and Kayden began searching for her immediately. She had just been there. Then she disappeared.

J. R. was playing in the entry hall when Griffin rushed in and quickly scanned the area. "Who ya looking for, Daddy?" he asked with a grin.

"I'm looking for Danielle, the girl who came in with Kayden. Have you seen her?" Griffin ruffled his son's hair.

"Do you mean the really pretty girl that looks like you, Daddy?" J. R. managed to look away from his game.

Kayden and Griffin looked at each other. Griffin thought what he saw in Danielle had been his imagination. He looked at Kayden for a reaction.

"It's probably just the hair, Mr. Vaughn," Kayden added.

"Yes, that girl." Griffin sighed. "Did you see her?"

"She left a little while ago. I walked to the door with her. I like her, Daddy. She's pretty and she smells really good. Will she be back?" J.R. returned his attention to the game.

"Hopefully she will be back very soon." Griffin ran into the study and grabbed the phone to call the gatehouse. She couldn't have gotten far. When the guard answered, Griffin said, "Stop the girl who's on the way out. She needs to come back to the house."

"I'm sorry, Mr. Vaughn. A girl left about fifteen minutes ago. Is there another girl on the way out?" the guard asked.

"No, never mind." Griffin hung up the phone and went back into the hall shaking his head, irritated but impressed. "She left fifteen minutes ago. I can't believe she was able to use her power on me, an adult vampire. I thought it was funny when she did it to you, but I figured it was because you're young. I have been shielding my mind for years." Griffin had this intense feeling of foreboding he couldn't comprehend. He had become a hard-edged man after the loss of his first family. He didn't take to new people, and he only really cared for his immediate family.

As soon as Griffin was sure the girl was gone, something began to turn in his gut. He knew it was his duty to look after the talented girl in that dangerous time, especially since she had no family. But it was more than that. He felt the need to protect her, to shelter her. The last time he had that feeling was a long time ago, in a dark alley when those pale eyes stared up at him from that same petite frame. That must be what was tweaking his nerves. Those eyes had reminded him of a lost dream.

"What do you mean, when she did it to me?" Apparently Kayden didn't see the humor.

"How exactly did you think you ended up sitting on the floor facing the wrong direction in my office?" Griffin smiled in spite of himself.

"She did that to me? Damn, I should have known. I saw her do it before." Kayden scratched his head. "What should I do now? Do you want me to go check the school?"

"No, she said she was going to an appointment several hours away. Do you have any idea where she was going?" Griffin asked.

"She didn't tell me, but I am going to search for her. I assume that you want her to be protected now."

"I think it's very dangerous for her out there alone. It's also dangerous for us if she ends up in enemy hands. She was able to enthrall both of us at once and hold it for fifteen minutes. She also has telekinesis and telepathy. If there really is someone after talented youth, she would be a target." Griffin scowled and tried to beat back the anxiety tightening his chest.

"I would like to be her guardian, Mr. Vaughn. She's a friend of mine, and I won't stand out in her circle. It will be more comfortable for her to have me nearby than a stranger," Kayden explained.

"That's right. Your father called me earlier and requested I put you on the job, if necessary. Congratulations on your entrance into the warrior class. I know your father is very proud. You'll be a fine warrior, maybe even a Wrath guard one day.

"This is an important assignment, Kayden, more so than I believed when I spoke to your father, but I always defer to Gage's judgment in these cases. I know you've been training with Gage your whole life, so I believe you're up to the task. I just hope you can keep up with her. But first things first, we're going to need to find her. You will need to practice guarding your mind. She could be slippery." Griffin was still in disbelief at how easy it was for her to walk out and disappear without a trace.

It was a long ride home. Dani worried about Kayden and Griffin. She hoped they weren't still frozen in the study. She pulled up to the curb in front of her house and fished out her cell to call Kayden. She understood the reason behind them wanting to protect her, but she wouldn't be hiding while they dealt with the situation. She wasn't a part of their world and had no plans to join the black-eyed freak club.

"Hello?" Kayden answered.

"Hey, Kayden, it's Dani. Are you guys okay?" she asked sheepishly. She was waiting for him to yell at her, but he didn't. He was kind, even playful.

"Yeah, that's a neat trick you played on us. We're fine, but I wish you had waited for me. I could have gone with you, wherever you needed to go. When will you be back?"

"Sunday afternoon. I'm sorry about what I did, but I have some personal issues that couldn't wait. Mr. Vaughn is kind to want to protect me, but I'm really not one of his people."

"Why do you keep saying that? He explained to me that you were raised outside of our society, but you're still one of us, and we protect our own. I can help you adjust to our way of life. Things will probably be much easier for you once you learn to let us help you. Really, Dani, you know I'm a friend, right?" he reasoned.

Dani chuckled. "I may be putting that theory to the test very soon. We'll see how accepting you really are, eventually. I gotta go, but I'll call you when I get back into town."

"You know you're cryptic and crazy, right?" he joked.

"Yes, I am, but would you have me any other way?" She couldn't help smiling. Kayden was just so easy to talk to.

"I'd be willing to give it a go." They both laughed. "I'm serious, girl. You can trust me. I'll protect you and your personal issues that make you feel the need to manipulate others."

"Thanks, Kayden. I guess maybe we could be friends," she said in a teasing tone. "I'll call you when I get home." She hung up before he asked where she was.

Next, she needed to get to the reason for her long drive south. Her mom had some explaining to do, and she wouldn't be dancing around the truth anymore. Dani needed to know exactly what and whom she would be dealing with.

There was a black BMW parked out front, so she figured their guest was already there. She thought she'd have a day to grill her mom privately before he arrived, but maybe she'd get more answers if she were on the spot.

Dani parked and climbed out of her car. As she crossed the lawn, a feeling of betrayal crept over her. Her mother should have told her about her father. She should have prepared her for this madness. She slammed the front door behind her so Tessa would know she was pissed. She'd never slammed a door or yelled in her life. This seemed like a good time to start.

She stalked into the living room, where a man stood to greet her. "Soleil?" he asked. She had no idea who he was or what a soleil was, so she kept walking.

Her mother was in the kitchen making tea, but she didn't turn around to look at Dani. "Would you like a cup of tea, sweetheart?" she stalled.

"Yes, I would like some tea, with a side of, *What the hell is going on!*" The attitude was out of character for Dani and not polite for a stranger to witness, but she'd had enough.

The man stood in the doorway. "Maybe we should sit down, and your mother and I can calmly explain the situation to you, Soleil." His manner was smooth and irritating.

"Who are you and what is a soleil?" Dani snapped.

"I'm Mason, your godfather, and I am sorry for calling you Soleil. That has been your name in my mind since you were born, and I'm having trouble adjusting to your other name. Maybe I should say your *real name*," he explained. He was handsome, and his voice had a calming effect.

Dani looked at her mom. "Are you trying to tell me even my name is a lie? I can't believe this shit!" She threw her keys across the room and went back into the living room to plop down in a chair sideways with her head hanging off one arm and legs over the other. Taking deep breaths, she calmed herself and stared at the ceiling, waiting for them to join her.

"I didn't think you'd be here until tomorrow," Dani told the man in a much more civil tone when he sat across from her on the sofa.

"It seems we have some very serious problems at home. I need to get back tonight," he explained.

"I guess you're talking about the crazy vampire snatcher?" she asked sharply.

He and Tessa looked at each other. "Yes, that's the problem I'm speaking of. Why don't we start with you telling us what you already know about that, and we'll fill in the blanks for you, Soleil. I mean, Danielle. I'm sorry."

"So that is my real name? Why was it changed, and why didn't you change our last name, too?" she asked Tessa.

"That's the name your father gave you. It is a unique name, so I changed it in order to make you harder to find, but I had trouble letting go of my married name. I was only trying to protect you."

"Alright then, I will tell you what I have figured out the hard way and from piecing together our past discussion about my father." She paused to gather her thoughts. "I know that my father is a vampire whose family didn't approve of him marrying a human. Something bad must have happened after I was born, because you let them believe we both died so they wouldn't kill us, or whatever. Griffin believed we were dead, too. So he married and started a new family." When she said his name, Tessa cringed.

"I guess I was a normal kid, until I came of age. Griffin explained to me that it is not unusual for abilities to be unknown until then. I guess when my abilities made an appearance, so did my need for blood. He wants me protected because my *awesome* power might fall into the wrong hands and put his people in danger. Does that about sum it up?" she finished sarcastically. By the looks on their faces, she'd just told them something they didn't know. Good—at least she wasn't the only one in the dark.

"Did your father recognize you?" Tessa asked slowly.

"I don't think so. He looked at me really hard. My eyes caught him off guard, and he made a comment about my scent, so it's probably just a matter of time. I thought his wife would pass out when she saw me. I look just like him and their son."

"Sweetheart, you have no idea how sorry I am you had to find out this way. I really did believe that you were mostly human and this wouldn't be a problem." Tessa and Mason went into an explanation of the events that led to them hiding from her father. Her mother cried through most of it, which made Dani feel like a heel for yelling at her. She didn't blame her for running after he agreed to remarry—or bond, as they say—less than a day after hearing of their deaths. What a slap in the face. Dani could feel her mother's sorrow from across the room. She still loved him. It made Dani furious with him and his family all over again.

"So many things make sense now. You never dated or married. The necklace and the story you told me. The lack of any family and your unwillingness to talk about my father is understandable. I just wish I had known before I started to think I was going crazy. I really did think I was insane when I started to dream about biting people and liking it." It was a weak apology, but an apology nonetheless.

"Tell me about the power you were referring to. Griffin said you're unusual?" Mason prompted.

"Yes, he was impressed and said I need to be under council protection until the kidnapper is found."

Tessa looked at Mason, obviously confused.

Mason addressed her. "Do you remember the story Griffin told you about his sister and my brother?" Tessa nodded. "It's happening again."

She gasped and went into the kitchen to hyperventilate. They could hear her pacing and panting. When she returned she'd calmed and pasted on a neutral face.

"Let's talk about why Griffin thinks you need protection. Show us what you showed him," Mason suggested.

Without saying anything, she lifted the coffee table, turned it in the air, and set it back down. They both laughed then. "You got that from your dad," Mason said. "He's been known to move people's cars and hide them as a prank."

They were both watching her. Without moving her lips she said mentally, *I know. He lifted my chair off the ground with me in it to demonstrate.*

"Holy shit!" her mother yelped, and Mason laughed again.

"I seem to be projecting some of my thoughts, but it's usually not on purpose. It takes effort to do it on command," Dani explained.

"That is a little more common among telepaths. I do agree that you should be protected, but as for having awesome power, I'm not convinced."

"Oh, I'm not done yet. Let me show you something." She went around to Mason and put her hand on his. "I can do it without touching, but it is clearer if I touch you. Close your eyes." Then she showed him the same thing she'd shown Griffin—all the events of the night she was attacked, in fast-forward.

Trying not to look shocked, he said, "So you *have* fed." He commented on the scene with Nathan. "That is quite a telepathic talent indeed. I don't think I even have a name for it."

Her mom cringed again at the mention of her feeding. "How many times have you fed?" she asked.

"Twice, and both times I got a little stronger. You might as well know too." She touched Tessa and gave her a tour of the memory as well. "I can also read thoughts, but it mostly comes to me in pictures. I did it to Lucas that day in the kitchen, Mom, and I did it to Griffin today. I think Griffin's major concern is my ability to control other vampires."

Both of them looked at her as if she had a third eye. Dani didn't know what to say, so she opted to show them again. Without touching either one of them, she reached out with her mind and replayed for both at the same time how she'd frozen Griffin and Kayden and made Kayden do silly pet tricks before that. Neither one of them seemed to be able to speak.

"I'm making a sandwich." She trotted off to the kitchen. She could hear them whispering, but Dani'd had enough for one day.

"So, I'm going to go back to school and try to pretend I'm not a black-eyed, bloodsucking freak," she announced, returning with a ham-and-cheese sandwich in one hand and a glass of tea in the other.

"I'd like to clear up this notion you have about being a freak." Mason was obviously starting to take her criticism of his race personally. "Vampires and humans have the same basic genetic makeup, with a few DNA mutations. We aren't dead and we aren't immortal. We need blood to survive just like we need food and water. We don't catch human diseases, due to our strong immune systems. We're faster and stronger, with more acute senses, and some of us have extrasensory abilities. These abilities are not evil magic but naturally occurring gifts caused by the fact that large parts of the human brain that are not used are active in adult vampires. We can live a very long time if we take care of ourselves, or we can die from massive blood loss, though our strength and healing abilities make us hard to kill. Now that we have that straight, I'm going to have to arrange for some security for you. If the monster out there taking our kids gets his hands on you again, he will kill you for your power." Mason was dead serious, and her mother began to slump over in her seat like she'd pass out. Dani was still trying to absorb the Vamp 101 he'd just barked at her.

Mason reached over and patted Tessa's leg. "It'll be alright, Tessa. I'll protect her."

"How do you plan on doing that without Griffin knowing who she is?" she asked him.

"Griffin has already offered her protection. I'm going to a council meeting tomorrow, and I'm sure Griffin will tell us about her. I will, naturally, offer my services to protect our newfound miracle child," Mason reasoned.

"I'm not going to stop going to school. If I can't go to school, I'll just stay home," Dani snapped.

"Danielle, the safest place for you now is going to be close to Mason," Tessa told her and turned to Mason. "She can still go to school since you live close, right?"

"I think I should go to this meeting and see what I can do without attracting attention to myself, unless you're ready for them to know about the two of you." He looked at them both.

"No!" Tessa shouted.

"Mom, I'm not ready either, but I don't think it'll be long before Griffin starts asking questions. I told him a huge lie, and he seems like the sort of guy who might try to check out my story. Especially after I put him under and ran away. How pissed do you think he will be?" She wrinkled her forehead.

"I'm afraid she's right, Tessa. It should be funny to see what happens when these two go head-to-head. She seems to have his temper." The corners of his lips lifted just a bit.

"It's this damn change! She was the mildest-mannered girl. She's changed so much in the last month. You see the red in her hair? It wasn't there the last time I saw her, and she has never raised her voice to me." Her poor mother began to visibly shake.

Dani went down on her knees in front of her and laid her head in her lap. "I'm sorry, Mommy. I wish I could take it back, but I don't think I can. I'm sorry I yelled at you. I was just upset at the shock of everything that's happened. I'm afraid," she whispered.

"You should both know we have security—a small army of warriors, actually. I'm sure they'll assign a couple to watch over you until we figure out what's going on with the kids." Mason was trying to console Tessa more than Dani.

"Great. I'm sure I won't stand out at all around campus," she spat sarcastically. "Is there anything special I should know? I was hoping for a handbook on vampirism and a secret handshake. If not, everyone would know about 'us.'" She drew out the last word. "I'm ready to get out of here for a while. This is all too much."

"Of course there are laws. Laws you must follow or face the consequences, just like in human society. You can't tell anyone about us, obviously. We don't kill. We only take what we need, and we erase the memory of those we feed from. Don't feed in public, if possible, due to the risk of exposure. You should try to feed every few days, by the way. Of course, you are unique, so you may be able to go longer, but I wouldn't wait until you are starving. That makes it harder to stop," he said solemnly and looked at her mother with an apology in his beautiful blue-green eyes.

"I don't know how to erase memories, and how am I supposed to get anybody to follow me? I've never seen a vampire feed in public or drag off an unwilling person screaming in terror." She was ashamed of having to ask in front of her mother.

"You have quite a gift for mind control. Just tell them to follow you and they will. When you're done, tell them to forget about you, unless it is someone you use regularly, which I suggest. If you have regular hosts, you won't have to hunt for blood. In that case, just tell them to forget that period of time. You should know that it can be a very sensual experience once you come of age. So it won't be painful for the human after the bite." Now he looked embarrassed for having to tell her that in front of her mom.

"Just so the two of you know, I was bonded to a vampire for two years. I do know that they have to feed, and I was bitten frequently, so I know exactly what you're talking about. There's no need to be bashful," Tessa scolded.

"Sorry, Mom, I actually didn't know you were married, or bonded. I'm still trying to figure myself out. I haven't had time to think about what this all means for you. Believe it or not, I can understand just a sliver of how you might have felt in the beginning. There is this guy I had been talking to, and after I decided I had real feelings for him, his fiancée showed up. He is going to be bonded to this mean, but absolutely beautiful, girl. He says it's been arranged by his parents and it's an obligation he can't get out of. So I won't talk to him anymore, because it hurts too badly. I guess it's better this way. I bet he wouldn't want me anyway if he knew I'm a half-breed freak, not to mention his family's reaction. I don't think anyone is going to want me or my mixed-up human-vamp babies."

"Danielle, I would be proud to have you as my daughter-in-law. I am proud to be your godfather, and your father loved your mother and you more than anything. He loved to feel you moving in your mother's belly, and the joy in his heart when you were born was overwhelming. I think you will feel differently about the future once all this is settled. I will grant you that my point of view is not common, but we'll find a way to work it out. You should focus on getting used to the change before you start worrying about other things."

Tessa was crying again, and Dani couldn't deal with it anymore. "Mom, I'm going to go see if I can find Lucas. I just need to think about something else for a while."

Tessa nodded through her sniffles.

"Mason, is there a number where I can reach you if I need to?"

He gave Dani the number. She called him after programming it into her phone so he would have her number. Before she left, he stood and hugged her. Amazingly, he smelled like summer. It brought a tear to her eye. She hadn't smelled anything like that since the last time she was with Chase. She couldn't speak, so she just left.

Walking down her street felt so lonely. She felt like an alien no matter where she went. She didn't belong in either of the worlds she was a part of, and nobody really knew her anymore. She didn't even know herself.

Twelve

It wasn't a long walk from her house to Lucas's, so Dani took her time. She had no idea what she was going to say when she got there, or why she was going to his house. Maybe she just needed to feel something familiar. She'd thought about calling him to see if he even wanted to see her but had changed her mind. If he said he didn't want to see her, she would just go home. The moon was full, and its light cast an otherworldly glow over everything. She felt like the alien she was. She wondered if there would ever be a sense of being normal or belonging again. She'd walked those same streets for years, but they felt so strange that night. The stars looked like strangers staring down at her, instead of the constellations she used to be able to name. She could see everything, just like it was daytime. That had changed since the night before, and vampire vision could be a plus.

Walking down Lucas's street made her heart start to pound. The last time she'd seen him had been a really bad day for her. She arrived at his house and anxiety tied a knot in her gut. All the downstairs lights were on. She could see his mom and brothers playing cards at the dining room table through the living room windows. She'd sat at that table with them hundreds of times and played more hands of cards than she could count.

She knocked and Lucas's mom opened the door. With a squeal of delight, she pounced on Dani for a hug. Lucas's mom smelled like freshly baked cookies. Dani actually wondered if her blood would be as sweet. What a sick thought to have about a woman who was like a second mother to her.

"Oh, Dani, we've missed you so much. Lucas has been a mess lately. I don't know what happened between the two of you, but I hope you can work it out. He'll be so glad to see you." She squeezed Dani tightly.

"It's good to see you too. Is Lucas home?" Dani backed away from Mary before she had any more time to dwell on the thought of tasting her blood.

"He went out for a while. Do you want me to call him? I know he'll run right home." She smiled brightly.

"I kinda wanted to surprise him. Do you have any idea where he would have gone?" Dani couldn't help smiling back.

"You could check the field behind the school. He's been spending a lot of time there at night. He says it reminds him of you, so he likes being there." Mary brushed a hand across Dani's cheek. "He misses you."

"Thanks, Ms. Mary. I'll check there before I try calling him." Mary hugged her again. Dani left the porch feeling a little brighter. A dose of home may have been just what she needed.

The thought of Lucas sitting in their field, staring up at the stars to feel closer to her, gave Dani's heart a squeeze. Maybe what he had done was just a drunken mistake. She was no angel. Chase had slept in her bed that night. In fact, she'd crawled all over him and offered him sex. A fact she hadn't remembered until after she had walked out on Lucas. Dani still wouldn't have remembered it if she hadn't been able to invade Chase's mind. Lucas had told her mom he was waiting for her to come to him because he knew he'd messed up. He was willing to wait for her forgiveness. Maybe it was time to let go and forgive.

She headed off toward the campus with a renewed hope for their relationship. Maybe everything had been so crazy because her other half was missing. Would he be able to forgive her for having sex with Chase? She would have to tell him. She only hoped he wouldn't want an apology, because she didn't think she could be sorry for the night she'd spent with Chase. She would need to get over what Lucas had done with that girl from the party, but she wouldn't worry about that yet. She would find him and bury herself in his familiar and comfortable arms. The whole world had gone off its axis, and she couldn't find her balance, no matter how hard she tried.

The school came into view, and Dani thought about all the days she'd spent roaming those halls. From the very first days, Lucas had been by her side. Hand in hand they trudged through two years of college, growing and learning together. Would anyone ever know her the way he did? Would anyone ever want to again? Would Lucas be able to get past this thing she had become and still love her? Of course, in the back of her tormented mind, Dani wondered what he would taste like. *Way to ruin it, idiot. Damn black-eyed freak.*

Trying to shake off that line of thought, she reached the back of the school. Behind the school sports fields was a line of trees. On the other side of those trees was their field. It was far enough away from all the street and house lights, and that made it a great place for stargazing. They'd spent innumerable nights out there, lying in the bed of his truck, looking up at the night sky, talking, and making out. She broke through the line of trees and, sure enough, Lucas's truck was parked on the far side of the field in the spot where they had always parked. She couldn't wait to crawl up in the bed of the truck with him. She missed him so much. They could get through this together. Dani ran across the field, unable to hold herself back any longer. She needed to be loved and forget all the craziness.

As she got closer to the truck, a strange scent hit her like a ton of bricks. It was like cheap perfume and beer mixed with . . . with sex. She couldn't go any farther. She stopped and listened to the sounds of a girl moaning and asking for more.

"Lucas," she breathed, "that's it, baby, right there." A female voice moaned her pleasure to him.

She could finally see what she'd missed in her rush to reach him. The truck was rocking.

"You like that, huh? I know you do," Lucas said in a deep raspy voice. He panted with his exertion. "I told you I had what you needed, girl."

Oh God. She had to leave. She couldn't hear it; couldn't know it. Why? Why would he tell her *no* time after time and do it so easily with a stranger?

She couldn't get her legs to move, as the truck began to rock faster. They both panted and made sounds of sickening pleasure. The few times Lucas made love to her he was always silent, never speaking or moaning. Finally her legs did move, but in the wrong direction. She walked toward the back of the truck while her brain screamed at her to run, leave. She didn't want to see it, couldn't see it.

Tears streamed down her cheeks, and she knew her eyes were black, because her sharp vision picked up every hair on his bobbing head when she rounded the truck bed. Night vision had turned into a curse. Her Lucas was on their field having sex with another girl. "I love you, Lucas," the girl said in a heated whisper.

"Yeah, I bet you do," Lucas replied with dirty innuendo.

Oh God. Hearing him use that tone with another girl made her sick. Seeing this was destroying any chance of her ever loving him. Her insides twisted with the pain of it. He was giving this girl what Dani had begged him for so many times. He must love her in a way he couldn't love Dani. She hadn't been good enough for that kind of passion. Dani actually heard the fissure in her heart when it cracked. The piece of her that belonged to Lucas shattered and divorced itself from the rest of her. It turned to dust and blew away in the wind with the smell of their lust and the sound of their climax. There was nothing in the human life she'd lived for twenty-one years to keep her here.

The stunned silence she found herself in was almost unbearable. She didn't know how long she had stood there before he saw her, but he had seen her. She must have looked like some sick, perverted stalker, standing there staring at the bed of his truck.

Lucas leapt from the tailgate, frantic and confused. The girl screeched something at Lucas that Dani couldn't understand over the blood now pounding in her ears. Lucas grabbed Dani's shoulders and started to shake her. Maybe she was in shock. After what had felt like the vacuum of space, all the sound and sadness flooded back into her at once. She looked up at Lucas. He was disheveled and beautiful, and he reeked of sex and beer.

"Baby, Dani, are you okay? Please, talk to me. I'm so sorry." He wrapped his arms around her. "How long have you been here? I'm so sorry. I didn't think you would ever speak to me again." He held her tight with her feet dangling and his face buried in the crook of her neck. "Please talk to me."

She regained some control of her body and pushed at him until he released her. The pissed-off girl in the back of his truck began to get dressed and yelled about how it was the last time he would ever get her out in that field. Between her comment and his obvious ease with her, Dani could tell it wasn't the first time.

Dani started to walk away, but he grabbed her arm, spinning her around. He could see her eyes in the bright moonlight. "Dani, what happened to your eyes?" He didn't run like she thought he would. He grabbed her again, hugging her tighter, but she pushed him away again.

More calmly than she thought possible, she said, "You should go take care of your girlfriend. I'm going home. Good-bye, Lucas." And they both knew that was good-bye forever. Dani backed away from him, taking one last look at his sandy hair and blue-gray eyes. He had been her savior, once upon a time, but he couldn't save her anymore. No one could.

"Please, I know you're upset, but we can talk about this. You broke up with me. I thought you didn't want me anymore. I was lonely and hurting," he tried to explain. The girl screamed at him from across the field to take her home.

"I don't blame you, Lucas. I understand now that I wasn't what you wanted, what you needed. What an ass I made of myself, begging for your affection. I begged you, Lucas." She shook her head in self-disgust.

"Are you crazy? She is nothing, nobody. Please let me make this better. It wasn't that I didn't want you," he sputtered.

"So what you're telling me is you gave away my love for nothing, to nobody? Just like when you came to see me at school. You hurt me to impress a bunch of guys you didn't even know and broke my trust with a stranger. I'm very sorry to know I was worth so little."

"You scared me, okay?" he shouted. "I know that sounds ridiculous, but something about you would always scare the shit out of me when we got close like that. I . . . I don't even remember most of the nights we spent together! I wanted you so badly but it was like I had no control of my own body and that is frightening. You make me completely lose myself. I know it sounds crazy but it's true. All of our intimate moments are foggy for me."

He tried to grab her hand while she continued to back away. Her calm cracked as tears overflowed, and she turned away from him. Dani moved quickly, but she couldn't stand there anymore with him trying to touch her with the hands he'd had all over that girl. She ran until she reached her street, her mom's street. She didn't live there anymore. She didn't belong. She stormed into the house, hoping her mom wouldn't see her, but no such luck.

Tessa stood by the stairs and got a full view of the black-eyed freak when she walked in. She staggered back a step. "Danielle, what happened? Are you alright?" She rushed forward to embrace her, but Dani didn't want to be touched.

On her way up to her room, she said, "Don't you mean Soleil?" and slammed the bedroom door.

Okay. That was uncalled for, but she was so damn mad at the world for lying and making her think she was something she wasn't, and it all started with her mother. She gathered everything that was of any importance to her from her room.

Tessa knocked on the door and walked in.

"Please don't touch me." She flinched when Tessa reached out to her.

"What's wrong, honey? Talk to me." Alarm rang in her mom's voice.

Dani paused to take a deep breath before she lost it. "I found out today that my whole life has been a lie. I have no idea who or what I am anymore. Even my name is a lie. I have to give up my freedom to be protected by people who are only going to reject me when they find out I'm not what they think I am. I have to hide from someone who wants to kill me, and I just caught Lucas having sex with a girl in the back of his truck. All I want now is to be left alone, please." She couldn't even look at her mom. Sanity was holding on by a string.

Tessa nodded and turned to leave.

"I'm sorry I yelled at you. I love you, Mommy," Dani apologized. She needed to remember that her mother had been living with this for twenty-one years. Dani wasn't the only one whose life was in turmoil.

Tessa looked back and their eyes met. "I'm sorrier than you could ever be." She shut the door behind her.

Shortly after that, Dani heard a knock at the front door. She should've expected Lucas to follow her. She should've told her mom not to let him in. Dani cracked her door and listened to her mom telling Lucas that she was busy and didn't want company.

"Please, Ms. Tessa, I have to see her. She doesn't understand," he begged.

There was a pregnant pause before she began. "Did she see you having sex with another girl, Lucas?" Mom asked very directly. He didn't respond, but she figured his face said it all.

"Then I think she understands perfectly. You have made your feelings known in a vivid fashion, and now I would like you to leave." She shut the door in his face.

He came around the side of the house and started yelling up to her window, just as she had expected. "Dani, please let me in. Let's talk about this. Please, listen to me."

She ignored him and hoped the neighbors wouldn't call the cops. She could go down and talk to him, but there was nothing left to say. It had been silly of her to go to him in the first place, thinking the familiarity of the past could help her deal with the unknown future.

Dani shut the window, lowered the blinds, and turned out the light. She collapsed onto the bed and let the sorrow take her under. There was sorrow for the loss of her first real boyfriend, but more than that she mourned the loss of the life she would have had if she were the human she'd believed herself to be. She would let the pain have its way with her. She could still feel Lucas out there. He stood beneath her window, hoping she would change her mind, praying she would let him in. She could hear his heart beating so hard in his chest. It was such a familiar sound. She'd listened to it with her head on his chest so many times. It called her to him, but for an entirely different reason now.

It was oddly comforting to know why Lucas had pushed her away so many times. He'd been afraid of her all that time. She'd wanted so badly to love him, but there was always something there between them. He'd felt the monster hiding inside her long before she did.

Dani cried until she could no longer breathe. Every time she thought she was out of tears, the dam would break and let loose another torrent. She wrapped herself around the hurt and let it drain her. She would never cry for her old life again.

She heard her mom come to the door a few times. Tessa sat outside on the floor for a couple of hours before she went to her room.

When the sun finally started to rise and throw shades of pink and gold across her bedroom wall, Dani got up and left her human life behind in puddles of tears and sorrow. Looking in the mirror was a mistake. She looked worse than she felt, but it was over. She took a quick shower and pulled her hair up. At least her eyes were back to their normal shade of blue.

She found her mom peering out the living room window. "He is still out there in his truck, sleeping," she said without looking at Dani.

"I know. I'm going to leave before he wakes up." She could hear him out there if she listened hard enough. He was having restless dreams. She made herself a bowl of cereal with extra sugar and a cup of coffee, light and sweet.

Tessa came in and sat across the table. She reached out and rested her hand on Dani's hand.

Dani looked at her mother and smiled. "I know, Mom. I'm sorry too. It's over now, so let's just move on from here. The past is gone and the present doesn't care if we're ready for it or not."

"When did you become so mature?" Tessa asked.

"That would be when the world I knew and everything in it disappeared. It's okay. I'm going to need to be grown up to deal with what's coming. They think they want me, the vampires. They think I am special. I'm going to let them believe that until this threat is gone. Won't they be shocked when they find out exactly how special I really am?"

"Danielle, everything is going to be fine. Mason and I will take care of things when and if this all comes out." She patted Dani's hand.

"Are you gonna take care of it if I spend the rest of my life alone? Are you gonna take care of it when I have to explain to some poor guy that our child will be a half-breed reject? Are you gonna take care of the fact that I feel like I'm trapped under the ice right now? I can see everyone else in the world on top of the ice but I'm underneath, in the place where nobody belongs, because I don't belong."

Tessa started to cry, but Dani couldn't comfort her. She had no comfort to share. She washed her dishes like any other morning. When she reached the front door, she called out, "I'll text you when I get back to school. I love you."

Walking by Lucas's truck on the way to her car, she prayed he wouldn't wake up. He slept with his face pressed against the window. She watched him for a moment but couldn't see the sweet guy she'd wanted so much when she looked at him anymore. He had become a memory in a box of photographs that she would leave behind, along with the rest of that life.

Nathan followed Dani all night, watching her every move. He hadn't been home since his run-in with her. She was able to identify him, and the hunt had been on ever since.

Living out of his van without assistance from his master was difficult, but he deserved the punishment. He would need to find a place to clean up and get some new clothes soon if he planned to follow her more closely. His master was angry with him for letting her slip away and causing her harm the first time around. Now the girl was under his surveillance until he found something useful to present to the master.

"He'll see how devoted I am when I get him what he needs to attain his goals," Nathan told himself.

He had watched the little slut leave the club the previous night to go to the boy's room. She didn't leave until the early morning. It had been so quiet and deserted on the campus that he'd considered taking her then, but he decided to wait. He had to figure out how to disarm her before he tried again. The drug he used on the other vamps didn't work the same way on her. He figured she would need a much larger dose than could be transferred by a feeding. He would continue to follow her and see where she would lead him. With any luck, he would find a chink in her armor.

Indeed, the girl was well connected, as the master had said. The Wrath warrior's son had come to retrieve her in late morning. Nathan couldn't believe it when they arrived at the home of the Vaughn family. She could be quite a prize indeed, if she had connections to the council. The master hated the council.

After less than an hour, she left the gated estate, and he followed her to the interstate. The bitch drove for over four hours without stopping. Good thing he had a full tank of gas, or he would've lost her. They'd arrived in a town called Perry Hall, and he dropped back to follow her through the winding town. If she saw him, the gig would be up, and she would call in reinforcements.

"No. I'm smarter than this little girl. She will not make a fool of me again," Nathan cursed.

Finally, she stopped in front of a perfectly manicured lawn, surrounding a little house on a quiet street. Nathan had to slump down and drive past her to avoid drawing attention. At the end of the block, he pulled over and watched in the side-view mirror.

She hopped out of the vehicle and stomped up the front steps, slamming the front door behind her. He was fairly sure he hadn't been detected. He got out and walked back down the street to investigate. Taking down the address and noting that the name on the mailbox was *Vaughn*, he decided to return to the car. He quickly ran to the convenience store they'd passed on the way in and returned with provisions to last a couple of days, if necessary. Getting into a better position, he hunkered down as the sun set.

A couple of hours later she left on foot, but Nathan didn't follow her out of fear that she'd see him. How far could she go on foot anyway? She would be back for her car before leaving again.

Just after the girl rounded the corner, a man and woman came out onto the porch. More specifically, a vampire male and a human woman. He had enough experience with vamps to know one when he saw one. They spoke with stern faces, until the male reached out and wrapped his arms around the woman. She seemed to sag in his arms and cry on his shirt. She pulled away from the vamp and straightened her clothes. She wiped her face and, after a few more words, the male got into a black BMW and drove away.

That was an interesting development. What could it mean? Who was the vamp? Maybe the woman was a donor or an employee, as Nathan had been. Then there was the last name on the mailbox. It couldn't be a coincidence that she'd left the Vaughn estate and driven to a home with the same name displayed on a mailbox—though that quaint little home wasn't what one would expect of a member of the Vaughn family to live in. That information alone was worth the drive. Nathan would wait her out and get to the bottom of that mystery. The master would have to forgive him after he returned with that valuable nugget and possibly the girl.

Relaxing back into his seat, he ripped open a bag of chips and popped the top off of one ice-cold beer, then another. Before he knew it, the twelve-pack and chips were gone, and the peaceful night sounds of the quiet neighborhood lulled him to sleep.

Hours later he woke and stretched, trying to return circulation to stiff limbs. The midmorning sun shone brightly through the windshield. *Damn it!* He'd slept all night and half the morning. Nathan checked his side-view mirror and cursed.

The bitch had left. Her car was gone. She must have snuck out while he was sleeping. He'd let her get away again! *Shit!*

Thirteen

Dani had several missed calls and voice mails. Mostly from her mom, who was totally freaking out because Dani didn't call in the allotted time it took to get back to school. The others were from Kayden and Mason. On the way across the courtyard, she called Mason. He answered on the first ring.

"I'm sorry. I was indisposed for a while and didn't hear my phone. I am on campus and heading to my room," she said before he could even say hello.

"You better call Tessa. She's freaking out and about to come searching for you herself. Then get in touch with Griffin and see what he wants you to do. I imagine he will send someone to pick you up, so you can't escape like the last time." Mason's words were clipped.

"I am not a prisoner, or one of Griffin's subjects, so I have nothing to escape from. He can kiss my ass. He hasn't missed me in the last twenty-one years. He can deal with it now," she clipped back.

"You have no idea what you're talking about, child. He is going to be devastated when he realizes who you really are. He suffered terribly when he lost you and your mother. I will likely lose his friendship when he finds out I helped hide you all these years, but that is a discussion for another day. Right now, I need to get you under our protection, or your mother is going to lose her mind," he scolded her.

She was walking down the hall to her room when her senses were assaulted by something unpleasant. She reached her bedroom door, which was open a crack. "Hold on, Mason. This is weird. My door is open, and something smells nasty."

"Don't go in! Leave now. I'm sure it's nothing, but I'd rather be safe than sorry. I'll be right over. I'm already moving." Dani heard the sound of a car engine starting.

"I have to go in. I have a roommate, Mason. She could be sick," Dani whispered and pushed the door open.

"You don't know who is in there. Just listen to me." She tiptoed into the dark room. Olivia's bed was made, and she wasn't there. But someone was in Dani's bed. She flipped on the bathroom light. The bathroom was empty. "Someone is in my bed." She crept forward and pulled back the blanket. "Oh God, Mason! It's a girl! She's dead!" She backed up to the door and slid down the wall, hyperventilating.

"Get out of there, now! Are you sure she's dead? Can we get help for her?" he shouted.

"No." Dani sniffed. "She looks like she's been gone for a while. I can't leave. She's one of us. She has fangs. I can't let anyone else find her like this." Her voice trembled so badly she could hardly understand herself.

"Damn it! It's our missing girl! I'm calling Griffin! If anyone comes in, you put them down until we get there. Do you understand? If they try to hurt you, kill them!" Mason said sternly.

"I understand. I'll do what I have to." She hung up and sat in the corner, fighting the urge to vomit.

Kayden had tried to call Dani twice, and she hadn't returned his message. She should have been back on campus by now, so he decided to go hunt her down. He found her car in the parking lot. The hood was cool, so she'd been there for a while.

At her door, he knocked, but she didn't answer. She was in there, but wouldn't open the door, and he could smell death. The sickeningly sweet smell of decay polluted the air, but it was still too faint for the humans to detect with their weaker senses. If she was harmed, he'd never forgive himself. She was his charge to protect.

The door was locked, so he calmed himself enough to use his mild telekinetic skills to unlock it. It was dark, and as soon as he stuck his head in the door, he found himself plastered to the wall with a tight stranglehold on his throat, only nobody was touching him. He struggled to no avail against the nothingness that pinned him there. Finally, the light came on, and he saw Dani, huddled in the corner with her hands out. She held him back in fear. As soon as she registered whom she was choking, she released him and ran into his arms.

"I'm sorry, Kayden, I'm sorry. It's just so awful, and I was afraid someone was coming for me." She was crying and shaking and, yes, she smelled strongly of the human male, but Kayden didn't care. She was letting him hold her.

"Shit, Dani. You scared the hell out of me. What's that smell?" he asked, holding her securely to his chest.

"She was here when I got back." She pointed across the room.

Kayden reeled back a few steps at the sight of a dead vampire in Dani's bed. "I have to call someone right now, honey. Just relax, and I will take care of it." He squeezed her and stroked her back. Then he noticed a girl asleep in the other bed. "Is she okay?" he asked.

Dani nodded. "My roommate showed up, so I had to put her down until this is cleaned up." She shut off the light telekinetically. "I don't want to see her," she explained. Then the door flew open, and Dani shoved Kayden into the corner to protect him. She threw her hands out in a defensive movement. They heard two thuds hit the floor and could only see forms in the light from the hallway. Kayden leaped around her and dragged the two bodies farther into the room while Dani shut the door.

"Turn the light on, Dani," Kayden said hastily. She turned it on from the corner with her hands still held out, and Kayden sucked wind. "Oh shit! It's Griffin and Mason!"

Dani immediately released them both from the nap she had induced and returned to the corner, while Kayden helped the two adult vamps up. The dead body on her bed clearly had Dani shaken.

"What was that?" the adults said in unison.

"Danielle is a little frightened, to say the least. At least she didn't try to choke you before she figured out who you were," Kayden said. The two men looked at each other, and then went to Dani in the corner.

Mason tried to help her up but she snapped at them, "Don't touch me! Do what you have to do, so I can release my friend and get out of here." She sniffled.

Kayden went to sit by her on the floor. She didn't seem to mind the small comfort he offered. She leaned into him for support and buried her face in his arm.

The men examined the body and the note that was left with it. It read, "You are next. No one else needs to be hurt if you come willingly."

The body belonged to another girl, also named Danielle, who had been missing for a week. Griffin and Mason carried her out wrapped in a blanket. They didn't need to worry about being seen. No human would notice a vamp who didn't want to be seen.

As soon as they were out of the room, Dani began to pack a few things. Kayden waited while she showered, and he was glad she had. She smelled strongly of human male and it was obvious she'd recently fed. When she emerged from the bathroom, she was wet and sexy in nothing but an oversize towel, and the scent of sweet lavender billowed through the air. *Damn it, she was hot!*

She grabbed some clothes and woke Olivia before heading back in to get dressed. It was weird. Dani didn't even say anything to her. She just touched her, and Olivia got up, gave her a hug, and left with a smile, like they'd had a whole conversation. On the way to his car, Griffin called to tell Kayden to take Danielle to Chase's home, where he had a room ready for her. That didn't make Kayden or Dani happy, and she snatched the phone from him.

"I've had a shitty damn week, and I am not going to put up with Chase tonight. There has to be another place to stay for a few days until I can get my head on straight, Griffin. If not, you may find that boy dead too," she snapped.

Kayden was astonished at her complete lack of respect for Griffin Vaughn. Nobody spoke to him that way.

"You can stay with me, if you like. I live with my parents, but we have a spare bedroom. It's not fancy, like the Vaughn estate, but it's home," he whispered in her other ear.

"I'm going home with Kayden. We'll check in tomorrow." She hung up the phone without saying good-bye.

"I'm really sorry you have to leave school for a while, but after today, you have to understand the need for it. I'll do my level best to stay out of your way. Honestly, I hope we can become friends. It'll make it easier for you to have me around." Kayden wanted to plant the seeds of friendship before he pushed her for more.

"I just need to think, Kayden. I've had my whole world rocked in the last twenty-four hours. I hope you can forgive my need for silence." Dani closed the conversation with a swift slam of Kayden's car door.

Fourteen

The ride out of town toward Kayden's house took about thirty minutes. She'd never really noticed Kayden's scent before, but being in the car with him brought it to her attention. He smelled earthy, like the woods behind her mom's house in the spring when everything was in bloom. The good thing about Kayden was he didn't need to fill the silence. He could let her think without needing to know what she was thinking about. She didn't want to talk about all the shit that was happening, and if she did, Dani couldn't tell him anyway.

Kayden pulled off the freeway and said, "We need to check in at the Enclave before we head to my house. I'm sure Mr. Vaughn has called my father, but I still think we should make him aware that you're in town. The warriors in the area need to be on the lookout for anything odd." The all-business side of Kayden was new to Dani. The more time she spent with him, the more intriguing he became to her.

"What exactly is the Enclave?"

"It's where all the warriors in this region report. Some of them even live there. Think of it as a cross between a police station and a military base."

At least she'd be close to reinforcements if the shit hit the fan. She thought it would be interesting to see a hive of warrior-type meatheads.

She supposed she shouldn't be so narrow-minded. After all, they would be protecting her and, from what she'd seen earlier, she needed it. Dani was just so pissed off. She was in the middle of a shit storm with no umbrella, and she was sick of it.

Kayden drove into a gated community, passing the armed guards, who didn't even make him pause. By the time they were up the short drive leading to the gatehouse, it was open, and the guards respectfully nodded at Kayden.

The new Kayden was such a surprise and not at all like the party hound she'd seen and heard about from others. Crossing the grounds was an experience. Indeed, there were a lot of warrior-looking men trotting around, but there were also a lot of families. There were moms and kids at the various playgrounds. People cooked on stationary grills, while other people gathered around picnic tables. The day was warm, and everyone took advantage of it. There were individual houses and buildings that looked like apartments with courtyards and gardens. In the center of the complex there were large buildings that she assumed were the training facilities. Kayden parked and exited the vehicle before he came around and opened her door. She looked at him in misery.

"Can't I just stay here, Kayden?" she pleaded with a pout.

"How am I supposed to protect you if I don't stay with you?" he smiled and held out his hand.

"I'm just not in a very good mood. I don't know if I can be polite." She gave in and took his hand. "I feel like hitting somebody. I feel like screaming and kicking and fighting." She finished with a growl.

Kayden stopped and looked at her. He smiled the bad-boy smile she was used to seeing. "If you wanna fight, this is the right place. I could find a hundred people willing to spar with you at any moment. Or maybe you wanna fight with me?" He raised one naughty eyebrow. "I wouldn't be opposed to doing some self-defense training with you. If you plan to fight fair, that is." He turned and started walking.

"Are you serious? You would spar with me? You would teach me to fight?" she asked, thrilled he didn't treat her like a defenseless girl.

"I would love to teach you to fight. It would make me feel better to know you could defend yourself if need be. As far as wanting to hit someone, I understand that completely. I come here frequently to spar in order to work out my anger issues. The only thing is, you can't cheat. No using your superpowers," he said with a grin as he held the door for her.

The building appeared to be a police station in the front. Long hallways branched off to meeting rooms and gyms with boxing rings. People wrestled on matted floors and played on basketball courts. They passed a huge pool and several saunas before reaching the locker room. She hadn't seen a woman since they passed the area of the grounds where the houses were located. Not one woman was inside the training facility itself.

"Are you ready to get your ass handed to you?" he asked playfully.

"I'm not dressed for it." She looked down at her jeans and sweater.

"That's okay. I'm sure I can find you something. Stay right here." He disappeared into the locker room. While he was gone, a group of large, mountain-looking men came down the hall in a loud cluster, boasting over a basketball victory, insulting each others' skills and manhood. When they noticed Dani they got quiet, and several of them stopped to interrogate her.

"What is a sweet thing like you doing hanging around outside the locker room? Wow. Have you boys ever seen a girl with hair like that? Are they power marks, baby doll? You look like you could be very, very powerful," the crew cut blond asked, flashing a smile that would melt the heart of any woman. He was man personified, and he knew it. He had a scar that started at the corner of his eye, stretched across his cheekbone, and disappeared under his chin. Somehow, the battle scar made him even sexier.

Alright. She was feeling intimidated and a little embarrassed with them all staring at her. Dani squeezed her way out of the circle and walked down the hall toward the front of the building. She was officially ready to fight. When she finally reached Kayden's car, she was glad to find it unlocked. Dani dug in her bag until she found a pair of yoga pants and a tight workout top and went back inside to change in a bathroom with no gender sign on the door. Ladies' rooms were unnecessary with no ladies. She changed quickly, excited at the prospect of taking a few swings at Kayden. Hopefully he wouldn't hit her too hard. Maybe he would hit her hard enough to knock her out for a few days. She could use the break.

"Damn it!" Kayden had taken a while trying to find her something to change into, but he'd told her to stay still. Where the hell could she have gone? She wasn't in the car or any bathroom he came across. There was no way anyone could get to her on the Enclave. What if she left on foot? No, she wouldn't do that; would she?

On the way back from his car, Kayden overheard a couple of guys talking about how odd it was to see a female in the training building. "What happened to the girl you saw?" he demanded through gritted teeth.

"A few of the guys stopped to give her a hard time, but I didn't stop. You know I can't stand Darren, and he was all in her face." The guy shook his head.

"Darren was with her? If you see either of them, have me paged!" Kayden didn't like the sound of that. Darren was a volatile bastard, and Dani was a firecracker. If he offended her, she would surely let him have it. Kayden ran back toward the locker rooms.

When he rounded the last corner, he found Dani leaning against the wall. Without thinking he snatched her up into his arms like a rag doll and hugged her.

"Where have you been? My nerves can't handle the way you disappear like that all the time!"

"I'm sorry, Kayden. I just went to get a change of clothes and got lost on the way back." She leaned back and put her hands on his chest. Her acceptance of the embrace made him feel oddly happy. He liked knowing she was comfortable with him.

"Yeah, Kayden, loosen up." Darren appeared from the locker room. "Danielle here was telling me you're going to teach her some self-defense. I told her I could handle it for you."

Kayden possessively slung an arm over her shoulder and pulled her toward a training room. "I've got it, thanks." Kayden couldn't stand the cocky bastard.

He pulled her a little tighter and ruffled her hair.

"Could you just try to make my job a little easier and not give me a heart attack before I'm twenty-two? I told you to fight fair. You didn't need to search for backup in case I kick your ass."

She smiled and pushed him into the wall. "I don't think it will be a fair fight if you get to use your arms, or your legs, for that matter. So I have to use what I've got." She squealed as he pulled her into a room with wall-to-wall floor mats like gymnasts use.

Kayden truly enjoyed the playful banter. "I think you should wear headgear. If I scratch that pretty face, I'll get fired."

Kayden turned for a storage closet and got a surprise when Dani hit him from behind with a blow to the back of the knee, taking him down. She pounced on him, putting him in a tight headlock with her legs wrapped around his waist so if he got up, she wouldn't lose her grip.

He didn't stand. He sat there on his knees, laughing his ass off at the effort she was putting into choking him. He reached up and grabbed her upper arms, dragging her over his shoulder. She struggled, to no avail. He put her in a bear hug that had her arms completely disabled.

"Now what are you going to do, little girl?" Kayden knew it was wrong, but damn he was getting turned on by their playful wrestling.

She smiled and leaned her face closer, like she would kiss him. When she was so close he could feel her breath on his lips, he closed his eyes. She head butted him, drawing blood from both his mouth and her forehead. Stunned, he released her. She jumped up ready to fight, with her foot in the middle of his chest, setting him off-balance, but only for a second. He would fight dirty, if that was what she wanted.

Back on his feet, he looked at her, really looked at her, for the first time. She bounced like a prizefighter in her light gray pants that barely covered her hips and a short black tank that clung to her like a swimsuit, only covering a small portion of her belly. She had defined abs to match the toned arms that currently held up tiny fists. Kayden was confused when he saw the bruises still visible on her creamy skin from her broken ribs. She should've healed long ago.

Her hair was a wild riot of dark waves and stunning streaks of white and red. Her eyes were so light blue that they were almost clear. She looked at him with a challenge in her aquamarine gaze. Damn, if she wasn't the hottest thing he'd ever seen. She stood, daring him to swing at her, as a trickle of blood ran down her nose from her forehead. He stepped forward with his long reach and an open hand. He slapped her before she could block.

"You better keep those hands higher." He walked slowly around her like a big cat sizing up his prey while she hopped and bobbed. He stepped in again and caught her other side, but she got in a right jab before he pulled away.

"Nice shot, very nice," he praised. It didn't hurt him, but he was pleased nonetheless. She could surely hold her own with a human. He really enjoyed watching her, but the amount of blood on her face began to concern him, and she had a big handprint on her left cheek. *Shit,* he'd left a mark on that pretty face. It was enough for one day, so he barreled down on her, turning her around, one arm twisted behind her. Her face was smearing blood on the wall before she could blink. He pressed his body against hers and whispered into her ear, "That's enough now, Dani. Calm down before you really hurt yourself."

He caught the scent of her blood so close to his face. It was dark and seductive, like a human, but sweet and floral like a vamp. *Holy hell!* He didn't know if he wanted to bite her or throw her down and make love to her. Maybe both would have been better. She went slack in his arms as a quiet sob began to break from her throat. The stress had finally cracked her outward calm.

"Don't cry, Dani. I'll let you kick my ass again tomorrow." He sat cross-legged and let her fall onto his lap, holding her like a baby in his arms. He held her there in the quiet of the training room. He liked being so close to her, and as much as he hated to see her cry, he loved being the one there to comfort her. He rocked her back and forth and whispered gentle encouragements until she was done crying. Then he used his shirt to wipe the tears and blood from her face.

From behind him, he heard the sound of a single person's applause. The loud clap of hands echoed in the empty space. He turned his body just enough to see Darren, sitting against the wall on the far side of the room.

"Bravo!" Darren exclaimed. "Now I know how you get the ladies to spread their legs. You behave like a caveman, just knock the hell out of them and drag them off." Dani stiffened in his arms at the sound of Darren's voice, and Kayden wondered how long he'd been watching. Jerk probably followed them from the locker room.

"Oh, don't you worry about my girl. She could flatten my ass anytime she wanted to. She's just fighting fair today." Kayden continued to inspect Dani's face and smiled down at her. "Don't you have a job to do, Darren? Or are you getting paid to be a Peeping Tom these days?" Kayden hopped up without releasing Dani. Quietly, just for her ears, he said, "You okay, Tyson?" Dani smiled up at him and nodded as he stood her on her feet.

Dani recognized the scarred face of the man slowly ambling across the big room. She'd seen him twice already that day, and he'd been flirty both times. He eyed her hard with hungry, unnerving eyes. Kayden looked tense, standing a few feet away from her, but the warrior called Darren looked as though he couldn't care less if Kayden were in the room.

"Are you?" Darren asked her.

"Excuse me?" She raised an eyebrow.

"Are you his girl?" He gave her a lopsided smile and inclined his head toward Kayden. Kayden took a step closer. Darren began to circle her other side.

"I don't belong to anyone, but Kayden is a good friend." She smiled at Kayden and was surprised at how true the words were. She could think of several times she'd been in trouble and Kayden had been there for her. He'd definitely endeared himself to her. Seriously, only a true friend would let you head butt them and then hold you while you cried.

"Are you promised to anyone?" he asked from behind her. She couldn't help noticing Kayden bristled at the question. He must have been asking if she had an arranged marriage in her future.

"I told you, no one owns me. Why do you want to know?" She turned to look at him.

"I want to know because you're beautiful, and if given the chance, I would take you for my own." He said it as if it were obvious. He stepped even closer and sniffed the air around her.

"You think you could take me?" she reply acidly.

Dani figured the man was trying to goad Kayden into a fight. What an ass. She bet that was how he got the scar on his otherwise handsome face. She refused to let him stand there doing his best to embarrass Kayden. She took a purposeful step toward Kayden and tucked herself under his arm, wrapping her arm around his waist. He smiled down at her. She didn't know exactly why she did it, but she pulled him down toward her and went up on tiptoes to place a searing kiss on his parted lips. He tasted like man and sweat. He bent lower, so she didn't have to stretch so far, and allowed her to explore his mouth more deeply.

She heard Darren let out an amused chuckle behind them. "Let me know if you want to learn to wrestle with a real man." There was no missing the sexual innuendo.

She knew in the back of her mind that she had made her point and should stop kissing Kayden. It felt good to kiss someone and not want to bite him. He was schooled in the art of tongue. He pulled her tightly against his long, hard body. Dani really liked Kayden, but he just didn't inspire the kind of need that took over her mind and body when Chase kissed her. Kayden was funny and comfortable to be around, just like Jared. But unlike with Jared, when she was with Kayden she didn't feel like she had to protect him, or feel the need to feed.

They were shocked apart when a throat was cleared and a gruff voice said, "Kayden?"

Kayden snapped to attention, releasing her so fast she stumbled. He crossed the room to speak to the stern-faced man before she could right herself. She watched them speak and chastised herself for kissing him that way, but she couldn't actually bring herself to regret it. Kayden turned and waved her over.

When she reached the men, Kayden put his arm around her waist. "I'd like to introduce you to my father, Gage Paris. He is the commander of the warrior class. Dad, this is Danielle Scott."

"It's a pleasure to meet you, Mr. Paris." She stepped forward, extending her hand. She cringed a bit at the use of Jared's last name. Gage was tall and very muscular, just like Kayden. His hair was dark with just the slightest hints of gray at his temples. His eyes were the same hazel green as Kayden's. Gage looked rather young to hold such a high-ranking position, but she hadn't figured out all the vamp stuff yet. She really shouldn't have tried to guess his age. He could have been hundreds of years old, and she wouldn't know. How old would she live to be?

"The pleasure is all mine, Ms. Scott. I'm very sorry we had to meet under these circumstances, but I hope you'll be comfortable in our home." He bent to kiss her hand. It was an odd gesture, but it felt genuine and right.

"Please, call me Dani. I truly thank you for your hospitality. I needed to get away," she told him honestly.

Gage took her chin in his hand and tilted her face up for a better look at the cut on her head and her bruised cheek. "How did this happen? It's a shame to mar such a lovely face."

"It's nothing, really." She smiled wryly. "I had some aggression to work out today."

Kayden looked sheepish.

Gage laughed and shook his head. "No wonder you and Kayden get along so well. Perhaps you're right, Kayden. I'll see you two later at home." He bent to kiss her hand again and looked at Kayden knowingly before he departed.

They stood there, uncomfortable for a moment before he asked, "Are you ready to head out? I bet you'd like to rest awhile before dinner."

She just nodded and went to grab her other clothes and phone from the corner.

The ride to his home was short and silent. Dani felt like some kind of vamp slut. She really enjoyed that kiss and wouldn't mind another. Kayden also looked lost in thought.

The house was set back off the road, down a long driveway and behind a row of concealing trees. She wouldn't have seen it from the road if she'd driven by on her own. The large, red-brick house sat on beautifully landscaped grounds with flower gardens on either side of the road and a fountain out front. Kayden parked in a huge garage that housed several other cars, motorcycles, and four-wheelers. He came around to open her door before he grabbed her bags.

The house was modern and unassuming inside. The first floor was open and inviting. The dining room table was huge with large, sturdy chairs. She could imagine the room frequently filled with warriors visiting from the Enclave.

The guest room was on the first floor in the rear of the house. He carried her things into the room and placed them on the bed before kissing her on the forehead. She felt comfortable with Kayden and his affectionate touch, as if he'd done it a thousand times.

"I think dinner will be later than usual tonight. You can relax, and I'll come for you when it's ready. There are towels in the linen closet if you want to clean up, Tyson. I'll be here if you need anything." He smiled and tilted her face up to examine the cut and the bruise darkening her cheek. He tsk-tsked and left the room with an obviously guilty expression for having hit her. It wasn't his fault. He had tried to get her to wear headgear.

The room had a king-size bed and looked more like a master suite than a guest room to her. She looked around, noticing the French doors that led out to the back of the house and a yard that looked as if it were used frequently for entertaining. There was an outdoor kitchen and a pool fit for an Olympic event.

Eventually she made her way to the shower in the large, marble bathroom, and wondered at Kayden's comments about his humble home. Sure, it wasn't as big as the Vaughn estate, but the home would be a dream come true for most people. She was so tired, the hot water made her eyes want to close. She found a fluffy terry robe in the linen closet and wrapped it around herself. Staggering out of the bathroom, she fell on the bed. The bed was like a cloud, and she quickly felt herself slipping into a blissfully dark oblivion.

Kayden knocked on the bedroom door at dinnertime. It'd been nearly two hours since he'd left Dani to get settled. She didn't answer the door, so he knocked again but heard nothing from inside the room. The thickness of her scent told him she was there, so he turned the unlocked doorknob and peeked into the dark room. He really hoped he wouldn't get choked again.

"Dinner's ready, Dani," he said into the darkness and drew in a lungful of her sweet scent. She didn't answer. He opened the door farther to let in the light from the hall. The light splayed across her on the other side of the bed. He entered to wake her. "Dani, dinner's on the table."

He walked around the large bed and froze in his tracks. She wore only a bathrobe and, dear God, it was open. He could see the luscious curve of one breast, and half of her nipple was exposed. Most of her left side hung out. Her bare leg drew his eyes all the way up her thigh to the triangle of feminine beauty he so desperately wanted to touch and taste. She slept so soundly, with her soft lips parted and inviting.

He remembered the feel of those lips under his when she'd kissed him. He'd been shocked but elated to have her willingly bless him with such hot affection. Her lips were so damn sweet. Not only did she smell like floral vanilla, she tasted like it, too. In the moments he was allowed to worship her mouth, he could smell the blood on her face and was so confused by the intoxicating allure of it.

He again thought of tasting her blood and making love to her at the same time. The thought shocked him. Tasting her would have bonded her to him for the rest of their lives, and he had never wanted that with anyone else. He had never really made love to anyone. He'd had a lot of sex but never actually loved anyone. Looking at her made him want to find out what that would feel like. He wondered if he could love her.

Stepping closer to the bed, he wanted to touch that creamy bare skin with his hands, his body, and his lips. He needed to leave, before she woke and caught him gawking at her like a pervert. If he woke her, she'd be embarrassed that he'd seen her that way. She must have been exhausted after the day she'd had, so he let her sleep. If she were hungry later, he'd get her some food.

Kayden left the room quickly, quietly securing the door, and went straight to his room for a cold shower. He needed to get his head on straight if Dani was going to be staying in his home. He would need to learn how to balance his desire for her with his duty to protect her as his charge.

Dani woke up hours later and couldn't believe how long she'd slept. It was ten thirty, and she wondered if Kayden had ever come to get her for dinner. She dug out a nightgown and put it on under the robe to go look for him. The house was completely quiet, and she felt like an intruder walking around their private space. She smiled, imagining Kayden growing up there. It was the home that had helped shape him, just like her home had shaped her.

Her tummy rumbled—unsurprising, since she hadn't eaten all day. A creaking noise sounded from out back. Dani crept to the kitchen window, imagining assassins creeping around the yard looking for a way to get at her. She didn't see anyone at first, until a small movement caught her eye at the far end of the yard. There was someone swinging in a hammock out there. An odd thing to be doing on a fall night, she thought, but the day had been warm, and the night was supposed to be the same. She figured a killer wouldn't stop for a swing, and she wondered if it was Kayden out there. She wanted to talk to him. Her mom and Mason hadn't told her much about life as a vampire, and she wanted some more answers about vampire behavior and protocol. Kayden knew she wasn't raised among his kind, so he might answer her questions without too much suspicion.

She crept out of the French doors in the guest room onto the back lawn. She was fairly sure it was Kayden out there, and if it wasn't, she just hoped it wasn't a crazed vamp hunter on a break.

She padded softly over to the hammock and was relieved to see that it was, indeed, Kayden. He didn't open his eyes, so he startled her when he said, "Good evening, Danielle."

After finding her voice, she replied in a breathy whisper, "Hello, Mr. Paris."

"What are you doing out here?" He opened his eyes and gave her a crooked smile.

"I was going to ask you the same question." She grinned back. It struck her that if she'd met Kayden before Chase, he would have been the perfect guy, as long as he was willing to give up his pursuit of other girls.

His lips stretched across his face, and she wondered if she'd projected that thought. How embarrassing would that be? She really needed to learn to build better walls in her mind. He scooted over slightly, extending his arm to help her climb in with him. She hesitated but climbed in with him. The hammock, it held them tightly against each other. He let her use his arm for a pillow. Again she felt a sense of comfort in his arms. It was quiet for a bit. She decided to let him speak first, not wanting to give the impression that she'd come to talk. He was very good at letting her think without pestering her, but she was beginning to feel guilty for crawling into the hammock. She was comfortable with Kayden, but she had the growing suspicion that he would want far more than friendship. That could be a good thing eventually, but she needed time to get her life straight first. "So, about that kiss today?" he interrupted her thoughts.

"I'm sorry if I offended you." She started to pull away from him, embarrassed. That was the one thing she didn't want to talk about.

"You didn't offend me, but you surprised the hell out of me. To tell you the truth, I've wanted to kiss you since that first night at the club, but Chase saw you first and made it clear that you were off-limits."

"Off-limits, huh? It's too bad you listened to him." She was a little annoyed by Kayden's easy acquiescence to Chase. Did everyone do what he said? "I guess it's bros before bitches, right?"

Kayden stiffened and looked down at her. "It's hard to explain, and I don't expect you to understand. You don't know our ways."

That was only the damn truth, but it stung her anyway. He was right. She was an outsider. She guessed she always would be. "You're right. I guess I'll have to learn as I go. I'm going to bed." Lord, she sounded like a pouty child, but she didn't have it in her to pretend all was well.

Suddenly she didn't care to explore the mysteries of vampirism. She just wanted to go to bed and forget they even existed. She rolled out of Kayden's arms and off the hammock, heading for the guest room.

Fifteen

Kayden reached the doors that led to the guest room but they were locked. There was no damn way he was letting her walk away without trying to explain himself. It was obvious he'd upset her, and he didn't like that feeling. He wanted to get closer to her, not push her away. When he'd held out his arms to her and she shyly climbed into the hammock, he'd wanted to shout a victory cry. She was letting him comfort her and it had been going so well, until he opened his big mouth. He should've just held her and kept quiet, but the memory of that kiss kept circling his mind. He wanted to kiss her again, and again after that.

He used his telekinesis to unlock the doors. She stood on the other side of the bed, hands on her hips, glaring at him. She'd removed her robe, and her modest pink nightgown distracted him for a moment. Damn it! She was sexy without even trying. When had neck-high, floral-print cotton become such a turn-on? He had to focus.

"Did you think that door could keep me out?" he asked.

"No. I don't believe that anything could keep you away from something or someone you wanted, Kayden." She put a huge emphasis on the word *wanted*. She crossed her arms over her chest.

"You don't understand, Dani. There are so many things you don't understand." He shook his head and raked a hand through his hair.

"You know what I don't understand? I don't understand how you could say you wanted me from the night you first saw me, then you just stood by and allowed him to hurt me. You knew he was engaged, and he was playing with me, but that was alright because I was off-limits to you. So what did you care if I got hurt, right?" The anger and hurt bled from her tone. Kayden wanted to cross the room and take her into his arms, but he could tell by her rigid stance that she wouldn't let him near her. He wanted to be the male she would want to be with. The best way to start being that male was to help her learn about his people. He could start with the truth about Chase. It wouldn't hurt his case, and he could start her introduction to his society. The fact remained that Chase was betrothed and off the market either way.

"In his defense, and mine, Chase wasn't made aware of the arrangement until after he met you, and I didn't know about it until after you stormed out of his place the day of the incident with Sam," he tried to explain without giving Chase too much credit. He stepped closer to her.

She stepped back. "I want you to tell me what you think I don't understand. I want to understand, Kayden." She hopped up on the bed like she was ready for a bedtime story.

Kayden watched her, trying desperately not to think of her on that bed naked and sprawled out for him. He realized he wasn't doing a very good job when his rod twitched in his pants. He knew what was under those clothes, and he wanted to get a closer look.

"I'll tell you what you want to know, after you answer a few questions of mine—deal?"

She didn't respond but seemed to be waiting for his questions.

"I feel like an ass admitting this, but I feel something for you and I like it. I want it. So don't play games with me." She lowered her head for a moment, breathing deeply, but didn't respond. He continued, "That day at Chase's place, you told me you're not what we think you are. What does that mean?"

No answer. She got up and went to shut the door that was still wide open, allowing cool air to pour in. She seemed to be considering her response carefully. She stood there watching him with those pale-blue eyes until he couldn't take it anymore.

Slowly, he approached her and wrapped his arms around her petite body. Just like when he'd held her while she cried earlier that day, he could tell something was hurting her, and he had to try to help.

"I just need to know if you felt what I felt when you kissed me today. Everything else can wait until you are ready to talk to me." He held his breath, waiting for her to break the painful silence.

Finally, she wrapped her arms around his waist and pressed her forehead against his chest. "I'm going to be honest with you, Kayden, because you promised to help me."

He nodded tightly in response.

"I'm not in a good place right now. I broke up with my boyfriend recently. I have this intense connection with Chase that I can't explain. I even find him in my sleep, and he tries to talk to me. He has been trying like hell to apologize, but it means nothing to me. It's an empty apology. He told me he wanted it to be only me and him, just before that girl busted into his room. Then, he had to admit he had some 'house' obligation to marry her or bond with her—whatever it is that you people do."

He interrupted, "You people?"

"Yes, you people. The whole race of people I was unaware of until I started school this fall. You think this shit has been easy for me? I was raised among humans. I never knew any others like me, and the human who raised me didn't know shit. My caretaker died, and I started school with no knowledge of others like me.

"I went to the club with my friends that first time and got all this special treatment. I came to understand later that it was because *you people* recognized me as one of your own. I had no idea who I was dealing with, until I was attacked." She shuddered and pushed out of his arms.

"All this stuff I can do didn't start happening until just before I started school. I have no one to teach me or explain anything to me. I thought I was going crazy. Griffin explained that it's normal for these things to be unknown until you come of age. Do you understand now why I'm so damn confused? This is a new world for me, and I don't have a single friend in it."

"I'll do anything I can for you," he vowed, and he found that he truly meant it. It wasn't an empty promise to get what he wanted.

"Don't say that until I finish." She paced back and forth across the room with her arms wrapped around her waist while she spoke. "I have feelings for Chase that I can't explain, but I wish they'd go away. I also enjoy being around you. You have been there for me several times, when I really needed a friend."

Kayden stopped her from pacing. He needed to touch her, comfort her.

"You make me feel safe," she whispered. "When I kissed you this afternoon, it started with teaching that jerk Darren a lesson and ended with me wanting more."

"I've wanted to kiss you since the first moment I laid eyes on you. I already told you that," he admitted.

She smiled weakly. "To answer your question plainly, yes, I'm attracted to you. You make me feel safe and not so damn alone, but I'm not ready for a committed relationship, not that you've asked for one, but I'm just putting it out there. I like you, Kayden. I enjoy your company. Who knows what tomorrow will bring?" She smiled and shrugged. "I think I'm gonna go try to find something to eat and go to bed. We can talk more tomorrow, if that's what you want.

I don't have anything left in me tonight." Dani opened the door that led to the hall and left the room.

Kayden went back out to the hammock. After only one day with Dani, he completely understood why Chase had gone a little nuts. He dozed off, looking at the stars and thinking of Dani and that hot kiss.

After having scorching dreams about pale skin, clear-blue eyes, and vanilla-flavored passion, Kayden woke to bright morning sunlight. He'd been outside all night. It was much cooler than the day before. After a shower and a few more minutes of debating whether or not he could share Dani, he went to knock on the guest room door. Why did the idea bother him so much? He had never been in an exclusive relationship. He was the bad boy, the loner. This should be right up his alley, but the alley was starting to feel kinda crowded to him.

"There you are. I was beginning to worry," Koren Paris said, wrapping her loving arms around her son. Koren was a tall blonde with blue eyes that were always smiling. She was such a contrast to his stoic father, but they balanced each other out. Kayden was beginning to notice things like that. He noticed things he never paid attention to before, like the way his mother could totally disarm his father and have the tiger of a man purring like a kitten within moments of arriving home. He wondered if that was what love did to a person.

Kissing his mother's cheek, he asked, "Why would you be worried, Mom?"

"Your father and Dani were trying to reach you, but you didn't answer your phone. They left without you. Gage was uncomfortable about removing Dani from your care, but she insisted that she go with them to search for the missing boy." Worry lines creased Koren's forehead.

"What? Where did they go?" Kayden was confused, and his pulse began to pound in his ears.

"Apparently the boy that's missing was reaching out for help. Like a telepathic SOS. He reached Dani somehow in her sleep. She woke your father and me before dawn, saying he was reaching out for help. He is trying to lead us to him. She said she could see the room he was in, and she was sure he was by the water from the smell and sounds she was picking up. That girl is really very gifted, and lovely, too."

"I know, she's perfect, Mom. Could you get to the part where they left without me?" Kayden's mind reeled while he listened to his mother recap the morning's events. "She went on a strike with the Wrath! I don't believe this! I never would have allowed this to happen! When did they leave? Where were they going?" Kayden ran toward his room to get geared up, and he dragged his mother along, demanding answers.

Kayden and Koren reached the Enclave not long after the returning Wrath teams. Before they left the house, Koren had gotten a call from Gage's secretary at the Enclave informing her that he would be tied up all day. The strike was over. She couldn't give much detail other than things had gone wrong. The Stafford boy and Danielle had both been injured during the rescue attempt.

Kayden sped the entire way to the Enclave and ran ahead of his mother when they finally arrived. Passing a wrecked vehicle, he noticed the blood smeared down the driver-side window and a small bloody handprint on the hood. He wondered if it was Dani's handprint, or one of the boy's. He wanted to rage at the idea of her being hurt. She'd said he made her feel safe. She'd said he was there when she needed him, and now she was hurt because he had failed on both counts.

Kayden went straight to the infirmary, where warriors waited for word of Dani's condition. There must have been fifty of them lined up in the hall. They had all gotten word of her bravery and came to lend their support. They all looked up at him when he rounded the corner, and Darren, who was a Wrath team leader, stepped in front of the door to the medical wing.

"Get out of my way, Darren!" Kayden growled as several other warriors grabbed him.

"No can do, Superman. The commander said to keep you out here until the warrior is patched up. He said you were too busy to care for your charge earlier, so now he will tend to her until she's ready to be seen." Kayden tried to free himself. Darren smiled, amused, watching Kayden struggle against the warriors who detained him.

Coming up behind the struggle, Koren stepped up. "You said a warrior is being patched up. Who else was injured?" She put a hand on Kayden's chest, willing him to calm down.

"Only the female was injured. She was the only one to see any action. I guess she didn't need all of us trained soldiers. The commander said she went after the boy like he was her charge to protect. She did what she had to do at the risk of her own life to save him. She was as much a warrior as any one of us. So the warrior, Danielle, is being patched up now." Darren spoke reverently of the girl, and the hall exploded with shouts of approval and agreement.

Several hours earlier

Dani tossed and turned fitfully in the plush bed. Every time she drifted off to sleep, she dreamed of a boy calling for help. He pleaded over and over for someone, anyone, to come release him from his prison. His fear seeped into her own heart until she woke screaming for help along with him. Dani panted and crawled to the bathroom to wash her face in hopes of chasing away the nightmare of being enslaved. His knowledge that he would die just like the others was a sour taste on her tongue. In her dream, his horror, his pain, and his fear were hers as well.

Dani jumped when the door to the guest room flew open and Gage Paris entered looking ready for battle. He wore pajama pants and his dark hair was mussed, but he looked every bit the soldier with his double-fisted guns, bulging muscles, and eyes the black of midnight. Her scream must have startled the entire house.

"It's okay!" She stepped out of the bathroom with her hands in the air. Something about having guns pointed in your direction makes a girl want to surrender in a hurry. "I'm so sorry, Gage. I had a nightmare and I screamed."

Gage's eyes continued to scan the room for danger. Dani stayed put while he checked the bathroom, the closet, and under the bed for hidden danger. When he faced her again his eyes had returned to the hazel that was so much like Kayden's, and his guns were lowered to his sides.

"I apologize if I frightened you, Danielle. We're all on high alert with the recent kidnappings." He looked away in deference to her modesty. She wore a nightgown that covered her from neck to knees, but he seemed embarrassed at seeing her like that. "Would you like me to send Koren in to talk to you? I'm sure the stress of recent days contributed to your bad dream. She's a great listener." He stepped into the hall, where he couldn't see her any longer.

"No, thank you, Mr. Paris, I'll be fine. I'm just going to get back to bed. I'm truly sorry for causing such a ruckus." Her cheeks heated. How embarrassing.

"Gage, is she alright?" Mrs. Paris called from down the hall.

"Everything's fine, Koren. It was just a nightmare," he called back. "Go back to bed, honey. I'll be right there." His voice softened when he spoke to his mate. "Good night, Danielle," he said to Dani as he pulled the door shut.

Dani climbed back into bed and sighed. She would never get back to sleep. Her heart still sped in her chest. She took a few calming breaths, trying to clear her mind of everything but the need for sleep. Closing her eyes, she focused on her breathing, taking deep lungfuls of air and releasing them slowly. She imagined all of her stress and worries being swept away by the oxygen so she could sleep peacefully. Her body melted into the mattress. Just as she began to drift off, the boy's faint voice reached her ears again. Only this time she was awake. She sat straight up in bed and listened closely. There it was again, just like her dream. She could hear someone calling for help.

"Where are you?" she asked the room, feeling insane.

Oh thank God! Someone heard me! My name is Christopher Stafford . . . He kept talking but his voice faded out.

Are you still there? she asked in a panic. This was clearly not a dream. Christopher was the name of the missing boy. Her telepathic ability was doing some good tonight, it seemed. He was talking to her.

I need help! That came through loud and clear. She just needed him to keep it up like that. *Okay! I'll keep it up!* he told her more loudly.

Dani leapt from the bed and began to pull on clothes. That last bit hadn't been said out loud. She was thinking it. So there was no need for her to talk to the empty room.

You just keep talking to me, Christopher, and I'll get us help. She tried to sound confident so he would stay calm and give her any details he could about his location. She opened the bedroom door and headed in the direction Gage had gone, calling Gage's name because she didn't know which bedroom belonged to him and Koren. He was sure to think she was as crazy as she was feeling.

Thankfully, Commander Paris—that was how everyone else addressed him—and his mate, Koren, believed her immediately.

They quickly searched the house for Kayden and both she and Gage tried to call his cell, but they got no answer. Christopher was sounding increasingly panicked, and his anxiety was rubbing off on Dani. They needed to go find him quickly before his captor came to claim him.

They left without Kayden and were at the Enclave in no time. During the car ride over, the commander activated a Wrath team and had them prepare to move out. The Wrath was an elite group of warriors trained to deal with the more dangerous situations that faced the vampire kind. If the warriors were like a cross between the police and the military, the Wrath was a cross between the human Navy SEALs and a police SWAT team. They were a deadly force. From what Koren told her, Dani got the impression nobody wanted to have the Wrath come down on him or her.

Dani concentrated on gathering every detail she could from Christopher, while his voice faded in and out. Christopher had no telepathic ability and hers was too new to her to be very reliable. She repeated everything Christopher told her so that Gage could hear, and Koren wrote it down on the back of an envelope she found in her purse.

The Enclave was a buzz of activity, and Dani absorbed it all in silence while she spoke to Christopher. When she finally focused on the commander's directions she realized she was going to be left behind while they took her notes and searched the area near the wharf that they believed matched Christopher's description. *Oh hell no!*

"All due respect, sir, but I'm going with you. I can't stay here and wait." She stepped into the commander's path with her hands lodged firmly on her hips. She would not stay behind. The room grew quiet and the men waited for the commander's response to her dictate.

"Look, Danielle, I commend your effort to help retrieve our victim, but you have no training. You would be a liability to our mission," he explained kindly and patted her on the shoulder. He tried to step around her but she blocked him again.

"In my admittedly limited experience, the closer to a person I am the better the, for the lack of a better word, reception, is for me. I may be able to lead you directly to him without the need to search each and every building in the area. Doesn't it make more sense to take me along for that reason? We don't have time to waste." She held his stare while he considered her reasoning. Finally he shook his head and reached around her for a flak jacket. He handed it to her, looking grave. Koren gasped.

"I agree that we need to find him as quickly as possible. Let's get you geared up. You can go on the terms that you remain in the vehicle at all times and do exactly what I tell you when I tell you to do it. Is that understood?" he asked her firmly. Christ, the man was scary as hell when he was in warrior mode. It was hard to believe this was the same male who spoke so gently to his mate.

"Yes, sir. I understand." She backed up.

"Have someone get us the smallest fatigues we have," he shouted and looked her over. He shook his head and muttered as he walked away, "They'll still be too big."

"I just tried to reach Kayden again," Koren told her, looking concerned. "Maybe you can try to reach him telepathically," she suggested.

"I thought of that too, Mrs. Paris. I'm afraid if I try it I'll lose my link to Christopher. I just don't understand it, or have enough practice to know if I can reach two people at once yet. It's too risky to experiment right now."

"Please call me Koren. No need for formality." She smiled gently. "I agree. You shouldn't take the chance of losing Christopher." Koren's eyes filled with tears. "If anything ever happened to my son." Her voice cracked. "I just can't imagine what the Staffords are going through."

Dani held on tightly as the truck sped through town toward the waterfront. When they reached the area where she believed they would find Christopher, the teams slowed to let her concentrate. "I can feel him, Gage. We're close. This is it! Christopher is in this building!" Dani pointed to an abandoned warehouse by the docks.

"Are you sure? Maybe we should circle the area again." Gage surveyed the street and surrounding buildings.

"I can't explain it. But I know he's here, and something is going on in there. He needs us now!" she shouted and tried to get the door open while the truck was still rolling.

The Wrath warrior named Garrett grabbed her around the waist and planted her back in the seat. His partner, Troy, rolled his eyes in annoyance and gave her a look that promised consequences should she try it again. The truck she rode in carried a standard six-man Wrath team, plus she and Gage, who drove. Two other teams followed in separate vehicles.

Most of the warriors were wary of having a civilian female on a strike, but Garrett and Troy seemed to have adopted Dani as a little sister. They taught her how to gear up properly in her flak jacket and thigh holster. While the rest of the teams gathered, they'd taken her into the firing range for a quick lesson. Good thing, considering she'd never held a gun before, and she wasn't sure she could pull the trigger on a person.

"You're staying here. We'll handle this. You stay out of sight in the truck. Do you understand? I have never lost a person in my charge, and I'm not going to start today." Gage telegraphed his insistence with his eyes in the rearview mirror.

"Yes, sir." She sagged back into the seat, defeated. Dani wanted to go in. She wanted to help find Christopher, not sit there like a scared little girl, but she'd promised to stay in the truck. She'd done all she could to help find him.

All the warriors entered the building as a fierce unit that she hoped would never come looking for her. Every one of the large men was a nightmare in black. The truck sat parked on the corner at an angle that allowed her to see two sides of the building. Not thirty seconds after the team disappeared into the building, a door on the other side opened, and three men emerged. Two men dragged a guy with his arms and legs bound. A beat-up dark gray sedan sped around the corner and stopped just long enough for everyone to get in.

"Shit! They're getting away." The car sped past the rear of the truck, and she knew she couldn't sit there and wait. If she lost him, they wouldn't find him again. Dani jumped behind the wheel and forced the truck into reverse to go after Christopher. Trying to keep the wheel steady at a rate of speed she'd never think of driving on the street, Dani grabbed the comm unit that was left in the truck and called Gage.

"This is Dani. Can anybody hear me?" It seemed like the voices of every male on the mission came back at once. "Christopher was brought out a side door, and they're moving out fast in a car. I'm following them in the truck," she said, spitting out the names of the cross streets she passed. She had to catch them before they got out of the industrial area. It would be impossible to drive like this when they were in civilian traffic.

Gage came over the radio. "Stand down! Stand down! Do not pursue! We're heading out!"

She ignored him, dropping the device. The bad guys drove toward the water. She knew they would have to circle back on the only other street that came away from the water. When the bad guys turned up ahead before they hit the water, she turned down a narrow alley between two buildings, racing to block their escape. She asked Christopher how many streets they passed before turning. His answer came loud and clear. Dani sent a fierce mental command for Christopher to brace himself for a collision, and she wished that she'd put on a seatbelt. It was going to be close. They hit the intersection at the same time, and the getaway car plowed into the front driver's side of Dani's truck. She flew forward, cracking her head on the windshield and banging her still-aching ribs against the steering wheel. It took her a minute to shake off the impact.

Two of the bad guys tried to get Christopher out of the car, and he fought them. The third slumped in the front seat. She felt the blood running down her face and the knot on her head, but she had to get out of the truck. Dani put all she had into a telepathic command to *STOP!* The abductors froze in place. "Move away from the car," she told them, and they both backed up and stared dumbly into the distance.

Cautiously, she crept over to free Christopher from the car. Thank God, he'd been wearing a seatbelt and wasn't injured badly. She would never have forgiven herself if her stunt had killed him. With the men disabled and Christopher out of the car, Dani grabbed the knife holstered along with the gun Gage had given her and cut the tape from his hands and feet. They supported each other, staggering back to the truck. She tried to back the truck out of the tangle of metal and shattered glass when another strike vehicle pulled up behind them. The Wrath jumped out with their guns drawn, ready for a fight. The last thing she remembered was leaning against Christopher in the front seat, while he thanked her and tried to get a look at her injuries.

After all that, she just wanted to sleep, and the annoying, constant beeping wouldn't stop. Her head felt like she'd cracked it against a windshield. Oh yeah, she *had* cracked it against a windshield.

Slowly, she pried her eyes open to find Mrs. Paris holding her hand. Kayden's mom ran out to the hall and called for help. The beeping that had woken her was a heart monitor. Mrs. Paris came back with a big smile and kissed Dani's cheek.

"We have been so worried about you, honey. You're at the Enclave, in the infirmary. You've been out for more than twenty-four hours."

"Christopher?" she croaked without much sound.

"Christopher is home with his family. You saved him. He's been waiting for you to wake up so he and his parents can come see you. We're all very proud of you," she praised. The room suddenly swarmed with nurses and a doctor. Koren backed away from the bed, smiling at her from the wall she leaned against.

"Kayden?" Dani croaked again.

"I'll get him as soon as the doctor is done. He's been waiting on pins and needles. His father has kept him away in punishment for not being there for you," she said sadly.

"Get him now. I need him now," Dani struggled to tell her.

"I'll go get him and make a few phone calls. Several people have been by to see you. Griffin and Mason were here most of the night. I think Chase is still here. I'll call Griffin and tell him you are awake."

Chase had been driving back and forth to the Enclave for the past couple of days since Danielle woke up. He had waited for hours after she woke to be let in to see her. When he was finally admitted to her room, it was a shock to see her and Kayden together. Chase stood by and fumed for days while Kayden hung over her, holding her hand and kissing her cheek, getting her drinks and running to get the food she liked when she had finally felt like eating. It was driving Chase insane.

Griffin had been there every time Chase visited, so Chase couldn't very well express his annoyance. It wasn't good for a future father-in-law to see his future son-in-law lose his mind over another female. Chase was still in a heated debate with his father over the betrothal. His father was insistent that Chase honor his house and do the right thing. Reneging on the agreement would cause an even bigger rift with the Vaughns. They had a financial and legal agreement. Both his father and Griffin were set on trying to fulfill the prophecy foretold by Griffin's sister before she took her life. Chase was frustrated, but he wasn't giving up.

He'd won a huge victory the day before, though. He'd convinced Griffin and Mason that the best thing to do was to go with the original plan of having Danielle stay with him. She would be close to school and would only need a warrior when she went out. His building was secure, and he had a room ready for her. Griffin arranged to have a nurse look in on her for the first few days.

Chase was happily on his way to pick her up. If Kayden was coming, he would have to follow them.

Her room in the infirmary was full of flowers and get-well cards. She was alone for the first time when Chase arrived.

"Are you ready to go home, Lovely?" Chase smiled his obvious pleasure.

"I asked you not to call me that, and your home is not my home. It's your fiancée's home, though, isn't it? How's she taking the news that I'm staying with you?" Dani quipped.

"Don't be like this, Lovely, please?" Chase sat on the edge of the bed and picked up her hand, looked her in the eyes, because she'd avoided looking at him for days. "You know I love you. You know I meant what I said to you, and I'm still working on my father."

"Did you mean the part about it being just you and me with no one else between us? Because when Griffin came to see me this morning, his wife was talking about your bonding ceremony. I didn't realize you were marrying into the Vaughn family." She pulled her hand away. "Just stop bullshitting me. That isn't how you treat someone you love."

"I suppose you think Kayden loves you?" he snapped.

"I think Kayden cares for me, and I know I care for him. If you're thinking of coming between us, you can forget it. I will call your fiancée and invite her over every day, if you mess with me. I can date anyone I damn well please." Dani closed her eyes and took a deep breath. Sudden tears streaked down her face. "I don't want to fight with you, Chase. You know how I feel about you, and half of my attitude is jealousy. This will be easier for me after you're bonded and you don't want me anymore. Please don't ruin the happiness I might have once you've moved on. If you really love me, don't try to hurt me any more than you already have."

Chase couldn't respond at first. It was the first time she had let him see her real feelings since she'd left his bed that night at the club. Just as he opened his mouth to tell her he wasn't giving up and neither should she, Kayden ruined the moment, entering the room and scowling at Chase beside her on the bed.

"Hello, beautiful. I see you are up and all dressed." He grabbed her hand and pulled her away from Chase and across the room to sit on his lap. "I have a gift for you." He kissed her, on the damn mouth, and rocked her in the chair. Chase thought his head would explode with rage.

Chase watched enviously, hating every brush of Kayden's hands against her skin. Every press of his lips to hers made him sick. He wondered if the jealousy she fought hurt her just as badly. She knew he would love Sam after they were bonded, whether he loved her at the moment or not.

"Alright, Lovely, are you ready to go?" Chase broke into their moment.

"Stop calling me that," she huffed.

"I haven't given her my gift yet. Relax, would ya?" Kayden eyed Chase. "You shouldn't be stressing her out, ya know?" he admonished.

"You didn't need to get me a gift, Kayden." She blushed and nestled against his chest.

Kayden handed her a box that contained a necklace with a warrior symbol hanging from it. "These are normally pins we wear on our dress uniforms, but I had it made into a charm for my beautiful warrior." He grinned.

"I love it! Help me put it on." She turned so he could hook the clasp around her slender neck.

It made no sense to Chase. She wasn't a warrior. She couldn't be a warrior, because they didn't allow women to join the warrior class. Kayden was just hanging his mark around her neck for all the males to see, and it pissed Chase off to no end. He needed to get her out of there and home with him. Some separation from Kayden was apparently overdue.

Another warrior entered with a wheelchair for Dani, but Kayden refused it.

"That won't be necessary. I'm going to carry the warrior out." The guy saluted Dani as if she were a high-ranking warrior and took the wheelchair away.

Kayden carried Danielle to Chase's car, whispering to her and making her giggle the whole way. There were tons of warriors gathered to wish her well and invite her back to visit or spar with them anytime. Two in particular, Garrett and Troy, seemed very familiar with her. Indeed, they had been spotted in her room every day of her stay in the infirmary.

Christopher Stafford was also there. He, too, had a gift for Danielle. It was a gold bangle he'd had engraved with the inscription *Angel of Wrath*.

Everyone admired her new necklace as Kayden carried her from person to person so she could bid her farewells. It must have taken an hour to get from the door to the car.

Chase hoped his Lovely would never return to that place again and was exasperated by the time Kayden gently placed her in the front seat and fastened her seatbelt for her. Kayden had lost his mind if he thought Chase would let him play his Lovely like he did all the girls he dated. They said their good-byes, and he promised to be at her side and on duty in the morning. Another warrior would be following them home because Kayden had been assigned elsewhere for the evening. Kayden shut the car door and walked to the rear, where Chase waited for him to disengage. Kayden put his hand out in a gesture of friendship, but Chase didn't take it.

"Come on, Chase. We grew up together, and you're still my best friend. You're going to be bonded soon, so you have no reason to be angry with me for dating Dani." Kayden kept his hand extended.

"I'm trying my damnedest to get out of the betrothal agreement. My father is fighting me, but I'm working on him. I won't let you treat Danielle the way you've treated all the other girls in your life. She's precious and above you," Chase countered. "She isn't one of your disposable females."

"She doesn't think she's above me. And I think you mean the way you treated her? Vowing your love to her, alone, just to get in her pants, so you could drop her when you bonded to Sam? Because of your games, she thinks she can't trust any of us. You ran her straight out of our race with your bullshit. I'm surely not going to treat her that way, Chase."

"This isn't the end, Kayden. I'm not bonded yet. If I can stop it, I will, and then you'll have a fight on your hands. A fight you can't win. She still cares for me, and you know it." Chase tried to smile, but he knew as things stood, he was on the losing end of this battle.

"She may still care for you, but she is with me. She kissed me, and then she came back for more. I'm not letting her go." Kayden put a finger on Chase's chest and pushed.

"She kissed you, huh? That's nice. Did she crawl out of your bed on weak knees?" Chase knew he was ten kinds of bastard for pulling the old kiss-and-tell, but Kayden needed to be put in his place. And that place was far from Lovely. Kayden's face drained of all color. "No? Well, she made love to me while her little human buddy Jared waited for her to return to their date. I'm not really impressed by your kiss." Chase pushed Kayden back.

"Do you two boys need to get in the ring and work something out?" Gage came out of nowhere to separate them.

Chase walked around to the driver's side and said, "No, sir, Mr. Paris. I have to get Danielle home, where she belongs."

Sixteen

There had been a steady stream of visitors for the past couple of days, but it'd been quiet that day. Dani received an invitation to a dinner party in her honor at the home of Christopher Stafford. The Stafford house wanted to show their gratitude for her efforts in the rescue. She didn't like the attention, but Mason said it would be an insult if she declined.

Mason had given her a lot of the answers to the questions she'd had regarding the council and how their justice system worked. He also explained more about vampire longevity. Vampires reached their prime at around twenty-five, and then the aging process slowed way down. If they took care of themselves and fed regularly, they could live for hundreds of years. The older a vampire got, the stronger he or she became. The young were much more vulnerable, until they came into their power. It seemed Dani's need for blood was brought on when she came of age and her powers started to kick in. He explained that baby vamps got blood cells from their mothers' milk, and they breast-fed longer than humans would consider normal. He'd been bringing bags of blood to the Enclave for her, but she'd have to learn to hunt soon enough. Obviously, she didn't need to worry about sunlight, crosses, or any of that other silly stuff.

According to their history, vampires were just creatures that evolved from the garden-variety human, like the missing link or something. Both species shared many of the same traits, but there were huge differences in metabolism, dietary needs, basic strengths, and abilities. Humans could be turned into vampires if enough blood was exchanged, but it was rarely attempted because the human died more often than not during the process. If it was attempted, it was usually done out of love. Made vampires couldn't have children, and the reasons why eluded their scientists. They also tended not to live as long as born vampires. He hadn't found any records of a vampire and a human ever having a child that survived. He had found a few very old references, but the mother and child had died in every case. It wasn't a problem anymore, because of the vampire's prejudice against humans. Humans were lower on the food chain and therefore beneath consideration for a mate, unless the human was turned first, but then children were out of the question. Mason believed Tessa had convinced Griffin to turn her if she survived childbirth, so they could stay together.

Her mom was going nuts because she had to stay away. Dani suggested she could expose her humanity. Dani had suggested her mom could give Griffin a call from the grave, but Tessa didn't want to do that. She was convinced that Dani would be scorned. As Tessa's biggest concern was keeping Dani safe until the vampires caught their villain, Dani wondered how long the charade would last. Someone was sure to notice her differences in time. She didn't heal as fast as a vamp. Her physical attributes were seriously lacking, but her mental gifts were over the top. Dani believed that had a lot to do with her mother's paranormal ability to see the future, and her father's telekinesis.

Jared had been begging to visit, and she'd finally agreed. Chase pitched a fit until she explained that either he would be a gentleman to her guest, or she would find someplace else to stay. He'd been trying hard to make her comfortable and rebuild their relationship. She couldn't be anything more than friends with an engaged man. He still insisted he was working to get out of the engagement, but she'd told him he shouldn't ruin the relationship between the two high-powered families over her.

Whoever would have thought Nightmare Barbie would turn out to be her half sister? She'd found that out the day she left the hospital. Mrs. Vaughn "the second" had perched herself on a chair in the corner of Dani's room, on her cell phone, going on and on about the bonding ceremony. She kept looking at Dani to be sure she was listening. Dani didn't know why Sarah had come to visit. Then it dawned on her. The woman was trying to relay a message without coming out and saying it. Sarah was there to make sure she understood Chase was taken. Dani got the memo loud and clear. Her life was moving on. She and Kayden had slid smoothly into a relationship she was comfortable with. He was her rock and the reason she hadn't run away screaming yet. He kept her calm and distracted her from all the things she couldn't change.

Kayden was now outside pacing the hall. Dani had just informed him that Jared was on his way, and he didn't like it at all. She suspected jealousy was the cause of Kayden's bad mood. She imagined the females he dated didn't parade their male friends around in front of him.

She reminded Jared to act like he knew nothing about the black-eyed freaky people. He said he'd act like he didn't know his own mother if it got him a visit with her. She really missed her friend and was so happy to finally see him again. It was going to be nice to spend time with someone who wasn't pressuring her for more than she could give him.

A knock on the bedroom door pulled her out of the morbid thoughts. She knew it was Kayden by his woodsy essence. "Come on in, Kayden," she called out.

He sulked in and flopped down on the bed, face first. She couldn't help checking out his butt. No wonder all those girls chased him around. The view from behind was almost as good as the front.

She plopped down next to him, face up, using his muscled arm for a pillow.

He simply breathed in and out, and she could feel the tension rolling off of him. "We need to talk," he finally announced.

Oh, shit. That didn't sound good. She didn't want him to break up with her over a friend, but if he couldn't trust her to have friends they didn't have a very good relationship. He made her feel normal, like she belonged with him. But she'd made it clear she needed time before she'd be ready for a sexual relationship. She just wasn't there yet. Not after being with Chase so recently. A guy with Kayden's reputation couldn't be expected to go without sex indefinitely. It was only a matter of time before he let her go.

"What do you want to talk about?" She sat up and waited for the other shoe to drop.

"Us . . . you and me."

He still didn't face her. Oh God. She was right. He was ending it. They'd only been together just over a week, and she didn't want to lose him.

"I'm listening. Are you going to look at me or what?" Anxiety made the words harsher than she had intended.

"I don't know why this is so damn hard for me. I've been dating since I was fifteen, and I've never had an exclusive relationship, but knowing you're spending time with someone else makes me crazy." He still couldn't look at her.

Here it comes. She'd have to decide to let him walk away and see if he came back, or throw herself at him before he made it to the door. He rolled over to face her with his beautiful hazel eyes burning a hole in her heart and said, "I think I'm falling for you."

That wasn't what she'd expected. The words needed to soak in for a minute. He watched her nervously, until the statement was absorbed. The smile she gave him felt oddly shy.

"I have feelings for you, too, Kayden. I just think we need to take it slowly." Why couldn't she fall in love with this man who wanted her and her alone? Her feelings for him grew every day, and maybe one day her attraction to him would become something more. He was the kind of man she needed and wanted in her life. She just had to convince her heart to get with the program. He took a deep breath and hauled her flush against his body, squeezing her so tightly it hurt her ribs.

"Ouch! I do still have tender ribs."

He instantly loosened up but didn't release her. "I was so afraid you were gonna laugh at me," he admitted, and his voice wavered a little.

"Why would I laugh at you?" She ran her fingers through his hair in an effort to comfort him. He was so damn cute when he got nervous. Truthfully, he was hot all the time, but the unsure side of him was endearing. As big and bad as he could be, he could also be sweet and vulnerable.

"Everyone says you're above me," he confessed, "and I'm not good enough for you. I'm afraid they're right." He blushed. The big strong man blushed in her arms.

"You know better than anyone else that I don't believe the class system you people live by. Even if I did, how in the world would I be above you? I come from no house at all, in a town without any other vampires. Hell, *I'm* probably beneath *you*. Maybe you should leave before my low-class upbringing starts rubbing off on you." She laughed and tousled his hair. "God forbid I should sully the son of the mighty Gage Paris."

"You're not funny. I guess because you're so powerful and beautiful, you've risen above the status of the warriors. Did you know that there's talk of you being voted onto the council when you get older, purely on the merit of your power? You're not even a member of one of the ruling houses. That would surely put you way above me," he explained.

"No. I didn't know that. But I do know they wouldn't want me on the council. I won't play by their rules. But that's a discussion for another day. For now, why don't you tell me what you came in here to say? Your anxiety level tells me that you're not done." She encouraged him to continue.

"I know I can't tell you what to do. I mean, we're dating, not bonded." Again, he couldn't look her in the eye.

She cut him off. "Even if we were bonded, you wouldn't be able to tell me what to do. In case you haven't picked up on it yet, I usually go my own way."

"If we were bonded, you likely wouldn't want to do this anyway, so I'd be pretty safe." He smiled and brushed her cheek. "I actually like that idea. I didn't think I would ever want to do that, but if you agreed to it, I would exchange blood with you right now."

When he said he would bond to her right then, the only thing that stopped her from saying, "Let's do it," was her half-breed nature. A bonding would solve half of her problems. Chase would no longer be a constant distraction. Kayden was well aware that she had feelings for Chase, and he was talking about bonding despite that. So it wouldn't be like she would be taking advantage of him, would it? She wished she had met Kayden first. Did it matter? It certainly wouldn't matter when Chase was bonded to Samantha.

She would have to tell Kayden the whole truth first. She couldn't go into something so permanent and sacred with secrets. Why was she even thinking about this? If he knew, he would probably change his mind about her entirely.

"Maybe that's something we can talk about one day when all of this madness is over and we can get to know each other without so many distractions," she told him shyly. He looked stunned. She was kind of stunned herself.

He pressed his face into her neck and breathed her in deeply. "I need to ask you not to have sex with Jared tonight. I know it's crossing the line, but if you care about my sanity or emotional well-being at all, you won't do it while I'm here. I can't leave after what happened to you. I have to stay nearby until my relief comes. I'll be honest, even if I got some relief, I don't think I could leave. Leaving you here with Chase is maddening enough, but knowing you are with a guy you're dating . . . " Kayden trailed off. Dani was shocked. He thought she was still dating Jared? No wonder he was so agitated about the visit.

"Are you gonna say anything? Or am I just gonna go crazy wondering what you're thinking about?" Kayden was on edge.

"I went on *a* date with Jared, one date, and we've never had sex. I hadn't planned to start now. I've fed on Jared, sure, but that's it." She was a little annoyed. She rolled away from him and faced the other way.

"Oh, I was under the impression that you didn't want a committed relationship because . . . well, because you were dating . . . more than one person. And he's human. And you like humans, you trust them, you know, more than you do us because you were raised with humans." He was stumbling through his explanation.

"Who gave you that impression? My life is too crazy right now, and I wouldn't put my human friends at risk. Things are too dangerous out there for me, much less for someone who couldn't defend himself." Shit. She hadn't thought before that moment that it could be dangerous for Jared to come see her. What if that crazy bartender was out there watching the building?

"Yeah, so I feel like a total ass." Kayden interrupted her thoughts. "Look, I know you dated Jared. I didn't know it was only once. And I know you've . . . been with Chase."

How the hell did he know that? Nobody but Chase knew that!

"It just made sense when you told me you weren't ready for sex that it was because there were other guys in your life." Yeah, she guessed that did make sense, if someone had suggested it to him.

Chase was interfering with her life. He had her locked in his home and he was feeding Kayden information that wasn't accurate. She would be having a chat with Chase about kissing and telling. She'd hate to have to tell his betrothed about their night together. But for now Dani had another very difficult task at hand. After Kayden left her room she called her godfather for some advice.

Dani's heart ached a little when she opened the condo door to find Jared's smiling face on the other side. He was a good man and great friend. Sadly, she would lose him today. Maybe not entirely—she would see him around campus when she returned to school—but the closeness they shared would be gone.

She stepped back to let Jared in, and Kayden's blank face came into view. He was on guard and trying to be professional. She could tell he'd believed her when she said she wasn't dating Jared anymore, but knowing she had gone out with him made leaving them alone hard for him. He was trying to give her some space, and she appreciated that. She smiled and blew him a kiss. One corner of his mouth twitched before he moved down the hall, farther away from the door.

She shut the door and turned to greet the only true friend she had. Jared swooped her up in a tight hug and kissed her cheek. "Damn, I've missed you, girl!" He put her down and looked her over, his expression becoming serious. "What happened? Why you aren't at school anymore, and why are you staying here with that jerk from the club? I'm sorry. I know you like the guy, but moving in so soon is a little much, don't you think?"

Dani pulled him back in for another hug. This was just too hard for her. She wanted to keep her friend. Jared made her feel like less of a freak. He knew about her and he accepted her. She'd attacked him and he still cared for her. But this new life of hers was far too dangerous for a human. She wouldn't . . . couldn't put his life at risk.

Dani stepped back and placed her hand on the side of his face. Touch made the rest of her abilities stronger, and she couldn't mess this up. She was going to replace Jared's memories of her with something . . . safer.

"Look into my eyes, Jared. I have a story to tell you."

Dani saw Kayden jump in surprise when the door opened and she exited with Jared just moments after they had entered the condo. She was hardly able to hold herself up when Jared hugged her again and patted her on the back. "We'll see each other around, right?" he asked.

"Sure, I'll give you a call," she nodded, masking her expression.

Jared stepped into the elevator with a smile and waved goodbye to her as the doors slid shut on their relationship. She'd lost so much of herself in recent days that her decision to remove Jared's memories of her secrets hurt deeply. He now remembered everything up to the night of their date, with the exception of the weird things that happened around her, like the opening doors and accidental mind reading. If asked, he would now tell people that he just wasn't that into Dani after their one date. She was just another girl who hadn't held his attention for very long. It was best for Jared not to have the responsibility of keeping her secrets.

When Chase arrived home, he was surprised to see Kayden sitting against the wall in the hall outside the penthouse. He'd seen his replacement standing watch in the lobby. Kayden was the only one who had access to the penthouse unless there was an emergency. The two of them didn't agree on much right now, but neither one of them liked the idea of the human boyfriend.

"Shit. Tell me that damn human guy isn't still in there with her?" Chase asked in disgust.

Kayden slid Chase a sidelong look and shook his head. "He's gone, but Dani wants to be left alone tonight. She said to make sure she wasn't disturbed. Not even by you."

"Okay, so I obviously missed something." Chase waited for more information, but Kayden just shrugged, not giving anything away.

"You can go home or hunt if you want to, Kayden. I won't be leaving until late morning. It's up to you." Chase unlocked the door.

Kayden got up and went to the elevator. "Tell her I'll be back at nine if she comes out before I return in the morning. Can you stay until I get here?"

"Sure thing, I won't leave her alone. See you tomorrow." Inside the condo, Chase loved the way Dani's scent lingered everywhere, just as it should.

In his room he stripped to his boxers and went to his closet for pajama pants. When he came back into his room, Lovely was standing there glaring at him. Damn it! She was always a beauty, but when she was angry the sparks in her eyes made her look like a goddess on the warpath. She wore ratty-looking boxer shorts and a Nirvana T-shirt. She was so damn sexy standing there with her fists on her hips and that little defiant chin in the air. His rod was swelling in his shorts already.

"Stop meddling in my business, Chase," she hissed.

"You are my business, Lovely. You just aren't ready to admit it yet."

"Did you tell Kayden about us just to hurt him? That was before I started dating him. Would you like Samantha or her father to know about us?" she threatened.

Okay. He could admit, if only to himself, that he'd been wrong for telling Kayden their personal business. But he'd been angry and damned jealous of Kayden's relationship with Danielle. He still was. He took a deep breath and her sweet aroma filled his lungs.

He could stand there and debate what he'd done to piss her off, or he could make good use of the hard-on she so often inspired. She was angry, but her eyes kept shooting to the tent in his shorts. He stepped closer and stared her down. They needed each other; more than that, they wanted each other. She took a step backward, but it was too late. He'd already seen the flash of heat in her eyes. That was all the encouragement he needed.

Chase wrapped a fist around the hair at the base of her skull and crushed her mouth with his. She resisted for a moment but he kept up his oral assault. The smell of her, the taste of her skin, made him harder than he'd ever been. Now that he knew how they could be together, he wanted her constantly. Her body called to every part of his and he meant to have her, now. Her back hit the wall, and he wedged a thigh between her legs. He nipped her lower lip and she gasped.

"Let me in, Lovely. I want to taste that sweet tongue."

She was panting and no longer trying to get away. Her mouth opened to accept him and Chase slid inside gratefully. Relief spread through his chest. They belonged together, and her body knew what her mind wanted to reject. He lifted her higher and pinned her to the wall with his hips. He pulled her shirt up over her head and he gloried in the sight of her lush, rose-tipped breasts. He laved one full breast first, circling the nipple with his tongue and then nipping at the tender underside, before moving to the other breast. Dani writhed and moaned so sweetly for him. He kissed her swollen lips, pinching her nipples and grinding his stiff rod into her softness.

"Tell me you want this, Lovely," he demanded. He needed her to say the words. She had to admit that she needed him too.

She blinked a few times. Her mouth opened and shut, but nothing came out. Chase's insides twisted. He kissed a path up her jaw to her ear, giving her a moment to make a decision. He wanted her, but he wouldn't let her pretend this was all his doing. Was he seducing her? Hell yes he was, but she was a willing participant and she needed to admit it to herself. The only way he could see to break down the wall she'd built between them was to show her that she hated their separation as much as he did.

Chase's voice sounded too husky to his own ears when he spoke. "You're so beautiful, Danielle. I want you and I know you want me too," he whispered into her ear. He kissed her softly. He thrust his hips against her again and she panted. "Let me love you."

She nodded her head and wrapped her arms tighter around his neck. Chase smiled. "Thank God!" he shouted. Dani laughed and for the first time she took the lead, nipping his lower lip before kissing him deeply. His tongue danced with hers. Her silky skin against his palm tantalized. He slid his hands down her thighs to push down her panties. His raging lust wanted him to take her right there against the wall, but his mind wanted to savor every inch of her luscious body. This time he wanted the taste of her heat coating his tongue and drenching his face.

Chase turned and crossed the room in several long strides. He laid her out on the bed like a feast, and he was starving for her. When he had her beneath him, he took his time exploring her mouth until she made little mewling sounds in her throat that made him crazy. He crawled farther down the bed, paying close attention to each breast until the tips were sensitive points. He kissed his way down her flat belly. She jerked when his tongue dipped into her navel and circled. Her hips jerked, seeking fulfillment when he breathed warm air over her wet mound. Chase nibbled her hip bone but bypassed her little patch of dark curls to nibble and lick the inside of her thigh, starting at her knee and slowly working his way all the way up to her slippery heat.

He slid his thumbs into her fold to open her to his view. He had to calm his breathing and grit his teeth. Her soft pink petals glistened with her desire. He needed to taste that desire. She shivered when he blew warm air over her mound. His first long lick had her squirming. Chase leisurely explored her with his tongue, delving deep and then retreating to tease her clit. His mouth roamed over the core of her need, sucking and lapping, not missing a single drop of her heat. She arched her back and moaned, lifting to meet him.

He suckled her clit and finally gave her what she needed when he thrust first one and then a second finger deep into her dripping channel. Chase brought her to a shattering climax but he held her hips tight, giving her no reprieve from his teasing until she boiled over into another release.

"Oh my God, Chase, I need you. I need to have all of you." She begged for him to possess her.

He didn't make her ask again. He wasn't gentle this time. He wanted her to experience the depth and breadth of his feelings for her. He kicked off his boxers and climbed up her body. He pressed the burning thickness of his manhood into her, deeper and deeper until she took all of him. She cried out his name and bucked against him.

"I'm going to make you shout my name, Lovely. I'm going to take what you already know is mine." He set up a ruthless pace, plundering her depths. She dug her nails into his back and pleaded. He wasn't sure what she was begging for, but he gave her all he had in long, hard strokes. He took her to the edge and let her teeter there, writhing, whimpering, while he teased her until the luscious agony gripped him by the throat and demanded its release. He let it take him and dragged her under into the violent climax his body demanded of them both. The sweetest thing he'd ever heard was his name on her lips when she did just as he'd promised she would. She screamed for him.

After their bout of loving, she'd insisted it would never happen again and scurried off to the guest room. That frustrated Chase. He'd thought he'd made some ground with Danielle, but she'd retreated as soon as the passion faded. He wished he could have convinced her to stay in his bed, but he had to take what he could get for now. He would work his way into her life in slow increments until she realized she couldn't be without him.

Chase decided to take advantage of his alone time with Danielle to show her another side of him. He got up super early and went out for groceries. To be safe, he directed security not to allow anyone other than Kayden to go to his penthouse while he was gone, and he checked in with the warrior who'd just come on shift in the lobby. He knew Danielle hadn't eaten dinner, so he hoped to entice her out of her room with the aroma of breakfast. Maybe after breakfast he could get her out for a little shopping.

When he arrived home, he turned on the radio in the kitchen and mixed the pancake batter from scratch. He used to cook with his mom all the time, but he never had the patience to cook just for himself. It was gratifying to cook for someone he loved. That must have been why his mother cooked for the family on a regular basis, instead of having the cook do every meal. He just hoped like hell Danielle would come out to eat.

The table was set, and the condo was filled with the smell of bacon and bananas. He was focused on making perfectly round pancakes, when Danielle walked up behind him. He turned with a plate full of his culinary creations and smacked into her, miraculously managing to avoid a spill. They both laughed and ended up standing there staring at each other. There was a new intimacy between them now that boded well for his chance of winning her over.

"What are you doing out here?" She checked out the spread appreciatively.

"Are you hungry? I didn't know what you liked, so I made a little of everything." Chase beamed back at her.

"I'm starving, and it smells so good." Her stomach growled in agreement.

"Good, let's eat. I have the table all ready." He went to the dining room with Danielle on his heels.

"What about Kayden?" She looked around, noting his absence.

"He hasn't returned yet. I'm on warrior duty for a while." He winked at her.

"You need to be on duty more often, if it means I get breakfast. I haven't had a good breakfast since . . ." She bit her lip in thought, and Chase wanted to soothe the hurt with his tongue. "Well, for a long time," she finished.

Chase sat close to her at the table. He suggested they do the morning paper crossword puzzle together. "It's something my parents do together," he said. She gave him a look that said, *Please, don't start,* so he said, "It's just a game, Danielle. My mom is really serious about it, but my dad always gives her the craziest answers. It's funny to watch. I just thought you might like to play."

She relaxed. Alright, it seemed she wanted to pretend last night hadn't happened. He could do that, for now. They ate, talked, and worked the puzzle. Somehow, they'd gotten closer and closer to each other at the table, until finally their chairs were so close their legs touched. They took turns writing the answers, and Chase's quips had them both in hysterics. The light in her eyes helped him understand why his father loved the activity so much.

Chase was quite proud of his culinary skills when she polished off her first plate with moans of pleasure and then finished off a second helping of everything. His Lovely wasn't one of those waifish girls who never ate. She had a healthy appetite and wasn't ashamed to eat in front of others. He was actually helping her unwind, and she seemed to enjoy his company. That was what they needed. Time to really get to know each other without outside distraction was crucial.

Of course, that was when the blissful morning was shattered. In the middle of a raucous bout of laughter, a shrill voice broke through the contentment.

"What the hell are you doing here with my man, again?" Samantha screeched and glared at Danielle over the table.

Danielle looked at Chase. "Let me guess. She didn't know I was staying with you, did she?" She put down her fork and the crossword puzzle.

"She didn't need to know, Lovely. You were placed here by the council for your protection. Her father is very aware that you're here and has been here to visit several times, as I recall." He put his hand on hers to encourage her to stay at the table while he dealt with Sam.

"What are you talking about? Daddy knows she's here? No damn way is this bitch staying here and skanking up our home." Sam stepped toward Danielle but Chase got between them.

"Sam, she is a guest in my home, so back off. And how the hell did you get in, anyway? I am so sick of your sneaky shit," he warned.

"Fine, I'll back off, but I'm going to wait for you in our room. If that bitch's shit is in there, she's gonna be missing some hair!" Sam threatened.

Dani'd had enough of this girl's mouth. She couldn't take it anymore. So she did the cruelest thing she'd ever done in her life. She told the crazy bitch the truth.

"You do know this is why he doesn't love you, right? He doesn't even like you. If he had the choice he would be with me, because he does love me."

Sam was shocked for a moment, before she came back, "He doesn't have a choice, so you need to stay out of our business and out of our bed," she snapped. Sam looked at Chase for a denial of what Dani had said, but none came.

Dani just smiled at her and said, "I hope that thought keeps you warm at night after you've bonded. I can't imagine having to force my mate into bonding with me. It's a good thing the bond is soul deep. Because if it weren't, he would spend every night he's with you thinking about me. I've been in his mind, and, believe me, I am all he's thinking about." Dani bumped Sam's shoulder on the way out of the dining room. She told Chase, "Thanks for breakfast," and slammed her bedroom door.

Chase did his best to keep the peace, but while he argued with Sam, his mind kept returning to Danielle. She had seemed so happy over breakfast. Damn Sam for ruining their oasis again.

Lovely had said things to Sam that were hurtful and true, but he knew it had also hurt her. Lovely lived with the pain of his situation just as he did. He could hear the anguish in her voice and sensed her hurt at having to stand by and watch the bonding happen.

No matter how hard she tried to push him away, he knew she loved him. No matter how many other guys she used to fill her time, he was the one she wanted. His suffering would end. Hers would continue. At least until she found a mate of her own.

Okay, that was harsh. Dani didn't know what had come over her, but that bitch needed to hear the truth. She should just gather her stuff and go back to campus. It wouldn't be long before Sam cried to her devoted daddy. He would put her out of there soon, anyway.

Hell no! She wouldn't leave! She'd stay there until they dragged her ass out, just to spite Nightmare Barbie. She was so pissed at the world. She felt . . . she felt like she needed to feed. Anger made her hungry. That's what she'd do. She'd take her chances and go hunting for the first time, and she would do it alone. Who was going to notice, anyway? She could pull her hair up or put on a hat to hide her hair. Chase and Sam were too busy fighting in his room to notice her leaving. Dani left a note on her bed.

Gone hunting, it read.

Looking at herself in the gleaming elevator wall, she was sure she could get out unrecognized, as long as Kayden didn't catch her. She'd found a skullcap in Chase's coat closet. Once she pulled the front of her hair back in a barrette and added the hat, her streaks disappeared. The trendy and slightly too-big sunglasses covered her eyes, and she wore a plain gray sweat suit. She wasn't a complete idiot, so she tucked the blade Gage had given her into a sock, just in case. She had her cell phone on her, but turned it off.

Exiting the elevator, she saw Kayden coming toward her, juggling coffee and donuts. Quickly, she turned and ducked into the lobby's ladies' room. She couldn't help but laugh when she thought of the hell Kayden was going to raise when he realized she was gone. As soon as the doors closed on Kayden, she scurried out without drawing attention. Dani wanted to wander the streets like a normal person and find some blood like a normal vampire, alone.

It was a beautiful fall day, and the streets were busy. She wandered around the town, ducking in and out of stores and taking in some daylight by the park, before ending up in a big bookstore with the big puffy chairs and quiet corners for reading. Her standard café mocha from the coffee joint made her think of mornings on campus. Funny enough, she found herself in the section filled with vampire novels and books about fairies and werewolves. Paging through a random book, she felt eyes on her. Trying not to be obvious, she returned the book, moving to get another, and turned slightly, trying to get a feel for her surroundings. There was a man watching her from a nearby chair. She'd just turned down the next aisle when he approached. He was older and very attractive.

He reminded her of Dr. McSteamy, only a little younger. He had tawny hair and blue eyes. Normally, she would have dismissed him as an older guy looking to take advantage of her naivety, but she was hungry. No time like the present to learn how to be a black-eyed freak.

"Do you like vampires?" he asked teasingly.

"Why yes, I do. I'm dating one, and another one is in love with me. I'm quite in demand with the vamp population." The truth-telling thing was fun. That was probably the second-worst move she'd made that day, and it was only noon.

The guy looked at her, wide-eyed for a second, until she cracked a grin, and he laughed. "You're funny and beautiful. Seriously, what are you looking for? Maybe I can help."

"Let me see what you're reading." She took his book and was surprised to see Anne Rice's *The Vampire Lestat*. That was too funny. "Maybe I'll buy this one."

"I actually have an extra copy at my place. I live just around the corner, if you would like to borrow it." He gave her a suggestive half smile. Could it really be so easy? She didn't even have to enthrall him to leave with her. Sweet!

"Alright, I'm game, if you don't mind. I promise to return it. I'm Dani," she said, shaking his hand.

"I'm Danny, too." He winked. "You can call me Dan or Daniel, if you prefer. I'll be expecting a review when you return the book to me, Ms. Dani. Maybe over dinner you can give me your opinion?" he flirted on the way out to the busy sidewalk.

Dani touched his arm on the way and scanned his mind for bad intention. All his intentions were of a sexual nature but no more than that.

He lived in a nice brownstone across from the park. Inside, they went to his study where, damn if there weren't medical school diplomas hanging on the wall. She *knew* he was related to Dr. McSteamy. He had a library full of books and went right to the one he was after, bringing it back to her and standing way too close for comfort. "So do you date vampires exclusively, or would you be willing to give a plain old human a chance?"

Starting to feel uncomfortable, she tried to joke, "If you can get the job done. Maybe I need to see what you have to offer." That was just what he wanted to hear. He led her happily to his big leather sofa and pulled her down on top of him. Shit, it really was easy.

"Just relax, Dan. I will do all the work." He moaned when she found the spot with her tongue. It was torture feeling his pulse tick against her tongue. Her fangs extended painfully. The experience turned instantly delicious when those teeth sunk into his succulent vein. He sucked in a sharp breath and clutched wildly at her waist. Then he went limp beneath her and moaned in ecstasy. Dani ordered him to be quiet and drank her fill.

Seventeen

Feeling energized and in better spirits, Dani strolled down the street. The fresh blood seemed to revitalize her in a big way. They'd brought her bags of blood that she drank like juice boxes. It helped the healing, but fresh blood was a different experience. Fresh blood was warm and deliciously thick, like hot chocolate. It filled her with a feeling of peace. She decided Dr. McSteamy might become a regular donor.

The busy streets were full of shoppers and milling pedestrians. After several long hours out, she figured it was time to check in. She shot a text to Kayden to let him know all was well and she'd be home when she cooled down. He tried to call her immediately. Turning the phone off really was the best idea. Enjoying her day out alone was an even better idea, and she wasn't ready for it to end yet. It was a beautifully cool, sunny day. She couldn't bring herself to go inside and hide from the world just yet.

Being stuck in the penthouse between Chase and Kayden was constantly taxing. After giving in to her desire for Chase the previous night, Dani was feeling the guilt of having cheated on Kayden. She would need to tell him. It would be better coming from her than from Chase. Either way he was going to be hurt, and for what?

Sam's appearance that morning had her feeling like a prize idiot. She'd let Chase make a fool of her. In the heat of passion she'd allowed herself to overlook all of the valid reasons she had for staying as far away from Chase as possible. In the light of day she'd been humiliated when his future bride had shown up and treated her like a slut poaching her man. To be honest, that was exactly how she felt.

She just couldn't go back yet. It was all too much. She often wondered what would have happened between her and Chase if he hadn't been engaged. His magnetism pulled on her constantly, and she feared the love she struggled to ignore would eventually take her over. It had been nothing for him to get her into bed both times he tried. She wanted to dislike him the way she pretended to, but her heart wouldn't allow it, and it seemed that even he knew it was all an act.

They needed to find the evil hunting them so she could get back to school and everyone else could return to their normal lives. Kayden would be assigned to something or someone else, and Chase would be happy with his beautiful new bride.

Dani was walking aimlessly when the sweetest little face peering miserably out of the window of a dress shop brought her attention back to the street, and she stopped. It was J. R., her little brother. The thought of that was funny, never having imagined she'd have a sibling. He saw her and came running.

"Danielle!" he exclaimed, wrapping his arms around her waist and hugging her like it was a natural thing he did every day.

"Hey, J. R., what have you been up to?" She tousled his hair.

"I heard you got hurt. I'm so glad to see you. Dad said you weren't ready for visitors yet." He smiled up at her, and she flinched at the word *Dad*. "Mom and Mrs. Deidrick are trying on dresses for the gala, and I'm bored. Are you coming to the gala?" he questioned unhappily.

"Are you going to be there?" Dani was distracted, pondering going in to meet Chase's mother.

"I have to go, and I have to wear a stupid tuxedo and everything," he huffed.

"If you think maybe you could save a dance for me, I would love to come," she cajoled.

"I can do that." He blushed. "I'm not a very good dancer, though."

"Good, I'm not either. We can dance badly together." Taking his hand, she spun him around like they were dancing, and he laughed, pink cheeked. She was curtsying to him when his mom came to the door in a temper. Sarah was lovely in a floor-length lavender gown that clung to her in all the right places. It felt like a betrayal to Dani's mother to admire her.

"J. R., I asked you to stay inside while I'm in the dressing room." She stopped when she noticed Dani standing there, midcurtsy. "Danielle, how are you? Griffin told me your injuries were still mending. We are all very proud of you for your bravery, dear, but I hope you'll leave the dangerous missions up to the men in the future."

Dani grasped the warrior charm hanging from her necklace and scowled. "Yes, ma'am. The next time I'll just let them take the kid without a fight. I guess it isn't my problem if someone else goes home dead. I'll just run and hide behind the men." She couldn't believe how old-fashioned and ridiculous their society was. She'd be damned if she was gonna turn tail and run just because she didn't happen to have a penis.

"Oh now, don't get upset," Sarah condescended, patting Dani on the shoulder. "Why don't you come in and meet Mrs. Deidrick? She and I were talking about how gracious it is of Chase to give you a safe haven in his home." She tugged Dani toward the door of the dress shop, and J. R. bounced in beside her. Mrs. Deidrick stepped out of a dressing room. At first, Dani thought she was a girl, due to her petite stature. Chase's mom was a beautiful brunette with hazel eyes. She wore a red, strapless gown with a slit up the side. The woman was only about five feet two, but she was lean and muscular. Her daily workouts were evident.

"What do you think of this one, Sarah?" she asked their reflection in the mirror and turned to address them directly when she saw Sarah wasn't alone. "Who is this lovely girl?" Dani blushed at her use of the word that was Chase's favorite nickname for her: *Lovely*.

"This is Danielle Scott. Danielle, I'd like to introduce you to Debbie Deidrick." Sarah did this annoying Vanna White gesture, as if she were presenting a gift or revealing a consonant or a vowel.

"It's a pleasure to meet you, Mrs. Deidrick."

Debbie stepped forward and shook Dani's hand firmly. "Please, call me Debbie." She smiled. "Are you going to the gala?"

"Yes, and she promised me a dance," J. R. spoke up at her side.

"At least one dance, but I'm hoping for a couple of dances. Is your dance card already full?" She mussed his hair again.

"No, we can dance all you want to." He blushed again. Dani really felt something for the boy. It could have been because she knew he was her brother, but she didn't think so. He had something special inside him, and Dani hoped for a chance to know him better.

"What are you wearing? Have you selected a gown yet?" Debbie wanted to know.

"I have no idea. I guess I better start thinking about that. Isn't it coming up soon?"

"It's only a month away," Sarah put in. "I believe Chase and Samantha are working on the final details today. They've been getting very close and working together as a wonderful team to bring this gala together. Don't you think so, Debbie? They will make a beautiful couple, when they're bonded." She must have felt the need to remind her of his engagement, again. "She and Chase are attending the gala, together. Do you have a date, Danielle?"

"I do. Kayden and I are going together." She plastered on a fake smile.

Debbie waved one of the shopgirls over and said, "Could you please bring some gowns for our friend to try on?" She turned to Dani. "What size do you wear, Danielle? A four, maybe?"

"I wear a size six, but you don't have to do that. I was just passing." Dani couldn't afford to use the restroom in that boutique, so a dress was out of the question.

"Don't be silly. Stay a while. It will be fun." She patted Dani on her shoulder and led her forward into the changing area.

An hour later, she spun in front of the mirror in a ruffled gown she would never wear in public and danced a poorly performed waltz with J. R. It was fun, and she was glad she'd stayed. J. R. returned to his handheld video game and she went back to the dressing room. She'd just slipped into the last dress the shop owner had brought her when she heard Sarah calling for J. R.

"J. R., where are you? Come out now. Mommy isn't in the mood to play hide-and-seek," she pleaded with the absent boy.

Turning to admire the gown, Dani heard a shrill scream from Sarah, who was somewhere near the front of the store. Dani ran barefoot in the beautiful gown to see Sarah and Debbie standing on the sidewalk. Sarah was in full panic mode, and Debbie crept forward with her hands up in a gesture that looked like she was trying to calm someone. Dani ran out the door, her heart in her throat, expecting to see J. R. injured. Her heart plummeted when the scene she came upon was far worse than she'd expected.

J. R. was in the back of a white van with the door open to the sidewalk. She wanted to vomit at the sight of her little brother wrapped up in the arms of the very same man who had attacked her in the club a few weeks back. She'd heard Chase say his name was Nathan.

Nathan held a knife to J. R.'s throat with one hand and a syringe full of milky-looking liquid pressed into his arm with the other. Nathan's arms were crossed tightly over the boy's chest to hold him still.

Dani stepped toward the van, but Debbie grabbed her arm.

"Don't move and don't even think about pulling any freaky vamp tricks! If I feel even a pinch, this kid is getting an armful!" Nathan was deadly calm. "Your friend said you weren't here, but I've been watching since before you left that house by the park. It's really not smart to broadcast the fact that you are unprotected, sweetheart. Not smart at all. You need to come with me, Danielle. You don't want to have this boy's blood on your hands, do you?"

Sarah was hyperventilating.

"Let go of the boy, and I will come with you," Dani bargained. She knew full well that if she left with Nathan, she wouldn't be coming back alive. The evidence of that fact had been left in the form of a dead girl in her bed, and the deaths of several other unfortunate young vampires.

"I've come face-to-face with your telekinetic freakdom once before. I won't let him go until I've secured you, and you're unconscious. All I have to do is depress this plunger to kill him for sure at this dose. So, I suggest you get your pretty ass over here, because one of you is coming with me to my master. I can take you alive, or I'll take him and wait to see if he ever wakes again," he threatened with a smile.

J. R. cried and looked at her with a fear that raked her heart. "It's alright, buddy. Don't be afraid." She tried to smile for him, while slowly moving forward. She was trying to work out how to disable that asshole without hurting J. R. Her power was new to her and it worked sporadically. If she tried to subdue Nathan and was too slow, he could kill J. R. She couldn't let him be taken instead of her. If she couldn't handle it safely, she'd have to surrender.

"Don't play with me! If you try anything, I will kill him! I have nothing to lose, and I will not fail again! My master wants you. I am gonna deliver, today. Get in the damn van. And after you're down, I'll release the boy." He tightened his grip on J. R. A thin rivulet of blood ran down J. R.'s throat where the blade bit into his skin. He breathed hard, and tears streamed down his round cheeks.

Debbie held her arm in a death grip. She didn't let go when Dani tried to go to the van. Sarah stepped up and knocked her hand off Dani's arm.

"Let her go, Deborah!" Sarah hissed.

Dani couldn't help smiling at the irony of the situation. "I thought you wanted me to let the men take care of things from now on, Sarah?" She got no response. Dani yanked the delicate chain from her neck and handed the warrior pendant to Debbie. "Please give this to Kayden. Tell him I'm sorry. Make him understand this isn't his fault. Tell him I wish I'd had the chance to see what we could have been together."

Slowly, she turned and walked to the van. Encumbered by the gown she wore, Dani crept in slowly, and the nightmare began. The two women outside looked on, holding their breath.

J. R. continued to cry, blood trickling down his neck. He tried to squirm away from the needle that stung his arm. As she brushed him, he looked up at her in horror. He didn't want her to go. He didn't want her to sacrifice herself for him, and it was plain in his sweet face. He was such a brave boy.

"Facedown on the floor, hands crossed behind your back!" Nathan barked.

"It's going to be alright, J. R. He isn't going to hurt you, honey. Don't worry about me, okay?" She soothed the whimpering child and complied with Nathan's orders.

"Shut up and don't move!" Nathan bellowed, just before she felt the sharp stab and burning in her thigh. It was the syringe. He had drugged her again, but this was different. She slipped away instantly. There would be no defending herself this time.

"Sarah, calm down. I can't understand you." Griffin was on his cell when he strode off the elevator outside of Chase's penthouse and knocked on the door. He had come to check on Danielle Scott. He'd done so frequently. Maybe too frequently, but she seemed to have a pull on everyone she came in contact with, including him. Griffin was fascinated by her abilities and felt a kinship to her he couldn't explain. Maybe it was the hair. He knew how tough it was growing up with that curse, but Danielle wore it beautifully.

Chase opened the door, looking less than happy to see him. Kayden paced a hole in the carpet of the living room.

"Put Debbie on the phone. I have no idea what you're trying to tell me."

Chase stepped back to admit him.

"What the hell is going on, Deb?" Griffin had the attention of Chase and Kayden. They both looked like they'd been waiting for trouble, and it had just arrived. Debbie gave him the rundown of the events that had just elapsed. "How is he? Dear God, how could this happen? How did he disable her? She's very capable of self-defense." Griffin eyed Kayden in anger and listened to Debbie's explanation. "I understand. All three of you need to get to Chase's place right now. I'll call Doc Stevens. Give me the license plate number." Griffin motioned for something to write on. "Alright, get moving. I'll send Kayden to meet you. You're right around the corner. See you in a few." He hung up and cursed before launching the phone across the room. He stood there, fuming for a few seconds. He looked back and forth between Kayden and Chase. "If you two are the future of our race, I'm afraid we're doomed. Do you know where Danielle is right now?" He waited a moment. "No, I don't guess you do. Let me tell you. She gave herself up to a madman in exchange for my son."

All the air was sucked from the room. Kayden blinked rapidly, looking suddenly ill. Chase fell back into the chair behind him and spent a moment trying to catch his breath. It was silent in the room as the three men contemplated the loss of the girl they'd only just found and didn't want to lose.

Chase spoke up first. "It's my fault, Mr. Vaughn. I was watching over Danielle this morning when Sam showed up. I was trying to diffuse the situation when Danielle disappeared." Chase held his head in his hands and rested his elbows on his knees.

"Did anyone think to go look for her?" Griffin asked.

"I searched the area," Kayden explained. "Chase stayed here, in case she came back. Her phone was turned off, but she turned it on long enough to text me that she was fine and would be back soon. So, I returned to wait for her here."

"Both of you, call your fathers and tell them that Danielle has been abducted. I'm calling in Doc. Debbie said J. R. was cut. Kayden, go meet Sarah and Debbie at the dress shop on Fifth Avenue off Main Street and escort them back here. Sarah can fill you in on the way back. Go, now." Griffin had to locate the phone he'd thrown. He walked into the room Danielle had occupied and shut the door for privacy while he dialed the Doc.

In her room, he was overwhelmed by the memory of his first love. The scent of her seemed to linger in that space. He had noticed it several times before. The similarity Danielle's scent bore to Tessa's was staggering to him. From time to time, Griffin could swear Tessa was still out there, somewhere. He thought he could feel her, but he dismissed it as wishful thinking and his deep love for her creeping up on him again. He had to look around the room. After he had lost Tessa and Soleil, the agony was too much to bear. Suddenly, he completely understood why his sister had committed suicide when her mate was murdered. The pain was like losing your soul. It was like losing the part of him that made him alive. It was like not having oxygen to breathe, but living to suffer in its absence. He bonded again immediately in an effort to stop the pain, but it was still there in the background. His bond to Sarah had never been the overwhelming love he hoped would wash away the pain. He felt Tessa's loss every day, in a whisper from a far-off place that said, "I'm here and I still love you."

He was still frozen in the past when Doc answered his call. "Hello? Hello, are you there, Griffin?"

"Yes, I'm here. J. R. has been injured in an abduction attempt. I need you to come to Chase Deidrick's place to have a look at him. When can you be here?"

He confirmed Doc was on the way before hanging up. Griffin sank heavily onto Danielle's bed. He shut his eyes and reveled in the scent and memories of the human woman who'd stolen his heart all those years ago, the woman who still owned his soul.

Kayden sat in silence at Chase's dining room table with his head down. He fought the cold pain in his chest and the tears threatening to shatter his tough-guy image. As soon as the call went out that Dani had been taken, all the warriors fanned out across the city to look for the van that had been used. It had been reported stolen, so the human police were also looking for the vehicle. The human police scanners were being monitored from the Enclave.

Mason and Griffin grimly discussed defense strategies for dealing with the attack that they could expect from whomever would be taking Danielle's life and power that night. How would they defend against someone who could put them down before they could even see him coming? How could they defend against someone who could disable an entire Wrath team at once with just a thought? How could they defend against someone who could read their memories and steal their defense strategies?

Kayden couldn't even begin to pay attention to Mason and Griffin or help plan the next move. His future had just disappeared. She had been stolen in broad daylight, off the street. He should never have trusted Chase to protect her. Chase couldn't even protect her from his own fiancée. Chase had shut himself in his bedroom. He blamed himself for Danielle's disappearance, and he should have.

Debbie entered the dining room with a bag from the dress shop. "Griffin, do you know how to reach Danielle's next of kin? We should notify them and send her belongings." Kayden lifted his head for the conversation.

"Actually, she has no family. There is no next of kin for us to call. Nobody out there will be missing her or wondering where she is tonight," Griffin replied sadly. Chase emerged from his room to stand in the doorway.

"I guess we should give her things to Kayden then?" Debbie walked to the end of the table and set the bag in front of Kayden. She patted him on the back.

"Why would you give it to Kayden?" Chase chimed in.

"She gave me a message for you, Kayden." Debbie turned to address Chase's question. "Her last words before she climbed into that monster's van were for him. She was so brave. She was trying to comfort J. R. the whole time. Right up until he stabbed that needle into her leg." She turned back to Kayden. "Do you want to go talk in the other room?" she asked him.

"No! Tell me now! What did she say?" he barked and then took a deep breath to calm himself. "I'm sorry. I didn't mean to snap at you. I'm just not dealing with this well, Mrs. Deidrick."

"It's alright, Kayden." She stroked his shoulder. "It was clear to me that you and Danielle had a special relationship. She told us you were taking her to the gala as her date, not just as a warrior escort. She was actually wearing the gown she'd tried on for the event when he took her. I guess I should have paid for that gown," Debbie said, her thoughts wandering.

"What did she want you to tell me, Mrs. Deidrick?" Kayden asked, trying to reel her back in.

Debbie reached into her pocket and retrieved the broken necklace with the warrior charm Danielle had given her and dangled it in front of Kayden. He took it and couldn't hold back the tears anymore.

"She asked me to give you this. She wanted you to know that she was sorry and said you shouldn't blame yourself. This wasn't your fault."

Nathan felt the glorious thrill of victory when he pulled away from the curb downtown with his quarry unconscious in the back. He'd stolen the van to pull off the abduction. It had gone perfectly. It had been too easy to grab the boy out of the store when he'd stood by the door, looking bored and obviously unattended. Nathan had received a call from a trusted source with information regarding the girl's general location and absence of any warrior protection. How the information was obtained didn't matter. He had been overjoyed when the call came in. He hadn't heard from his master since the day his master had tossed him unceremoniously onto the street. This was Nathan's chance to get back into his master's good graces.

It was a stroke of luck to witness the exchange of affection and playfulness between Danielle and the unknown boy she embraced. It was just what Nathan needed. He knew she wouldn't let anyone harm a kid, if she could prevent it. All he had to do was get his hands on the kid, and the girl would follow. He hadn't done too much damage to the kid. He'd cut just enough to make the girl move faster at the slightest trace of blood on the kid's neck. He had released the boy as soon as she was out, and slammed the door shut, racing away from the scene. He ran a red light to prevent either of the two witnesses from following him.

In the rearview mirror he could see the girl sprawled on the floor in her fancy gown. He laughed, thinking to himself that she was even gift-wrapped. On the other side of town was an abandoned warehouse near the port. His master used it as a holding tank for his men and hostages, as needed. Nathan would go there to get in touch with his master via his guards. Without a valid phone number or address for his master, Nathan had no other option. The area was quiet, but he proceeded with caution. He knew they would see him coming and attack if he weren't careful.

Rounding the last turn, he was shocked to see yellow police tape across the main entrance to the building. He pulled over and went to try the door. It was unlocked, so he pulled down the tape to enter. The place was vacant. There was no one to report his capture to or help him get in contact with the master. What was he going to do with her? Shit, he wasn't sure how much of the drug he had left, but if he couldn't get her to his master, he was sure he had enough to kill her. He wouldn't allow anyone else to steal his glory and turn her in, and he knew he couldn't hold her once she woke. He cursed and stepped out of the warehouse. Nathan opened the driver-side door and climbed into the seat a second before a shot rang out, shattering the window and spraying glass and hot metal into the van.

Eighteen

Chase couldn't take it anymore. They didn't even have a body, and everyone was acting like she was already dead. She'd only been missing a few hours. The warriors and Wrath were still out searching. Kayden, the mighty warrior, should have been out there with them, but he was apparently happy to sit there and be the grieving widower to a girl who didn't even belong to him. It pained Chase that he'd driven Danielle right into Kayden's arms, and there he sat, clutching her shirt to his face.

If he really loved her, Kayden would know she was still alive, the way Chase did. He would feel her energy buzzing in his mind. If he had ever really felt the depth of her soul, he would know her heart still beat strong.

Taking a deep breath, Chase entered Danielle's room. Her scent was so strong in there, it took his breath away. He hadn't been in that room since she moved into his home. The pajamas she'd worn during breakfast were lying across the bottom of the bed. There was a bottle of pink nail polish on the bedside table that matched the shade of the toes he'd admired while she sat with her feet propped up on the chair at his side. Her closet door was open, and he noticed that her clothes were hung neatly by color from darkest to lightest. He didn't know why, but that made him laugh. He opened one of her drawers, and all the socks and underwear were organized in a similar fashion, neatly folded and separated by graduating color.

Even her dirty clothes were already separated and ready for the laundry room. She just hadn't seemed that anal to him.

Chase flopped down on the bed and decided to see if he could reach her. They had a connection, and if he tried hard enough, maybe he could find her. Chase realized that he was grasping at straws, but it was worth a shot. He concentrated on her and called her to him in his mind. He reached out further and further to find the unique sound of her voice. Chase concentrated on the sense of oneness they shared when they were joined and communicating, as if they were two parts of a whole.

He had to smile when he thought of how she would think of him, unaware that he could hear it plainly. But her ability to control her projections was improving, much to his dismay. She said he smelled like happiness, sunshine, and love. He wanted to be all those things for her and more.

Time passed with no response. The fear built again. Chase demanded she respond to him, but there was nothing but dead air.

He couldn't sit there waiting for news any longer. He got to his feet and went back to the dining room. "She's still out there, Kayden. I can still feel her. I love her and I'm not going to stop looking until I know she's really gone. I know you care for her too." Chase put out a hand to his oldest friend. "Let's go. We can cover twice as much ground together."

It was unfathomable to Mason. His son, Chase, and Kayden, who'd been his son's best friend since childhood, seemed to be in competition over his goddaughter. Mason wondered if they would fight over her if they knew she was half-human.

He should have told them everything, but he didn't. It would do more harm than good now if Danielle was really gone. So many lives would be affected. And for what reason, if she wasn't there anymore? Griffin's bond to Sarah would have been in question, because he had already been bonded to Tessa. Griffin's reputation would have been damaged, due to the scandal of having had a human mate. Griffin would have also likely killed Mason for keeping the secret all these years.

Tessa would blame him. He'd promised to protect Dani, and he'd assured Tessa no harm would come to her under the protection of the warriors. How could he tell her mother that Dani was gone?

He needed to go to Tessa. This wasn't something he could do over the phone. But he was hesitant. Chase was right. They didn't have a body. What if she fought her way out? What if she was released, like the Prince girl had been? On the other hand, if his child were missing, he would want to know now, not when it was all over. Tessa had been through so much pain in the past twenty-one-plus years. He did not want to put any additional stress on her until he had some solid facts to tell her.

Chase had come to him repeatedly, looking for a way out of the betrothal to Samantha. Mason believed Chase was in love with another girl, but Chase had never told him the girl's name. Mason hated to see his son so unhappy, but the union was very important to the houses and the future of the nation. At the time Mason consoled himself with the knowledge that after Chase was bonded, he would be happy, and he wouldn't think about the other girl anymore.

If he'd known before that Danielle was Chase's new love, it would have changed everything. Tessa would need to be willing to go public with their story, but he was sure Dani's happiness would be the most important thing to her. Danielle was Griffin's daughter too. Chase could bond to Danielle, and it would have the same meaning as if it were Samantha, with one exception: Dani wasn't a full-blooded vampire.

How would Griffin feel about the switch? Mason suspected Sarah would lose her mind if Chase selected the half-breed child of Griffin's secret first union instead of one of her girls.

Mason was focusing on what could have been, instead of the reality of the situation in front of him. He would need to help his boy mourn the loss of his first real love if she didn't come home. It all brought to mind the memory of the agony he'd felt in Tessa's touch, the agony he'd felt in Griffin so long ago. Chase was clearly in love with Danielle. Mason had never seen him so passionate about anything in his life.

Debbie came to sit with Mason.

"Did you know about Chase's affection for Danielle?" she asked, taking his hand. God, he loved his mate so deeply. He prayed he'd never know the kind of loss Griffin had suffered and that his son was now possibly facing.

"No, but I did know he didn't want to bond with Samantha because of another female." He threaded his fingers with hers.

"I spoke with Danielle about Chase earlier today. I was taken aback by her description of him. I intended to speak to him about her. Maybe talk to you about having her moved from his home, because of the way Sarah was reacting to her staying with Chase. Seeing his behavior makes me ashamed of myself for denying him love. I guess it's too late now. Even if it weren't, we need him to honor our agreement with Griffin."

And there it was. Even if Mason had known about Danielle and Chase, he would still hold him to the engagement, because there were too many variables and what-ifs concerning Danielle. They had agreed to do all they could to fulfill Leann Vaughn's prophecy. She said a child from the house of Vaughn and a child from the house of Deidrick would bond in love and bring an end to the fear of their children and the pain of their loss.

It might have been crazy to believe it would work, but the children were worth the risk. Mason had to believe that fate would take over and bring about any changes that needed to take place without his further interference.

Every warrior who was on duty, and many who weren't, including Kayden, spent the day out patrolling and sweeping the surrounding area for the stolen van used by the vamp hunter. Dani had become an unofficial warrior, due to her bravery and self-sacrifice. There was an added urgency to the search because they were looking for one of their own. Warriors were a loyal sort. Most of them lived side by side and raised their families in a close-knit community, a true brotherhood. As Dani was their first little sister, they were a bit protective of her, but she was more than a little sister to Kayden.

None of the single warriors believed Kayden would hold on to Dani for very long. There was actually a pool going with guesses as to how long it would take Kayden to screw it up. Kayden didn't give two shits what anybody thought of him but Dani.

He'd nearly collapsed when he believed she was gone forever. It had taken Chase's reassurance that she was still alive to shake him from the daze he'd sunken into. He couldn't sit there waiting for news. He had to go out and get her back. After a day of unsuccessful hunting, coldness had settled over Kayden. It was a chill he suspected would never recede if Dani wasn't found very soon.

Sitting at a red light with his bike vibrating beneath him, Kayden was lost in thought, and he almost didn't notice the white van cross the intersection in front of him until the hair on the back of his neck stood up. Chase saw the van at the same time and reached over from his bike to tap Kayden's arm and nod toward it. He and Chase had temporarily put aside their differences to join the hunt, and it looked like their refusal to stop searching might have just paid off.

They turned to follow the van on its journey across town. When he was close enough to see the van's plates, he knew they had their man. Actually, it was the woman he was after. The man was going down for his actions. Of course he knew his orders were to apprehend the assailant for questioning and punishment by the council, but the guy was a proven danger to the vampire race. Too many of their young were dead because of this asshole. He was human, not a vampire, so he had no true right to a trial before the council. The first clear shot Kayden got, the bastard was going down hard.

The van finally pulled off onto a side road. It would be harder to follow him without being noticed on their bikes, but the good news was there were only a few roads leading in and out of the area by the port. It seemed like a good time to call for backup. Kayden called the Enclave dispatch center with his position and positive ID of the suspect's vehicle. That place would be crawling with warriors soon enough. He took one road, and Chase split off and took the other.

All he needed before taking this bastard out was confirmation that Dani was still in the van. If not, he would beat her location out of the vermin.

After giving the van enough space to reach its location, he followed and found it parked outside of an abandoned warehouse. He moved in on foot. The driver was nowhere in sight, so he pulled the pistol from its holster hidden under his jacket and crept around the corner keeping as low as possible, until he reached the back of the van. Peeking in the window, he could see Dani sprawled facedown on the otherwise-empty floor of the van.

The door of the warehouse slammed against the wall, and he heard some unintelligible cursing from the front of the van. Perfect. The bastard would never know what hit him. Kayden waited for the piece of shit to climb into the vehicle. Without hesitation,

Kayden crept up to serve his brand of justice, but he was too late. A shot rang out from just to Kayden's left, shattering the window and striking the ex-bartender in the head. One shot, and it was over.

Kayden turned with his gun still raised and ready to fire. Chase stood there, still wearing his helmet, and the sight of Nathan's corpse reflected in the black glass of his shield. They both lowered their pistols and Chase flipped up his shield. He stared blankly at the male he'd just killed. Neither the council nor any warrior would hold the shooting against Chase. It would be simple to explain the need to secure the hostage at any cost. They would say the guy had attempted to flee, again. He would have driven away in another moment if he hadn't been stopped. Kayden would corroborate the story for Chase. Kayden was just pissed he hadn't moved faster and taken the shot himself. Shit, he had years of training with his father, and he hadn't even heard Chase creep up on him.

They turned their attention to the back of the van. Opening the door, they found Dani barefoot in a black gown. She was beautiful, even in her disheveled state. He and Chase checked her over for injuries that would prevent them from moving her. She seemed all in one piece, but unconscious. Empty syringes were scattered around the back of the van. Kayden wondered how much of the drug Nathan had given her. So much for being the superwoman with fangs everyone believed her to be. She was vulnerable and fragile now.

Any minute the others would arrive, and surely Kayden's father would be leading the cavalry. Chase holstered his gun, clearly in shock. As far as Kayden knew, Chase had never fired a weapon in his life, and today he'd killed a man in defense of the woman they both loved.

Kayden saw other vehicles begin to filter in from different directions and surround the scene. For the second time that day Chase reached out his hand to Kayden. They held each other's forearms, just like old times. They'd brought her home together, but their truce would end the moment Dani was safely delivered to the Enclave.

Nineteen

Dani had been unconscious for two days. Kayden sat at her bedside, holding her small hand in both of his and listening to the steady beeping of the machines connected to her. The helplessness was overwhelming. He was supposed to be a warrior. He should have been strong and fearless. He'd been anything but that for the past several days. He'd been scared to death of losing her.

Warriors were supposed to protect their charges and deal with losses as they came. He'd failed at both duties and was waiting for the consequences. His father had likely not approached him yet due to Dani's condition, but he'd the distinct feeling he would be relieved of his charge.

Doc had him talking to her and trying to reach into her mind the way Chase had, but it didn't work. Kayden had never done it before, but he wanted it to work so badly that he refused to take a break at all. He'd even allowed his mother to bring him bags of blood, instead of heading out to hunt. It was unthinkable to him before, but it was better than leaving her again. It worried Kayden that Doc spent so much time at the Enclave tending to Dani. It was out of the ordinary and made Kayden wonder if he was holding back information regarding Dani's prognosis.

"How is she doing?" Doc queried when he and Griffin entered the room.

"No changes," Kayden replied, moving to allow Doc to look

her over. Doc went through the normal exam he had performed several times a day.

Griffin stepped up to the other side of the bed and ran his hand through Dani's streaked hair. "How are you doing, kid? Can you hear me?" Unexpectedly, her heart rate picked up, and the beeping of the heart monitor became faster. Doc and Griffin looked at each other.

"Danielle, can you hear me?" Doc asked, and again her heart kicked.

"Maybe he's right," Doc said to Griffin.

"Who is right? What are you talking about? Do you think she can hear us?" Kayden asked. A look passed between the two elders. There was something they weren't telling him. "What is going on?"

"Kayden." Doc seemed to steel himself for a fight. "You know Chase has been here waiting to see her."

"Here's the problem, son." Griffin came around the bed and rested a hand on Kayden's shoulder. "Chase says Dani has been trying to talk to you since yesterday, but she can't reach you. He can hear her, as long as he stays close. She's been reluctant to talk to him, but today she says she's lost. She can't find her way out of wherever she is in there, and she can't reach you to help her get out."

A light came on in Kayden's head. Memories of seeing Chase and Dani in Chase's bed, Chase holding her mostly naked body, rushed into Kayden's head and burned him. "It's comparable to a coma in some ways, I believe." Doc shook his head. Dani's heart rate kicked again, and Doc took her hand. "The brain will shut down to give itself time to heal. She's in there and she can hear us, as we suspect some coma patients can. Sometimes they wake up spontaneously after years of being under. Sometimes it just takes the right trigger to get their brains firing again." Then he looked past Kayden to Griffin. "We are going to need to try a blood transfusion, or she won't have the strength to fight. She hasn't fed in at least three days." He left the room at a clipped pace.

It was quiet for a long time. Both men stood and watched the sleeping girl. "Something my father taught me comes to mind," Kayden said. "Being a warrior means making decisions in the best interest of your charge. Being a mate means doing that, plus putting your mate's needs before your own. I know what needs to be done. I just hate the idea of not being able to provide everything and anything my female needs." He looked over his shoulder at Griffin.

Kayden sat there, brooding over the idea of Dani being in close physical contact with Chase. Kayden never had a jealous thought in his life, until Dani came along. She made him crazy and possessive. He'd dealt with her living under Chase's roof in the past for her safety, because he'd had no choice in the matter. But giving Chase permission to touch her made his skin crawl. What else could he do? Her needs were more important than his jealous pride.

"I won't be gone long, baby," he whispered next to Dani's ear. "I guess I'm gonna need to go, so you can get some help. I'll be back soon." He kissed her lips softly and turned to Griffin. "Tell my father I'm going to take a break. Please have someone call me if she wakes." Kayden left the room with one last look over his shoulder.

In the hall, Chase paced and listened to the soft whimpering in his mind. He could feel her confusion and distress. She was getting further and further away. His Lovely was lost and couldn't find her way out of the darkness. As time passed, she became completely silent. Even the soft whimpering faded away. Chase was deep in thought, trying to talk to Danielle, when Koren startled him, poking her head around the corner.

"Alright, let's see what you can do. Kayden's out of the room, but who knows for how long, so let's get moving." She prodded him into action.

Chase's heart leapt in his chest, and he tore down the hall ahead of Koren. At the door to Danielle's room, he was met by Gage, who gave him a stern look that was clearly a nonverbal threat. All Chase cared about was getting to Danielle.

The room was dark and quiet, except for the beeping of the heart monitor. She looked so small and fragile in the bed that was meant to hold warriors three times her size. He lowered the bed rail and pulled off his shirt. The last time, Doc had said skin contact might help. He crawled into the bed next to Danielle and began to search, reaching out to her verbally and telepathically, as he had before. His bare chest against her arm, holding her hand and resting one of his on her forehead, just like before, he called to her.

"Lovely, I am here now. Can you hear me? I've come to find you." He said it over and over again, until he noticed the heart monitor beeping faster. He lifted his head and said, "Danielle, can you hear me? Come toward the sound of my voice."

Then, it started just as it had before. First, he got pictures only. She was flashing clips of J. R. with a knife to his throat and a syringe in his arm. It felt like a question, somehow.

"J. R. is fine. He didn't even need stitches, but he's been worried about you. I think he's still here with Griffin. If you wake up, you can talk to him."

Then, he listened but there was no sound. He saw flashes of her memory of being loved and pleasured in his bed. Then the next morning when they'd had breakfast. It felt warm and happy. She was enjoying their time together. He saw himself through her eyes and was surprised at her view of him. He could feel the affection for him that she usually suppressed. Then, he saw Sam wearing her best bitch mask. "Don't worry about Sam. I'm very sorry you felt the need to leave alone because of that situation. I blame myself for what happened to you, but none of that matters now, Lovely."

I was hungry. I needed to feed. That is not your fault, Chase, she acquitted him.

"I hear you now, Lovely. Keep moving toward my voice. Doc says you should try to visualize an exit door. It may help. We can find the door, together." It had been too long since he'd heard her mental voice.

I don't want you taking the blame for my crap. He heard her agitation with him, and it was wonderful. He would take what he could get, even if it was annoyance.

"You wouldn't have left alone, if not for the rude interruption, and I left you in order to deal with her."

He felt a flash of something hot and angry from her. *She is your mate. What else are you supposed to do?* He could feel her getting closer to him.

"She is not my mate yet, Lovely, and you know I don't love her. You know I only want you. I wish you would give me a chance to rectify the situation, before you write me off. I think I'm making some headway. I've got my mom on my side now.

"Please come to me. We can talk about this later. It's time to get you out of there. You need to feed and so do I," he coaxed.

Then, he had the strangest sensation of being touched, but it was in his mind. She grabbed on to him and held tight. There was no way to explain being telepathically embraced by another person. Especially one he craved so deeply. She wrapped herself around him, and he held on to her for dear life. It was like floating in a dark cloud with her very soul snuggled to his chest. They just hung there, unspeaking, entwined with each other's thoughts. He heard her take a deep breath, and her eyelashes brushed his cheek. He didn't move a muscle. She felt too good in his mind to release her and not be allowed to touch her again.

"Thank you," she said aloud.

"Shhh . . . Don't speak, Lovely. Just let me hold you a while longer. As soon as they realize you are awake, they'll make me leave." He kissed her swiftly and nibbled her ear.

"We've got to stop meeting this way. I don't like this damsel-in-distress business," Dani smiled up at him and croaked, her voice rough from disuse.

"I don't mind. It's the only time we spend together anymore," he chuckled.

"I'm going to miss seeing you." Her smile faded.

"You don't need to miss me, Lovely." He brushed her cheek again.

"I can't stay in your home any longer. It is not fair to either of us to continue interfering with the progression of each other's life. You need to start thinking about your mate, and I'm in the way. Do you know the last time I was here"—she gestured around the room—"your future mother-in-law sat in that chair for two hours, making wedding plans in front of me. She wanted me to know who you belonged to. When I was at the dress shop with her and your mom, she made sure to rub it in my face again and do all she could to make sure she brought the bonding up with Debbie every chance she got. She thinks I am a threat to her daughter's happiness. I did some fishing of my own and learned that there are serious and lasting financial and social penalties for breaking a contract. I don't want to cause you any more trouble than I already have." A single tear slid down her cheek. She wiped it away quickly, blinking away the evidence of her sadness.

Chase's eyes were wide with disbelief. No wonder he'd had so much difficulty getting closer to Danielle. She'd been dealing with interference from Sarah, Sam, and Kayden.

Ever since her last brush with death a week before, Dani had camped out at the Enclave. She moved out of the infirmary and into a private room with its own bathroom. It was meant for high-ranking visitors to the Enclave. It was like a nice hotel room but more comfortable, with a sofa and a little kitchen area. Koren had it all arranged for her. Dani believed Koren had picked up on the tension between Kayden, Chase, and her. Koren had graciously found a way to give Dani some space to breathe.

Kayden was none too happy when he was removed from her detail. His father had said it was a conflict of interest. Gage told Kayden he couldn't properly protect a person he was so attached to. Kayden was going out on patrols with other warriors and rotating the duty of guarding the council members' homes as well.

Dani was assigned to Darren, which only aggravated Kayden more. But she couldn't find a fault in the guy, other than his conceited nature. Kayden was leery of the reasons why Darren was her guardian. Darren was a Wrath team leader and by rights shouldn't be expected to take on a charge.

Dani found Darren to be pleasant, and appreciated the fact that he didn't hover. He checked in with her several times a day and only really followed her when she needed to leave the Enclave, unless she was going to Kayden's house, in which case she had Kayden and Gage to babysit her. She didn't resent being followed, after the day at the dress shop. She'd climbed into that van believing she was going to die. She didn't die, but not waking up had been even more terrifying.

Darren had also been teaching her to use a gun in his spare time. "Anyone you can't stop with that pretty little brain of yours will stop when you pump some lead in their ass," he told her.

Dani was anxious beyond all reason. She had been invited to be Kayden's date for the bonding ceremony of his cousin. She couldn't wait to get out of the Enclave for a while. It was also exciting to see how the bonding thing worked, and Kayden promised to explain everything to her. She was nervous about meeting so many of his family members and other vamps in general, because she was still expecting some supervamp to come along and know with one look that she was a fraud. She tried to remember she had never claimed to be anything other than herself. Everyone just assumed, and she went along with it, but that wouldn't matter much when it all came out.

The ceremony would be a formal affair, so she decided on a tea-length, deep-purple dress with intricate beading on the bodice for the evening event. Koren said it was a perfect choice and gave Dani a gorgeous updo, braiding the streaks to show them off in an elegant twist that she arranged effortlessly. Just as Dani slipped into her heels, there was a knock at the door. Her date was right on time. But as soon as she opened the door, it was obvious there was a problem. Kayden leaned against the doorjamb in his fatigues, not at all appropriate wedding attire.

"Good God, you're gorgeous." He swept her up into a tight embrace.

"Why aren't you dressed?" she asked, trying to catch her breath.

"I have to go cover for a warrior whose mate is having a baby. They told me an hour ago. Being the low man on the totem pole really sucks." He began to lead her in a dance to music only he could hear. They spun around her room and laughed.

"I can't believe I have to let you go out looking like this without me." He poked out his luscious lower lip in a cute little pout.

She was totally charmed when he looked at her so adoringly with those beautiful hazel eyes. He had been sweating, but his natural woodsy scent was still wonderful. Dani couldn't help putting her face in his chest to breathe him in.

"I guess I'm not going either. I can't go alone, and I don't want your dad to have to worry about me all night instead of dancing the night away with Koren. She's really looking forward to the evening."

"Fine by me." He perked up. "Do you need help getting out of this dress?"

Things between them had been progressing quickly—more quickly than she preferred—but it seemed like Kayden had been pushing harder to move things to the next level since her release from the infirmary. Kayden was a gorgeous man, and Dani was well aware that he'd never had trouble getting a woman. She wasn't ready for the next step, but she feared losing him if she didn't get her head in the game soon. Judging by his hard length pressing against her hip, she was swiftly running out of time.

He kissed her and toyed with the spaghetti strings on her dress, slipping them from her shoulders, her dress falling to the floor. She stood before him in heels, a black thong, and matching push-up bra. He sucked wind. She stood there like an idiot, gaping at him. A low growl that was actually frightening rumbled from his chest. He pounced on her before she even saw him move, pressing her into the mattress and crushing her lips to his. His tongue explored her mouth, tasting her thoroughly. The growl became a purr, and he licked down her neck to the cleavage overflowing the bra and nibbled her ample curves. Kayden had her from zero to nearly nude in the space of a moment.

She pushed on his chest, but he was engrossed in his task. "Kayden, I don't think I'm ready for this just yet." Just as he pressed his mouth to her breast, a loud knock at the door shattered his trance and he seemed to remember himself. He lifted himself and looked down her body, then into her eyes, like he was begging for permission she just wasn't ready to give.

The knock came again, more demanding this time. "Danielle, are you ready to go? We need to leave if you don't want to be late." A deep voice vibrated through the door.

Kayden froze. "You have got to be kidding me." He went to the door with his shirt untucked and in obvious disarray. He cracked the door. "What are you doing here, Darren?" He scowled. Dani hopped up off of the bed and rearranged her clothes.

"I was directed by Gage to accompany Danielle to a bonding tonight and try to blend in, so as not to embarrass her. Since you're not going, and Gage's attention will be on his mate, he wants her to be escorted. Your parents are waiting for us in their car. Tough break for you, dude." Darren was smug.

Kayden clenched his teeth. "She isn't dressed. Give us a minute." He slammed the door.

"What's that about?" she asked while hunting for a shoe that had ended up under the bed.

He returned to nuzzle her neck and looked her over appraisingly. "You are perfect. Let me at least walk you out?"

She grabbed her clutch and shawl. "Did you hear Darren?" he asked with a scowl.

"If you want me to stay home, I will. It's not a problem," she assured him, looking toward the door. She knew he hated the time she spent with Darren.

"No, I don't want you to sit here bored because I have to work. Besides, I know Mom is looking forward to introducing you to her friends and our family. Apparently no one believes I'm capable of maintaining a steady girlfriend, and she's proud to have such a lovely example to rub their noses in." He brushed her cheek and continued down her collarbone to the swell of her breast, testing the weight and kissing her senseless.

"If he touches you, I'll kill him," he whispered against her ear.

"I won't be allowing anyone to touch me." She grinned.

"Gage is about to leave. Should I tell him we'll drive separately?" Darren bellowed, rapping hard on the door.

Kayden shot an angry look at the door and hissed, "In your dreams." He lifted Dani against his chest and walked to the door, nuzzling her neck and making her squirm. Darren moved from the doorway to allow them to pass. Kayden carried her halfway out of the building like that, until she lost a shoe. He went down on one knee to put it back on for her, like she was Cinderella. Darren rolled his eyes and made impatient noises. Kayden was showing off to prove a point, but Dani didn't mind. After the way Darren had acted the first time she came to the Enclave, he deserved to be put in his place.

Driving away from the Enclave, as Kayden watched from the curb, hurt her heart. He looked so downtrodden. Dani nearly asked them to stop the car so she could get out, but Koren was happily chatting away about all the people she couldn't wait to introduce her to. Kayden was right. Koren would have been upset if Dani had stayed behind.

It wasn't a long ride to the place where the bonding was being held. The house reminded her of the Vaughn estate, but Koren said it was a country club of sorts—a members-only club to keep out unwanted human witnesses to blood exchanges and feedings that happened there regularly.

They were escorted to their seats in a room that was similar to a chapel. It was beautifully decorated with bare, white trees from the last pew all the way to the front on both ends of each row. Entering the center aisle reminded her of the trees at school that arched over the walkway and touched like lovers reaching for one another. Everything from ceiling to floor was covered in sheer, white fabric, and all of the flowers were white. The whole room was illuminated by white candles. The effect was stunning. It was like a winter wonderland by candlelight.

She couldn't help noticing the way Gage and Koren snuggled together and looked at each other lovingly. Dani had to work hard at pushing all thoughts of Chase from her mind. She missed him terribly, and seeing all of the happy couples in the room had her imagining the impossible again.

When the music started, and the doors in the rear of the chapel were opened, everyone stood and turned to see the bride. She was gorgeous in a white, old-Hollywood-style gown. It was beautiful, not puffy or frilly, but elegant and sleek. Her short, brown hair finished the look with finger waves. She carried no flowers, but her left arm from the elbow to her wrist was woven with white ribbons hanging at long lengths. The bride held the loose ends between her hands.

The groom also wore a suit of pure white. He waited anxiously at the front of the chapel.

There were no bridesmaids or groomsmen. Only the bride and groom stood in front of their friends and family to share their devotion to each other. There wasn't even a preacher, but an elder member of the council, who introduced himself as Lloyd Vaughn, standing before the couple. Dani suddenly realized that he must be her grandfather, and she had to catch her breath.

"Friends and family, we are here to witness the bonding of these two people, who have agreed to enter into a union of mutual love and spiritual solidarity of their own free will for eternity. In this life and the next, they will nurture one another's mind, body, and spirit. Please join me in celebrating the miracle of their love and the future they will build as mates and best friends for all time."

His rich, joyous voice was so sincere. It made everyone smile at the honest beauty of the coming ritual. He bowed to the couple and left them at the altar. When he stepped down, Dani saw the white-draped table displaying two small ornamental daggers.

The bride and groom faced each other with bright smiles. Dani had to pull out a tissue when tears of joy began to slide down the groom's face. The couple joined left hands as if they would shake hands. The bride wrapped the lengths of white ribbon hanging from her arm around their joined hands and up the groom's wrist and forearm.

"Elliot, I vow to love you for the whole of my existence. I vow to protect you to my last breath. I vow to cherish the gift of your returned love for all time. I vow to always remain grateful for the man who will from this day forth be the one and only mate of my soul." She smiled through happy tears and beamed up at her mate.

The groom smiled down into the face of his bride with unmistakable admiration. He wrapped the lengths of white ribbon that hung from his wrist around her arm and up her wrist and forearm before he began to speak.

"Krista, I vow to love you for the whole of my existence. I vow to protect you to my last breath. I vow to cherish the gift of your returned love for all time. I vow to always remain grateful for the woman who will from this day forth be the one and only mate of my soul."

They both reached with their free hands for the daggers on the table. Dani had no idea what was about to happen, and, frankly, she was nervous. Both the bride and groom lowered their heads and pressed the blades to their lower lips, making the slightest of cuts. Then they put down the daggers. They lifted their faces and Dani saw the thin lines of blood on their lips. They kissed for a long minute, sharing the very source of each other's lives. They tasted the very essence of the other's being.

She was transfixed by the intimate exchange. The couple broke apart and stared at each other in wonder and awe of the moment. The room erupted into cheers of happiness and laughter. Everyone began filing out into the lobby, but the bride and groom never moved. They just stood there, looking into each other's eyes.

Dani was confused. In a human wedding, the bride and groom always left first. Darren leaned down with a wrinkled forehead and asked, "Is this the first bonding you've attended?"

She nodded.

He whispered, as he led her toward the rear of the chapel with a hand on the small of her back, "This is a very powerful moment for the couple. They'll need a few minutes alone before they can share each other with the rest of the party."

Before she left the room, Dani turned to look at the couple one more time. They stood with their lips still just inches apart, gazing lovingly at each other, as if the rest of the world no longer existed for them. There seemed to be nothing but the two of them and their eternal bond.

Twenty

The celebration after the bonding was much like she would have expected at a human wedding reception. There was a cocktail hour in the lobby while the newly mated couple enjoyed some time alone. Dani was introduced to practically everyone. Koren was so proud to show off her son's girlfriend and the newly dubbed "Angel of Wrath," who was oh so powerful, blah, blah, blah. Dani really hated the attention.

Darren had stuck close, seeming to assess everyone she encountered without being obvious about it. He looked like all the other very attractive, well-built vampires at the ritual. But she was sure most people knew who he was by their cautious reactions and unwillingness to get too close to him. He had a bad reputation for being short-tempered and overly aggressive. He didn't seem to enjoy his duties of the evening, given the wary looks he shot around the room and the exasperated sighs he released from time to time. She felt sorry for ruining his evening with his babysitting duty.

After making a full circuit of the room, she tried, unsuccessfully, to pry herself away from Koren. Darren took a moment to stare aimlessly out the window onto the beautifully moonlit grounds. Dani was reintroduced to several couples she'd already spent time chatting with, until she managed to back out of the group.

Someone grabbed her hand and pulled gently to turn her around. She expected it to be Darren, but it was odd for him to take her hand. He had a way of leading her around by the small of her back, but he had never taken her hand. To her surprise, she found Chase at the other end of her arm. She hadn't seen him until then, and, Lord, he was gorgeous in a dark suit. He flashed that devilish smile that made her look too long at his lips and remember the taste of sunshine and happiness.

"W-what are you doing here?" she stuttered.

He shifted his eyes toward Darren, who still had his back to her at the window about ten feet away. He winked and pulled her quietly out of the crowded room and into a darkened room that wasn't being used for the event. It was quiet but for the faint sounds of the partygoers and kitchen staff busily preparing for the meal to come. He didn't say anything at first. He just looked at her from below those long, dark lashes, his ocean-blue eyes lighting a flame in her core. Dani turned pink under the heat of his obviously appraising stare. Still holding her hand, he spun her around and pulled her into an embrace that lifted her feet up off the ground, her ankles crossed and feet dangling.

A nervous giggle escaped, and she wrapped her arms around his neck.

He broke his silence with a barely audible whisper. "I've missed you, Lovely. You're so beautiful. I just had to touch you. I needed to hold you. It's been awful for me since you left." He took a deep breath, nuzzling at her neck and sending chills down her spine. He seemed to enjoy having that effect on her and kissed the gooseflesh on her shoulder. "You smell just like heaven, a vanilla-and-lavender heaven."

"I didn't see you at the ritual," she stated stupidly. Why, oh why, couldn't she feel this giddy, brain-cell-robbing passion for Kayden?

He put her feet back on the ground but did not back away. "Elliot is a friend of mine. He was among the group of guys I grew up with. I spent a lot of time with Kayden, and his cousin was often around. I skipped the ceremony because . . . " He paused, looking like he hadn't meant to really answer.

"What?" She prodded him.

"I didn't think I could handle it. I knew you and Kayden were coming, and I didn't think I could watch the ritual and not think about you. Then I would have to see you with him." He looked away.

This was bad for both of them. She had to get away from him. Why had she followed him to this darkened room? "I'm sorry, Chase. After your own ritual, it won't be a problem for you anymore. Then I will be left to suffer alone." She smirked and tried to pretend it was no big deal. "Don't be offended when I don't attend your wedding. Not that I was expecting an invitation anyway. I better get back before they call out the guard to look for me." She pulled out of his grasp, but Chase caught her arm and tugged her deeper into the shadows.

"Don't be like that, Lovely. We don't have much time. Let's not argue."

His thumb brushed across the pulse in her wrist. It was a comforting gesture, but as he continued to stroke her pulse with the pad of his finger, her body began to ache. She wanted him to caress her entire body with those strong, restraining hands.

"Let go of me." Her voice wavered. It sounded more like a question than a demand.

"No, I won't. You don't really want me to release you, Lovely, do you?" He tangled his fist in the loose curls at the base of her skull and tugged, forcing her to look up at him. Her lips were parted, her eyes wide and full of the same longing that tormented him. She wanted him just as badly as he needed her. She was fighting it, but he couldn't hold back the wave of hunger that rolled over him. His mouth lowered to hers and she made no move to get away from him. He nibbled and licked, tasting her vanilla sweetness until she gave in to his gentle but sure assault. She made a little humming sound in the back of her throat and sucked his tongue into her mouth. That had him instantly hard.

Chase slowly backed her toward a pillar and pressed her against it. He released her hair to lift her higher, wedging her right where he wanted her. Danielle's hands fisted in his hair and pulled. Chase felt out of control. He hadn't intended to seduce Danielle when he tugged her into the vacant dining room. He just wanted to hold her for a moment, touch her, and try to numb some of the ache that had taken up residence in his chest since she moved out of his condo. But once he had her alone, it was all he could do not to rip off her sexy little dress and show her whom she belonged to.

They held each other tight, completely letting go of their senses. The murmured sound of voices, the clanking of pots and dishes from the kitchens, and her inhibitions all faded away when he began to rock his hips against her soft, heated center. Danielle's legs parted for him and he pressed in tighter, enjoying her quite moans of pleasure when he rocked against her, hitting her sweet little clit with every thrust.

Chase's heart thundered in his ears. Their gasping breaths mingled and their tongues tangled. Danielle pushed back against him, rubbing herself against his stiff rod. Oh God, she was going to come for him, and Chase was sure he would follow her and embarrass himself for the first time in his life.

She was so sexy, so lush. Chase was addicted to the taste of her. She pulled away from their hot joining of mouths and moaned his name over and over while she bucked against him and found her release. He breathed deeply and gritted his teeth to hold back his orgasm while she rode out her passion. Chase smiled, once he was sure he could hold it together. Giving her pleasure was an unexpected gift and something he would be thinking about for a long time. He kissed her face, her eyes, and the corners of her mouth while she came down and regained her breath.

She stared up at him like she had no idea where she was, and that gave him the greatest pleasure. He liked knowing he could affect her the way she did him, leaving her breathless and off balance. Chase had just stepped back and righted her clothing when one of the double doors to the dining room banged open and Darren charged into the room.

The door flew open and Dani jumped like she'd been caught with her hand in the cookie jar. Darren looked ready to kill. This was the warrior who frightened and intimidated almost everyone he came into contact with. It was a side of him she hadn't yet seen. He spotted them and stormed over to sweep her up in one arm and turned in a protective stance to scan the room, gun at the ready in the other hand.

"No need to pull a gun. We were just talking." Chase stepped back, hands up in surrender. Dani was grateful Chase didn't argue. This wasn't the time or place for a scene.

Darren didn't respond to him. He backed out of the room and set Dani on her feet in the hall. Holstering his gun, he looked her over in an oddly possessive way and seemed to be checking for injury. By that time, Chase was watching from the doorway. Darren straightened her dress where it had ridden up a little from him snatching her up so abruptly, then tucked a stray curl behind her ear. She was still dazed by what had just happened between her and Chase. She hadn't really registered the oddity of Darren's behavior until he took her chin in his hand and checked her face, for what, she didn't know. Then he took her hand and tugged her back toward the party.

"It is time for dinner. Let's get seated, and I will get you a drink." He smiled and walked faster.

She looked over her shoulder at Chase, who was about as astounded as she was by such an unprofessional exchange. As if he touched her that way regularly. Chase followed them down the hall, making low growling noises.

The dining hall was decorated similarly to the chapel, with arches of trees and white cloth covering every surface. The striking difference was the lighting. The room was bathed in red. It was a sharp contrast to the winter white of the chapel. The red light washed everyone and everything in a beautifully sensual glow. Darren pulled out her chair and she sat next to Koren.

"I was wondering where you'd gotten off to, sweetheart."

Darren went to the bar. Chase was watching him disdainfully from the doorway.

"I was talking to Chase in the hall." Gage's head came around like a whip. She saw no sense in hiding the fact that she'd been with Chase. It was likely that Darren would mention it.

"I hadn't seen Chase. I didn't think he was going to attend." He scowled.

"He told me Elliot, Kayden, and he had grown up together. He was happy to come celebrate his friend's joyous day with him."

"He will be celebrating his own joy soon, from what I have heard," Koren added. "He will be bonded to Griffin's daughter. That'll be a happy day for both houses," she prattled.

Dani could see Gage watching her for a reaction to her comment. She was careful not to give him one, even though the reminder stung painfully. Especially after the time she'd just spent in Chase's arms. Dani was ashamed of her inability to control herself in his presence. She also now had the added guilt of having stepped out on Kayden again.

Darren returned to the table with two glasses of red wine. Good thing, because she needed a drink. She put the glass to her lips and was shocked when the delicious red liquid exploded in her mouth.

"This has blood in it?" she sputtered.

"It does, so take it easy. The mixture of the blood and wine goes to your head. Would you prefer I get you something else?"

"No. It's good. I just didn't expect it." She blushed. Blood made her hot and giddy. Maybe it made her too hot for that gathering, but one glass wouldn't hurt.

"Please forgive me. I forget you're not familiar with our customs. Did anyone explain the ritual to you beforehand?" he inquired.

"No, I don't know much about it, but I am curious about the process. Kayden was going to explain some things to me tonight."

Music began to play, and couples shuffled out to the floor. It was beautiful instrumental music that somehow sounded classical and modern at the same time. Gage rose from his seat, and, with an elegant bow, he extended his hand to his mate, who took it with a joyful smile of pleasure. Darren explained that the first dance was meant for the mated pairs at the celebration. They took the floor before the newly mated couple. It was supposed to bring luck and wisdom to the couple when they took the floor and absorbed all the residual energy and joy left by the experienced mates. The amazing sight of all the tenderness and love on the floor from so many couples warmed the rest of the room. Dani wished the human race was so lucky to mate for life and love to the end, the way vampires did.

Darren wrote on a small slip of paper. She had noticed the papers and a pencil at the center of the table when they sat down.

"What is that?" she asked.

He grinned and looked at her from the corner of his eye, dropping the paper in a box carried by the bride's mother. "It's another tradition I'm surprised Kayden didn't inform you of beforehand. All the single men and women write the name of another single person they would like to dance with on the paper, along with their own. No one will know which one requested the dance except the couple, and oftentimes they have both requested each other. You must dance with everyone who writes down your name. It's bad luck for the new couple if you refuse. It isn't free, though. You must pay for the privilege of the dance, and all the money goes to the new mates. So you are doing a great service to them and bringing them blessings of prosperity. The female's mother collects the requests, and the male's mother will come around with a list of people in order of the amount they paid to dance with you. The male and female who bring in the most money for the new mates will dance the second dance along with the bride and groom, and then everyone else is invited to join the couple on the floor. Many beautiful maidens have gone to a bonding ceremony single and left having met their future mates due to this time-honored tradition."

Dani nodded. "Humans have a similar tradition, except you pay for the privilege of dancing with the bride or groom. The maid of honor, another human tradition, wears an apron, and people drop money into the apron before dancing with the bride or groom for a minute. It usually only lasts a couple of songs, and people line up for a dance that is symbolically supposed to bring wealth and prosperity to the marriage."

Darren smiled at her.

"Does that amuse you, warrior?" she asked.

"You amuse me. You speak so lovingly of the race we are all taught to think of as beneath us. You make a lovely ambassador for the human race." He touched her cheek, making her turn a little pink. He had no idea how much of a true ambassador she was. "There is no way anyone will get to dance with the *bride* or *groom*." He repeated her terminology. "They will be inseparable for weeks to come, too wrapped up in the building of the bond to be away from each other."

Dani went to refill her drink and enjoyed the lovely warm glow of the room and the happy faces on the dance floor. Darren didn't follow her, and she was grateful, until a dozen pairs of eyes burned through her. She was stopped several times by people politely inquiring about her "mating" status. That must have been vamp for marital status. She finished one glass of wine while speaking with a lady who shamelessly promoted her son, who sat at a nearby table with his head hung in shame and embarrassment. Dani took a third glass minus the blood.

At the table, Koren laughed and shook her head. "Kayden is really going to wish he'd come tonight. People wouldn't be nearly so bold, if he were here." She giggled again.

"What do you mean?" Dani was lost again. Not to mention a little buzzed.

Darren chimed in, scowling, "I have a feeling your dance card filled up quickly. Every guy in the room is dying to spin you around the floor and tell you of the wonderful attributes and talents that would make him the perfect mate for you. I believe the bride and groom will be in your debt for the donations they'll receive on your behalf. Maybe they will name a child after you." His tone was laced with arsenic, and his eyes swept the room.

"Oh. Why do you think they will want to dance with me?" Great—she really didn't need anyone else's interest. She had enough trouble already. Dani was willing to bet her fangs she'd be back in Chase's arms before the night was out.

Gage was on his cell phone, telling Kayden what a lovely evening he was missing. He informed Kayden of Chase's presence and Dani's presumed-full dance card for the evening. She never would have taken Gage for an instigator, but he seemed to enjoy provoking his son.

"Don't be silly, Danielle. You're the most beautiful maiden here and not yet bonded, not to mention powerful. You're quite a catch. Gage shouldn't be torturing Kayden like that. I hope those heels are comfortable, honey." Koren seemed to have no fear at all of Dani being stolen away from her son.

The newly mated couple enjoyed their first dance and soaked up all the love and joyful energy left on the floor by the mated couples who had danced before them. The mothers of the newly mated couple went through and made dance cards for people with requested partners. After dinner was served, the music kicked up again, and the groom's mother began passing out the dance requests. The mother of the groom stopped at their table and beamed at Dani.

"Are you Danielle, the warrior?"

She nodded, grasping the warrior pendent that rested in the hollow of her throat. She wasn't a warrior, but she was proud to be an honorary member.

"Our family owes you a debt of gratitude for your presence this evening. You are the maiden who has brought the new mates a small fortune. You will be called to the floor very soon." She handed over the dance card and hugged Dani tightly.

Dani handed it to Koren, not even wanting to see what was on it. Koren's eyebrows shot up into her hairline, before she handed it to Gage. Gage shook his head and handed it to Darren before retreating to the hall, she assumed to call Kayden. Koren followed, scolding him.

Darren examined the card, cursed a blue streak under his breath, and handed it back to her. She had sixteen dance requests. Chase was her first dance, and he'd also secured three more dances throughout the night. Darren was the second dance. He must have paid a pretty penny in an attempt to be first and wasn't happy at being thwarted. It was worse than she'd imagined. Darren turned his chair in the direction of Chase's table and was shot flames from Chase's eyes across the room.

Chase leaned back in his chair, smiling and fiddling with his phone. Dani's phone chirped. Oh, shit. She had a text message.

Tell him there's no room for another warrior in your life. You're upgrading to a male who can outbid him. He shouldn't have interrupted us, Lovely. He's your guard, not your boyfriend or your mate.

"I assume that message is from him?" Darren inquired, still trying to ignite Chase with his eyes.

"It is. Why are you behaving this way? Why would you pay to dance with me, Darren? How did Chase know you would?" She stiffened.

"Did he send a message for me?" He avoided answering by asking another question.

"It doesn't matter. Please, answer my questions." He was really pissing her off.

Darren snatched her phone off the table and started hitting buttons. She tried to take it back but he pushed her hand away.

"You have no right to mess with my phone! It's an invasion of privacy!"

Chase stood on the other side of the room, watching the exchange and sending Dani telepathic question marks.

"I am seeing to your safety, little Wrath," Darren growled. He gave back the phone, only after looking at all her recent text messages. "I requested a dance because I enjoy your company and I was sure if I asked, you would give it to me freely. But this is a bonding celebration, and I am a male of tradition. So I paid for the right to dance with the loveliest maiden here. I am behaving in a protective manner because it's my job," he insisted.

She didn't have time to respond to that load of bullshit before she was called to the dance floor to meet the bride and groom. Darren shadowed her to the floor. The male who was called for the traditional dance having brought the couple the most money was, of course, Chase. The sound that came from Darren behind her was not friendly. He stayed close, all the way across the floor, and introduced himself to the happy couple after they were introduced to Dani. They obviously already knew Chase. The music started, and Chase twirled her around Darren before he had a chance to leave the floor. She was really sick of testosterone-filled vampires. It was a waltz, and Chase seemed surprised that she had no trouble keeping time and danced with grace.

"You're a wonderful dancer, Lovely," he praised her.

"I guess the warrior class can hold their own, after all," she retorted.

"Stop that. You know that comment wasn't a shot at you. Darren was way out of line," he explained.

"It might as well have been a shot at me. You do realize the warriors are actually above me in social standing, according to your people. So how do you think that makes me feel?" Embarrassment and stress colored her cheeks.

"Here we go with 'your people' again. Lovely, there will never be anyone above you. Just ask every male here clamoring for a moment of your time. Hell, I'm not even going to tell you what I paid to have the honor of your time."

"Shut up and dance, Chase. I am tired of hearing people tell me how special I am. You people have no idea who I am. When this danger passes, and I know no one else will be hurt because of me, I'm leaving. I'm transferring to a school someplace far away from this bullshit," she snapped in midspin.

"You don't mean that." He stopped dancing and looked at her in disbelief.

"Hell if I don't! I'm sick and tired of being hurt by people who are supposed to care about me. You claim to love me, but you don't. You don't have any idea what it means to love, Chase. I have begged you to stop doing this to me. It hurts me to be near you. I lose myself in you and the way you make me feel, just to be immediately reminded every time that you can never be mine.

"I fight the urge to come to you every day, because in the end I'll be nothing but a memory to you. I won't be bonded anytime in the near future. In my world, people don't do that until they're in love. My people don't have a magic ceremony that forces two souls together. We have to find our spouse's soul and hold on to it with love and hard work. So when you head happily off into the sunset with Nightmare Barbie, I'll still be feeling the feelings you're going to forget. I'm trying to move on with my life now, instead of waiting for you to forget me."

She walked away as the song ended and everyone was invited to join the dance. She left the hall, going straight out the front door and around the side of the building to a patio area. Dani needed to get away from the crowd and from Chase before she made a fool of herself by having a public meltdown. The air outside was clear and cold. It felt good on her temper-heated skin. She realized Darren was watching from a safe distance, but he didn't approach, so she ignored him. She wasn't strong enough to live in that world. For a girl with so many admirers, she was very much alone.

She made it through the rest of the evening uneventfully, performing all her required dances, with the exception of the ones with Chase. He never came back to claim his rewards for donating such a price to the new couple. He wordlessly danced with the string of girls who requested his attention, then he disappeared. Dani was polite and spoke socially with her dance partners. They'd paid for it, after all.

When she was ready to leave, Darren had a car take them back to the Enclave before Gage and Koren. He was wise not to speak to her in the car.

When they reached her room he said, "I'm sorry for ruining your evening. It wasn't my intent."

She didn't respond before shutting the door in his face.

Chase was stunned by Danielle's intentions to leave the area. Talk about double-edged swords. She all but told him she loved him, but she was going to leave because of him. Chase hadn't meant to hurt her. He just couldn't help getting excited at the opportunity to hold her and soak up some of her sweet attention. He could have had lots of time with her, but after her speech, he didn't have the nerve to approach her again. He should have. What if she left, and he never saw her again? He would regret being a gentleman then, wouldn't he? To know he'd never hold her again, would never smell that delicious scent of hers again, or hear her soothing voice again, would kill him. To never again see those ice-blue eyes surrounded by rich, dark hair with flashes of the proof of her natural power. The thought put a cold spot in the center of his chest. He wanted her so badly, but all he seemed to be able to do was hurt her.

She danced so elegantly. He could still see the proud length of her slender, alabaster neck, her hair all up, and nude shoulders daring him to taste them. The way the red light played off of her skin was amazing.

Watching her dance with all those other guys was maddening. He guessed they had also decided to take advantage of Kayden's absence. She smiled and spoke politely to the would-be suitors, thanking them for being so generous to the new couple. Chase, on the other hand, was rude and too focused on what Dani was doing to even speak to the ladies he danced with. After all the time she'd been away from him, he tried to absorb everything he could without getting close enough to upset her again. Like a damn junkie trying to get a fix, he hung on her words, her expressions, the way she moved. He fixated on the way her lips moved when she spoke, and waited anxiously for glimpses of pale blue, when her eyes turned in his direction.

He was so whipped. He could have any girl crawling all over him. Instead, he was in bed alone, thinking about what it was like to have her pressed against his chest in the dark, giggling in his ear and happy to be with him. His mind replayed having her in his bed with him and moaning his name. He missed her in his home every day. Damn it! Chase was sick of living without her. He was closer and closer to walking away from his family. It seemed like that was what it would take to be with the woman he loved.

The phone in Kayden's bedroom rang, and he answered on the first ring. He was hoping it was Dani in a better mood. Kayden had gone straight to Dani's room when his shift was over the night before. She answered the door but wouldn't open it more than a crack. His fear was that his aggression earlier in the evening had put space between them. He didn't know what had come over him. She was so hot in that dress. He'd kissed her, and the next thing he knew, he had her nearly nude and trying to push him away.

Oddly enough, it was Chase calling. "What do you want, man?" Kayden asked rudely. He was in a shitty mood and nothing Chase had to say was going to make it any better, but he kept talking anyway. Chase filled him in on all of the gritty details from the night before. It had been a hell of a night, and Darren had totally crossed the line and behaved like he was on a real date with Dani. It was a problem they both believed needed to be dealt with.

Then Chase had added fuel to the fire by insulting warriors and harassing her.

"I see. Thanks for the call. I think I may need to pay a visit to Darren," Kayden said darkly, before hanging up the phone.

Kayden stormed through the Enclave in search of the elder Wrath guard. He was seeing red and ready to fight. Darren had gone too far, and Kayden intended to teach him a lesson in how to respect boundaries. He found his father in the hall and quickly filled him in on the information he'd gotten from Chase.

"I'm going to kick his old ass!" Kayden shouted.

"Well, there's a problem with that, son. He's gone, and so is Dani. Darren came to me this morning with the news that Dani was gone, and she didn't let anyone know she was leaving. Apparently he put a tracking device on her car for just such occasions. I don't know where she's heading, but Darren left two hours ago to follow her, and she hasn't stopped driving yet. She has at least an hour lead on him. He called me to check in just before you showed up. Don't bother to ask. You can't follow them. You have duties to attend to here. Darren is dealing with his charge, and I won't allow jealousy to disrupt life at this Enclave. Do you understand me, son?" Gage ordered sternly.

Kayden looked at his father with confused anger. "I want to know where she is and what's going on."

"I guess she'll call you when she is ready for you to know. Otherwise, you need to let Darren do his job." Gage walked away.

Twenty-one

Kayden stomped away from his father, trying to hold his tongue. It was difficult to separate his father from his commander, some days.

"Oh, I almost forgot." Gage turned around to stop Kayden. "You've been assigned to shadow a visiting representative from down south. You need to meet her at the hotel where she's staying. They'll have the address and room number at the dispatch office."

"A hotel? Why not stay on the Enclave?" Kayden asked.

"I was told she isn't comfortable staying in such close proximity to all of us lusty males." Gage rolled his eyes.

"Great. I bet this'll be a peach of a day." Kayden sighed.

"You should expect it to be a late night. She's leaving in the morning, so she has a lot to accomplish today. Try to be a gentleman. Your mother socializes with ladies from all over the country. I would hate for her to be embarrassed." An uncharacteristic grin cracked Gage's face. "You know, she had the best time parading your girlfriend around last night. She was delighted to have everyone dote over her son's selfless warrior girlfriend with unmatched talent and beauty to boot," Gage said warily, almost sarcastically.

"Oh God, Dad, tell me she didn't. I should have gone. Dani hates all that attention. Between Mom, Chase, and Darren, it's no wonder she ran." Kayden couldn't believe his mother would be so insensitive after all the crap Dani had been through. He'd never get

Dani to move back to his place, if that was what she'd deal with every day.

"Well, since you've been voted least likely to succeed by her social peers, it's nice for her to have something to brag about," Gage bitterly defended his mate.

Kayden just ran his hands through his hair and headed to the dispatch office. His instructions for the day were vague. All he was given was an address for the hotel and a room number. He wasn't looking forward to playing chauffeur all day, and the fact that he hadn't heard from Dani had his nerves frayed. Kayden decided to give Chase a call. He was sure Chase had been holding back that morning. Kayden would try to rattle his cage a little, but all he accomplished was getting Chase worked up about Dani taking off. There was definitely more to the story, but Chase wasn't sharing.

Still fuming, Kayden headed to the hotel to collect his charge for the day. He would be holding doors and driving some snob around all day instead of looking for his girl. It pissed him off that everyone from his parents to her damned Wrath guard took turns kicking the legs out from under her, and Kayden was the one to pay for it.

Why hadn't she called? Was there more to the situation with Chase than Kayden was aware of? Did she care so little for his feelings that she would up and disappear without a word? Had he unknowingly done something to hurt her? Had Chase and Darren filled her head full of his past adventures with other women, until she was disgusted by him? The questions and worries swam widely around his head, and Kayden had no idea how he was going to get through the day with his sanity intact.

He reached the hotel room and was surprised to find the door ajar. He knocked and waited but there was no answer. He knocked again and called into the room.

"Hello. Ma'am, are you ready?" There was still no answer. Something felt wrong about it to Kayden. He pulled his weapon and slowly entered the room. It was quiet. The light was on behind the locked bathroom door. He knocked on the door.

"Are you alright in there, ma'am?" He did not want to have to kick the door in to find some old lady dead on the toilet. Suddenly, the light went out and the door flew open. Kayden jumped back and raised his weapon in the sudden, total darkness. All he could see was the silhouette of a small person standing away from the open bathroom door.

"Is that a gun in your hand or are you just happy to see me, warrior?" A very sultry and familiar voice crept out of the darkness, and Dani stepped into the doorway. Kayden's heart almost stopped with the shock and joy of seeing her beautiful mouth turned up in a half smile. He holstered the weapon and pulled her into his arms. For a minute he couldn't speak; he could only breathe her in and be thankful for her presence and safety.

"You scared the shit out of me. I thought you left me, Angel," he huffed with relief.

"I am the Angel of Wrath, remember? My wrath is mighty today. I'm sorry, but it was necessary subterfuge. I wanted you all to myself, and I had to remove a few obstacles to satisfy my needs. I hope you can forgive me." She snuggled into his chest.

Kayden was just glad to have her in his arms. The anxiety of the morning melted away.

She pulled him to a chair and pushed him down before climbing into his lap and resting her head in the crook of his neck. Now, this was what he wanted. This was the most openly affectionate

Dani had been without him pushing for just a little more than she was giving.

"Tell me what happened. I know you had a bad night, but this is a little extreme." He was confused. Who was Darren chasing if she was here, he wondered.

"I couldn't sleep last night, so I went for a walk. I was passing the indoor basketball court when I heard my name, so I stopped to listen. I guess Darren was also having trouble sleeping. He was still in his suit and pacing back and forth, talking on his phone. I don't know who he was talking to, but he asked if the tracking device on my car was enabled yet. I was already good and pissed off, so that was the straw that broke the angel's back. Did you know they were tracking me?" She looked at him with narrowed eyes and an edge of annoyance in her voice.

"I had no idea until this morning, when Dad told me you were gone. Dad didn't know until Darren told him that tracking you down wouldn't be a problem. Does my dad know you're here?" Kayden asked.

"No. I pulled some strings with his secretary and the duty clerk to fabricate a false visitor and get you assigned to me." She snuggled even closer and practically purred, nuzzling his chest. "I went out and found the tracking thingy in my car. It took me a while, but I found it. I thought it would be on the outside of the car, but it was tucked up under the passenger seat."

Shivering under her tender touch, Kayden rasped, "Where is Darren?"

"I have no idea. I tossed the tracker through the open window of a tractor-trailer that was delivering food to the mess hall. The plates on the truck were from Alabama." She shrugged and smiled.

Kayden could do nothing but laugh. Angel of Wrath, indeed. He could just imagine Darren finding the truck, and he wondered how long it would take him to figure out she'd duped him. Darren thought he was so damn smart, and she had him chasing his own flea-bitten tail.

"He was a little more than an hour behind the signal a few hours ago." He chuckled.

Dani had a full day planned for them. He took her shopping and sat back in the chair while she modeled for him. Then they had lunch at a café near the park. Both picked an entrée and placed the plates in the middle so they could share. She played with her food and talked animatedly about how good she was getting with a gun. Her dark hair fell in waves over her shoulders, and she absently tucked a strand of white hair behind her ear.

Kayden admired every little nuance of her posture and speech and the way she used her slender hands to speak. His heart swelled when, without a thought, she reached a hand across the table and laid it on his, like that was where it belonged, while she smiled and talked about his dad teaching her to box. Kayden was a bit jealous of all the time she'd spent with Darren and his dad on training exercises. He had always been so busy with his daily rotations.

It struck Kayden that he'd never really spent time with a female like this before. He'd taken females out and did a lot of partying with them. Usually he had two objectives, blood and sex, and it depended on whether his date was human or vamp if they were both fulfilled that night. He was obviously not going to take blood from another vamp. That would have been like death by marriage, but if he found a nice human female, that was different. He could take care of all his needs and strip the girl's memory, so why bother with dating?

No one before Dani had ever been able to catch and hold his attention. She sat across the table, and he had no hope of pulling his attention away from her. He was enthralled with every move she made, and he hung on her every word. Shit. He was in big trouble. This new territory was the most frightening thing he'd ever experienced. This female was capable of crushing him, and he didn't like it all. For the first time, he wasn't in control. He couldn't just walk away from her and not care. He couldn't imagine a future without her anymore. Oh God, it was really bad.

Dani pulled him from his deep thoughts when she said, "So what do you think? Are you in?"

"Huh?" he asked.

"You haven't been paying attention to me at all, have you?" she pouted.

"On the contrary, I was actually mesmerized by you, Angel," he confessed.

Watching Kayden, she realized how much he'd changed. Kayden had been affectionate, playful, and protective since the beginning of their relationship, but he was different now. Kayden had always been a lady's man, and she was very aware of that. It was amazing that he was willing to wait for her to be ready before broaching the topic of sex. More so that, as far as she could tell, he hadn't been with anyone since the day they first kissed. She couldn't say the same.

Dani watched him watching her all day. He watched her lips as she talked and her hands when she touched him, and, obviously, he watched her body.

She looked across the table into eyes full of tenderness. He said he was mesmerized, and as she drew circles on the top of his hand with her fingers, she believed him. He was not the cocky, devil-may-care party animal of the past. He was stunningly handsome, strong, patient, and affectionate. What else could a girl want in a guy? If she didn't have the constant longing to be near Chase, she believed Kayden would have her heart by now. He did, in many ways, if she were to be honest with herself. He made her feel happy and safe. He relieved some of the aching need for Chase. She missed the days when he was her guardian and with her all the time.

Being a warrior wasn't a nine-to-five kind of job. He went where they needed him, when they needed him, no questions asked. It was very much like being in the human military. On the other hand, maybe absence did make the heart grow fonder, because she surely felt his absence when he was gone.

"What are you thinking about so intently?" He leaned across the table and kissed her bottom lip.

She couldn't find the smile he deserved to see. "The future." Her tone brought seriousness to the simple statement. "It's been a dangerous topic of thought for some time now."

"Do you see me when you think of your future?" He brushed her cheek.

"That was actually my very line of thought—you and the future. I've been too wrapped up in death and drama to imagine anything but surviving. I'm not even going to school anymore, with the exception of some online courses. It's going to take much longer to graduate if I'm forced to keep this pace. Today, I find myself imagining other possibilities." She held his hand to her cheek and turned her head to place a kiss in his palm. He closed his fingers, as if to save the kiss.

"Do you know that I adore you? This has been a huge adjustment for me. This relationship is like nothing I have ever known. I don't really know what I'm doing, but it feels good. I hope you can be patient while I figure out how to be a good boyfriend. Everyone is waiting for me to screw this up and fall off the wagon, so to speak. I do know that I'm not the best you could do in a guy, but you are the only female I think about anymore. I would do anything to make you feel the same way." Kayden was obviously referring to the ever-present shadow of Chase Deidrick.

It made her heart ache. She was doing them both an injustice by withholding pieces of herself for an engaged man. She had to break free of the limbo she'd been in to move on.

After lunch, they strolled through the park hand in hand, not really speaking much. They enjoyed each other's presence, both of them working through things in their own heads as they meandered. Dani's cell phone rang. She looked at Kayden and shook her head in disgust.

"Is it Darren?" he asked.

"Worse. It's Chase, again." She turned off her phone and dropped it in her purse. She would check for messages from her mom or Mason later.

When they arrived back at the hotel Dani almost felt like her old self again. The day of shopping, strolling, snacking, and otherwise just hanging out was such a relief from all the recent drama. Kayden deposited her bags in the room's closet while they talked about where to go for dinner. They saw a pub during their travels that he'd heard had the best wings in town. That sounded good to her. She rummaged in her overnight bag for a pair of jeans and a sweatshirt and kicked off her heels. This day had been exactly what she needed and she wasn't ready for it to end.

She spun around to head into the bathroom to change out of her dress and slammed into Kayden's solid chest. He grabbed her shoulders to steady her, and they both laughed. When the laughter subsided, he was still holding her, and they just looked into each other's eyes. Lord, he was a beautiful man, and in that moment she wasn't thinking of school, or her mom, vampires, or humans, she only thought of how good it felt just to be with Kayden. Simultaneously they leaned forward and their mouths crashed into each other. It was a searching, frenzied kiss that had them both heaving in moments.

Kayden's hands roamed down her body and brushed back up her bared thighs. Her dress slid quickly over her head and sailed off to the corner, and she was laid out on the bed before any sane or logical thought had time to form. Kayden never left her mouth or gave her time to second-guess their impulsive actions.

Her taste and smell were so overwhelming to him. She was like the most fragrant summer meadow and the sweetest-smelling confection all at once. He had never wondered what another vamp would taste like, but he wanted to taste her. It was the undercurrent of hunger he had for humans, but it only happened when they were intimately kissing and touching. Her purely feminine heat brought out strange desires he couldn't understand.

Kissing him more deeply, her lithe body rose from the bed to rub against his. His insides turned molten with the need to finally claim her. She dug her fingers deep into his hair and clung to him. Kayden had her stripped to her panties, but he was still fully dressed. Her full breasts filled his hands while her mouth traveled up his neck to nip his ear. He ripped off his shirt and sent it flying.

Dani explored his chest with her hand when the sound of their mingled breathing became stereo in his head. Kayden shook his head when images of himself blinked behind his eyelids. The air between them became an earthy, woodsy, springtime scent mixed with leather and gunpowder from his time on the firing range that morning.

She rose up to kiss him, and Kayden tasted his own flavor on her tongue. Oh God! She was projecting. This would never last if he had to contend with both of their passions.

Twenty-two

Dani didn't know she was projecting until Kayden told her with an aching moan. She was overwhelming him with a telepathic overflow of emotion and sensation. She was projecting her feeling into Kayden, so she concentrated on cutting off the connection between them. He sighed with relief. Then Dani felt an odd interference, like static on a radio, and the set of Kayden's face and his posture changed completely. His eyes went wide and he sat back on his knees.

"Are you okay?"

He didn't respond. He looked like he was struggling to get away from her but couldn't. She leaned up on her elbows and shook her head to clear the static and the confusion it caused.

That was when it happened. The experience went from frenzied and passionate to a nightmare in the space of a second. Kayden lurched forward and wrapped his hands around her neck, choking her. She pitched and bucked but he held her tight.

Dani looked into his eyes with betrayal and hurt overflowing and spilling in the form of tears. He was wringing the life from her body, painfully.

"Isn't this sweet?" a deep voice came from the bathroom. "You two look so much in love. Or maybe it's just good old-fashioned lust. It's too bad he's going to choke you with his bare hands. He'll live the rest of his life knowing he incapacitated you and watched while I carried you away to your death. However long that may be. Once you're disabled, I'll take you to the master. He'll drink in your energy and absorb your whole bag of tricks. I bet you don't even know half of what you're capable of yet."

A large male came around the side of the bed and sat in a chair across the room. Someone had been in the room that whole time. He'd been listening to everything.

Dani shifted her eyes to the chair but couldn't see the person in the shadows, except for his large mass and black clothes.

"Your lover is going to watch helplessly as you slip through his fingers yet again. Of course, he won't remember my face later. That would ruin my career. You know, I could make him not remember what's happening now, but that wouldn't be any fun at all. He should be made to suffer as you suffer under him. He has been quite a poor guardian indeed, hasn't he, Danielle?"

She looked back up at Kayden to see tears run down his face and drop onto her chest.

Can you hear me? she asked telepathically.

He blinked frantically at her in response, as if it was the only free movement he had left. He couldn't stop, and she couldn't force him off of her bodily. She was mentally strong but physically nowhere near a full-blooded vamp. Dani tried enthralling Kayden so he would release her. Then she used telekinesis to lift Kayden away, but his fingers didn't loosen their grip on her. When that didn't work, she tried to mentally push at their attacker. Nothing worked. The room began to fade around the edges. She gasped for air and fought against the steel grip of Kayden's fingers crushing her larynx.

"You see now that you're not the only vamp with the ability to control the minds of other vamps. There are a few others that I know of, but most of us don't make our abilities known, so we can't be exploited the way you will be. The master doesn't even know the extent of my ability. He only has my word that I'll bring you in at the first opportunity. I guess it couldn't hurt to give you a little Mind Control 101, since you're bashing at me so ineffectively. You're going to die today anyway. You see, once a vamp has another vamp under mind control, they block out everyone else. It's first come, first served, just like when we manipulate humans. So you can't overcome my grip on his mind. Thanks so much for releasing his mind at just the right time. You were blocking me.

"Also, the fact that you conduct mind control makes you impervious to it yourself, and likewise for me. So you can't control me in order to save yourself." He leaned forward and rested his forearm across his knee, bringing his face into light. He was a warrior. She'd seen him around the Enclave many times but had never been introduced to him. He'd seemed like one of the guys who didn't approve of a woman living among so many men. He smiled at her.

"You recognize me, don't you, beauty? I've been watching you, as many of us have. We're everywhere, little girl, and we watch your every move. I've enjoyed watching you work out and play at being a warrior princess. As if you could defend yourself against me with a pair of boxing gloves. It's really a shame such a delicious creature has to die. I would love to show you the darker side of life, but the master wants you desperately. It's become sort of a thrill for him to chase you, to play cat and mouse. You've been great fun, but it's time for the game to end."

She had to try getting free one more time before she passed out. Kayden would never forgive himself. It seemed as if he could hear her, so she looked into his eyes and reached out to him.

Kayden, I'm gonna try again to lift you off of me telekinetically. I can't hold out much longer. Her mental capacity was waning. She used all her strength to try lifting him, but his hands were so tightly wrapped around her neck she couldn't break free. The dark warrior in the corner laughed at her efforts. Kayden's eyes were tortured and shining with tears of anger.

Plan B, Kayden. I'm going to try breaking his concentration in hopes it will help you move. If you feel any release, I need you to take off and go for help. Do you understand? I need you to leave so he can't use you against me. It was getting darker and speaking to Kayden was difficult.

Lack of oxygen was finally taking its toll. She went limp under Kayden. Her eyes were open and unseeing, as his tears continued to fall on her face. The dark warrior jumped up from his seat to evaluate her condition. He wasn't supposed to kill her. He had to deliver her alive, or the master couldn't take her energy. He removed Kayden's hands from her neck and checked for a pulse.

That was all the distraction she needed. Danielle threw Kayden's body toward the door, then threw everything else in the room that would move at the warrior. The chair he'd been sitting on struck the back of his head with force, and unbalanced his concentration enough to give Kayden a chance to run.

She caught a second wind when she realized Kayden was safely out of the room. She scrambled off the bed. Everything, from the mirror on the wall, the brush she left on the dresser, to the lamps, pummeled the rogue warrior. She cursed a blue streak when he attempted to cross the room toward her. She used her few remaining seconds to call out to as many people as she could, not knowing if it would work from so far away or if she could reach someone she'd never touched telepathically before.

The telepathic mayday call was for Kayden. Her targets were Gage, Chase, Griffin, and Mason. Then, the huge man was on her. She could hear Kayden, through their brand-new connection in her mind, screaming for her to follow him. She couldn't. It was going to be a fight for her life, and either she or the warrior was going down. She refused to be taken alive again. If her power was what they wanted, she would make sure they lost it, in the end. Her strength would not be turned on her friends and family, or anyone else, for that matter.

He had the advantage of strength, but she had telekinesis, and neither of them could use mind control on the other, so it was going to be a brawl. Every time he slammed her, she threw him. If he hit her, she bombarded him with the various objects in the room. He tried to hold on to her, but she had enough training with the warriors at that point to make herself a hard target, and the battle raged for what seemed like an endless time. Broken glass, broken furniture, and blood riddled the room. Finally, he got her by the throat and tried to finish his earlier mission. It was working. She was exhausted, and he was choking the life out of her.

"I'm going to have some fun with you before I turn you over, beauty," he hissed into her face. "You've excited me with all this foreplay. I'll have to satisfy my hunger for your sweet little body now. Would you like to be awake for the fun? I promise you all those little boys sniffing around your skirt haven't nearly given you what you need."

He pushed the length of his body against hers, and the ridge of his huge erection pressed into her belly. Nothing but her panties had remained by the time the beast descended on her and Kayden in bed. That seemed like hours ago, but in actuality, it had been only minutes since Kayden fled the room in search of help. After fighting in that state of undress, her body was cut and battered, and she was all but defenseless. There was no damn way he was getting anything but his ass handed to him that night. She prayed that help was on the way and gathered every ounce of energy she could muster. The warrior released her throat and held her against the wall with his body, while he did his best to get her panties down. The violation made her so angry the building energy in her gut bubbled over. She reached up to grab him by the neck. She wanted him to feel the same pain he'd inflicted on her. He would see her little body was not his to touch as he wished. In an explosion of fury and terror, she unleashed the overflowing energy that throbbed inside her. It launched them both across room. Her hands still around his thick neck, they hit the far wall with force and slid down, until the full weight of his body crushed her to the floor.

Kayden had to wait for reinforcements to arrive before he could return to Dani's room. It killed him to leave her there, but she was right. That guy could use him against her, and it would be two on one. She wouldn't be able to beat those odds. He sat on the curb with his head in his hand, the image of her delicate neck wrapped in his huge hands replaying over and over. It was one of the worst experiences of his life. When she went limp under him, he thought he'd murdered her. She'd looked up at him with the blank eyes of a corpse, and he knew he'd killed her.

Her thoughts and senses reached out and crept into his mind. He saw himself through Dani's eyes. He'd felt the deep affection and connection she felt for him. He knew exactly where he stood in her mind. There was the consuming passion that enveloped them both, but beyond that was trust and devotion he knew he hadn't earned. He sat there reliving that time and praying that she'd survived without him.

Up to a certain point, he knew for sure she was still alive, because he caught her thoughts and brief glimpses of the scene through her eyes. He guessed, since Dani allowed him into her mind, their connection hadn't been truly severed. He intercepted vivid flashes of pain and battle. The last thing he saw was a huge man crushing her against the wall. Her thoughts ran toward a dark place Kayden didn't want to imagine. The assailant was going to violate her before taking her away. Try as he may to reach her, Dani was silent.

The entire ordeal had lasted twenty minutes, but it had been an eternity since he'd left her in the room with that man. Kayden hadn't seen the man, because he wasn't able to turn his head, but he saw recognition in Dani's eyes when she looked at him. The man had said he'd watched her train. He was a warrior, one of his brothers. No one else would have access to the Enclave's training facilities.

All at once, everyone converged on the scene. A Wrath truck pulled up and males poured out. Chase sped onto the lot with Griffin hot on his tail, Mason in the passenger seat. The people at the front desk looked frightened and confused when the mass of black-clad, gun-toting males entered the lobby. On the way up to the third floor, Kayden filled in his father, and the rest of the men listened intently. Chase looked like he would vomit when Kayden relayed having been in bed with Dani and distracted when the attack hit.

They had to kick the damn door in, due to the key card locks. The room was a disaster, and, at first, they didn't see her. Only the body of a huge vampire male that was facedown at the far end of the room. Once the room was secured, and they were sure no one else was hiding in the room, they crossed to the body on the floor.

"Help me! Danielle is under this piece of shit!" Mason called.

It took several Wrath guards to lift the huge male off of her, and the shock wave that crossed the room was tangible. He was a well-known Wrath leader in full uniform. There was a large chunk of glass protruding from his back, and blood coated the floor. The glass had come from a light fixture that was crushed into the wall. He'd died from blood loss. She'd killed one of their own. He was a loner and a mean bastard to work with, but nobody had ever suspected he was a traitor. The warriors started rumbling about the law and the expectation of a trial, should the girl survive. Kayden ignored them and slid to the floor at the bottom of the bed.

Griffin and Mason were in a meeting about the betrothal agreement when a scream for help and vivid pictures starting bombarding them both. There was no doubt in Griffin's mind who had been calling them. They were already in the car and deciding where Danielle was when Kayden called, pleading for help. At the hotel the scene was far worse that he expected.

That sweet child was nude. The only scrap of cloth on her was the panties that had been pushed down to her knees. Her body was covered with cuts and bruises. Her neck was the worst-looking injury. Griffin grabbed the blanket off the bed and covered her before he scooped her up off the floor and laid her across the bed.

"Somebody get her some clothes. Kayden, get your ass over here and help me dress her," Griffin barked. He could see Kayden leaning against the end of the bed in bewilderment. Danielle look like death, but she was still breathing.

"She's not dead, Kayden." Chase then let out a huge sigh of relief from the doorway. Griffin leaned over the girl on the bed and examined her neck. It was clear she had been strangled, and more than once. It struck him as he looked down at her dark hair all spread out with the white and traces of red fanned through it that she did indeed resemble his family, and him in particular. It sent an adrenaline-charged sense of protective fury shooting through his veins. His head spun, and that's when he heard it. That voice in the back of his mind that whispered sweetly to him at night. But it was no whisper of devotion and love. It was of devastating loss and pain. It was a heartwrenching cry of agony that clawed at his chest, until he was forced to take the girl up into his arms and hold her against his chest. He sat on the bed, rocking her, and listened to the pained whimper in his mind.

It's okay. She will be fine. We will fix this, I promise, he told the voice. He was truly beginning to think he was going insane. When had he started responding?

Several warriors, along with Mason and Chase, looked at him in confusion. He continued rocking the girl and holding her tight.

Mason's cell rang, and he cursed under his breath on the way out the door. Danielle stirred in Griffin's arms, and he pushed the hair out of her face.

"Hey there, sunshine." She opened her eyes and looked at him. Those ice-blue eyes were breathtakingly pale and bright at the same time. She laid her head back down on his shoulder.

"You came for me. You heard me," she rasped. The sound was like gravel in her damaged throat.

"Of course I did. I'll always come when you call me. We are kindred spirits, sweet girl. I hear you clearly when you call." He comforted the trembling slip of a girl in his arms. Everyone looked at him. It was so quiet. Everyone wanted to hear her explanation.

"He wanted to take me to the hunter. His master, he called him. He had to take me alive, so they could drain me later. We fought until I couldn't fight anymore, and then he tried to rape me. He wanted to teach me a lesson before he turned me over. I would rather die than be taken alive or raped. He said they're everywhere, and they watch every move I make. He's a warrior, Griffin. I saw him every day, but he never talked to me."

"I know, Danielle. Don't talk anymore. Kayden is here to help you get some clothes on, so we can get you out of here," he soothed. Her eyes shot open and the name came soundlessly across her lips, but it was unmistakable and tears began to flow instantly, as she tried to search the room with her eyes until she found him.

"Kayden!" She reached for him, and Griffin stood to allow Kayden to sit and hold the girl. Griffin transferred her to Kayden, who promptly nuzzled his face into her hair and murmured comforting pledges of love and apologies for failing her. Chase left the room as if it were on fire. When the body of the rogue warrior was removed, Griffin cleared the room to allow her privacy to get dressed and gather her things.

The Wrath had left, but Gage stayed behind to give the desk clerks and human police officers who had been called for a disturbance a thorough mind scrubbing. Chase paced the hall and cast glaring looks at the door that concealed Danielle and Kayden. Mason's phone rang again and he ignored it. Griffin stood outside the door and pondered the strange sense of recognition he felt, not to mention the faraway cry in his mind that had since faded.

"We have a huge problem here, Griffin," Mason said without looking at him. "People, warriors in particular, and council members whose families have been protected by this warrior, are not going to be happy when they hear of his death. You know the law, Griffin. We'll have to take her to trial."

"I can't believe this shit," Chase murmured, more to himself than to anyone else.

"I don't even think she realizes she killed him, Mason. Did you see her? She was brutalized and bloody. How can we fault her for defending herself against abduction and rape? We can't do that to a girl who has sacrificed herself repeatedly to protect our children," Griffin cursed.

"If the rest of the council calls for it, we'll have to comply. Murdering another vampire carries a death penalty, and the other warriors are not going to stand for the death of one of their own without investigation, no matter what she says happened. I just think we should be prepared for all possibilities."

Griffin knew Mason's reasoning was solid. They needed to be ready to appease the public and convince the rest of the council to see things their way if this went south.

The elevator door opened and Darren leapt out, followed by Gage, who was explaining the situation. Darren held on tightly to his barely leashed rage. He pushed the broken hotel room door open to find Kayden sitting on the bed with Dani on his lap. This pissed him off even more. That little shit shouldn't have the right to touch her. Kayden couldn't even keep her safe for a few hours. He wasn't worthy of holding her shoes, much less her.

"You wanna tell me what the hell you were doing that you could have missed an assassin in the room? Some warrior you are!" Darren barked.

"If you must know, we were in bed, and Dani began projecting. We were a little distracted." Kayden tucked her face into his neck.

Danielle gingerly got up from Kayden's lap and grabbed her duffel bag. Darren put an arm around her waist and guided her to the wall, removing her bag from her shoulder and tossing it on the bed. He pulled a pair of handcuffs from his belt and said, "I hate to do this to you, but it's necessary."

Kayden jumped up to protest, but Dani halted his efforts. "It's alright, Kayden. I've been catching everyone's thoughts, so I was kind of expecting this. I didn't realize I killed that man. I don't understand how I could have killed him, but I did." Tears ran down her face. "I know I'm not above the law. I did nothing wrong, so I'll go quietly," she sniffed.

"You don't need to cuff her, Darren." Griffin stepped forward. Mason and Chase came to back him up.

"Yes, I do. There are warriors downstairs in the parking lot. The news of a dead warrior spreads quickly, and they expect justice. If the public finds out that a warrior was killed with no recourse, there will be lawlessness and open season on the warriors." Darren glared at Kayden.

"I think if she gets special treatment because of her relationship with everyone here, it will send the wrong message to the rest of the warriors regarding their importance to our society. We defend *all* in our race. If our leaders don't defend us against the possibility of foul play, it will drag down morale and cause mixed emotions. It's too bad she was left alone with no witness to her assault."

He cuffed Dani's hands behind her back as loosely as possible. Her wrists were so small she could wiggle out of them with some effort and a few bruises. Every other man in the room looked on in shock. The "Angel of Wrath" looked directly at each of them with those stunning ice-blue eyes that overflowed with tears as she passed them on the way out of the room. Each one of them felt the sting of her grief for having taken a life, and her fear of the consequences rolled off of her in palpable waves. She was so overwhelmed that she couldn't stop herself from projecting her pain into their minds, and each one of them wavered under the strength of her emotions.

Chase stepped in front of the doorway and wrapped his arms around Dani's shoulders. He was surprised, and a sweet pain shot through him when she laid her head on his chest and nuzzled her face against him, embracing him the only way she could with her hands bound behind her.

I love you, Danielle, my Lovely, he told her telepathically, stroking her hair and back.

She blinked away more tears and sent back into his mind, *And I will always love you, Chase. I will still love you, even after you've forgotten me in the throes of your blood bond.* Danielle told him the truth of her feelings, minus the attitude she normally used to deflect her pain. Darren nudged her to get her moving, and she was pushed against Chase to get past him.

I'm sorry you witnessed all of this between Kayden and me, but you and I were over before we even got a chance to start. My heart can't handle missing you anymore. I can't continue longing for something I will never have.

The words rang in Chase's head. She was guided past him and down to the elevator by Darren and Mason. Chase spun around and put his fist through the wall of the suite.

Danielle continued. *I'm telling you this now, because I've been scanning the minds of our group and those downstairs. Mason and Griffin can't help me, and the warriors downstairs are the dead warrior's Wrath team. He was their leader, and they want blood, my blood. None of them knows me, because he kept them away. He was very good at deception, Chase.* The sound of his name on her mouth, or in her thoughts, made him warm, but he could also feel her fear. *I might die for this crime. I just want you to know that as long as my heart beats, I will love you.*

Chase felt Danielle's mental walls go up to block him when he stepped into the elevator. He wanted to tell her so many things, but she threw up an iron curtain in her mind that he couldn't get around.

Darren was still angry with Dani for her stunt from the morning, but he couldn't stay pissed at her while she stood there handcuffed, so fragile and bruised, with tears streaming down her cheeks. He knew he'd been an ass at the bonding, and he also knew she wouldn't like having a tracker on her car, but he had to protect her to the best of his ability. After his performance the previous night, she probably thought he was being controlling. He didn't blame her. He couldn't believe he had taken her cell phone and looked at all her messages. What had gotten into him? Once they were on the elevator alone, he turned her around and lifted her into his arms.

"I'm so sorry about last night and the tracker. I was such an ass. I was just trying to keep you safe, I swear." Darren had been doing his job, for the most part.

"I forgive you, Darren," she said, her voice gravely from the strangulation she had endured. "And I am sorry for the stunt with the tractor-trailer. If not for that, I wouldn't be in this position."

"Can you quickly tell me what happened, so I can start trying to put out fires? I'm a jerk, I know, but I'm also a very old and well-respected jerk. Not to mention feared, in some cases. I can deflect some of the flack with some well-placed diplomacy."

He needed the whole story right now. "Showing you would be easier for me right now. Is that alright?"

Darren nodded uncomfortably. He didn't like people messing around in his head, but if she was just sending and not receiving, he would allow it. The elevator door opened to the lobby, and he carried her off and over to an out-of-the-way grouping of chairs in the corner. People watched with interest as he sat the handcuffed beauty in the chair. "Do you need me to do anything?"

"Thoughts are easy, but if I want to show pictures, it's easier and less choppy if we are touching. So, if you put your hands on my skin, it will help me relay things more clearly," she explained.

Darren got to his knees in front of her and wrapped a hand around her bicep.

"The warriors outside are thinking I was having an affair with that guy and that this was a crime of passion. They are so confident in his ability to defend himself that they're thinking I stabbed him in the back or did something underhanded to take him down. So I am going to show you the whole day. This is hard for me, because you will also be able to feel my emotions and maybe even physical sensations." She couldn't meet his eyes.

"It will be okay, Danielle. I have lived a very long time, and I'm sure you aren't going to show me anything that will surprise me. Just relax, so I can get the whole picture. It's the best way for me to defend you."

Without another word she started. He had been wrong about her ability to surprise him, and she didn't disappoint. She didn't start in the morning. She started the night before at the bonding. She let him see himself through her eyes, and he could feel the anxiety he made her feel. He saw himself snatching her phone, stalking her on the way to the dance floor, and the rough, almost bruising, way he'd held her when he finally got the dance he had paid for. He could smell his scent mingling with hers while they danced, and he saw his own shadowed eyes daring her to pull away from him. If that was his idea of how to win over a woman, he wasn't nearly as wise as he gave himself credit for.

She went through the rest as he wandered over the sights, smells, and sensations in his mind. Seeing Kayden pawing all over her made him angry, but when they finally reached the part that mattered, Darren was sickened. The fight was brutal, and she was nearly nude the whole time. Pride swelled in his chest at her use of the skills she'd been taught in training, and relief washed over him in the end when he knew she had no intent to kill the warrior. Rather, she was trying to get him to kill her, because she wouldn't be taken alive or raped. She hit the wall in a blast of energy, and that was it.

When it stopped and he opened his eyes, she looked over his shoulder. He turned to find the group of men from upstairs taking in the scene between him and Dani. He got to his feet.

"The battle she fought on her own was nothing short of hell. I don't know how she's still breathing, much less walking." He pulled her up from the chair and began pushing her toward the front door. "I think we should have Doc come look her over as soon as possible. Let me take her out alone so they don't think the council is favoring her, given there are two members present. The anger and tension is at a critical level out there, so I want you to keep watch. It could go downhill quickly."

They all followed them to the door and stopped to let Darren escort her out alone. There were at least twenty warriors milling around the parking lot, and they all looked at her with disgust, but Darren stayed close behind her, his expression daring them to make a move.

Twenty-three

Hiding behind the wall separating Tessa's living room from the dining room, Mason had narrowly missed being hit by a half-full pitcher of lemonade that flew past his head. He hadn't seen Tessa so pissed off since the day he told her Griffin was going to be bonded to Sarah.

"Honey, just calm down and let me tell you what's going on," he pleaded with her.

"Oh, I know what's going on, Mason! You are just like Griffin! You make promises you have no intention of keeping, and to hell with anyone who gets hurt because of your betrayals! You promised to keep her safe!" she screamed. Tessa paced like a caged animal.

"I don't see how tearing up your own house is going to help this situation, and I have other important things I know you will want to be aware of." He peeked around the corner and a plate flew past his head.

"Are you going to tell me they might kill my daughter? I have been dreaming about her execution for a week, Mason. I usually keep my mental distance from Griffin, but I felt it when he found her hurt and naked! He may think he's going insane, because I have been all up in his shit! I hope he suffers for being so damn blind! How could he not know she's his baby? How could he let them hurt our girl?"

"I think she's in love with my son," he blurted.

"That's nice. When she is publicly executed, he can watch and suffer along with me. Or is he like the rest of you, with no heart to speak of?" she growled. "I thought she was dating a warrior. Why do you think she loves your boy?"

"She has been dating Kayden, and I wasn't aware that anything had ever happened between her and Chase, until the dress shop incident. I know she loves him. When they took her out in cuffs today, Chase stopped her for a hug that was too intimate for a girl who is supposed to be angry with him. So I took the liberty of stepping up to help guide her from the room. I touched her and felt the love and need between them," he confessed.

"Oh my God! Chase is your son? Holy shit! Do you know what that means? I have to sit down! My heart can't take this!" She fell back into a chair.

Mason slowly entered the dining room. "Has she spoken to you about Chase? I wouldn't have put her in his home, if I'd known it would cause her pain. The day she went missing, there was tension between Kayden and Chase over who loved her more. Griffin was stunned, but he held his tongue."

"He was stunned because Chase is going to marry his daughter. *Nightmare Barbie* is what Dani calls her."

Mason and Tessa compared notes about the relationship between Dani and Chase as well as the wedge it had driven between Kayden and Chase. Mason explained the betrothal agreement and reminded Tessa of the prophecy the Vaughns and the Deidricks were attempting to fulfill by bonding Chase to one of Griffin's daughters.

"The engagement is actually an arranged marriage based on a vision given by Griffin's sister. Do you know the story?"

"I know that years before I met Griffin, your brother was killed by someone trying to do the same thing that is happening now. He was kidnapped and killed for his powers. Griffin's sister was secretly bonded to him. She killed herself rather than live without him," she said quietly, with respect for the loss of his brother.

"Actually, my brother killed himself because his kidnapper was going to kill him and use his power to capture Griffin's sister. The two of them were indeed secretly bonded, and he knew if he were already dead, the kidnapper wouldn't be able to take his power. When Griffin's sister—who was precognitive like you—realized her mate was dead, she wrote a vision of the future before she followed him to the grave." A tear slid down Mason's cheek. Tessa crossed the room and hugged him tight. "She said a child from the house of Vaughn and a child from the house of Deidrick would bond in love and bring an end to the fear of our children and the pain of their loss."

"So when it started to happen again, you and Griffin decided to force together your children in hopes of fulfilling the vision. Little did you know your children had already found each other." She sighed. "It just wasn't the daughter you expected."

"The funny thing is, if your timeline is correct, Chase had no idea he was promised to one of Griffin's daughters until after he met Danielle. That makes me feel a little better about his behavior. It saddened me to think he was capable of leading a girl on for his own selfish pleasure."

"You said one of Griffin's daughters, not Nightmare Barbie specifically?"

"Her name is Samantha. Chase had a choice between the twins, but Sam can be very persuasive. Not to mention she's beautiful, hence the Barbie reference. To answer your question, no, it didn't have to be Sam. So if it is known that Dani is Griffin's daughter, I could break the engagement between Chase and Sam without causing a house feud. Sarah would lose her mind, but that is something for Griffin to deal with."

"I think it's more important for her to survive your faulty penal system first." Tessa put her hands over her face. "They're going to kill her, Mason. I have watched it every night for a week. You can't imagine what it's like to watch your child die."

Mason stroked her back. "I know I've let you down, Tessa, but I'm going to make this right. Not only is she my godchild, but I also believe she holds the key to my son's future happiness and the fulfillment of the prophecy. I need you to understand that if it comes down to it, I will expose her identity. They will be much less willing to execute the daughter of a councilman."

"Or, they might kill her on the spot for being an abomination to your race who would muddy your bloodlines," she retorted.

Griffin was arguing with Gage when they entered the area known as "the hole."

"I'm sorry, Griffin. I don't like it either, but we must follow the letter of the law. She killed another vampire, so I have to detain her until the council passes judgment. Kayden is losing his mind, and Koren won't speak to me, but I'm sworn to uphold the law."

"Do you have to detain her in a prison cell? You know she isn't going to run," Griffin growled.

"I know no such thing. She was on the run when the murder took place. To be honest, I think this is the safest place for her, given the tension around here," Gage returned.

"You know damn well it wasn't a murder! She was defending herself! Did you see her? She didn't do that to herself!" Griffin snarled.

"The fact remains that our law states that any vampire who kills another has committed murder and must stand trial. Self-defense can be achieved without killing your attacker. This is what others will argue," Gage calmly explained.

As they reached the door before the row of cells, Griffin took a deep breath. He didn't want to see Danielle locked in a cell. He had been unmercifully haunted by the voice in his head since he found her the day before. It asked him over and over again how he could be so blind. It demanded he protect this girl and care for her like one of his own, like a daughter.

When he reached the nine-by-nine jail cell, the sight of that sweet girl, so petite and fragile looking, huddled in the corner at the far end of the metal slab they called a bed, broke his heart. She had her legs tucked up to her chest with her arms wrapped around them. She seemed so small curled around herself like that. She looked like a child. Her face was turned away from him, so he couldn't see the bruises at first.

"Do you want to stay out here or go in with her?" Gage asked.

"Lock me in. I'll call for a guard when I'm ready to leave."

Dani gingerly got up from the bed and approached the bars when she heard Griffin's voice. Her lips were split and her eyes blackened from the fight. Her nose had a cut across the bridge and looked as if it could have been broken. Worst of all was the sight of her neck. It was black and blue with the marks of repeated strangulation. Gage stepped into the cell and took her chin in his hand, turning her face from side to side trying to assess her injuries.

"You look like a prizefighter who forgot to fight back. I thought I taught you to keep your hands up," he accused, shaking his head. He heard the cell door locking behind him.

It was distressing for Griffin to see her pretty face marked. She wrapped her arms around his waist and buried her face in his chest.

"Thank you for coming. Did you bring a camera with you?"

"Yes, I brought a camera, but I'm not sure what you want it for." He hugged her a bit uncomfortably and loosened when she winced. "I'm sorry."

"I need your help. It's a little embarrassing, so I needed to ask someone I trust." She stepped back with a blush. "I think it will help my claim of self-defense if I document my injuries before they heal. I have no idea how long it will take to get to trial," she paused, "so I need you to take the pictures." Danielle backed up and asked, "Can you do that for me?"

"Yes. It's a shame I didn't think of that. Are you sure you don't want me to find a woman to do this?" He knew she would have to remove her shirt.

"I don't feel safe with the others here, and I'm not comfortable with Kayden doing it. He's having trouble looking at me. He feels responsible for my injuries, particularly the marks on my neck. I don't want to make him see the rest of my injuries," she explained.

"Alright then, if you're sure; let's get it over with so you can rest." Griffin pulled a thin digital camera out of the inside pocket of his suit jacket. Danielle moved back against the wall and pulled off her shirt. Griffin tried not to look shocked at her battered torso. The girl had scrapes, cuts, and huge bruises covering her entire body. He did as she asked and took pictures of her as proof of the brutal attack.

The council chamber was housed in a building that also contained the Hall of Records and a library. It was where their history, family trees, laws, and disciplinary hearings lived shoulder to shoulder in a huge, round building with a domed roof. The council chamber was a round room in the center of the building that was surrounded by a marble hall. The room was floor-to-ceiling Carrara marble. There were five sets of double doors that led into the chamber from various angles. The library and Hall of Records ringed the outside of the building, along with private councilmen offices. Inside the chamber there were rows of curved, dark wood benches all directed toward the rear of the room and the long tables occupied by the council. The council passed laws that affected their entire race and passed judgment on those who broke the law. Their law was very strict, and punishment was swift and exacting. Because of those consequences, it was unusual for vampires to break the law. The benches were full of curious vampires and angry warriors, waiting to witness the fate of the vampire youth known as Danielle Scott.

She'd killed another vampire, and that was the most heinous of all crimes. Even worse, she had killed a warrior. It was the human equivalent of murdering a cop or a soldier. The crowd was aflutter with rumors of everything from a crime of passion to Danielle's inability to control the power she was rumored to have. Most of those people had not met Danielle. For that matter, most of the council had not met her, either. The vampires were leery of the claims of her power.

In the front row sat all of those who cared for Danielle and several who did not. Chase sat with Debbie's arm around him. He was haunted by Danielle's last words to him. She loved him as much as he loved her, and she would suffer for that love. Debbie knew the pain of her son revolved around Danielle, but he wasn't willing to talk to her about it. So she sat in silent support.

Griffin's family sat on the other end of the row. Samantha sat in silent joy at the possibility of the death of the bitch who plagued her happy future. Sarah couldn't care less about the girl either way, as long as she stayed away from her daughter's fiancé. Brandi Vaughn looked at her mother and twin sister in disgust. Neither one of them cared what happened to the girl who had willingly risked her own life to keep her brother, J. R., from harm.

Koren and Kayden sat close together in stunned silence, amid the rumors and laughter that spun around them. They knew the truth and would not stop until those fools heard every word of it. Kayden was ashamed he'd let Dani down, again. Every time he looked at his hands, all he could think of was how they had looked wrapped around her neck, choking the life out of her while he watched, screaming inside for forgiveness the whole time. Christopher Stafford, his mother, Veronica, and older brother, Donovan, sat in the second row behind Koren and Kayden.

A hush came over the crowd, and everyone stood when the council entered from a door centered behind the long table they presided from and moved to take their seats. The current serving members were Lloyd, Adele, and Griffin Vaughn, Seleste, Seth, and Mason Deidrick, and Alexander, Ayden, and Kane Stafford. In front of each seat was an envelope containing pictures of Danielle's injuries and pictures of the warrior Lance's body, her statement, and the statements of the first responders to the scene, including Kayden's.

Once everyone was seated, Danielle was led into the chamber by Gage on one side and Darren on the other. Darren stood very close, with his arm linked with Dani's shackled arm. He whispered words of encouragement to her. Both Chase and Kayden shot up to their feet in surprise at the sight of her arms and legs in shackles. She looked exhausted and so small in an oversize Enclave sweat suit and chains joining her hands and legs. Being flanked by two huge warriors only amplified the effect. They led her to a long table between the council and the front row.

Several people murmured at first sight of her. The streaks of white in her hair were an ancient sign of great power that was very rare indeed. Griffin was the only other vampire they'd ever seen with the coloring, but the red running through the white was nothing they had ever seen before.

Adele and Lloyd gave each other looks of suspicious worry when they got their first look at the girl who had caused so many waves of late. They both thought the same thing: She looked just like Griffin, right down to the streaks. Griffin looked out over the crowd. Someone moving in the hall caught his eye. The person came in the main entrance, and the wind blowing in from outside carried the sweet scent of vanilla to him, but no one entered the chamber. He shook his head, thinking it must have been Danielle. She had that lovely sweet scent of vanilla and lavender.

Kane Stafford, who was the great-grandfather of Christopher, began the proceedings.

"Ms. Scott, you stand accused of murdering Lance Brown, a well-known and respected Wrath leader. The penalty for killing another vampire is death by beheading. How do you answer these charges?" There was a long pause while the crowd murmured accusations before she answered.

"I murdered no one. I was defending myself. Lance was accidentally killed during his attack on me." She raised her chin in defiance of the charges. She was scared to death and trying not to cry in public like the little girl she was.

"We have reviewed the photos you provided, along with the other statements, but it has always been the opinion of this council that a person does not need to kill in order to defend. We need to hear your explanation for this grievous crime," Kane returned. Murmurs of agreement rippled through the crowd.

"I had no intention of killing him. In fact, I didn't think it was possible for me to do so. He broke into my hotel room and hid in the bathroom. He assaulted me and my future mate after surprising us in bed.

"He used mind control to sneak up on me by using Kayden to choke and hold me down. After I got Kayden out of the room, Lance beat me senseless. I only tried to hold him off until Kayden was able to get reinforcements. I also sent out a distress call to two members of this council and my friend, Chase Deidrick. If I wanted to kill someone, I would not have called for two prominent leaders of this society to come witness the aftermath."

"That isn't possible. We cannot use mind control on each other, only on humans. How could the warrior have caused Kayden to choke you?" Seleste, Mason's mother, scoffed. She didn't seem to like the elder Stafford.

"I understand from my brief exposure to this society that some of my powers are unusual, but I assure you it is possible. The warrior laughed at me for assuming I was the only one with the ability to control other vampires. He explained that a lot of vampires don't make their powers publicly known. He said it's easier to get away with things if no one knows what you are capable of, and harder for your gifts to be exploited."

"Could you please explain to us what you mean when you say you sent out a distress call?" Lloyd spoke up without looking up from his paper as he took notes on her comments.

"I have the ability to speak telepathically with others and pick up on their thoughts and feelings. I've been told this is a more common ability. I've found the more familiar I am with the person, the easier it is for me to reach him or her from a distance. Chase, for instance, had come to my rescue and had been able to help me on two separate occasions when I was drugged and having trouble coming out of the mental hold the drugs had on me. He and I have shared a lot of mental conversations, so I can call him easily. I can also hear him if he calls out to me, as long as I'm not too distracted. I have demonstrated my power for Mason and Griffin in the past, so I am also able to find their unique mental signatures with my mind. When Kayden and I were threatened, I called out for help," Dani explained.

"That's interesting. Were you able to do this all at once? Could you demonstrate this ability for us? I understand you have a great many talents that we might like to witness in order to substantiate your claims," Lloyd asked.

"What would you like me to do? I can also send my memories to you. I could probably show you blow for blow what happened that night if you like," she offered. Lloyd called Darren to the front and gave him two pieces of paper from his notepad and two pens. Lloyd instructed Darren to give paper and a pen to Chase and keep one for himself.

"If she is able to use mind control on us"—Kane gave a disbelieving look—"I don't feel that she can be trusted. She could put anything she wants in our heads and we would believe it. And if such a thing is possible, why didn't she use this ability to stop Lance without killing him?" Kane spoke up again. Danielle was surprised to get such opposition from the house of a boy whom she had saved.

"Lance explained to me and Kayden, while I was being choked to death"—the hostility and agitation in Danielle's voice was plain—"that you cannot use this power on another vampire with the same power. He couldn't influence me, and I couldn't him, because we have a natural shield against each other. He was very forthcoming with information, because he believed that he would be turning me in to his 'master,' and I would be dead by the end of the day," Danielle explained with venom in her voice. "Also, he explained that it is a first-come, first-served ability, just like when we enthrall a human. He took over Kayden and was shielding him against my influence. Basically, once he had a hold of his mind, I wasn't able to use my ability to stop the attack."

The crowd erupted into an angry denial of the claim that Lance had been reporting to an outside entity.

"She lies!" one warrior shouted.

"Lance was a good man. She shouldn't be allowed to defile his memory!" another warrior agreed.

Griffin stood, demanding silence and respect for the chamber and council. As he stood scanning the room, he saw someone in the hall again, watching from a shadow. When he looked closer, the person moved quickly.

"I believe this is a good time for a recess. Anyone who cannot hold their tongue should not return to the chamber," he bellowed.

He tapped Mason on the shoulder and motioned for him to follow quickly. Griffin needed to know who was lurking in the shadows. It could have been a traitor there to report the outcome of the hearing back to the rogue vampire at the root of all the mess. If so, they were going to beat some information out of the bastard. The two men shot out into the hall, as a side entrance door shut behind someone who made a quick retreat.

"Did you see that?" Griffin shouted over his shoulder to Mason.

"I think we have some unwanted company. Let's go introduce ourselves, shall we?" Mason pushed the door open in time to see a figure darting across the lawn toward a parking lot. They put their supernatural speed to use and were on the stranger in seconds.

Griffin reached the intruder first and tackled him to the ground. Facedown and covered by an oversize coat and a ball cap, the person was totally obscured. Griffin was surprised at the slight size of his quarry, until he flipped him over. Rolling off the person he pressed to the ground, he began repeating to himself, "It's not possible. It's not possible."

The person crawled away.

Griffin got quickly to his feet and snatched the person up, knocking off the ball cap with a swat of his hand. Dark blond hair spilled from under the hat, and eyes of angry ice looked up at him.

It was Tessa.

Twenty-four

Griffin stood, holding his dead mate, the love of his life. She'd been snatched by the cruelest of fates. He'd been robbed of her love and the life they were building together, along with the beautiful baby girl she had given birth to just days before. How could he possibly have been looking into the ice-blue eyes that had haunted his dreams for the past twenty-one years? The weight of touching her, smelling her sweet vanilla scent, and seeing the fire in her eyes was more than he could handle. He went to his knees and dragged her down with him. Wrapping her tightly in his arms, he began to sob and tremble with the power of his emotions.

"I really hate to break this up, Griffin, but we need to move, before we're seen." Mason patted him on the back.

"It's my Tessa. She lives, Mason. They lied to me. My Tessa . . . is here, in my arms," he said in a tearful rasp, rocking her in his arms.

Tessa pushed away from him and snatched her ball cap off the ground to tuck her hair back under it.

"Your Tessa? I am not your anything, Griffin Vaughn!" she snapped. "You have a replacement family, remember?" She started to walk away but stopped to come back and look down on him. He reached for her hand, and she allowed him to take it and kiss her palm, looking up at her from his submissive position. She was the only person who had ever ruled over him. He had gladly submitted to her whims in the past. He would do anything to please her.

"I can't believe you could look at that girl and not know she was your baby, Griffin. I have looked at you in her face for twenty-one years. How could you see your own face with my eyes and not know? Why can't you feel that she is yours?"

"Danielle? She is my Soleil? She has been here with me all these months? Does she know who I am?" he sputtered, pulling her hand to his lips. He breathed in the unforgettable scent of her skin. Tessa was alive. Their baby girl had survived. Griffin's mind struggled to accept what was right in front of him. His chest was tight with joy and relief, but it was tainted with the knowledge that she had left him behind. How could she do that to him, to them?

"Griffin, we really need to move, man," Mason interjected. Griffin was in the grass on his knees in plain view of anyone who passed the exit door to the parking lot. Griffin turned his face toward Mason and wondered why his friend didn't seem the least bit shocked by Tessa's reappearance.

"Yes, she knows exactly who you are." Tessa took a deep breath, and the tears began to flow. "And how could you not know I was still waiting for you?" she whispered. "How could you agree to bond to another less than a day after you heard of my 'death'? How could you not hear me calling to you night after night for all these years? You better make this right, Griffin Vaughn. You promised to love and protect me and our child forever, and you have failed miserably. I expect you to make up for it now by proving her innocence. Get your ass in there and make this right!" Tessa pulled her hand from his and walked away.

"How will I find you again?" he asked anxiously. He couldn't imagine watching her walk away. If it was a dream, he didn't want to wake up, ever.

"Our child knows how to find me. After she's freed, she will call me. I'm taking her away from these people you would allow to kill her in cold blood, the same way your family would have when she was no more than a day old. If you allow them to harm her, I swear, there will not be a place in your world or mine that you will be able to hide." Tessa got into her car, slammed the door, and pulled out of the parking lot.

Mason went to help Griffin up off his knees and brush him off. Tears still streaming down his face, Griffin watched Tessa's car disappear down the road.

"Did I just dream that, Mason? This can't be real. I must be asleep, or crazy."

"You're not dreaming, my friend. Now, you need to pull yourself together so we can go take care of your daughter. She needs her dad right now." Mason pushed him back toward the council chamber.

"You knew they were alive!" Griffin grabbed Mason by his lapels. It was clear that Tessa's appearance had not been a surprise for him. Mason grabbed Griffin's huge wrists to stay his attack long enough for a short explanation.

"I did." Mason calmly tried to explain. "I'm sorry, Griffin, but I didn't know what else to do. I can explain it all later. Right now we have to get back inside."

Almost everyone had returned to his or her seat, and Danielle was being led back into the chamber by Gage. Lloyd wouldn't allow Darren to go with Danielle. He said he didn't want his experiment ruined by her cheating. She suspected Lloyd wanted to see the extent of her powers while he had an excuse to force her cooperation.

A guy she'd never seen before was at the large front table looking over the photos she had submitted. She watched him with interest, wondering who he was and why he was so interested. He was a stunning man who looked to be a little older than Kayden. Of course, that meant nothing. He could be very old, and she would have no way of knowing. He was statuesque, lean, and not overly muscular. He wore a tailored suit that reminded her of Griffin's polished style. He had wavy hair the color of raven wings, and eyes so dark she couldn't tell the pupils from the irises. His skin tone was that of a well-tanned Italian god. Damn. If she didn't already have enough trouble, this guy could surely inspire some more.

Chase caught her staring and followed her gaze. He walked swiftly past her to snatch the pictures from the guy's grasp. Danielle wore nothing but a bra and panties in the pictures. "Get your jollies off one of your pets, Van. Danielle is way out of your league," Chase snapped at the guy. The guy smiled widely at Chase and reached for another pile of pictures on the table. Completely indifferent, he continued to look over the photos. Chase tried to take those, too. Without even looking up, the guy put his fist in Chase's chest, and Chase stumbled back. Danielle could only imagine the guy was from one of the ruling houses, because everyone else had a healthy fear of Chase. Chase's family was powerful, and he would one day serve on the council. Tall, dark, and mysterious just swatted him away like an annoying bug. Chase's eyes went dark in a way she had never seen before. He was truly pissed and went all black-eyed freak in the space of two seconds. Dani jumped up and went to put herself between the men. Shackled and cuffed, she put her hands on Chase's chest.

"Please don't do this now. I can't handle any more drama. It's not worth it." She tried to soothe him with circular stokes of her fingers on his tight abs. He looked down at her, and the black bled from his eyes. Telepathically she said to him, *Please, baby.* His features softened at her endearment.

"I'm sorry, Lovely. I just don't like him looking at your body in those pictures." Chase pulled her into an embrace and buried his face in her hair. Of course, that was when Kayden entered from the rear of the chamber with Griffin and Mason. Extracting herself from Chase's arms in order to avoid a war, she turned to look at the stranger. He watched her intently with one eyebrow cocked and a half smile on his full lips. She stepped forward and Chase stepped with her, putting his chest against her back and a hand on her waist in a possessive movement. Dani could see Kayden on the move toward them and Mason rushing to catch him. She pushed Chase back away from her, but his hand remained on her waist.

"I apologize if I have offended you, Ms. Scott. My name is Donovan Stafford." He reached out, took her cuffed hand, and bent to place a kiss on her knuckle. "Christopher Stafford is my little brother, and I am forever in your debt for saving his life. I will assist in any way possible. I'm a lawyer. I was only trying to find an angle of defense. Please, forgive me." He lowered his head in respect.

The council began to filter in, and Kayden watched in frustration from the front row, where Gage and Mason had pinned him.

"If you come up with anything, let me know," Dani said wryly. "They didn't exactly offer a public defender, and I couldn't tell which ones were the vampire lawyers in the phone book."

Donovan laughed at her sense of humor at such a critical time. She was led away by Chase while he glared at Donovan, who went back to looking at the pictures. Chase pushed in her chair for her when she sat at the defendant's table and went back to his seat. Griffin stopped by her table and looked at her meaningfully, before moving on to the council table. Danielle thought he looked sick, and his eyes were red. Was he angry with her? Great. She couldn't afford to lose an ally on the council.

"Alright everyone, let's get this over with one way or the other. Ms. Scott, are you ready to proceed?" Lloyd spoke up over the crowd.

Danielle nodded nervously in response. It quickly became quiet in the chamber.

"I want you to write down a sentence and give the page to Gage. Then, send the message to everyone the paper was given to, so we can evaluate your ability to send a distress call to multiple people," he instructed.

Danielle immediately complied and handed the paper over to Gage. Then she watched as Chase, Gage, Griffin, Mason, and Lloyd all wrote. All at once, they held up their papers to show the rest of the council and the crowd in attendance. They had all written the same thing: "I am innocent." The crowd buzzed.

"Impressive," commented Ayden Stafford. He was a tall man with the same jet-black hair as Donovan, pulled back in a ponytail at the back of his neck. "I'm interested to see you use mind control on one of us. Can we get a volunteer?"

"I don't see how that would serve to prove Ms. Scott's guilt or innocence," a voice from behind Danielle spoke up. Donovan stepped up to the table next to her. "No disrespect, Councilor Stafford, but I don't believe show-and-tell is going to resolve this issue."

He looked at Danielle. "Did you use mind control on the day of your attack?"

"No, I did not. I used telepathy to call for help and telekinesis to fight off the attack." Danielle liked the fact that he said "your attack" instead of "the murder."

"I see," he replied, and walked toward the table to pick up a few pictures. There was an audible hiss from Chase and Kayden as Donovan looked over her nearly bare body.

"You are correct, Donovan. I don't think we need her to demonstrate her abilities for our entertainment. This is a trial, not a circus." Griffin glared at Ayden.

"Tell us about the attack, Danielle," Donovan asked. Danielle gave the room a blow-by-blow description of the fight.

"Are we to believe that at your young age, you have the power to lift yourself, along with a large male warrior, across the room? That would be impossible for a healthy youth, much less one who was in a weakened state of injury," Adele scoffed in disbelief.

"May I demonstrate?" she asked with a cocky grin. "I will need a 'large' volunteer."

"I will volunteer." Kayden stepped up to the table and placed his hand on Danielle's. Then he smiled at Dani and teased, "Take it easy on me." She gave him a weak smile in return. They walked hand in hand to the floor between the council table and the rows of observers. He turned to her, and she placed his hands on her shoulders. Looking deeply into his eyes she levitated the two of them up off the floor, and the room buzzed.

"Hold on," she whispered. Suddenly, they flew across the room together and stopped in a sudden jolt just before they hit the wall. Kayden gasped. She giggled and gently spun the two of them in circles a few inches off the floor, as if they were dancing, all the way back to the center of the floor.

"You are very strong indeed," Griffin beamed.

"You are not injured anymore, child. You are very impressive, but you are no longer injured," Adele pointed out.

Danielle walked up to Adele, her chains clanking, and pointed to the pictures on the table. "These were taken yesterday morning. I still have broken ribs and extensive bruising." She pulled up her sweatshirt to just below her bra, showing Adele her black-and-blue torso. Then she pulled down the turtleneck she wore under her shirt to expose the handprint-shaped bruises around her neck. That got the council's attention, and she regretted showing them her still-injured body. Shit! Vampires healed more quickly than she did. They were going to ask questions.

"Why aren't you healed, child?" Kane asked, stunned.

"I don't heal as quickly as others." She didn't know what else to say.

Donovan came to her rescue. "I have been reviewing the photos of you and the ones of Lance's body. Why do you think it is that you are so battered and the only real injury to Lance was the laceration to his heart and lung? The doctor's report states a large piece of glass was stuck in his back, causing him to bleed out."

Danielle walked back to her seat while she tried to think of a reasonable answer. She was scared to death. Even if they acquitted her of the murder, they could still kill her for being a half-human abomination. At least that was what her mother feared. Then, the only explanation she could think of popped into her head, and she hoped they would buy it. The whole room waited for her answer, and her heart pounded in her throat.

"I have only been able to come up with one explanation. I don't heal as quickly as others, and I am also lacking in speed and strength." Danielle paused and looked around the room. She was publicly admitting her weaknesses and the differences between her and the full-blooded vampires she faced. This could have been a huge mistake, but it was the only way to plead her case.

"On the other hand, I am far more psychically capable than others of our kind. I believe that my telepathic and telekinetic strength caused a deficit in my physical ability," she speculated.

"So during your altercation with Lance, the only weapon you had was telekinesis?" Donovan asked.

"Yes. There was no way I could fight him off physically for very long, and there was no way to control his mind. All I could do was hit him with things from around the room and try to toss him across the room and evade his grip. I was just trying to hold him off until help came. That is, until he said he'd had enough foreplay, and it was time to take what he wanted before he gave me to his master. When he tried getting my underwear off, I decided that I'd rather die than be raped or let anyone use my power to hurt others. I was so afraid of dying. I put everything I had in me into pushing him off of me. I put my hands around his neck to choke him the way he was choking me, and we both hit the opposite wall. He landed on top of me when we hit the floor, and I passed out."

Danielle hung her head in shame as the tears she fought won their battle and overflowed her eyes.

"I didn't mean to kill him. I didn't think I was physically able to do him any harm. I was hoping he would kill me rather than take me away," Danielle sniffed.

"Councilor Deidrick, what did you find when you and Councilor Vaughn reached the hotel room?" Donovan inquired.

"We kicked in the door to find the room destroyed. Lance was on the floor on the far side of the room. I was rounding the bed to help him when I noticed a small arm under him. His body was completely covering Danielle, except for her arm. She was unconscious, and Lance was dead. She was bloody and battered with her underwear down around her knees," Mason answered.

"Lance had no visible injuries with the exception of his back wound, and he had no pulse," Griffin added. "Danielle was devastated when she realized he was dead."

The chamber was completely silent, as everyone took in the information and tried to make sense of it all. Danielle rose from her seat to stand before the council table. "May I show you what happened? I can show anyone who wants to volunteer." Both Lloyd and Kane stepped to the center of the floor before her.

"It won't be like watching a movie. It's more like flashes in time. You will feel what I felt emotionally, smell what I smelled, and hear what I heard. Do you still want to do it?" she asked them.

"We can handle it, child. Show us your proof, but know that it may not be used to prove your innocence. We have not decided if we can trust your talents," Kane said condescendingly.

Danielle nodded and stepped forward. She grasped the wrists of both men and concentrated on the evening of the attack. She showed them her and Kayden entering the room alone and just a glimpse of them in bed, just before he started choking her. Then she let the rest of it flow with as much detail as she could muster.

Every blow and every word came though her, and she felt them flinching under her touch at the fear that was heavy in her heart.

"Unbelievable," Lloyd exclaimed. When she looked up, they were both looking at her like an alien they'd like to dissect.

"The council will take a recess to deliberate this matter," Lloyd said to the crowd without taking his eyes off Danielle. "Does anyone else have any further questions?" he asked the rest of the council members. Everyone declined. "Ms. Scott will be taken into custody until we have a verdict."

Gage and Darren stepped up, and each took one of Danielle's arms and started to propel her toward the door leading to the rear of the chamber. She locked eyes with Chase. Love and concern he felt for her shone in his eyes. She wanted to give him some kind of comfort, but she just didn't have it in her. She knew it would be hard on him if she was executed, but he would survive. He had family and a fiancée to get him through it.

Chase leaned his elbows on his knees and put his face in his hands.

Darren put his arm around her waist once they were in the hall. She allowed him to comfort her for a moment.

"It looks good, Dani. I think they believe you, and Donovan was a lot of help."

"Don't give her false hope, Darren," Gage said from the doorway.

Dani entered the cell, and the door slammed behind her. Gage continued. "You know the sentence for killing our kind is death, no matter what the reason. If they don't make an example out of her, there will be hell to pay, and they know it. Whether they believe her or not means nothing. I have seen them sentence others to death for lesser crimes. She should be prepared for that."

"Gage, can I talk to you for a moment?" she asked.

He nodded and walked over to the cell. She gave Darren a dismissive look, and he stepped out into the hall.

"I realize that you're being standoffish due to your position. I also know it must be hard for you to do your job when your family is hurt by it. I just want you to know that I understand, and no matter how this ends, I don't hold it against you." She reached through the bars of the cell and placed a hand on his chest. He covered her hand with his much larger one.

"I know I won't get a chance to say good-bye." Danielle choked back a sob and closed her eyes in an effort to stave off the stinging tears. Her throat felt swollen. She lowered her face and said, "If I die . . . if I die, please tell Kayden I'm sorry for leaving him. Tell him this isn't his fault. There was nothing he could have done that day. Tell him I wish we could have had the future we were dreaming about." She pulled her hand back through the bars and went to curl up in the corner of the cell.

Gage stood outside of her cell and watched her huddle in the corner before he resumed guard duty.

A short time later, when she was led back into the council chamber, the buzzing of the crowd burned in her ears. She could hear the thoughts of the vampires, as if they were screaming at her. Frightened and full of sorrow, she staggered under the weight of all the words flying at her. There was a dazing mix of hatred, love, disgust, and concern, blowing in circles like a tornado in her mind. The imaginations of her opponents showed her their thoughts of her execution, and it made her blood run cold. It was too much.

Darren tried to steady her. "Are you alright? Never mind—that was a stupid question," he said while rubbing circles on her back. He helped her to her seat, and she fell into it. She laid her head down on the table.

It was so loud. They hated her, and they loved her. They wanted her to die, and they wanted her to live. They wanted to see her pay for a death, and they wanted her acquitted. The room was split down the middle between those who feared and distrusted her and those who wanted to protect and shelter her. Her heart pounded with fear and panic. She didn't know why everything was so sharp and loud. The emotions flying around the room were painful as they assaulted her mind. She was nauseous with overwhelmed senses. The council entered the room and took their seats. The room went quiet, but the buzz in Danielle's head remained. Mason stood and spoke.

"It has been the precedent of this council to punish the murder of our kind with a death penalty. We have reviewed our historical record of such cases for the last two hundred years, and we found only fifteen cases. In each of these cases there was clear intent to murder the victim and cover up the crime. In most cases, there was more than one defendant due to the sheer force it takes to really injure an adult of our kind. So, we find ourselves walking a fine line between protecting our people, continuing to uphold a strict justice system, and upholding the idea of justice itself."

The crowd murmured and fidgeted on the edge of an outburst. Danielle clutched her head in her hands and moaned. She wished they would go ahead and kill her already. Lloyd took the floor and continued where Mason left off.

"We have clear evidence that the death of the warrior was not intentional and was likely brought on by his own foolish choices. There is a rogue on the loose who is gunning for our young. Ms. Scott has been holding the attention of this evil one due to her unique psychic powers. The fact that she has been living in fear for her life for an extended time also must have a bearing on our decision. Danielle has put her life on the line twice to spare the lives of our children. This is quite a sacrifice, considering she was not raised in our society and has no connection to us that would elicit such a response. These were purely selfless acts. Given that two members of the council were summoned to the scene by Danielle in a cry for help proves that she was looking for assistance in subduing her attacker without causing him harm." Several people in attendance balked at the use of the word *attacker*. "The scene they found on arrival is consistent with the details relayed by Danielle and Kayden. Danielle was not alone in the assault, as her future mate was in the room to witness the intent of the warrior."

Her opponents in the room began to see where this was going, and several let out cries of anger and disgust. Danielle couldn't take the noise and animosity any longer. Her head pounded with it, and she was about to be sick with the stress of the whole situation. With blood pounding in her ears, she suddenly stood and shouted, "Shut up!"

The council looked at her in confusion. Then they realized that she had frozen the entire audience. Everyone was perfectly still and quiet. She sat back down, panting with a sigh of relief. Finally, it was quiet enough for her to hear the council and her own thoughts.

"What have you done, Danielle?" Griffin asked.

"Their thoughts are so loud. I can't take it." She was still massaging her temples and holding her head in her hands. "I need to hear what you're saying and they are screaming anger, hate, love, and compassion at me all at once. I can't take any more," she panted.

"When was the last time you fed, Ms. Scott?" Mason inquired, but she didn't answer. Mason approached her seat and lifted her head to examine her face. "I believe the stress and lack of blood is overwhelming her," Mason said to the rest of the council. "I will call for a human to assist after the hearing concludes." To Danielle, he said, "I need you to release the room so we may finish the hearing. Then we'll get you some blood. Do you understand?"

"Yes, sir," she replied, as her head lulled to the side and the crowd began to hum once more, as if they had never stopped.

Twenty-five

Danielle was relieved when the crowd hushed in surprise at seeing Mason standing over her. He'd been sitting in his chair a second ago.

"Is she alright?" Kayden stepped up. He brushed her cheek with the back of his hand.

"I'm fine. The noise is more than I can take right now," she said, and she held his hand to her cheek.

"May we continue now?" Kane drawled. "This chamber is a place of law, and it demands the respect of our kind. Keep your comments to yourselves or be permanently ejected. Please, continue, Lloyd."

"All the evidence in this case points to the fact that Danielle Scott and Kayden Paris were hunted down and attacked with the intent of handing Danielle over to a rogue. It is the opinion of this council that if we punish Danielle for Lance's death, we will also have to punish any warrior who kills one of us in defense of our laws. We have been hunting the rogue and would not hesitate to kill him if he were located. Lance fell in with the wrong side of the law and paid the ultimate price for that mistake. It should be understood that this does not give free rein for any vampire to kill another. We will judge crimes on a case-by-case basis and will not hesitate to strike down any that break our law. If we had apprehended Lance with proof of his betrayal, we would have executed him for the crimes ourselves," Lloyd finished.

Kane scowled as if he didn't agree with the ruling. "It is the opinion of some council members that this should not go unpunished." Kane stood to add, "Therefore, Ms. Scott will be removed from the Enclave and no longer live under our protection. I find it unfair that warriors would have to defend a person who killed one of his or her own, whether it was justified or not. She also claims that there are more traitors in our warrior class. If she cannot trust our warriors, she does not deserve to benefit from their protection."

Darren came up out of his seat at that, and Gage grabbed his arm to pull him back. "She will live, warrior. You should be happy with that."

"But for how long?" She heard Darren ask Gage.

"Danielle, do you have anything to say in response?" Griffin asked.

The room was still buzzing with agitated warriors, others who looked forward to watching her execution, and people who were so relieved to know it wasn't going to take place. Her head throbbed with it.

"I am grateful for the understanding of the council. I am truly sorry for hurting or offending anyone. I would never willingly bring harm to another. I hope I can be forgiven in time. I also understand the warriors not wanting my presence in their Enclave. I hope that when I leave, they will remember my appreciation of their past protection. I also hope others in your society will remember my efforts to keep the children safe. The person hunting us will likely find me. If it is possible to keep my powers from being used to do any harm to you, I will, because I promise you that if he gets them, you will all regret this day. Even if I am rejected by your society, I will still do my best to protect the young." With that, she leaned back in her chair and nearly collapsed.

Griffin jumped from his seat and leapt over the table to go to her. The crowd buzzed. He lifted her from the chair and carried her out into the hall. He gave Mason a meaningful look that was acknowledged. She needed blood.

Darren, Kayden, and Chase all followed closely behind as Griffin carried Dani to the room used by the council to relax during recesses or for other meetings that didn't require the use of the chamber.

Placing her limp body gently on a leather sofa, he glared at Kayden. "When was the last time she fed? Were you not taught that our males provide for and protect our females?"

"I don't know when she last fed. She's very secretive about it, almost like it embarrasses her. She mostly uses bagged blood, because she's so confined to the Enclave. There aren't any humans milling about there for her to charm. I have only seen her twice since she was arrested. She didn't want me to see her like that," Kayden confessed.

"It doesn't matter now." Griffin was furious. Nobody had taught his baby to properly care for herself, and the guilt of his failure to be a father to her stabbed at him painfully. "All of you, get out. Mason went to find her a human, and I'm sure she won't want an audience. Darren, you are dismissed from your charge. Return to Gage for your next assignment. I will figure out how we are going to protect her from now on."

Mason stuck his head in a side door. "Get out, now!" he said to Chase and Kayden, who were still lingering around the main door to the hall. Indignantly they left, closing the door behind them.

Griffin tended Danielle, trying to get her positioned comfortably on the sofa. He waited for the human Mason had procured for Danielle to appear.

Mason locked the main door and went back to the side door he had entered and instructed the human to lock the door.

"Get over here," Griffin growled when the door shut.

Footsteps came right up to his side. He tilted Danielle's head back to accept the blood and reached for the human's arm, tugging the person to her knees. Quickly slicing across the human's wrist, he pulled it to his daughter's mouth. He didn't care if Danielle drained the human dry, as long as she woke and opened those beautiful eyes so he could adore her. "Be still," he told the human.

After a moment, Danielle reached for the arm and held it to her mouth.

"That's right, baby. Take what you need. Mommy is here now. I won't let them hurt you anymore." Tessa brushed a hand over Dani's hair.

Dani's eyes snapped open, and her mouth stilled.

"No sweetheart, don't stop. You're not hurting me."

Griffin gaped at her.

"I didn't know it was you, my love." He reached out a hand to touch her cheek, but she moved.

"Don't touch me, Griffin," Tessa snapped.

After a few more deep draws, Dani licked the wound on her mom's wrist to close it. She sat up and stared back and forth between her mom and Griffin. Griffin was looking at her mom longingly, as if he wanted to wrap her up in his arms. Tessa looked at Griffin with hurt, angry eyes.

"Thank you, Mom," she interrupted. "How did you get here?"

"Your father caught me stalking the halls of the chamber trying to listen in on the hearing. I tried to leave and wait for you to call me, but I couldn't. I was in my car in the parking lot when Mason called me and said you needed blood. I told you to start feeding more often. I know you don't like it, but you must feed, Danielle. Feeding every once in a while is not enough to sustain you without you going all black-eyed freak on me."

Dani smiled at her mother's use of her description of the vampire race.

Griffin got up off his knees and began to pace behind the sofa. "So let me get this straight. Mason is close enough to you that he had your cell number? My daughter has been here with me all this time, and no one thought I deserved to know? You have been alive for all these years, and I didn't deserve to know my child? She has had no one to properly teach her, and you didn't think she deserved any better than that? You let me suffer and mourn for you all this time and didn't care?"

Danielle looked from her mom to Griffin and back. The look on Tessa's face said she was about to explode. Dani didn't particularly want to be a witness.

"I think I'm going to go find Kayden. Thank you so much for helping me, Mom. I will call you later. I'm going home with you. I have no home here now, and I don't think it's safe for my friends if I go back to school. I love you." She kissed her mother on the top of her head and went to the door. When she opened the door, she saw Sarah and Sam in the hall. She pushed the door shut before they saw her.

"Shit! You guys may want to continue this later. Sarah and Sam are in the hall waiting for you, Griffin."

Her mom went around the other side of the sofa and looked up into the eyes of the man she loved so deeply. "Mason saved me and Danielle."

"Her name is Soleil," he said through his teeth.

"Mason gave us a safe place, where your family couldn't find us, until I went out on my own. He made sure they would believe we were dead so Dani and I could be together. He knew you would come to me as soon as you knew where we were. So we waited for your parents to find the fake evidence of our deaths. It was torture. I spoke to you all day, every day. I cried to you all night, every night.

You didn't answer me. You never answered me." She blinked, and tears flowed over her lashes.

"When they finally told you of our deaths, Mason was sure you would call him immediately, but you didn't call him. The day he came to tell me you were going to bond to Sarah, you were supposed to meet him. He was going to bring you to me, so we could find a way to get you out of your engagement. I don't understand why you couldn't tell it was a lie. I have felt you every day of every year, but you couldn't feel me. I have never loved another, never touched another." She paused, taking a deep breath.

"I wouldn't allow him to tell you. If you cared so little for me and Soleil that you agreed to remarry less than twelve hours after hearing of our deaths, then you never really loved me." She backed away from him. "But I never stopped loving you. How dare you stand in judgment of me, you unfaithful bastard! As for being close to Mason, I left our safe house the day you bonded to that woman. I never spoke to him again. Until she started college this fall, Dani was a completely normal human girl. When her power took her over, I had to ask for help. Not that I need to explain myself to you. Why don't you go to your wife and family and leave me to mine?"

Dani leaned against the door, big tears falling on her shirt, as she took in her mother's pain. Griffin didn't seem to be able to form any sort of reply to her mother's rant. He backed away slowly. Dani moved to allow him to leave, but he stopped at the door and looked her over. With a weak smile, Griffin tucked a strand of white hair behind her ear and kissed her on the cheek.

When he left the room, her mother crumbled onto the sofa.

Dani swiftly crossed the room and held her tightly while she cried for a while. This whole experience had to be devastating for her mom. She'd put on a brave face in front of Griffin, but seeing him again had clearly taken a toll on her. Dani didn't know how to ease her pain. The best she could do was to be a shoulder to cry on whenever needed.

There was a knock at the door to the main hall. "Angel, I saw Griffin leave. Are you alright in there?" A deep voice came from the other side of the door.

"It's Kayden," she mouthed to her mom.

Then there was a knock at the side entrance Tessa had come in. "Lovely. Are you well enough for a visitor?" That door wasn't locked, so she quickly pulled the hood up over Tessa's head and mouthed, "Chase."

Tessa rolled her eyes. "I'm heading out. Call me as soon as you can." Tessa put her head down so she was completely covered and opened the side door.

Dani watched Tessa retreat through the crack in the door. Chase had begun to walk back down the hall and was halfway to the exit. He stopped, suddenly turning his back toward the doorway as Tessa passed him. He grabbed her by the arm and pulled her to his chest in a tight hug.

"Lovely, you frightened me. I think we should have Doc come have a look at you. You've been through a lot and you aren't feeding properly."

Dani stepped out into the hall, hoping he would see her and release Tessa. She cleared her throat, and his head snapped up to look at her. She went back into the office. Confused, he dropped her mother as if she'd burned him and ran down the hall to meet Dani. Dani felt sorry for the guy. She assumed Chase had smelled her mom's similar scent and had mistaken Tessa's nearly identical body frame for her.

"Lovely, I thought that was you," he stuttered.

"Nice to know you can't tell me from some other chick. That's true love for you, huh?" She grinned at him. He looked relieved that she wasn't angry.

"She smelled just like you, baby. I'm sorry," he apologized.

"I just fed from her. She likely has my scent all over her." She'd been through a terrifying experience, and as much as she knew she should stay away from him, Dani really just wanted to lean on Chase for a minute. She wrapped her arms around his waist and buried her face in his chest. He sighed and laid his cheek on top of her head, squeezing her back and rocking just a little.

That was how Mason found them. Chase must have expected Mason to be angry, but he didn't release her. The pink that spread across Chase's face when he saw Mason was precious. She couldn't help smiling at him. If they could be together, she didn't think anything would ever come between them. There was a connection that pulled on her constantly and made her want to hold him, touch him, and kiss him. It was hard work to stay away from Chase. She wished she could be his friend. She wished she could allow herself to be with him until his bonding, but she couldn't. It hurt too badly already.

"Why didn't you tell me the girl you wanted to break your engagement for was Danielle?" Mason shut the door and looked from her to Chase.

"I didn't think it would matter, Dad," Chase returned. "You saw me arguing with Kayden after the dress shop incident. So I didn't think it was a surprise."

What did he just say? *Dad?* Mason was Chase's father? That meant . . . Oh God, what did that mean? She stepped away from Chase and fell back on the sofa with a flop.

"It matters very much, actually. There are some things the three of us need to discuss, but I think it would be better if we didn't do it here. Dani and I are going to have a talk and then we'll meet you at your condo." Mason ushered Chase toward the door.

Dani had never known Mason's last name. Mason and Chase had never acted particularly close when she saw them together. Every time she'd seen them together, it was during a time of stress, so she didn't pick up on their relationship. Chase had never called him Dad before. Would he tell Chase who she was? No, he couldn't do that.

"No, Mason. There's nothing for us to talk about," she insisted.

"But, honey, things could be different." Mason crossed the room to sit by her and take her hand. The look on Chase's face was so hopeful.

"You can't. I can't. No," she sputtered. "Chase, could you leave me alone with Mason?"

"Hell no! I want to know what's going on here! What are you two talking about?" Chase stood firm, unwilling to give them privacy.

"Mason, do not make me freeze him. I can't deal with this. Do you have any idea what I've been through today? And there are other things we need to think about before you start jumping the gun." She was gruff.

"Chase, wait for me in the chamber." Mason was annoyed.

"No! You guys can't do this to me. I deserve to know what's going on!" Chase's eyes flared black.

"Please, give me a moment with Mason," she begged.

Chase dragged her up off the sofa to wrap her in a tight hug. "I know this is no excuse to you, but I have a duty to my house and to my people. I don't know how to walk away from that. I don't know how to fight a prophecy, Danielle. I'm supposed to stop this rogue and save our kids. I don't know how to undo that, but for you, I was trying." He kissed her lightly and left the room, dragging his feet as if he were forcing himself to go.

It was quiet for a few moments, while both she and Mason sorted out their thoughts. Then he asked, "Why don't you want me to tell him? Because I have to tell you, I have never seen him behave that way. I'm not even sure that was my son. I also think you should know that your mother and I believe the prophecy Griffin's sister gave us refers to you and not the other Vaughn girls."

"You're grasping at straws with the prophecy. If he's meant to be with one of us, he will be, no matter what. He professes his love to me, but he chooses her every time. He's never told her he wants to be with me. For all you know, she is the one he needs. I'll tell you one thing. I will be damned before I bond myself to a man out of obligation to some prophecy. If he doesn't love me enough to choose me, no matter the consequence, I don't want him. If you tell him who I am, then he will use it as his reason for breaking up with Sam. What if it's her in the prophecy, Mason? What if it isn't even Chase who is meant to fulfill the prophecy? Don't screw with fate any further. If he leaves her because of who I am, I will live the rest of my life wondering if he would have married her. Either he makes this decision on his own or I won't have him. Don't forget that we have no idea what Griffin is going to do now. He knows who I am, but that doesn't mean he'll claim me publicly. That would tarnish his family's reputation," she argued.

"These are valid points, but things would go more smoothly if we helped them along. If Griffin knew you and Chase were in love, he would see the connection to the prophecy and be more likely to take the risk," Mason returned.

"You just don't get it." She crossed the short distance between them and cupped his face. "I won't be second best, Mason. The men in my life will choose me for no other reason than they can't live without me, or I will not have them. If my father is too embarrassed to claim me as his child for no other reason than that he is proud to have me as a daughter, then I will not force myself on him and his family. If Chase doesn't pick me over her, prophecy be damned, it isn't enough for me. And have you thought of the fact that Chase has no idea I'm human? He may not want me after he finds out that little tidbit."

"You're half-human," Mason countered.

"I'm human enough for it to make me weaker than your kind, and he's not going to want my mutt babies," she whispered.

"You are much stronger than our kind in many ways. As far as babies go, I think that is the whole problem here. You're afraid he is going to reject you when he finds out you're human. You won't let him get close enough for it to matter. Also, you don't want your children to suffer the rejection you feel. I love you, Soleil. I love you no matter what you are, and he will too." Mason pulled her into his arms and rocked her.

"I need to think, and I need you to promise to keep a lid on this until we see what Griffin is going to do. Please take my feelings into consideration. This is my life, and I won't live it for people who could reject me for being beneath them. When the time comes, I will tell Chase I'm human. I also have to think of Kayden. So please don't push me." She stepped out of his arms and walked away.

Twenty-six

After her disagreement with Mason in the council chamber, Dani wandered down the corridor, feeling like her head would explode. He wouldn't see her point of view, and she wouldn't give in to his wishes. She could clearly see where Chase got his pigheaded nature.

She needed to get back to the Enclave to retrieve her things, but she didn't want to ask either of the men in her life for a ride. They were the reason for the persistent pounding in her head, so she was on her own. The chamber doors were still open, and two deep male voices could be heard echoing off the wall-to-wall marble. Of course, Chase and Kayden were both waiting for her. They were actually being agreeable and behaving like old friends instead of archenemies. Seeing them that way reminded her of the reason for their estrangement. They could both really use a good friend, and she was the wedge between them. She'd screwed up everything she'd touched since meeting those men.

"Do you need a ride? I promise not to ask any questions about your health or badger you to bond with me." Darren scared the shit out of her when he interrupted her spying. He looked over her head at Chase and Kayden.

That sounded like the ticket to her. She left with Darren, not stopping to say good-bye to the double trouble waiting for her. She needed to be alone with her thoughts and figure out the next step. It took no time to pack at the Enclave, and Darren kept watch at the door, in case any of Lance's men decided to exact their own revenge.

Dani found the sunburst necklace her mom had given her the day she left for college hanging from the lamp switch, where she always put it before crawling into bed. That day seemed like ages ago. She put the necklace on and smiled at herself in the mirror. It no longer mattered if Griffin saw the necklace.

Darren offered to take leave from work and go with her. He wanted to protect her from the danger they both knew would be coming, but she couldn't let him do that. That was her punishment, and she would deal with it. He walked her to the car, where both Chase and Kayden waited and looked quite perturbed.

"I'll call to check on you tomorrow. You can call me whenever you like." Darren surprised her with a hug and a kiss placed on top of her head before going back inside.

"I can't leave you alone for a second without some loser thinking he can grab on you, can I?" Kayden asked jokingly, but the undercurrent of jealousy was clear.

"He was just being kind. He believes I'll be dead before he sees me again. Every time I leave the Enclave, they catch me. This time, I won't be coming back. If I get into trouble, the cavalry won't be coming to save me. It's all gloom and doom, right?" She laughed nervously.

"Where will you go?" Chase asked.

"I'm going to stay in my hometown for a bit, until I get some things figured out. I can't go back to school and endanger my friends, and I don't want to impose on anyone here or put them in danger, so I think it's the best idea." She was still trying to convince herself of that and feared bringing trouble to her mother's door.

"You need to come home with me, angel," Kayden sweet-talked. "You have your own room and two warriors to watch over you. Mom is already buzzing around in anticipation of having you there." He took her bags and put them in the trunk of her car.

"Your house is the first place they will look for me, Kayden. If anything happened to Koren because of me, I would never forgive myself. You and Gage can't be there all the time with your crazy schedules," she reminded him.

Opening the driver's door, she watched Chase, who was leaning on her hood and looking at the ground. His head was full of questions about the conversation from earlier, but she couldn't deal with him.

"I just want to tell you both that I'm sorry for all the trouble I've caused you and your families. I wish the two of you could find a way to be friends again."

Chase turned to her then. "You sound like you're not coming back. You are coming back, aren't you?"

She looked at them both and gave a halfhearted smile. She didn't know what to say, and she couldn't make any promises. A black sedan pulled up behind her car, drawing all of their attention. Both Chase and Kayden moved to stand in front of her, as if they thought the bad guys could possibly have made it onto the Enclave. Griffin stepped out and sauntered up to them, carrying a small shoulder bag.

"May I speak with you privately, Sol . . . Danielle?" He corrected himself before he let loose what she affectionately referred to as her baby-vamp name. Shrugging their shoulders, both the guys walked a good distance away from her car to give them privacy.

She said nothing but went to stand before him.

He reached out and lifted the charm from around her neck to inspect it. "I gave that to your mother the day we were bonded." He smiled wistfully.

"She gave it to me recently." He turned it over to look at the inscription. "I guess the center of your universe shifted to another star," she mused.

He looked at her sharply and a tick started in his jaw. It was a low blow, but her heart still ached for her mother, and he was the cause of so many years of her suffering. On the back of her car he opened the bag he'd been carrying and pulled out a gun.

"You have learned to shoot, correct?" He loaded the gun and checked the safety. "Can I assume there are no children in your mother's house to find a loaded weapon?" He glanced at her from the corner of his eye.

"I have a gun already, thank you. Gage gave me the one I practiced with."

He winced at her dead tone and put the gun back in the bag. She shouldn't be that way. They'd become friends, but this day, the knot of raw emotions couldn't be untangled. Since he now knew who she was, she felt the need to share some of her frustration at his absence in her life.

"There are some other things in there you might need. You can look through it later." He put the bag over her shoulder. She opened the bag to peek inside. There was the gun, a box of bullets, and, below that, several stacks of hundred-dollar bills.

"What is this, Griffin? I don't need your sympathy or a handout. I'm still the same girl I was yesterday, and you don't need to provide for me now any more than you have my whole life." The bag fell to the ground.

He grabbed her hand before she could get away. "Listen to me, Soleil. If they find you, you will need to run. Trying to run with no money is very difficult. If you use cash, you can't be tracked. It isn't a handout. It's a backup plan for your safety. Please, take it," he urged.

"No, thanks. I'll deal with whatever comes." She extracted her hand from his grip and walked to the driver-side door. "Maybe I'll see you around."

"Tell me something?" he asked. She paused without turning around. "Is Scott really your last name?"

"No. It's Vaughn." She chuckled. "I picked Scott on a whim the day I met you. It was the last name of the guy I was dating at the time, and I needed a different name. Mom was terrified your people were going to kill the half-breed abomination when they figured me out, so she told me to pick an alias."

"And your mother?" he asked, embarrassed.

"We have the same name. She said, whether you abandoned her or not, she was still bonded, and she would keep her husband's name." That hit him hard. From her periphery vision, she saw him lean on her trunk and hang his head. "Can I ask you something?" She struck while he was still weak. "Are you going to publicly acknowledge me as your daughter?" Too afraid of the answer, she still didn't turn around. His head came up, but he looked away.

"I don't know what to do yet. I need to speak to your mother."

"Mom has nothing to do with it. Either I'm your daughter, or we go on like we have been, and you can forget you ever met me. You can't have it both ways. It's up to you. I won't interfere with your family either way." She dreamed of him being so overjoyed to have her back that he took her into his life and his home to love and protect just like the rest of his children. That wasn't going to be.

"You are my family, Soleil. Please be patient with me for a few days while I get my head on straight. I got the shock of my life today, and I'm just trying to remember how to put one foot in front of the other."

"No problem, Dad. Take all the time you need. You can have another couple decades if you like." The hurt and agitation in her voice betrayed her efforts at nonchalance. She slid in behind the wheel and drove off before either of the guys saw her go. She couldn't say good-bye to either of them.

She'd been home for almost a week with no trouble in sight, except for a run-in with Lucas. His mom ran into her at the grocery store, and before Dani could finish shopping and pay the cashier, Lucas was on her. He wanted to talk about mistakes and misunderstandings. That seemed to be the theme of her life of late. The contrast between the constant drama of being in vamp society and the constant calm of being at home was a shock to her system. Of course, there were still the daily phone calls from the vamp world. Koren tried to convince her to stay with them. Kayden's influence was obvious in those conversations. He called several times a day, trying to get an address out of her so he could visit. But the chance of him being followed was too great.

She hadn't heard a word from Chase or Griffin, but Mason called her mom every day. Dani knew Mason was mad at her. She was sure Chase wanted answers that Mason had sworn to keep secret. Mason didn't agree with her reasoning, but he would keep his word. Tessa said it was hard for a parent to see his or her child hurting, especially if something could be done to stop the pain. Darren called too, but she wasn't answering. She didn't trust that he wouldn't use his spy mojo to track her location.

The day of the gala quickly approached, and she was supposed to go, but without security, it would be dangerous. She did have that lovely new gown Debbie had sent her after the dress shop incident. It would be rude not to go and make use of her gift, but that wasn't a good-enough reason to risk the lives of everyone around her.

"Hello, Earth to Danielle? Are you there, Danielle?" Tessa asked from the other side of the breakfast table.

"Huh? I'm sorry, I'm just . . . I don't know what I am," she confessed.

"Well, could you answer the door for me while you work it out?" She raised an eyebrow at her from over her newspaper. Dani shrugged and went to the front door but didn't see anyone at first. She stepped outside to find her dear old godfather reclining on the porch swing. She grabbed a coat and went to sit by him, waiting for him to start in on her about Chase and Griffin.

"Are you ready to go yet?" he asked, putting an arm around her shoulder. "The Staffords are giving you a dinner party tonight. It would be rude of the guest of honor not to show up."

"What? I don't know anything about a party tonight. I don't think it's a good idea for me to go back. It's not safe for anyone involved," she sputtered.

"Let me worry about that, my sweet. Tonight you will stay with the Staffords and tomorrow we will talk some more. Now, go get your things." He smoothed a hand over her head.

"I don't have anything to wear to one of your fancy parties, Mason," she dithered.

"That's not what your mother said when we spoke," he coaxed. Tessa stepped out onto the porch with an impish grin.

"Do you want me to go with you?" Tessa asked.

"Why? So you can hide in a hotel room the whole time and sneak around in the shadows? Why are you two pushing me like this?" She felt cornered and wanted to lash out at them both.

"You have things to sort out and you can't do it from here. Trust me. Running from a problem doesn't make it go away. It will catch up with you sooner or later, even if it takes twenty-one years. You're better off dealing with it now." Tessa looked out over the brightening morning sky and nodded as if she'd just convinced herself of the rightness of her words.

"Let's go gather your things." She held open the screen door, not accepting *no* for an answer.

It took six hours to get to the Stafford estate and another two hours for Dani to settle the butterflies in her stomach. She wasn't ready to face those people again. A knock at her guest room door startled her. She opened the door to find Donovan smiling widely. He was in much more casual attire than when they first met. His jeans and tight black T-shirt showed off his lean, muscular body. It should have been considered a crime against women to look so good without the slightest effort.

"I almost didn't recognize you without your bracelets," he joked. It took a moment before she realized he meant the handcuffs she'd been wearing when they met. "If it's possible, you are even more breathtaking than last I saw you. Maybe it's the blood that has brightened you so sweetly."

She blushed. He was smooth and such a honey. He was hot in a manly, worldly way, like Mason, only yummier. That could have been because Mason was like a parental unit to her.

"Can I help you, Donovan?" she asked when she finally found her voice. He stared and made her squirm.

"Please, call me Van. Mother asked me to tell you the guests are arriving and cocktails will be served soon. When you're ready, I will escort you downstairs. I believe your date is already here, but my mom is old-fashioned. There is no way he's getting up the stairs to escort you himself." As he spoke, he looked her up and down, and suddenly she felt naked.

"Are you going dressed like that?" She pointed to his jeans. "If so, I won't have to put my heels on."

"No." He chuckled. "My mother would die twice. I was just about to go change. Just dial extension eight when you're ready. My room is around the corner, so I will be directly over to retrieve you."

"Thank you." She didn't know what else to say. Van sauntered down the hall like a cat on the prowl as she closed her door. She slid on the slinky, black, backless dress her mother had given her and a pair of heels with straps that wrapped around her calves to tie on the side. They looked kind of Grecian. She decided that putting her hair up was best with the backless dress. Looking at herself, she wondered if her mother had lost her mind. Did she want every man in vampire society sniffing around her skirt?

She called Van, but before she reached the door, she thought of her starburst. It was perfect. Dani opened the door just as Van began to knock. He was gorgeous in an Armani suit with his wavy hair slicked back. She had to control her smile while they looked over each other with approval.

"I think you should ditch that dude downstairs and stay on my arm all night. On second thought, you should stay next to me forever, Ms. Scott." He had a way of quickly undressing and burning a girl with his midnight eyes.

"I would hate to deprive all the ladies in your life of your presence. It would be a shame not to share such a stunningly masculine treat," she purred, and pulled the door shut to step out into the hall.

He smiled a little disbelieving smile. He was obviously not used to being shot down. He'd probably flattered hundreds of girls with that line, and she knew it was a line. He put his arm out and led her to the top of the stairs. The sounds of conversation, soft music, and clanking glasses rose from below. She paused to take a deep breath, hating being the center of attention.

"Are you alright? If you're not feeling up to this, I can take you back to my room and make it all better," he teased her. His idea of "better" would be her ruination for sure.

Darren was pissed. They'd cancelled Danielle's protection detail and hung her out to dry. Couldn't those fools see that they'd signed her death warrant? Did they want to see her dead? He was forbidden from following Danielle while he was on duty. All he could do was spend all of his time off with her, and that wouldn't leave him much time for resting or feeding. He would love it if Danielle was willing to let him feed from her. That would be delicious, and the thought of being at her neck made him hard. He would leave the Wrath and protect her for the rest of his life if she would agree to be his mate. If they were bonded, the others wouldn't matter to her anymore. That was his plan the night of the bonding they'd attended together. He'd hoped to convince her he was a better male than the rest of the population that begged for her attention. He'd gone from romantic warrior to jealous wannabe boyfriend that night in the space of a moment, when he found her in that dark room with Chase. When Chase had started texting her from the other side of the room, Darren had lost his mind. That was a huge mistake. He'd screwed it all up.

She was out there unprotected, and he had no idea where she was. Neither did anyone else. He didn't even know if she was still alive, because she wasn't answering her phone. The council had seen to it that most of the warriors didn't care one way or the other. It made him sick, and his mind went around and around with the possibility that some rogue bastard could have already taken her, and he hadn't been there to protect her from the fate she was sentenced to, just because she'd been born an incredibly powerful being.

He had to find her and do his best to make her his. It was the only way he could protect her all the time, the only way he could keep her to himself. After they were bonded, she wouldn't think about the others anymore, she would only think of him, want only him, be with only him. He would do anything for her now. He couldn't imagine how much more he would love her after she was his mate. He was going to do whatever it took to take her for his own.

His cell rang, and he jumped. It was a friend he sparred with regularly. Darren was glad he called. Getting out some pent-up aggression sounded like a damn good idea. "Hey, what's up, Todd? You ready for a fight?"

"No, man. I got some info I thought you would be interested in. Several warriors, including Wrath, have been assigned to keep a perimeter around the Stafford estate tonight. They waited for the last minute to call extra security, because they're trying to keep things quiet. They are having a dinner party to thank Danielle Scott for saving their son. I know the two of you got close when she was your charge. I thought you might be interested."

The sound of her name made Darren's heart leap. She was alive and well, and back in town.

"I owe you big, man. I'll let you beat my ass for a change the next time we meet in the ring." He leapt off his bed and ran for the shower.

Twenty-seven

Kayden waited anxiously at the bottom of the stairs for Dani to appear. He hadn't seen her in what felt like a year and needed to see with own eyes that she was safe and whole.

Chase was on the other side of the room, watching from a safe distance, a weird thing for him. Normally, he would be jockeying for position at Danielle's side. He'd even struck up a conversation with Kayden when he arrived. Maybe Dani's request that he and Kayden try to be friends again had affected him. Chase hadn't been the same since the day of the hearing, and it was nice to talk to the friend he missed so much.

Dani was not going to like the party. It was supposed to be a small dinner party, but the entire council and their families were all in attendance, as well as Kayden's parents, Doc Stevens, Melinda Prince and her family, not to mention that overbearing jerk, Darren, along with a handful of single male vamps. Kayden was sure Veronica Stafford was trying to find a more upper-class mate for Dani.

He smelled her before he saw her. The delicious scent of floral vanilla hit him like a wrecking ball, just before she stepped into view. She was a dream in black with her hair swept up beautifully in a purposefully messy updo. Her white hair gave her what she would call a "Bride of Frankenstein" look. She was on the arm of Donovan Stafford.

Kayden looked over to Chase, and they shared an annoyed look. They couldn't stand that arrogant prick. It figured he would be the first one Veronica would push at Dani. Veronica had been trying to reform his playboy ways forever, and Dani was just the girl to make a man rethink his way of life. Hell, Kayden himself had joined the warriors just to be closer to her. His playboy status had rivaled Van's, but that had all changed the day Dani kissed him.

Everyone turned to watch the couple descend the grand staircase in the foyer, where cocktails were being served. Danielle's face flushed the sweetest pink, and Kayden couldn't resist anymore. By the time she was three-quarters of the way down, he went to retrieve his girl from Van's arm and take her the rest of the way himself.

Dani smiled his favorite naughty half smile and took his arm, happily before she kissed his lower lip by way of a greeting. It took his breath away that she cared enough for him to make it clear to the rest of the room that she was with him in a subtle but sure way.

"I'm pleased to be in your arms again, Angel," he told her quietly, and his heart melted when she proudly took his hand. Never having been insecure by nature, Kayden hated the feeling that others believed he wasn't good enough for Dani. She'd told him several times how ridiculous that was. She believed she was beneath him in that respect. She was born of an unknown family and raised by a reclusive human family servant. Kayden was from a long line of the most respected warriors in their history and was a fine warrior in his own right. She always had a way of dispelling his worries with a simple word and batting those long, dark eyelashes at him.

Kayden decided before Dani left the Enclave a week before to ask her to be his mate and bond to him. The only problem was he was aware of her aversion to bonding at such a young age. Having been raised in a human society, she found it hard to swallow that people wouldn't wait until they finished college and had established themselves first. In vamp society, it wasn't unusual for the young to have a bond arranged by their families and carried out at an early age. Chase was twenty-one and Samantha only eighteen, but they would be bonded within the next year or so. The point was, Kayden didn't want to let that night pass without telling Dani how he felt and what his intentions were toward her. He even bought her a traditional human engagement ring and was willing to take part in the human custom of an engagement period, if that helped to settle her nerves. He just needed to know that she was his and always would be.

Kayden hung back and allowed Dani to entertain the crowd that assembled to wish her well for her bravery and celebrate her acquittal. She was a trooper and swallowed her agony at being the center of so much attention. He would think she would be used to it, with everyone always trying to revolve around her.

In the far corner of the room, Chase looked about as unhappy as Kayden had ever seen him. Sam hovered over him and spoke animatedly to several younger vamps about how happy they were to be promised to each other. She tried to get Chase to commit publicly to a date for their bonding ceremony. Chase wouldn't even join the conversation.

Noticing Chase watching Danielle intently, Kayden decided to step a little closer. He placed a hand on her beautifully bare back, and Dani immediately responded to his touch by leaning in to his side. Veronica did her best to introduce Danielle to the cream of the vamp crop in attendance for her mating pleasure. Veronica was really trying to find her a suitable bond mate, but Dani wouldn't release Kayden for even a moment to give anyone the chance to make her an offer. It made Kayden even more sure that solidifying their relationship would be the right thing to do. People should be bonded for love. He loved Dani. It wasn't about a connection or prestige between them. He knew Dani wasn't in love with him yet, but they had a solid foundation to build on. Their bond would be strong and they would both be happy in the end.

Chase couldn't have been more annoyed with the situation. His Lovely was right there, and he couldn't even speak to her. He couldn't even move in her direction without Sam cutting him off. She did everything possible to keep them apart, and it worked. Every so often, Danielle looked at him, and he saw her longing. Someone who didn't know her as well as he did would have missed it, but he'd been in her very soul and could tell what she was thinking by the slightest expression, turn of her head, or the set of her jaw. Chase had convinced himself that seeing Sam hang on him, spouting happiness and love, hurt Dani, so she clung to Kayden for support.

Chase's mind returned to the first night he saw Danielle after the shit storm Sam caused between them in his bedroom. Dani had been injured by the physical beating she received from Nathan and the emotional beating she received from him. Chase had practically dragged her to his suite in the back of the club with the excuse of needing information to help recover another missing girl. He'd been so angry when he saw that human boy touching and kissing his Lovely.

She'd told him that night, *I need his comfort to help me stay away from you. I have wanted you since the night I met you. I can't get you out of my head.*

That was all Kayden was to her. A friend who dulled the pain Chase caused her. He was sure Danielle had true feelings for Kayden, but she wasn't in love with him. When she looked at Kayden, Chase didn't see the burning want he saw in her eyes when she looked at him, but seeing their cozy familiarity made him sick. How was he ever going to survive it?

"May I speak with you privately for a moment, son?" Mason cut into Sam's discussion with a group of women regarding where she would like to honeymoon.

"Yes, sir," Chase groused, angry with his father for keeping secrets. Mason knew a lot more about Danielle than he'd ever let on. The problem was he wouldn't share the information, and that really pissed Chase off. Whatever they kept from him was life changing. He knew it. How could his father allow him to suffer that way? Chase followed his father to the study and flopped down in a chair by the fireplace.

"We have a problem. I was just speaking to Gage. It seems that your boy, Kayden, has some big plans for tonight. It's only fair that I forewarn you." Mason's tone was thick with dread.

"What kind of plans?" Chase turned to glare at the closed door separating him from Lovely.

"Gage says Kayden can no longer tolerate being separated from Dani. Kayden told his parents he would ask Dani to be his mate tonight. He hopes to be bonded to her immediately so they will be inseparable." Mason frowned.

Chase growled and his eyes went instantly black with rage.

"I know you're angry with me for keeping information from you, but there is one thing I will tell you, and the rest is up to you. If she accepts him and becomes his mate, it will only be to stop the pain she feels over you. It happens frequently with our kind. In fact, I will share a secret with you and trust you as my son to keep it to yourself always." He paused again and took a deep breath. "Griffin was bonded before Sarah."

"I didn't know that." Chase was surprised by the revelation.

"Neither does Sarah. That's why it's a secret. His first mate was, well, she wasn't up to his parents' standards, but he loved her so much he bonded to her in secret." Mason knew he was on the edge of betraying Dani's trust, but he would do his best not to cross the line. He might not agree with her reasons for keeping the secret, but he did understand them. She wanted Chase to choose her no matter the cost. She didn't want her mating to be the product of a vision revealed by a heartsick girl, before Dani was even born.

"What happened to his mate?" Chase asked.

"She died in childbirth along with the baby. Griffin couldn't handle it. Before he went mad with grief, he agreed to accept the bond his parents arranged for no other reason than to stop the pain of his loss. He thought Sarah would replace his first mate in his heart and stop his torment."

"Did it work?" Chase stood to pace the floor in front of the fireplace.

"I don't think so, not as well as he wished. He still mourned, and his relationship with Sarah has never been what he had with Tessa. Some kinds of love can never be washed away. You know that Griffin's older sister and my older brother were secretly bonded, right?" Mason inquired.

Chase nodded.

"When David killed himself to protect Leann from being harmed by his power, her grief was so profound she committed suicide and followed him to his grave." Mason took a moment to tuck that painful memory back into the corner of his mind where he kept it. "The point is, Danielle may be willing to do anything to stop her pain. I know the two of you have not been bonded, but the connection she feels with you is as strong as any bond I've ever witnessed. Griffin and Tessa were madly in love already when they bonded. The bond gave them a mental connection that you and Dani already share, but it didn't force them to love each other. It was the best kind of bond, one done out of love instead of obligation or as a means to end suffering."

"Why are you telling me this, Dad? You know I don't want Sam, but you're forcing me into a bond. So why torture me?" He sagged back into the chair.

"I just want you to know the difference between pure love and a blood bond. If she bonds to Kayden, she will forever be bonded to him, but her true heart belongs to you. Also, I didn't want you to be taken off guard if he decides to ask her publicly." With that, Mason went to the door. "Take a minute to gather yourself and rejoin the party, before Sam starts searching for you."

Dinner was an absolute nightmare. Chase and Sam were seated directly across from Danielle and Kayden. Danielle wouldn't look at him at all, and every time Kayden shifted in his chair, Chase thought he was about to go down on one knee, like the human males did when they asked a female to be their mate. It was something Danielle would appreciate, given her human tendencies after being raised among them.

"Chase, are you listening to me?" Sam interrupted his thoughts.

"How could I not listen to you, Sam? You never shut up," he said dryly, for her ears only.

"What the hell is wrong with you? People are going to think you're not happy," she chided.

Chase leaned into her ear and whispered, "That would be because I'm not happy. The more you push me, the more you are pissing me off. I am being forced to be your mate, Sam. I am by no means in love with you, so don't expect me to smile and pretend that I am. I may be many things, but fake is not one of them."

Of course, the moment that he touched Sam would be the moment Danielle would decide to watch him. Not good. He had been trying not to embarrass Sam. On the outside that would have looked like an embrace. She quickly looked away when he caught her looking.

"I love you too, baby," Sam crooned, as if that was what he whispered to her. The sting was plain on Danielle's face, and she didn't look his way the rest of the meal.

Veronica had music playing and dessert set up in the glass sunroom. It was a beautiful night without a cloud in the sky. People danced under the stars in the comfort of the warm atrium. Oddly enough, Sam detached herself from Chase's hip, and Kayden was nowhere in sight. Chase was on his way to ask Danielle for a dance when Brandi stopped him.

"I need to speak with you. It's very important, and we need to move quickly." The look on her face said he wanted to hear what she had to say. He grudgingly agreed and followed her to a hall just outside of the kitchen.

"Wait here, I'll be right back," she said, before she shot back out toward the atrium. To his great surprise, when she returned, Danielle was with her.

"What is going on here, Brandi?" Danielle asked her, perturbed.

"Follow me quickly." She ducked into a back stairwell that seemed to be meant for servants. Chase shrugged his shoulders at Danielle and followed Brandi. Danielle walked ahead of him, and it took all of his willpower to keep himself from running his hand down her bare back. At the top of the stairs, Brandi made a hushing gesture to the two of them and led them into a dark bathroom that connected to a bedroom. He could hear voices through a cracked door. Brandi pushed the two of them toward the door so they could hear. She left them alone. Confused, they listened.

"What's your point, Sam? I'm sorry Chase isn't in love with you, but I really don't see how that's my problem." It was Kayden's voice. Danielle stepped closer to the door with interest.

"My point is that we had a deal. You get that slut out of the way. You get what you want, and I keep Chase so busy with gala preparations and planning our bonding that he has no time for her," Sam quipped.

Chase and Dani looked at each other. What the hell was this? Kayden and Sam had been plotting together to keep them apart?

Chase wanted to kick the damn door down and strangle them both for their deception. He reached for the door, but Danielle grabbed his hand to stay him.

"First off, if you call my girl one more name I'm gonna crack your ass, female or not! Secondly, don't try to manipulate me. It won't work—" Kayden was cut off.

"Bullshit, Kayden! That day in Chase's lobby before lunch with my dad, you agreed that Chase shouldn't get to string her along until our bonding. You agreed that you would court her, and I agreed to keep him away as much as possible to give you a chance. Don't tell me you don't remember that conversation."

"You are twisting my words, Sam. I still don't see your damn point! Why did you drag me up here? Dani is going to start missing me any minute," he growled through his teeth.

"You're such a fool. She isn't missing you. I'll bet you my sizeable trust fund that the two of them were whispering in the corner as soon as we walked away."

"Danielle doesn't even pay any attention to him anymore. I have done my part in your so-called deal. I love Dani, and she cares for me. I plan to ask her to be my mate. Chase is your problem," he returned.

"Ha! You can't even say she loves you. What a joke. She is in love with Chase and you know it. If we don't keep them apart, we will both lose."

Dani's face flushed. Chase was over the moon. He realized it wasn't just his imagination or wishful thinking that made him believe she wanted him. Others could see it as well.

"I promise you now that if I can't have Chase, you will not have that freak of nature you call a girlfriend! If you don't keep her out of my way and away from Chase, I will tell her about our little deal. She will hate you. And from the looks of all the men just dying to crawl up her skirt, she will not be alone for long! You'd better lie, cheat, and steal. Do whatever it takes, Kayden." She paused and let out a little chuckle. "I do have to tell you, I was impressed when you joined the warrior class just for her. I wonder if she will appreciate the fact that you changed your entire life around just to keep her away from Chase." Sam was just about snarling.

"I joined the warriors because I didn't trust anyone else to protect her. Yes, I used my father to get assigned to her detail. That was because I care for her and her safety. I didn't make the first move on her. I was only keeping her safe. She came to me first," he snapped.

Chase was a little hurt to know that Kayden hadn't been making that part up just to hurt him, but he remembered what his father told him about the extent people will go to in order to ease their pain.

Kayden continued, "Unlike you, who will never see a day that Chase willingly kisses you until he is bonded to you by blood and his free will is taken from him, I will not deceive her. I love her. I'll tell her myself the things I've done, before I ever dishonor our relationship with the kind of games you play."

The sound of skin hitting skin echoed in the bathroom. Sam had slapped Kayden. Chase was so angry he couldn't take it anymore. He was ready to rip the damn door off and kill both Sam and Kayden for playing games. He couldn't imagine how it was upsetting Danielle. As much as he hated to admit it, Danielle had genuine feelings for Kayden, and the conversation in front of them had the smack of another betrayal. Chase believed that Kayden had real feelings for Danielle now as well, but had it started out as a game? First, Chase himself lied to her by omission, and then she learned Kayden was scheming with Sam.

"I'm going to go tell her you did all this to please me. You've always wanted me, and I tricked you into distracting her, so I could get closer to Chase. But I can't tolerate your sexual appetite any longer, and you won't let me go," she said, in a voice tinged with fear and regret, as if she were acting out her part to Dani. Then, in her usual bitchy tone, she said, "I bet she'll believe we're lovers, given your reputation. I have sources that say you haven't even screwed the girl yet. You have to be getting it somewhere if not from her." She started for the door.

"You won't tell that lie. She'll tell Chase, and that will ruin your chance at love with him," he scoffed.

"She won't tell him, Kayden. She loves him too much. She knows he has no choice but to be my mate, and she won't tell him something that will cause him pain. She is way too good and selfless for that. Especially if there is nothing he can do about it but suffer the humiliation of believing that both the women in his life were with you." She opened the door to the hall. "I guess it's back to slumming with humans for you, my friend."

Chase pushed the bathroom door open to reveal their hiding place. He saw red and couldn't hear another word out of her deceitful mouth. The look on her face was one of sheer disbelief and trepidation. Chase had never seen her look afraid in all the years he'd known her, but she was trembling with it. She'd been caught red-handed. Chase crossed the room toward her but just before he grabbed her—to do what, he didn't know—Mason and Griffin stepped into the doorway.

Brandi was a crafty little thing. She had the two of them listening at the door in the hall. They'd heard the whole thing. "I think it's time for us to sit down and rethink the bonding arrangement we've made, Mason." Griffin cursed as he grabbed his daughter by the arm. "Samantha is not yet mature enough to handle a real relationship."

"Oh please, Daddy! What are you going to do? Force him to mate with the mouse that Brandi is?" She was incredulous.

"Why not? I was forcing him to mate with you, remember? I'm sure he would rather have an honest mate," he came back at her.

Brandi's triumphant laughter echoed down the hallway.

Chase looked over his shoulder at Danielle. She was beautiful and shattered. She leaned against the bathroom door, her face toward the floor, tears hitting the marble tiles. All he'd ever done was hurt her, and she was hurting again.

"You deserve better." That was all he could say without breaking down himself. He couldn't comfort her or himself. He was trapped. The more he tried to break free, the more damage he did. Kayden and Sam had done their part to add to her misery. Maybe she was right. She could be happy someplace else, someplace faraway from him and the rest of the people who did nothing but hurt her. She deserved far better than his people could offer.

Twenty-eight

She couldn't believe what was happening around her. How could Kayden be so deceptive? Dani thought he really cared for her. He said he loved her, but he'd lied to her. He purposely pursued her to leave Sam an opening with Chase. Was there anyone in the world, besides her mom, who would ever really be able to love her? She didn't think so. Her own father wouldn't even recognize her as his daughter for the world to see. It said a lot about how everyone would react to what she was, when her own father was too embarrassed to claim her.

On the other hand, she had lied to all of them. How could she be angry with Kayden for his behavior when she allowed him to fall for her knowing he had no idea what or who she really was? Talk about the pot calling the kettle black. He would not profess his love so readily, once he found out the truth.

As far as Griffin went, it hadn't escaped her attention that she could be bonded to Chase as one of Griffin's daughters. But he didn't see her the same way he saw his other children. Dani was a disgrace to his house and to his kind.

Chase would have to know who she was, before he was bonded. She was sure in the cold light of the truth, Chase would also turn away from her. She realized she would never have true love. No vamp or human would ever want a half-breed mutant bride. Who could blame them? Imagine the stigma a child of hers would have to live with. The sting of rejection touched her every day since she'd learned her true heritage. How could she ever do that to her children? It was time for her to leave that place and the people in it behind. She could continue to live with her mother. Some people never married and remained childless by choice. Why not her? Dani was sure it would get easier after the first forty years or so.

Everyone left Kayden and Sam's meeting place except for Kayden, who watched her cry all over the very expensive-looking marble floor. If he had nothing to say, she didn't either. She would leave and all of it would be over. They could return to life as it should have been, and she would learn to deal with the pain until it faded.

She made it to the hall before Kayden caught her and forced her against the wall. The fierce look on his face was a frightening sight. Was she projecting again? Had he heard her thoughts? She worked hard to control that, but when she got upset, her control slipped away.

"I am in love with you, Danielle," he snarled. "Do you hear me? Of all the things you heard in there, remember that. I love you, and I gave in to a career I wanted no part of in order to protect you and keep you close to me. I am not afraid to tell the world the way I feel. I was not willing to let even my own happiness get in the way of being with you. Chase would not move to upset his precious family and public image to claim you as his own. He says he loves you, but he watches you suffer for him."

Kayden lowered his head and claimed her lips. His honeyed tongue dripped all the right words, seeking hers, tasting of lust and fear. He held her face in his warm hands and tilted her head to just the right angle for his exploration. He released her suddenly and went down on one knee, right there in the hall. He looked up at her with fear in his shining eyes. He pulled a box from his jacket pocket and opened it to reveal an engagement ring. It was the perfect, sparkling, one-carat, human expression of love that all girls expected when a man proposed. Her mouth fell open. He hadn't lied about asking her to be his mate.

"Danielle, I love you. I want you to be my mate. I understand that you are not yet in love with me, but I have enough love for both of us. I will wait for you to be ready, as your much-loved human custom requires, if that is what will make you trust me again. I will do whatever it takes."

The sincerity and overwhelming emotion in his cracking voice clawed at her heart. It was what she wanted from Chase. Kayden was willing to do whatever it took because he loved her that much. But it wasn't fair to him that she didn't feel the same.

"Kayden, you have no idea what you're asking for. You have no idea the secrets I hold in my heart. It suffocates me. I'm not what you think I am." She pulled him to his feet.

He pulled her to his chest, forcing her to look at him. "You told me that once before. I didn't care then, and I don't care now. I know exactly what you are. You are beautiful, smart, and strong. You put the needs of others before your own. You suffer in silence to protect others from the same suffering. I don't know what's going on with you, and I don't care. Dani, please, bond with me right now. I will make the pain stop. I will love and protect you always, and you will love me. We can end this here and now. Will you be my mate?" His voice was hoarse, and his body trembled against her.

"I can't do that if you don't know the truth." Dani was about to spill the truth when he cut her off with a hot kiss.

"I don't care," he said against her lips. "I will love you no matter what your big secret is. Tell me later, after I make you mine, forever." He waited for an answer and didn't want to hear her excuses for why he shouldn't want her.

The pain in her chest was intense. She was so afraid, but she believed him. She believed he loved her, and he begged her to let him love her, while the source of her pain slunk off into the night without even a second look in her direction.

"Why do you want to be bonded to someone you know isn't in love with you, Kayden?" She needed to understand him.

"Why don't you tell me why you want to be bonded to someone who refuses to put you first?" he countered.

"Because, I'm in love with him," she answered, and his point hit home.

"And I'm in love with you." Kayden smiled. "I know you care for me."

"I do; I love you. It's just not the same as what I feel for Chase. I can't explain it, Kayden. I know you're perfect for me, and I've wished many times that I could forget him and move on with you. I know I shouldn't want him. I shouldn't love him, but I do. No matter how hard I fight, it's still there, haunting me."

"Our bond will fix all of that, Dani. We won't be lopsided for long. He won't haunt you anymore," he encouraged and stroked his fingers lightly across her face.

"You need to know everything about me." She had to tell him.

"I don't. I know everything that could possibly matter."

She couldn't feel like she was using him. She thought about her life and wondered if she would be like her mother, lonely and wanting the same man forever, a man who'd moved on without her.

"Alright, I will be your mate, Kayden," she heard herself say from a distance.

He drew in a deep, ragged breath and picked her up to bury his face in her neck. "You will not regret this. I will make you happy; I swear it."

"Do you have a blade on you? Or would you like to bite me?" Dani wanted it done. She was done second-guessing.

He pulled back, a little surprised. "Now? You will be my mate, right now?" His eyes shone with joy.

"If you're willing to trust me without knowing everything about me, then I will trust you to mend my broken pieces," she explained. With happiness and adoration overflowing from his very being, Kayden led her back into the bedroom.

"I will give myself to you, and then I will go tell the world! Nothing will ever separate us again. I've been in agony since you went away." He rushed around the room, searching for something and babbling. He came to the bed with two braided lengths of fabric used to tie back the curtains.

"Take off your shoes and climb up on the bed. Sit on your knees, angel." He beamed at her and went to lock the bedroom door.

She could do it. She could, and she would. In a few moments, it would be over, and she would start a real relationship with a man she would love, who would love her back. Chase's face would no longer haunt her. His touch would no longer burn her. She wouldn't need her father's acceptance. Her husband, her mate, would love and accept her proudly for the whole world to see. She could do it.

Her shoes discarded, she climbed onto the bed and watched Kayden remove his shoes, suit jacket, tie, and holster. He pulled a blade from a pocket on the holster and went to the bathroom. He came back with a couple of towels and some alcohol swabs. Cleaning his very sharp-looking blade, he watched her.

"Don't be afraid. I would love to bite your sweet neck, but I will wait until you're ready to make love with me for that honor." He climbed up onto the huge four-poster bed. On his knees, he smiled down on her and pulled the pins out of her hair so it fell around her shoulders. "I'm so damn happy. I can't believe you are my one true mate." He kissed her deeply, then took her left hand and placed the stunning ring on her left ring finger. "I wanted to honor the human tradition of a ring. I hope you like it. I will, of course, wear one too, to show the world I am yours."

"I never thought I would get married in a black dress." She looked down at herself and laughed nervously.

After admiring her hand with his ring on it, Kayden tied a length of fabric around her wrist, the same way he had tied one around his. The blade was open on the bed between them. He grasped her hand as if they would shake hands. She'd seen it done once before at the bonding she'd attended. He wrapped his length around their hands to bind them together, and spoke in a low, husky voice.

"I vow to love you for the whole of my existence. I vow to protect you to my last breath. I vow to cherish the gift of your returned love for all time. And I vow to always remain grateful for the woman who will from this day forth be the one and only mate of my soul."

Her heart pounded, and he was as calm and content as she'd ever seen him. The decision he made would affect the rest of his life in ways he couldn't understand, but he said he didn't care. With a deep breath and shaky hands, she wrapped her length of fabric around their hands and repeated his vows.

"I vow to love you for the whole of my existence. I vow to protect you to my last breath. I vow to cherish the gift of your returned love for all time. And I vow to always remain grateful for the man who will from this day forth be the one and only mate of my soul."

Kayden pulled her to him by their joined hands and held her to his chest. His eyes were overflowing. He sat back and picked up the blade. She watched him lower his head to cut himself and knew she couldn't finish this unless he knew the truth. She couldn't do it to him just to end her own pain. The blade touched his lower lip.

"I'm human, Kayden." She blurted it out. His eyes shot up to her face, incredulous. "It's true. I'm half-human. That means our children would be part-human. I couldn't let you do this until you understand that fact."

"You can't be human. This isn't funny, Dani." His forehead knit into a scowl.

"It's no joke. My mother is human, and my father is a vampire." She stopped short of confessing her father's identity. "His family wouldn't accept us and wanted us dead. We were an embarrassment. So my mother faked our deaths to stop them from killing us. I am apparently a disgrace and an abomination. I was a normal human baby. I didn't start showing signs of vampirism until the day before I left home for college. I never tasted blood until the night Nathan attacked me."

"That's when you came of age." Kayden put the blade down and watched her, wide-eyed and confused. She could see the wheels turning in his head. He had to decide right then if she was worth it to him.

"I had no idea why I was getting such special treatment the night I met you at the club. You guys knew what I was before I did. I'm weaker than you, because I'm human. I'm mentally stronger, because my mother is psychic and my father is telekinetic. I don't heal as fast as you. I can get drunk. I have no idea how long I will live or how our kids will turn out. I assume they will be more vamp than human when we combine your full blood with my half blood, but I can't be sure. That is the truth. I could have waited another minute, and it wouldn't have mattered to you. But I couldn't damn you to a life full of the stigma of a human mate without your consent. It's up to you now. You said nothing I could say would change the way you feel. Was that true or will you abandon me now, too?"

He watched her for a long moment. She knew what was about to happen. She was going to lose her only true friend. She did love him, but not enough. She was not *in* love. The fact that losing his friendship hurt her more than losing his love proved that she didn't deserve that love. The tears of pain and disappointment began to stream down her face. He took her in, looking for clues that would have given her away as a human. There weren't any. To her surprise, he picked up the blade and sliced his lip.

"I love you, Danielle." He smiled and handed her the blade. "Nothing else matters."

She took the blade and followed his lead, placing a shallow slit on her lower lip. They were really going to do it. He loved her no matter what. Kayden went up on his knees, she met him chest to chest, and she waited. She would let him come to her. It had to be completely of his doing. He leaned his face to hers and paused, blood running down his chin onto his crisp white shirt. Her blood dripped onto her chest. He looked into her eyes and hesitated.

"I can't do it," he whispered in a shattered voice. "I love you, but I just can't do it. I want normal, healthy kids and a mate who will live as long as I do. I just can't." He pulled back from her then.

Angry and hurt, she wiped the blood from her face. "So much for all that bullshit you were spouting in the hall. So much for the vows you just spoke to me. . . . *grateful for the woman who will from this day forth be the one and only mate of my soul.* I am still the same person I was five minutes ago, Kayden." She struggled to get the damn ring off of their still-joined hands. He watched her struggle, while silent tears streaked down his cheeks.

Chase made it to his car, before he turned back to the house. He couldn't leave his Lovely like that, so upset. She must have felt so betrayed by Kayden, and Chase had done nothing to comfort her. He'd just stalked off to lick his own wounds.

He went back to the party and walked around the crowded first floor but couldn't find Danielle anywhere. Out in the atrium, he found Mason.

"Have you seen Lovely?" he asked his father.

"Why do you call her that if she doesn't like it?" Mason inquired.

"She's too lovely to be called a boy's name. She didn't mind the nickname, until I hurt her," he returned.

"She never came back to the party. I really don't blame her. That girl gets kicked every time she's down." Mason shook his head.

"It seems that way, doesn't it?" Chase reflected.

"Oh, you don't know the half of it," Mason quipped under his breath.

"What I would like to know is how you know so much and why you won't share your information." Chase scowled at his father.

"Maybe she's still upstairs. Come to think of it, I never saw Kayden leave, either." Mason avoided the question.

"What about Sam?"

"Griffin rushed his whole crew out of here as soon as he had them all gathered, and bid his farewells to the hosts. Brandi made sure to spread the news about the breakup between Dani and Kayden, so the guys are buzzing with anticipation for her return. No doubt, it was another Vaughn girl attempt at keeping Dani away from you. You may want to warn her if you find her."

Darren approached the two Deidrick men. "Mason, I'm going to look for Dani. I know we aren't supposed to be protecting her, but she has been missing too long for my liking. She is too precious to lose again."

"You don't know anything about her," Chase mumbled on his way past Darren. He had to find her now.

"She is a friend of mine. I've spent more time with her than you and your sorry-ass ex-buddy combined. I taught her to shoot a gun, to defend herself hand-to-hand, and drive a car like she stole it if she was ever being chased. What have you done besides hurt the girl? You don't need to answer, because I already know you haven't done shit. So don't question my motives!" Darren growled.

"Well, why don't you tell us how you really feel, Darren?" Mason stepped between them. "I am always breaking up a fight over that girl. I can't wait for the rest of the guys to get in on the fun."

"What do you mean?" Darren groused.

"Oh, you didn't hear? Danielle is a single girl again, and every man in a twenty-mile radius has been informed that our own little supervamp is accepting applications for a mate. Brandi thinks she is a matchmaker of a sort. Maybe we should all fan out and find her. She could have a line of applicants by now," Mason joked. Chase glared at his father. He could not believe he'd just told Darren, who was known to want Danielle, that she was single. Darren went to search the lower level of the mansion.

"Why did you tell him that?" Chase asked his father, annoyed.

"He was her warrior. Why do you care? I didn't see you trying to comfort her. If you won't do it, there are plenty of guys who will." Mason hit him low.

"I'm going to check upstairs. Maybe she is in her room." Chase ground his teeth.

At the top of the stairs, he checked several guest rooms, until he found the one containing Danielle's belongings and her delicious scent, but no Danielle.

He checked the upstairs library, which was empty, and had a sickening thought that she could be in Van's room. Begrudgingly, he knocked on the door.

Van answered, looking disheveled. He indeed did have a female in his room. Chase inhaled deeply, ready to pounce if it smelled the slightest bit like his Lovely. It didn't.

"Forgive the disturbance, Van. Have you seen Danielle?" he asked politely, since he knew she wasn't in his room.

"No, but I'm flattered you thought to check my room. She doesn't seem the type to fall into bed quickly. I'll need to work on her. A challenge is always fun, isn't it? I believe she'll be worth the fight." Van paused half a second, as it dawned on him that this was the last place Chase would look, so she must have really been missing. He buttoned up his pants and asked in a much more serious tone, "When was she last seen?"

Chase was just trying not to kill the bastard. "She is not one of your throwaway girlfriends, Van. Stay away from her."

"Yeah, yeah, I know. Whatever. Trust me. I wouldn't throw that one away. How long has she been missing, and who is looking for her?" he asked again.

"No one has seen her in about thirty minutes. Darren is searching the first floor, and I have searched this floor."

"Has anyone called the gate to see if she left?" He went to the phone by his bed and rang the gatehouse to question the guards. "She hasn't left the grounds. No one has left the party the through the gates yet." Van took off on his task, and Chase went toward the rear stairwell that he and Dani had followed Brandi up earlier that evening.

On the way past, Chase tried the door to the room Kayden and Sam had occupied earlier, but it was locked. Why hadn't he checked that room first? She was probably still holed up in there. The adjoining bathroom door was still open. Relief washed over him when her scent hit him hard and he heard her whimpering cry.

"Lovely, are you still in here? Let me walk you to your room." He stopped with a jolt, and his relief was washed away by overwhelming grief at the scene in the room. Blood. Danielle's blood and Kayden's, mixed.

It couldn't be. Kayden didn't deserve her. How could he have talked her into it? She was way too smart for that.

His father's words echoed in his head again. "The point is, she may be willing to do anything to stop her pain. I know the two of you have not been bonded, but the connection she feels with you is as strong as any bond I've ever witnessed. . . . If she bonds to Kayden, she will forever be bonded to him, but her true heart belongs to you."

Kayden and Dani were on the bed together, their hands bound. He held her and murmured to her, while she cried on his shoulder. There was a blade on the bed, and Kayden had blood running down his chin and on his hand. He was inadvertently rubbing the blood down Danielle's back as he stroked her gently. Why were they crying? Was their brand-new bond so strong and overwhelming already? Every chance Chase had with the only girl he ever loved, the only girl he ever wanted for his own, was shattered, because he'd walked away and left her to fend for herself with the only man who'd bothered to stand by her. Again, Kayden had been there when Chase wasn't. This time, Chase would pay with his very heart and to the depth of his soul.

"What have you done to her? Why is she crying?" Chase held on to the doorjamb to keep himself from going to her.

"Get out, Chase! You drove her to this! She is not ready to deal with you or anyone else yet! Leave!" Kayden continued to pet her, and she cried louder.

The shouting brought Mason in through the open bathroom door to investigate. He looked for Chase to tell him Danielle's car was still on the grounds. Mason looked as stunned as Chase felt at the scene he found.

"Chase, you need to leave the room. You're intruding on their private ceremony. Move it, now," his father demanded.

"Mason. Mason, please help me. Please, Mason," she whimpered, and leaned away from Kayden. Kayden's cut was already healing, but Dani continued to bleed down her face, neck, and chest.

Kayden's shirt was covered. "I do love you, Dani." His bottom lip quivered. "You know I do. Don't do this. Maybe I just need some time to adjust."

Mason moved to the bed, and Dani fell back to lean against him, trying to put distance between her and Kayden. She rolled toward Chase but didn't open her eyes. Chase was finally able to look up again, and what he saw made no sense. Her face was not the face of a happy new bride but a mask of despair. Mason untangled the couple's hands. He looked at Kayden.

"She told you." It wasn't a question but a statement.

Kayden answered anyway. "Yes. How do you know?"

"I suppose she would have told you had she wanted you to know. If you value her at all, you will keep your mouth shut." Mason had her hand free and used the bloody blade to remove the fabric from her wrist.

"Mason," Dani sobbed. That was all she could manage.

Once she was free, he scooped her up like a baby. Her beautiful hair was matted with blood down one side, and it hung almost to Mason's knees.

He looked angrily at Kayden. "Look what you gave away. How could she possibly not be enough for you? You're both fools," Mason told Kayden and Chase. He carried her out of the room. In the hall, he passed Van, Gage, and Debbie.

"Holy shit! Is she hurt?" Van rushed forward.

"Back off, Stafford, this isn't your business. Gage, go help your boy, he's in the room I just came from. Debbie, my sweet, help me with Danielle. She'll need a woman's touch." Debbie followed him dutifully and shut the door behind them when they entered Dani's guest room.

Chase was still on his knees by the bathroom door when something hit the carpet in front of him. He picked it up. It was a beautiful, blood-covered ring. Kayden had planned ahead and changed his mind at the last minute. He'd been a kiss away from forever, and he'd turned her down. Dragging himself from the floor, Chase approached Kayden, who was locked in a thousand-yard stare. He held out the ring for him to take.

"What could possibly have been so bad that you would refuse to be her mate? I thought you loved her?" Chase asked quietly, with honest curiosity.

"I was just thinking that very same thing." Kayden continued to cry, and the combined blood and tears soaking his chest would stain his heart forever.

"I don't want to go. Please, don't make me go." Why must Debbie and Mason torture her? It hadn't even been a week since the botched bonding. "I get into trouble every time I go out in public. Do you want to see that again? I thought you loved me."

"Of course we love you. That is why we want you to have some fun and stop hiding from life. I can't understand how hard this all must be for you, but life goes on, and you are too precious not to live every second to the fullest," Debbie replied. They looked at each other's reflection in the mirror, while Debbie used an iron to place huge ringlet curls in Dani's hair.

Dani was glad when Mason told her he'd been forced to fill his mate in on all the gory details of the secret he'd kept from Griffin and her for all these years. It had been a burden for him to keep such a major event from her for all that time. Debbie had been upset with him for a few days, but she just wanted to help Dani adjust to her new life. Debbie didn't care that Dani was human. Mason and Debbie only had one child, and Dani could tell Debbie was happy to have a girl around the house, for a change. They'd spent the past few days watching chick flicks, eating ice cream by the pint, and talking smack about men.

"Don't forget, you have a date for tonight, and he will be devastated if you stand him up," Debbie reminded her.

A slow grin crept over Dani's face. "How could I forget? He's probably the best man in the entire world. Of course I can't stand him up."

"Your hair is done, your makeup is perfect, and your gown has been steamed and is waiting in the closet. Now, I have a gift for you." Debbie handed Dani a small white box.

"Debbie! You shouldn't have. This isn't necessary." She hated receiving gifts when she was in no position to give gifts. Christmas was going to suck.

"Don't be silly. Your godfather and I can give you gifts whenever we like. Open it," she demanded. Dani ripped into the satiny, white gift wrap and opened the box to reveal a pair of gold, dangly earrings. There were three sunbursts hanging from delicate gold chains. In the center of each of the suns was a sparkly diamond. Debbie had given Dani back her necklace, which she'd cleaned up and polished. The new earrings were identical to the necklace, except for the diamonds.

"This is too much. I can't accept this."

"You can, and you will," Mason said from the door. "Your date is here, and he looks as nervous as a cat in a room full of rocking chairs."

Dani hugged them both, before they left her to dress.

Dani's heart melted at the sight of her date pacing in the foyer. He was so handsome in his tux and tails. He even had a corsage for her. She practically skipped down the stairs to meet him.

"Are you sure you don't have a prettier girl you could attend the gala with? I'm not sure I'm up to the standards of such a handsome young man," she teased.

"There could never be a prettier girl than you, Dani." He hugged her waist. Her little brother was adorable. "I'm going to hog you all night, so the boys leave you alone. I will protect you." He gazed up at her with the cutest look of stern determination she'd ever seen.

Twenty-nine

I said I'll do it! Now back off! We have an agreement! I completed half of my task, and the other half will be done on schedule. You better hold up your end, or I will kill you where you stand!" The defiant shout filtered through the speakers of the limo's phone.

The rogue laughed at the threat coming from a lovesick idiot. "You know, for such a strong man, you have become quite soft. I'm really not sure what it is about that girl that turns every vamp in town into putty for her little hands to mold at will."

"I'm not being molded. I'm taking her as I am and making her what I want her to be. She will love me, and she will obey me. You just better make sure there's still breath left in her when you give her back to me, or I will expose you in an instant, damn the consequences I will pay!"

"I guess you can't see how weak you have become in pursuit of the fledgling. The fact that you are willing to sacrifice your name and freedom to avenge a child you will have to force to love you with a blood bond is very telling," the rogue taunted.

"The fact that you have been chasing the very same girl and coming up empty for months is also very telling. You have thrown everything you've got at her, and she slips through your fingers every time. You're not above me, and don't you forget it. You need me to get what you want as much as I need you to get what I want. I will be your trap, and you will be my alibi. Just don't be late, or we'll miss our window." The call disconnected.

Idiot. He would drink until he had his fill of her power. If she had any blood left, he could have it. A lovesick male wouldn't stop him from reaching his goals.

It was the night Kayden had been looking forward to for months. He was supposed to be at Dani's side. They would have entered the gala hand in hand. He even wore the damn tux she'd picked to coordinate with her dress. She'd gotten a kick out of making him wear purple, but it was only the vest, so he let her have her way and ordered the deep royal purple. He could have replaced the vest before that night, but he actually hoped she would see it and know he still wore it for her.

He hadn't seen her since Mason carried her out of the room, covered in blood and sobbing. Never had he known such pain or been so ashamed. He'd willingly given her up, and for what? A few DNA strands that made her a little different? She was a demi-vamp, and she was perfect, beautiful, powerful, and full of love. He still loved her. Those DNA strands wouldn't change that, no matter how badly he wanted it to.

She'd bared her deepest secret to him, and he'd smacked her away. She had tried to tell him she was different, but he thought he loved her enough to overcome any differences. All she had to do was wait a few more minutes, and none of it would have mattered to either of them. They could have kept her secret. Nobody could tell. He couldn't tell the difference until her blood flowed from her lips, and the thick scent hit his nose. There was just the slightest hint of sweet human lifeblood mixed in with her powerful vamp essence. Maybe that was why her scent was so attractive. She had that sexy vamp pheromone tinged with a delicious human sweetness that made him so thirsty he burned to be nearer to the source.

Kayden was outside when her limo pulled up. He'd heard she had a date, but he knew it wasn't Chase. Chase was already inside and way too happy, because Sam and Brandi were both staying home.

Kayden didn't know how he was going to deal with seeing her on the arm of another man so soon after she vowed her life to him. She had looked him in the eye and handed over her very soul to be his mate. He would watch other men enjoy her company until she found a mate. He wasn't sure what would be worse, watching her date a string of males, or knowing the soul she had promised to him belonged to someone else, because of his stupid prejudices.

The driver opened the door, and she climbed out in a gloriously sheer, strapless, royal-purple gown. The bodice shimmered and drew attention to her. Oh, man. When the light shone from behind her, he could just make out all of her luscious curves. She didn't try to hide her hair, either. She showed off her unique streaks in big, flowing curls. How was he going to learn to live without her when just looking at her ripped him apart?

Chase paced the ballroom floor. He'd worked hard putting that gala together, and it would be a special night indeed. Big things were in the works for the night. Griffin had a special announcement planned, and Chase had some important news to share with Lovely. He'd stayed away and given her space to deal with her sadness over Kayden. Of course, he was sure that was going to take longer than the few days that had passed since he last saw her. Staying away when he knew she was under his parents' roof in the room next to his childhood bedroom had been tough. Hell, the rooms even had an adjoining door! He'd wanted to comfort her and coddle her. He wanted to shower her with all the attention he should have given her from the start, but his father counseled patience, so he'd waited until that night to speak with her.

The place was already almost full, and her seat was still empty. Chase had to make some last-minute seat changes when his mother called to inform him that Dani had a date. There was space at the table because he'd overlooked moving Kayden away from her. It would have been miserable for her to sit with him all night. It didn't make Chase happy that he would have to sit across from her and her mystery date all night, but hopefully after they spoke, it wouldn't matter.

"Would you please sit down a minute? You're wearing holes in your shoes with all the back-and-forth," Griffin said lightheartedly. Griffin seemed nervous, yet more energized than Chase could ever remember seeing him. Mason said his mood was due to the coming announcement Griffin planned to make.

"I've never been so worked up in my life." Chase took the seat next to Griffin.

"Love will do that to you. It brings the greatest joy and happiness, and the greatest pain, simultaneously." He clapped a hand on Chase's shoulder.

Chase felt Griffin's grip on his shoulder stiffen, and he followed his gaze to the staircase where the guests were entering. At the top of the stairs was a vision with flowing dark hair accentuated by curls of white and red. Her date had his head held high. Seeing the two of them together was a little unnerving. They looked like they could be siblings.

It was no surprise that Kayden followed her at a safe distance. He kept an eye on everyone around her, still in warrior mode. Hopefully, between himself and Darren, who was also going to be casing the joint for trouble, they could get her through the night with no incidents.

Danielle descended the stairs in a graceful sweep of sheer fabric and natural fluidity. The room stopped to watch her, and the crowd hushed a little. Most of those people hadn't met her yet. She was an oddity and the core of a lot of rumors. She had power people didn't understand, and the death of a warrior at her hand didn't help any. Ignorance bred prejudice, and it was an ignorant crowd. She and her date reached the table, and he pulled out her chair for her. Before sitting, she bent to kiss his check and made the unflappable little guy blush bright red.

"Good evening, everyone." She addressed the whole table and was met with smiles and happy greetings from all but Sarah, who was oddly reserved. Normally she would flit from table to table, gossiping with the rest of the Stepford wives.

Casual conversation went around the table, until Chase could no longer stand the wait. He had to speak with her. He rounded the table and asked J. R. if he would allow him to speak to his date for a few moments. Griffin and Mason shook their heads, and there was an exchange of cash. It seemed as though a friendly wager had been placed on how long it would take Chase to lose his composure and approach her. J. R. looked at Dani to see if she was okay with it before responding. She nodded her agreement.

"Don't keep her away too long, because she needs to relax and have fun, not worry about people who make her sad." J. R. eyed Chase cautiously.

"Well said, J. R. Very well said." Griffin patted his boy on the back.

"I promise to return her to you promptly." Chase bowed politely to her little protector.

As Chase put his arm out for Dani, she rose from her seat with the grace of a goddess and followed his lead to a room overlooking a garden with a view of the city lights off in the distance. She said nothing. She crossed the room and looked out over the scenery, as he knew she would. It was why he had picked that room.

"I'm sorry for the pain you've suffered," he started, but she cut him off.

"I don't want to talk about Kayden. I already had a run-in with him outside, and I've reached my bullshit quota for the week," she quipped.

"I don't want to talk about him, Lovely. I want to talk about you and me."

She didn't say anything, but she rolled her eyes in a way that showed she had heard that line before, too.

"I just need you to hear me out."

She huffed out a reluctant agreement.

"The other night, I realized what an ass I have been. I have wasted precious time and caused us both undue sorrows. I listened to my sense of duty instead of my heart. I can't stand being away from you, and I want the chance to repair the damage I've done. I know that you may need time to get over the past, and I am willing to wait as long as it will take for you to allow me into your heart again." He was quiet for a moment, expecting her to respond. He paced behind her, unable to keep still.

"That isn't going to go over very well with the family. Your newest fiancée may not appreciate the gesture. Nothing has changed, Chase," she said flatly.

"Oh, but it has, my Lovely. After the nightmare of the other night, I met with Griffin and my father. I told them I'm in love with you and will not take a mate I don't love to satisfy their need to fulfill a prophecy. I told them to disown me if they must, but my heart belongs to you. I refuse to suffer without you any longer, unless you don't want me. But I won't bond to one of the Vaughn girls. I want you and only you for my mate."

"How did they take it?" she asked quietly.

"Better than I thought they would, actually. I was expecting Griffin to lose his mind and my dad to disown me, but they didn't.

My dad hugged me like he was proud of me, and Griffin asked if I am as big a fool as Kayden. I told them that there was nothing about you that could change my heart. Griffin said that's what Kayden thought, too. He said if you accepted me, it wouldn't be long before you tested my sincerity. I just wish you guys would let me in on the big secret," he pleaded.

"It isn't just mine to tell, Chase. There are other people I have to think about."

"Just like me, you have worried about others for too long. When will you allow yourself to focus on your future happiness?" he encouraged.

She was still looking out the window into the distance. He couldn't take the silence, the rejection, not again. Chase grabbed Danielle's slender shoulders and jerked her impeccably styled body back against his raging heat. She gasped. She was his, damn it! His! And he wouldn't lose her again! He refused to accept *no* this time. His ingrained sense of propriety, his responsibility to his house, be damned. This female, his female, was worth the loss of his title, his future position on the council, and everything that came with it.

"You can deny me now, but I will have you, Lovely." Chase couldn't resist running his lips up the slender column of her exposed neck. His gums ached with the need to penetrate that delicate skin and claim her forever. "Tonight." He paused to taste the tender lobe of her ear. She shivered and squirmed in his hold, breathing hard. "I'll give you a choice. After this I won't be held responsible for what I do, Danielle. You've held me off for long enough."

She began to sputter a protest and fight his hold, but he cut her off and tightened his arm around her waist, pinning her length to his. The last thing he wanted was to give her reason to rehash his sins.

Chase was slightly embarrassed by his quickly hardening shaft. Damn it, this was a serious discussion, but he couldn't stop his body from reacting to her nearness. The smell of her was an aphrodisiac.

He knew she could feel his solid length pressed into her ass through the thin material of her elegant gown.

"I know. I know you had valid reasons for turning away from me, but that's all over now. This is about now, today, tomorrow . . . always. I'll give it all up. I *have* given it all up. For you, my Lovely. I don't want this life, not anymore. Not if I can't have you."

Danielle turned in his arms, and Chase saw the tears in her eyes. He took her face in his hands. "Lovely, please don't cry."

"Shut up and kiss me. I will be your mate, if you can love me for who I am. It's all up to you now, Chase." She pulled his head down to hers.

"I know who you are already. You are my Lovely, and I wouldn't have you any other way." Chase growled. He felt her passion for him pierce him deeper than he ever thought possible. All of the pent-up emotions flowed between them. Chase gasped when he felt her open the mental block she'd built between them, and she began to pour all of her longing and need for him through the connection. He hadn't expected such an immediate physical response from her. Hell, he'd just hoped she would listen to his plea for forgiveness, but she was rubbing against him and purring softly. The sheer fabric of her gown slid sensually over her luscious curves. How could he not respond to her passion and obvious need?

"Damn, Lovely. I've been dreaming about feasting on this mouth and claiming these sweet curves."

He was overwhelmed and a bit dizzy when she pushed him against the wall and began to unbutton his pants. She was ferocious in her need.

"You don't need to do this now, Lovely. We have plenty of time to love each other." Dani slid her hand down to cup him, and hummed appreciatively. Like a starving man, he devoured her lips, her jawline, her neck and back up to the spot where he desperately wanted to sink his fangs and lap at her blood.

"I may not live to see tomorrow, Chase. Just being here is dangerous for me and everyone around me. You want to talk about the future, but I need your love today, right now. Love me now, Chase. You just gave me the one thing I've been waiting for. All this time I've been waiting for you to choose me. I needed to know you loved me enough to choose me over all the expectations others had of you. Now that you have, I need the rest of you. All of you." She panted and stroked him.

Dear God, yes, he wanted to have her here and now. He hadn't been able to think of much else. He gave in and let her have her way with him. Not a shy bone did she have when she slid his pants and underwear to his knees and forced him onto the sofa. She was so damn sexy, and the scent of her arousal made him dizzy with lust. She went down on her knees before him and wrapped her hand timidly around his shaft, examining him curiously. He panted and prayed for the power to resist spilling in her hand. Chase could tell she'd never done that before, and that somehow made it even hotter. Her head lowered, and that hot pink tongue lapped at him, exploring the flavor and texture of him, teasing, tracing the veins, but not quite giving him what he needed. She took him into her mouth, suckled shallowly at first, then deeply and slowly she bathed his shaft with her tongue until he begged for her mercy.

Rising slowly, she pulled up her dress to reveal a total lack of panties. He stiffened even more and the head of his rod throbbed. She straddled his hips and dug her hands into his hair.

"Are you sure about this, Lovely? I can wait until I have a bed to love you on." Shit, why had he said that? He needed to be inside of her now.

Her answer came in the form of the slick sliding of her body against his eager erection, over and over. She was very sure. Chase massaged her breasts, fondling until her nipples poked through the fabric of her gown. She circled her hips and teased him with her moister and delicious aroma. He was so close to her core, but damn, not quite close enough. She tortured him with slippery, mind-numbing friction, until finally, she reached between them and slowly, inch by inch, she drove him home.

It was too much. The physical and the telepathic connection between them made it possible to feel their lovemaking from both sides. He felt his pleasure, and hers. He felt his body stroking hers and her body gripping around his, all at once. He tasted himself on her tongue and her delicious sugar on his own.

She panted and moaned her pleasure into his mouth. At that moment, the most possessive and primal urge to claim her for his own bubbled up in his gut. He turned to place Danielle beneath him on the sofa. He stroked into her forcefully, proving to himself in the most intimate way possible that she belonged to him. He kissed her roughly, possessing her mouth to remind her how badly they needed each other. He delved deeply and caressed every part of her he could reach to scour away the memory of every other male's touch.

He rode her to the peak, whispering to her over and over, "You are mine, Lovely. You are mine."

Chase twisted his hips to search for that special spot that would break her. She gasped when he stroked it, and Chase showed her no mercy. He pounded again and again, dragging his head across the bundle of nerves. Her body gripped him like a tight, rippling fist, and they tumbled over the abyss together, shouting and gasping. Holding on to one another, they spun out into oblivion, blew apart, and came back changed forever.

Time passed wordlessly, while she lay peacefully across his chest, sated and relaxed after a heated joining. He was actually nervous about how things would be between them from that point forward. Would she be willing to show the world their love? Would she need more time to herself? Then there was the matter of the big, earth-shattering secret she was hiding. He didn't want to ruin the moment with questions she might not be ready to answer, so instead he asked, "So, what was the secret you were going to share with me?"

"I'm not ready to tell you yet. I just want to enjoy you for tonight, but you should know that it is life-altering stuff. It could make you change your mind about me in a hurry."

"I wish you could trust me enough to let me in again." He brushed her shoulder with the pad of his thumb and delighted at the chills it sent down her arm. "You can tell me anything."

"How about we make a compromise? I'll tell you a small secret today and work up to the big stuff later. Is that acceptable?" she bargained.

"I'll take what I can get."

She nuzzled his neck. "My name isn't really Danielle." His head popped up.

"What?" he snapped.

"You see, if this is your reaction to the small stuff, the big stuff is going to make you run, screaming." She pulled away, and he instantly missed the warmth and intimacy of their contact.

"I'm sorry, Lovely. Please come back. I promise to behave myself."

Just then there was a knock at the door, and Danielle hopped up and scampered into the bathroom to freshen up, muttering about damn nosy vampires. Chase hurriedly tucked himself back in, buttoned his pants, and opened the door. It was Darren.

"Is she in there with you?" he asked. "Never mind, I can clearly smell her." He pushed past Chase and began pounding on the bathroom door. "Let's go! Griffin is waiting for you to make his announcement."

"You need to relax and back off. We'll be out in a minute." Chase pushed him away from the door.

"I was sent to retrieve her, and I'll be taking her with me." Darren pushed back.

"You are not her warrior anymore. You are no more than an invited guest at this gala. She is safe with me, and you will leave this room or I will have you removed from the building," Chase told him through clenched teeth. "Take your pick. I vote to toss you out on your ass for interrupting our privacy, but the choice is yours." Chase was good and tired of the warrior's power trip and bully tactics with Danielle.

"Leave now, Darren!" Dani said from the other side of the door.

"The lady has spoken." Chase opened the door.

Darren stomped off down the hall.

Several minutes later, Chase and Dani walked hand in hand back to the ballroom. He hoped she wouldn't drop his hand and move away when they reached the ballroom, but he tried to prepare himself for the possibility. Their connection was still forcefully humming with the flush of passion. "Are you going to tell me what your name is, or are you trying to kill me with suspense?"

"My birth name is Soleil."

"Soleil? Like the sun?" he asked.

"I knew you wouldn't like it. It's a stupid name, right?" She flushed pink.

"I love it, actually. It's just unusual. Do you know its origin? Maybe it's a family name?" He was curious.

"My father named me Soleil, because he was sure the world would revolve around me." She lowered her face and flushed even darker.

"Don't be embarrassed." He lifted her chin and kissed her nose. "That's very poetic. I assume your father was precognitive, because he was exactly correct." Dani stopped to show him her necklace.

"My father gave this to my mother the day of their bonding." He looked it over and smiled. She pointed to her earrings. "Your parents gave me these today. Aren't they beautiful?"

"They're lovely on you, Soleil." He loved being able to use her given name. It was much more fitting than that boy's name she used.

She looked around warily. "Please be careful with that name, by the way. It's a secret, remember?" She poked his side.

Chase was so happy to be able to touch and play with his Lovely the way he wanted to, he didn't think twice when they entered the ballroom with his arm wrapped around her waist to keep her close.

She didn't pull away. In fact, she nuzzled his chest with her still-flushed face. They earned several dirty looks, and Kayden came up out of his chair at the sight. The band was playing, so Chase playfully danced with Soleil across the floor. Yes, he would be using that name as often as would be allowed.

Before they reached their table, Griffin got up from his seat. Sarah followed and grabbed his arm, obviously frustrated. Chase didn't miss the irate, sidelong scowl Sarah gave Danielle. This announcement was obviously going to be memorable. Sarah continued to hiss under her breath at Griffin.

"Chase, I need you to stay with me, okay? Whatever Griffin says, no matter how you feel about it, please stay with me. I may need you to hold me up." She actually broke into a sweat.

"Lovely, I will never leave you again, if you let me stay close. What's going on?" He dragged her chair closer to his, so she could lean against him. She looked ill. He handed her a glass of ice water. Was it time for the big reveal? Chase assumed he would hear the secret from her in private.

Griffin shook off his mate and went to the podium. He asked the room to be seated for some announcements.

"You're about to get your second secret of the day. Please don't be upset with me." She looked at him with a plea for mercy on her creased brow.

"Is this what upset Kayden?" he whispered, as the room got quiet.

"No. He has no idea about this. Don't be surprised if he jumps out of his seat again."

That actually made Chase feel better. Kayden was in the dark, right alongside him. Chase caught Sarah glaring at the back of Soleil's head. She was obviously not in the dark, and she was pissed off.

"Ladies and gentleman, we have two joyous announcements to make. The first is mine and the second will be made by Deborah Deidrick."

Everyone at the table looked at Debbie. She shot a wicked little grin at her mate. Mason's eyebrows shot up. Good to know his father didn't know everything either. Sarah got up and left the room.

"This is a momentous occasion indeed," Griffin revealed. "I do not intend to answer any questions on the subject, now or in the future. But I want to share my joy with everyone. This is the perfect venue, given the number of us that gather for this annual celebration. I hope you will all be happy for me and my family."

Dani hung her head and Chase pulled her closer to him.

Griffin continued, "I was secretly bonded as a young man." The room hummed with the news. "I believed that my first mate and child died in childbirth, until very recently. Just days ago, I found out through a stroke of luck that the girl you know as Danielle Scott is actually my long-lost baby girl. Danielle, come, be welcomed by our community." Griffin beamed at her. She felt sick. "I would like to formally introduce my daughter, Soleil Danielle Vaughn."

Chase was ramrod stiff in his seat, and yes, Kayden stood in disbelief across the room. It all fell into place. Chase's first instinct when he met Danielle was correct. That hadn't been a fake ID used for getting into clubs. Her last name really was Vaughn, as her driver's license stated. Chase shared a glance with Kayden and knew they remembered the same thing and added up the facts. Danielle was the child from the House of Vaughn who would join the House of Deidrick. Together, they would stop the deaths of the children and bring their families back together. She was his soul mate. They were meant to walk together throughout life. That was why they shared such a strong mental and physical connection.

In his daze, Chase missed Danielle walking to meet her father, until she spoke to the crowd. Jeez, it wasn't that bad. He had to get it together. He rushed to stand behind her and support her in any way he could. Chase missed everything she said, until the end.

"I have an announcement of my own to make. Chase Deidrick has asked me for my hand, and I am honored to accept him as my one true mate. We will be bonded as soon as we are able." She took his hand and dazzled the crowd with her smile.

The crowd reeled. Most were happy and cheering; some were less enthusiastic. Debbie jumped up and darted to her son and hugged him. Danielle had just told the world she belonged to Chase, and his heart was so filled with the rightness of it he could hardly breathe. Griffin put a hand on Chase's back to steady him, and Danielle wrapped an arm around his waist.

"Isn't this what you wanted, boy? Don't you want my girl to love you the way you love her? Isn't that what you told me?" he whispered.

"Yes, sir. I just didn't know she was your girl. It would have made for a much less stressful day for me had I known." And with that, Chase's world righted itself, and he wrapped his arms around the star that his life would forever revolve around. Soleil. He never wanted the embrace to end, so he carried her back to their table, refusing to release her. She was forced to sit on his lap.

"Debbie, my dear, would you like to put the icing on our family cake?" Griffin gave her the floor and went to stand beside Mason.

When Debbie began to speak, Griffin had to put a hand on Mason's back to keep him in his seat.

"My news is a surprise to everyone, except my new daughter-in-law-to-be. She was with me when Doc called yesterday to inform me that Mason and I are expecting our second child." Debbie beamed at her mate, who was grinning from ear to ear. The room engulfed their table. The well-wishes and expressions of welcome overflowed.

Dani managed to get in a dance with her fiancé and several with her date, who had been patiently waiting for his sister's attention. She stepped away from the floor for a breather and a drink. Darren grabbed her arm and quietly pulled her to the hall, practically propelling her with the force of his movement down the corridor.

"I just got a call from the perimeter team. The rogues are moving in right now. We have to move. They're coming for you," he demanded.

"Wait, what? They're coming now? We have to warn everyone. I need to get Chase." Danielle tried to go back, but Darren stopped her.

"They are after you, not everyone else. If they all stay where they are and don't have a reason to panic, they won't get caught in the crossfire. What do you think Chase is going to do if he goes with you? That's right. He is going to get hurt trying to defend you. But it's up to you. Go get him if you like." The sarcasm was thick and annoying.

"No. Let's move. Do you have a gun I can use?" she groused, and gathered up her flowing gown to continue in the direction he pushed her. Damn it! Why couldn't she have this one night to celebrate with Chase? She moved faster to keep up with Darren. She'd never forgive herself if anyone at the gala was hurt because of her presence at the event.

"Just stay close and I'll keep you safe." The place was like a maze. They made so many lefts and rights, she was lost. Finally, he stopped by a set of heavy double doors.

"In here. It will all be over soon." She walked through the door first. It was dark and it smelled like mildew. The door banged loudly shut behind her and she jumped. Something didn't feel right. She saw movement in the corner and knew they weren't alone. Dani turned to run. Immediately both of her arms were grabbed and restrained. She stunned her attackers with a mental surge of anger and put them down in a flash.

"Run, Darren!" she shouted, not wanting him to be injured, or worse.

"You behave, and no one else will need to get hurt! You don't want me to hurt your mommy, do you?" The voice echoed around the room and froze her in her tracks. It looked like a locker room of some sort. An oddly familiar-looking man stepped out from behind a wall. She was sure they'd never met, but she couldn't shake the feeling of recognition. He had her mother by the neck. Tessa was bound and gagged, and he held a gun to her head. She wasn't struggling, and she looked vacant. She was enthralled.

"This puts a damper on your party, doesn't it?"

He looked over her shoulder as Darren entered the room. "I'm impressed, Darren. You got her here so fast I wasn't quite ready for you. You're right. She really does trust you, or at least she used to. I bet you'll have a hard time getting her to follow you anywhere, after this. Though I couldn't have done it without you."

"Shut up!" Darren shouted at the stranger.

Dani looked into Darren's anguished eyes. He was so handsome. The spiked blond hair and the scar that ran down his cheek belonged to her friend and protector, but he was a stranger. He'd brought her to the monster, the rogue.

"You did this to me? How did you find my mother?" she asked while sending out major distress signals. She might not be able to fight physically, but she would do all she could to get her mother out of there alive. Chase had already heard her call and was getting the others. She was so close to his mind that he watched flashes of the action through her eyes, and she could feel his rage.

"I thought your parents died." Darren was truly confused. "We'll discuss that later. It's going to be fine, Danielle. I can explain." He pulled her to him and began stroking her hair. She flinched. "He says if we give him the power he wants, he will leave you alone. He will go away, and we can be together. He will leave you alive, and I will feed you my blood, until they bring the blood bags I already have on standby. We will be mated and live in peace together. You will forgive me for this, once we are bonded and he is no longer hunting for you. I have to wait in the hall, until he's done, but I will be back in a moment."

"You have lost your mind. Don't you know he has to drain me completely to take my power? He is going to kill me." She shook her head at his stupidity.

"He has to drain you to take all of your power? You are very strong. He doesn't need it all. You have me to protect you." Was he seriously trying to soothe her? He actually believed that shit?

"And you think he's going to stop at some of my power, when he can easily take it all?" She extracted herself from his arms. "As soon as you step out that door, I'm as good as dead!"

He caressed her cheek. "You'll see, Dani. It will all work out. And I know you care for those two boys, but the life I will give you, the passion I have for you, is far beyond what a pup can offer. When you wake later, we will talk more. Now it's time to get this over with, so I can take you and your mom home." He stepped out into the hall, leaving her to her death.

Two men stepped up and took Tessa from the rogue. Tessa's eyes stared off into the distance, unseeing. They could do anything they wanted to Dani, and she wouldn't fight. She couldn't fight.

The man was tall and brooding with dark hair, broad shoulders, and sunglasses. He was every bit as large as Vince. He waited for Dani in the darkness of the abandoned locker room. His voice made her skin crawl. It was the man who'd killed so many young vampires, and that night it would be her life gushing down his throat.

"Come now, sweet. These men have been instructed to kill her if you so much as think of fighting me. I will do my best to leave something for Darren to work with, if you don't struggle. It won't take long."

He manhandled her to her knees before sinking his fangs into her neck. His bite was excruciating. It wasn't sensual and hot, like it should have felt. It burned like fire, spreading out from her neck. He tried to make it as painful as possible. She could hear his thoughts, as they were connected. He was full of rage and vengeance. She didn't want it to be the last thing she heard. Her world was too full of love to allow the end to be so tainted.

She continued to talk to Chase. Chase had been yelling in her head and trying to get direction the whole time, but she'd gotten so turned around getting here. She told them to find the locker room. Time had run out, and all she could do was say good-bye. Chase refused to let her finish. He wouldn't let her go. He was coming for her, but it would be too late.

It's too late. Can you still hear me? I can't hear you anymore. I love you, Chase. I love you.

Thirty

Finally, he had the slippery little bitch, and he intended to make her feel every ounce of frustration she'd caused him. She would hurt while he took pleasure from absorbing her very force of life and the power she didn't deserve. Why would a half-breed mongrel be so gifted? He knew she wouldn't fight or run, as long as he had her mother. That idiot, Nathan, was good for at least one thing. He'd reported the location of a home belonging to the girl and a human servant. Once he realized it was the home of her mother, everything fell into place. It wasn't easy to nab the female from her home. She fought like a madwoman. It had taken his strongest telepathy to contain her. She had a strong mind for a human.

Triumphantly, he grabbed the girl and sank his fangs deep into the tender flesh of her neck. She smelled and tasted like the best of both worlds. She tasted of the power and sensual grace of a vampire mixed with the delicate sweetness of a human that drove his kind insane with hunger and want.

Ravaging her greedily, he began to notice the sensation of emptiness that human blood always brought him. He'd drained many of his kind and was always overtaken by the exchange of power. A vampire's power rushing into his body was an extreme high. In the case of draining a female, the experience usually ended with sexual release from the sheer heat and power of the experience. While the little morsel was very warm and attractive, the heat of power was missing. He pulled harder at her vein to derive all he could, but all he got was blood. No power. The rogue was exasperated, but he kept at her neck. It couldn't be possible, after all that trouble that she wouldn't give up the treasure he sought. Could it? Was she capable of blocking his gift? He needed her psychic abilities and he needed them immediately!

Then, it began to dawn on him. He pulled away from her neck and looked at her mother hanging limply in the arms of his men. The human was special. She had supernatural powers of her own. Why hadn't he thought of that before? He dropped his prey to the ground in a fit of temper. He kicked her in the gut. The seat of her psychic power was human! Human power enhanced by her coming of age as a vampire! He couldn't absorb human power, only vampire! He already possessed the telekinesis she wielded. The bitch was of absolutely no use to him as anything but a tasty snack! He roared to the rafters.

He felt no exchange whatsoever. Even the short-lived bond he usually attained from drinking another vampire was absent. He never worried about the bond because his prey usually died. He learned long ago that even if they lived, the bond would fade. The nature of his gift wouldn't permit him to experience a real blood bond. He kicked her again and let out a string of curses that could've made Satan blush.

The sound brought Darren back to the room. He took one look at the heap of pale skin and slightly blue lips at the rogue's feet and advanced on him with vengeance in his heart.

"You weren't supposed to kill her! We had a deal!" Darren bellowed, and grabbed the rogue by the neck. They flew across the room, hitting a row of lockers with such force it knocked the air out of them both.

"She's not dead yet! Can't you hear her worthless heart beating? You should let her die. She is a half-breed piece of trash, so diluted with humanity I couldn't even reach her power! Let the bitch die!" he cursed into Darren's face. Darren was visibly taken aback by his statement.

"Humanity?" He paled.

"Oh, did I forget to mention she's the half-blooded whelp of a human woman? Her mother is right there. Smell her. Hell, taste her if you like. They're almost identical." The rogue was amused by Darren's astonishment.

"Now you have a choice, because she is about to die. Do you save her and bind yourself to humanity in the body of a lovely demi-vamp, or do you waste your time fighting me? Do you really want the filth of a human mate tainting your bloodlines? Or does she die without your blood to save her? The choice is yours now, Darren. Because she won't live long enough for more help to arrive," he taunted.

Darren released him to go to Danielle. He knelt beside her to feel for a pulse. "How sweet. You really meant all that crap you were spouting earlier. But do you want her badly enough to overlook your prejudices toward humanity? Don't you think it's a bit like falling in love with cattle? I mean, I love a good steak but I don't want to screw the cow."

Darren said nothing. He stared at her, vaguely aware of the rogue retreating to evade capture. He let them go. Brushing the hair from around her face, he tilted her head, not wanting to take any more blood than was necessary, and used his tongue to lick her wounds and heal them before he began to lap up the blood on her neck. That would be enough. A flash of heat and need spread through his veins. He could feel the bond already. His soul tried to creep into Danielle's, but she was so weak. He was sure he could already feel her essence inside him, like a faint whisper, and his heart quickened.

It was his fault, and he would spend the rest of his life atoning for his actions. She would forgive him, in time. Her heart would demand it, once the blood bond took hold.

Darren ripped open his wrist, and blood splattered all over both of them. He opened her mouth and let his life run past her lips, but she wasn't drinking. She wouldn't swallow. Blood ran out of her mouth and down the side of her face to drip on the floor. He sat down hard and pulled her into his lap. Putting his wrist back to her mouth, he massaged her throat to help it go down, but she didn't swallow on her own and blood continued to run out of her mouth. Frantic, he began to sob and tilted her head back to allow the blood to flow down her throat. If she died, it would be his fault. Danielle's blood in his body made him throb with pain. He could feel the pain the rogue had caused her, and he knew the betrayal she'd felt when she realized what he'd done to her.

After several moments of coaxing, she finally began to stir. She tasted what she needed and he gave it freely. Her eyes still closed, she lapped at his wrist until she finally found the strength to grab hold of his arm. His relief was staggering, and his sobs turned to tears of joy.

"That's right, Danielle. Drink. I promised I would make things right. The rogue will never touch you again, and we will have a long life together," he practically cooed at his new mate. "The others will also leave us alone. They never deserved your affection, and now you are all mine. I will give you the world, and we will never speak of them again."

His eyelids began to droop. She was draining him, taking too much, but he could stand a little more. His mate needed it badly, and every cell of his body demanded that he provide for her.

She stopped sucking, and he fell back onto the cold floor with her in his arms. Neither of them was able to move. He drifted off into a dark bliss with her sprawled, unmoving, across his chest. His last thought was of lying in his bed with her in the same position after the love they would make when he finally got her home.

Chase wanted to introduce the love of his existence to the world. She'd been dancing with J. R., who he just found out was her little brother, but he couldn't find her on the floor. It was the most incredible night of his life. Lovely had agreed to be his mate. He'd learned that she was Griffin's daughter, which meant he could have the girl and honor his family obligations. To top it all off, his parents were having a baby. He was going to be the best big brother, and his Lovely would be a wonderful big sister.

He continued to mingle until he crossed paths with Kayden. They just looked at each other, neither man knowing what to say to the other. Chase knew Kayden was hurting, and he didn't want to say anything to offend him or make it worse. They'd had differences, but Chase still loved his lifelong friend, even when they were fighting. Chase was jealous as hell that Kayden was so close to his Lovely, and it blinded him to everything else. Chase remembered the pain of losing both of them and clearly understood the sorrow swimming in Kayden's eyes.

Kayden put his hand out to Chase. A gesture of friendship was a good place to start over. Before Chase could take his hand, a deafening scream ripped through his head. Chase went to his knees, holding his ears. He looked up to see Kayden bent at the waist, holding his head. Griffin and Mason came running with the same pained expressions.

"Where the hell is Soleil?" Griffin shouted, as if he were trying to shout over the voice in his head. Some people could hear it, but most of the room carried on as if nothing was wrong. Danielle screamed angrily. There weren't even words, just rage-filled cries. Chase calmed himself and reached for her.

"Lovely, where are you? Why are you crying?" She didn't answer at first, but she sent visual hints. Was it a locker room? There were other people with her. A shadowed man held a woman around the neck. He couldn't see the man's face, but everything else was clear. Chase didn't recognize the woman.

This place is like a maze. I'm not sure how I got here. I think we may have passed underground into another building. I don't know where I am, but I can't fight them. They have my mother, Chase. Tell Griffin they have Mom. She projected so loudly that Griffin, Mason, and Kayden all heard her. Griffin went stiff, and Mason looked ill.

We're coming. Try to hold them off. Chase would sniff her out. He ran to the hall and followed his nose like a bloodhound. A wave of anger crashed over him, as Darren was revealed to be the traitor who'd handed her over to the rogue. Darren thought he could force his Lovely into being his mate! A sound of helpless rage ripped from Chase's throat. The four men tracked Danielle like prey. It seemed as if Darren had led her around in circles to confuse her, and anyone who followed them. Chase continued talking to her, until he lost her to blood loss and the pain the rogue had inflicted. The last thing she said was, *I love you, Chase.*

Those words echoed through his head, and he held on to them like a life raft. It took forever, but finally the trail ended at a locker room door. Chase burst through the door, and the scene they found was a nightmare he would never forget.

Darren had done it. He'd allowed the rogue to drain her nearly to death, and then he'd stolen Danielle's blood and forced his own blood down her throat to save her life. They were a mass of tangled limbs on the floor. It was disgusting how much they looked like lovers, so entwined with each other. She sprawled across his chest with her purple gown tangled around her knees. Darren was very pale, but he held her tightly to his chest.

"Go after the rogue!" Chase shouted at the warriors who filed in behind him. "That way!" He pointed toward a dark corridor leading away from the locker area.

Rage like nothing he'd ever know pumped through Chase. "I need a gun!" He pulled Danielle out of Darren's arms and held her limp body to his chest. She was still alive, but her heart beat erratically. "Somebody get me a damn gun, now!" he bellowed.

"You can't have a gun, man. He's a vampire." One of the warriors tried to calm Chase, but he was far beyond reasonable now. At that moment he didn't give a shit about the law. Darren had betrayed Danielle's trust and used her love for him to lure her away.

He heard Kayden go down on his knees behind him. "I'm going to be sick. Losing her to you was one thing. She loves you." Kayden paused. They both realized the love Danielle had for Chase would have been killed, murdered by her bond with the warrior-thief. Her freedom to choose her one true mate had been stolen from her.

"She loved you." Kayden's use of the past tense stabbed at Chase's heart.

There was nothing he could do about his broken heart or the loss of his one true mate. But he could give Darren a taste of what it felt like to be helpless and have someone take advantage of that weakness. Chase handed Danielle over to Kayden and proceeded to kick the shit out of Darren. Chase beat him until he was sure Darren would feel every injury the rogue had dealt Danielle, tenfold. Chase was panting and practically frothing at the mouth when the warriors finally dragged him away.

"Tessa, baby, wake up." Griffin shook her and lightly slapped her face. The rogue must have had a very strong telepath in his ranks. Griffin had tried many times in the past to enthrall Tessa, but her mind was too strong for him to control. Mason hadn't been able to breech Tessa's mental barriers, either. It would have taken an extremely high-level telepath to take her down. "Tessa, can you hear me? You need to wake up now. Our baby needs you." He shook her again. His hands burned where he touched her. Griffin's mind was scattered, but his body wanted to acknowledge the woman it had craved for so many years.

Tessa's eyes fluttered open, and the slow smile she greeted him with melted his heart. She looked the same as she had all those years ago, and watching her wake with a relaxed, languid smile reminded him of what life had been like when he was in love with his enchantress of a mate who could see the future in her dreams. She was the most beautiful woman he'd ever known, and she still had the ability to crush him with the simplest of gestures, even a smile or the brush of her hand on his face. She touched him in a way that made him long to keep her, to make her his, all over again.

"I've missed you so much, Griffin. I wish you were here with me. My dreams always end too soon, and I have to mourn you again each day." She snuggled against his chest and pulled him down to brush her lips over his mouth sensually. "Don't leave me yet. You feel so real."

It was more than he could have ever wished for. Not only did she still live and breathe, but she loved him and longed for his touch the same way he longed for hers. As wonderful as it was, he had to wake her fully, so they could tend to Soleil.

"Tessa, I am here, and you need to wake up now. Soleil is hurt." That did the trick. Her eyes snapped open. Griffin jumped to his feet with Tessa still wrapped in his arms, and carried her to Danielle's side.

"How did I get here? What happened to my baby?" Tessa asked Chase.

He didn't get a chance to answer before Darren came to life. Weak from blood loss, and battered from meeting the wrong side of Chase Deidrick. His swollen eyes shot around the room, searching for his mate. When he found her in Chase's arms, a growl erupted from him.

"Take your hands off my mate, Deidrick. Or I will kill you!" He struggled to stand and stumbled in Chase's direction. "Give her to me now!"

"She's not yours! You betrayed her with the monster who wanted her dead. Am I supposed to just hand her over? Hell no! I won't give you another chance to destroy her." Chase got to his feet with Danielle in his arms, and Kayden stood between Darren and Chase.

"We won't hand her over to you, traitor," Kayden snarled.

"Tell us who the rogue is, Darren. Tell us now and maybe we'll let you live." Griffin demanded.

"I have no idea what you're taking about, Councilman." Darren smirked through blood-covered lips. "I saved her life. You should be thanking me. It's just too bad she didn't have protection to get to her sooner."

"I saw what you did, you lying sack of shit. I know you brought him here. Danielle told me everything. You let him in and if it's the last thing I do, I'm going to make you suffer." Chase was ready to go at the traitor again. It would be more satisfying now that Darren was on his feet.

"I did no such thing, and you can't prove it either way. I saved her life here and that's the truth! You will give her to me, or I will see you judged by the council. Whether you like it or not, I have committed no crime. She is my mate, and council law says I have the right to speak for her when she cannot speak for herself. You may not come between bonded mates, *ever*. Now give me my new mate, or I will have Gage haul your ass to the Enclave in chains!"

Mason was in a rage and being held back by Griffin. His eyes black with anger, he flashed his fangs. "Don't threaten my boy! Trust me. The council will be the least of your worries!"

Finally, Gage and several other warriors arrived to diffuse the situation. "Arrest him, Gage," Chase demanded. "He lured Danielle to the rogue, so he could drain her for her powers in exchange for the chance to force a blood bond." Chase tried to remain calm, but his heart was breaking. When Dani woke, Darren would be all she wanted in the world. It was unlikely that she would turn on her mate, even if he'd betrayed her.

"Is this true, Darren?" Gage looked incredulous.

"I did no such thing. I got a call from the perimeter guard that we had a breach. I tried to get her to safety, but we were captured. I saved her life. She is my mate, and I want her now, Gage. Do your job and make them hand her over." Darren was practically frothing at the continued sight of his mate in the arms of another man.

"Unfortunately, Darren is correct. Our laws do not cover this situation, because Dani is alive. We have no right to keep her away from him, and he can have you jailed for attempting to do so. We don't have many laws, but the ones we do have are very clear, and coming between bonded mates is a major violation." Gage delivered the facts with his usual stony expression, but every muscle in his body was tense and his hand continually tightened on the butt of the pistol at his waist.

"What if he takes her, and she dies later? We will never know what happened to her. Do we even know if she can live without her power?" Tessa asked Gage.

"He actually wasn't able to absorb her abilities. He almost killed her trying, until he realized—" Darren said, but Chase spoke over him.

"He couldn't because she's human. All the pain she endured was for nothing. He didn't know she was human." Chase was back on his knees and stroking her hair, as Darren snarled continuously. This was it. He wouldn't ever hold her again. He couldn't protect her from her own mate. Everyone looked at Chase, stunned.

"He actually did know she was human," Darren said, "He had kidnapped her human mother, after all. He just didn't know her psychic power was seated in her humanity and amplified by her vampire coming-of-age. He said her mother was psychic. That's why he couldn't reach her gifts," Darren admitted.

"You knew she was half-human?" Mason asked Chase.

Chase didn't look up from his Lovely when he answered, "Yes. I've known since the day we found her beaten at the club. When Doc asked me to try to reach her subconsciously, we spent a lot of time speaking telepathically, and she gave me access to her beautiful mind. Because she was weakened, she wasn't able to hide anything from me. Her gifts were so new to her, she couldn't control her projections. I knew then I would have to protect her from the things in our world that could harm such a fragile being. Just to be sure I wasn't crazy and misreading her mind, I had Doc run her DNA from the blood samples he'd taken from her. He verified it for me. She was so afraid of vamps finding out and killing her. I knew she would tell me, when she was ready. I wanted her to tell me the truth. It didn't matter to me, Dad. I need her, love her. No matter what kind of blood runs in her veins, she will always be my Lovely." Chase's throat closed around the agonized scream trying to escape. He fought the tears burning the backs of his eyes.

"Why didn't you tell me?" Kayden snapped.

"I told you, I was protecting her! It was her right to tell people when she was ready and not before. It's not like she told me willingly. I couldn't betray her. She told you she wasn't what you thought she was." Chase shook his head. "She was absolutely correct. She is so much more than I ever thought she was."

"She said we could have human kids, and she didn't know how long she would live. I was afraid, and it will be the biggest regret of my life." Kayden left the locker room and stalked down the winding corridor.

Even Darren had been able to accept her for what she was, and Kayden had pushed her away. A knot of guilt began to form in his gut. If he hadn't been too afraid of the unknown, Dani wouldn't be suffering. She would be his mate, his to protect regardless of any council dictate, and this never would have happened. He'd failed her yet again.

Chase could do nothing to easy Danielle's pain. She let out a scream and began to thrash about in Chase's arms. Her eyes were open, but she didn't seem to be seeing anything.

"What is wrong, baby? Mommy is here now. Shhh . . . " Tessa tried to comfort her, but she continued to twist in Chase's arms and clutch at him in pain. Chase whispered to her, and Gage tried to hold Darren back.

"Give her to me now!" Darren demanded. "Why is she burning? It hurts!"

"What is happening to her, Griffin?" Tessa was panicked.

Danielle seemed to come around a bit and clutched Chase's arms. "Chase! It hurts!" She gripped him to her like a lifeline. "Don't let them hurt me anymore!" She was begging, gasping for air, and panting.

"I know it hurts, baby. It will be over soon. Just hold on, my lovely Soleil. I will stay with you." He soothed her and rocked her like a baby in his arms. He looked up at Darren with disgust. "She will never forgive you for this. You have taken a precious part of her that she will mourn forever."

"What is happening to her?" Tessa frantically tried to soothe her daughter.

"She is changing, Tessa. Darren had to give her so much blood to save her life that the vampire blood is trying to overtake her human blood. There's a war raging inside her body. This is usually done in stages so the person can adjust slowly, with a better chance of survival, but she was forced to bypass a more gentle transition," Griffin explained. "Our baby is losing her humanity. I didn't know if it would happen, given she was already a vampire."

"No. She was perfect and precious just the way she was." Tessa fell into his arms, weeping.

"I want her now, Gage. She needs her mate," Darren growled. Gage went to Chase and held out his arms to cradle the suffering girl.

"We must hand her over, son. I don't want to arrest you or anyone else here."

Gage removed Dani from Chase's tight grasp, but she clutched at him, trying to hold on. "Don't let them take me!" Dani held on to Chase and pleaded with him. His heart was shattering, but he had no choice. Bitter rage coated his tongue and choked him when he was finally forced to release her. Gage took her and handed her to Darren, who immediately walked away, murmuring comfort and praise to his mate.

Chase wanted to die. He had just gotten her back. He experienced heaven in her arms, just hours before. He had been bathed in the smell and taste of her. They were true mates, already bonded by love, ready to seal that commitment with blood. Finally, she'd held him in her arms and shared her mind, body, and soul with him, all at once. Her scent still clung to his skin after the bliss of their lovemaking. But she was gone. The sun had been forever snatched from his sky. His world would not be allowed to revolve around Soleil.

Dani awoke suddenly. Confused, she looked around the strange room and the huge four-poster bed with sheer curtains around it.

Where the hell was she? She got up unsteadily. Her legs felt like noodles, but other than that, she felt great. What had happened? Something important lingered around the edges of her memory. She had no clue where she was. Making her way to the door, she saw herself in the mirror. Great, she was all black-eyed freak again. No wonder she felt so weird. She was starving. The door opened, and Darren stuck his head in the room.

"I knew you were up, Danielle. I felt your mind stirring. I've been so worried." Darren embraced her and stroked her face lovingly. "Would you prefer I call you Danielle or Soleil?" What the hell was up with that? He needed to cut out the inappropriate contact.

"I don't care what you call me. What do you mean you felt my mind stirring?" That was passing weird. What was she doing with Darren, wherever *here* was?

"Okay. Since Danielle is the name I have used the most, I'll stick with that, unless you change your mind. You look hungry. Come back to bed, and I will let you feed. I have been anxious to feel you at my neck since our bonding." Darren led her back to the bed. He was acting weird. The super-cocky warrior suddenly seemed needy, even desperate.

The world suddenly tilted on its axis as the memories flooded back. He'd betrayed her to the rogue. He let the rogue rip her throat out. She should have died, but he'd saved her with his own blood. Oh no, please no! She couldn't be his mate. She loved Chase. She couldn't do it.

"You've been resting for several days. You lost so much blood. But Doc said your body just needed time to adjust to the change. It was very hard on you, due to the speed with which it was done. Doc said if you hadn't been half-vampire already, you would have died." He came to stand between her legs where she sat on the edge of the bed. "You can imagine that everyone is very upset with me, but I don't care. I love you, and you are my mate." He paused and looked at her sheepishly. "Are you angry with me? I'm sorry for the way I went about it, but I knew he wouldn't let you live in peace until he got what he wanted."

"I'm so confused. What changed about me? I think I still feel my power, but I feel so weak." She needed to get her head on straight, and Darren looked at her as if she were his most prized possession. It was creepy.

"He wasn't able to take your power, because it was rooted in your humanity. Your gifts came mostly from your mother and were, shall we say, activated and amplified by your father's blood when you came of age. The rogue can't absorb human powers," Darren explained while pushing her farther back on the bed.

"I guess I understand that, but I don't understand why you think I've changed." She tried to crawl away, but he had a tight grip on her.

"This is going to be hard for you to accept, but honestly, it's for the best. We'll be able to live a normal life, without people looking down on us for your flaws." He stalled a moment, searching for the right words. "You were so weak and close to death when I found you. I had to give you a lot of blood to save you." He peeked at her from below his long lashes and tried to crawl over her on the bed, but she forced him back.

"Tell me what happened, Darren," she demanded, letting the acid she felt leak into her voice.

"You've been made fully vampire. The amount of blood it took to keep you alive overwhelmed your human blood. You've lost your humanity, so you don't have to worry about what people think of you anymore. We don't even need to tell them you used to be half-human. Now that you're perfect, the past is the past. Now come to me, love. I want to feel our bond more clearly." He was so matter-of-fact about it, as if he were talking about his day at work. He'd killed the most important part of her, the part of her that had been nurtured by her mother from birth. Was she supposed to thank him and be accepting because of a forced blood bond? Was she supposed to be happy that he forced her to bond with him, instead of the man she wanted to spend her life with?

"You're a bastard!" She leapt off the bed and began to pace. "I thought you cared about me. I thought we were friends. How could you do this to me?"

"Danielle, please calm down. I never meant to hurt you. Your anger with me stings. It hurts me when you think hateful thoughts. Our bond will help you accept this, if you relax and let me in. I have been struggling to reach you since we bonded. Please come to bed so we can be whole," he pleaded, pacing behind her. He tried to lead her back to the bed.

"You can feel my feelings?" Something wasn't right.

"I can feel rough edges of them until you get upset. Then it stabs at me. I can feel the sweet warm light of your soul, but I can't enter, yet." He was almost pouting. The bastard was pouting like a child.

She thought about that for a minute. Shouldn't she be able to feel him? Shouldn't she need to be near him, if what they said about bonding was true? She should have been bathing in their love and devotion, but she wasn't. What she wanted to do was run. She wanted to cry for her lost humanity. She wanted to rage and scream to the heavens for vengeance. The last thing she wanted was to be anywhere near Darren.

Dani fell to the floor and began to sob. She'd had the world in her hands, and he'd snatched it from her. He'd plotted to destroy her happiness in order to create the phony love he imagined they would have. He'd disregarded her hopes and dreams to please himself. It took time, but slowly her tears turned to laughter. Darren rubbed her back and tried again to coax her onto the bed. He hadn't noticed the change in her mood.

"Don't cry, Danielle. This will pass quickly. I promise you, it will," he consoled.

Picking herself up off the floor, she looked at him with the absolute loathing she held in her heart for him, and he was taken aback.

"It has passed, Darren. In fact, it was never there to begin with." She froze him where he stood. He wouldn't move, until she was long gone.

"You thought you could drown my love for Chase with a forced blood bond? You thought I would wake up and fall into your arms gratefully and give you my soul and my body?" She laughed and wiped the tears from her eyes. Darren began to realize what she was telling him. His lower lip began to tremble with the tears he held back.

"Let me tell you something. Your lies and tricks were no match for my humanity. You may have stolen my human blood, but my human heart remains, and that heart belongs to Chase Deidrick. It was his when you changed me, and it still belongs to him. We have a deep connection that has nothing to do with blood and everything to do with one soul that lives in two beings. You say you can feel me? Guess what? I feel nothing but disgust for you."

Chase gathered everything in his apartment that reminded him of Lovely. He couldn't think of her anymore. He couldn't keep torturing himself with thoughts of her warming someone else's bed and sharing another male's life. He'd have thought that a heart could only break so much before there was nothing left, but his just kept crumbling with no end in sight. He had to remove her memory from his home. He stripped the pretty peach bedding from the guest room and the girlie towels and shower curtain he'd hung to make her feel at home. Then, he pulled the bedding from his bed because he could remember exactly how her pale skin contrasted with the dark gray of his sheets.

He went to the kitchen and wanted to toss the dishes they had eaten from together. That reminded him of the dining room table he would need to replace. Every time they'd sat there together, he would imagine laying her on the table and taking her body. He would need to cancel his newspaper subscription, because the crossword puzzle was too painful to look at. He needed to get rid of his high-tech stereo system, because she could never figure out how to work it. When she finally had given up and let him turn it on for her, the cute little wrinkles in her annoyed brow were almost enough to break him. He'd done his best to pretend he wasn't watching the sexy sway of her hips when she danced and cleaned the house that didn't need cleaning, because he had maid service, but she had gone stir-crazy. He opened the coat closet, where her jacket still hung, and her scent hit him like a wrecking ball.

Ah hell! He couldn't stay here any longer. He would need to sell the whole damn condo and everything in it. He would go to his parents' house, until he found another place of his own. He grabbed his coat and went to the elevator, wanting to leave behind the wonderful and painful memories, along with all of his belongings.

The elevator door opened, and he thought he was losing his mind. He wanted his Lovely so badly, his depraved mind must have projected her there. She was in the elevator, smiling at him, with visible fangs. Her eyes were black, and she wore a long, silky, pink nightgown and slippers. She stepped off of the elevator and continued to smile up at him. If it were insanity, he would take it. When she reached out and touched his face, he realized that she was real.

"You're here." He held her hand to his cheek and breathed her delicious scent deeply into his lungs.

"I'm here, and I love you. I need you, Chase. I need to know if you still need me. Can you love me knowing I lied about who and what I am . . . what I was? Can you love me now that I have been changed? I need to know, because you are my one true mate, my sanctuary. I don't want to live this long life I'm facing, if I can't face it with you." Her heart was in her eyes when she looked up at him. Truth rang in every word that left her lips.

"If this is a dream, I better never wake up. Why are you here? How are you here? Aren't you supposed to be happily bonded right now?" He was too afraid to be hopeful just yet.

Danielle pulled him down into her kiss, and she projected the events of her morning with Darren into Chase's mind. He needed to see in his own mind that it was for real. Word for word, he listened to what she said, and their connection allowed him to feel her emotions and listen to her thoughts unfold before him. Nothing else needed to be said.

He never stopped kissing her as he led her back into his home, their home, and took her straight to his bed . . . their bed. He removed her nightgown, marveling at the ivory perfection of her body. Her soft curves fit the hard planes of his body perfectly. He took his time, tasting every inch of her and greedily inhaling the sweet floral vanilla.

He stroked her damp heat with his tongue until she begged him for more. She needed more of him, and he would give her all of himself, forever. Sliding into her slippery darkness, he impaled her over and over, until she shattered in his arms. He whispered promises of a forever love that needed no blood. They could live their entire lives unbound, and the love in his heart would never change. He made love to her slowly, dragging out the pleasure with long steady strokes, until they were both spent and exhausted.

But Chase wasn't done with the center of his universe, his Soleil. He carried her to every part of his home he had tried to erase the memory of her from, and made love to her all over again.

Epilogue

Six months later . . .

"Are you sure you want to do this?" Dani asked Chase one more time.

"Yes, for the millionth time. I want to do this, but I'm beginning to think you don't."

Dani knew she was frustrating him. She'd asked him this question many times over the past months. "Why would you say that?" She felt like he'd slapped her.

"You keep waiting for me to back out. Maybe that's because you want to back out and don't want to hurt me. So you're leaving it up to me to get cold feet." He glared down at her.

"You know that's ridiculous. I want you to be my bonded mate more than anything. I'm just afraid it won't work on me again, and that's not fair to you. What if you bond to me, and I can't bond to you? I don't want you to resent me for being faulty and ruining our relationship." She'd already told him that a thousand times. The blood bond had worked for Darren, but it hadn't affected her at all. Darren had approached her on the street several times and regularly sent her notes requesting a face-to-face visit to discuss their mating. It was insane. Doc said it was a form of the mating madness that took over vampires whose mates had died. They would lose their minds to grief for a time. Not many vampires could withstand the loss of a mate. The difference for Darren was that his mate was still alive. So he held out hope. He just wouldn't accept that she wanted nothing to do with him. Dani's greatest fear was that the bonding failure would happen again with her and Chase. What if something was really wrong with her? Doc had no explanation for why the bonding hadn't worked. They could only speculate. She loved Chase and she never wanted him to feel shorted. She never wanted to let him down.

"Soleil, I am already bonded to you, and you to me. I realize that we are taking a risk, but I believe things will be fine now that you are fully a vampire. We have no history that refers to a human-vamp hybrid and the bonding ritual, but you don't have any of that tasty human blood left to interfere." Chase was quiet for a time, while she fretfully eyed him.

"My dad told me the story about Griffin and his first mate before I knew about Tessa and you. He told me some kinds of love could never be washed away. He said he knew the two of us weren't bonded, but the connection you feel with me is as strong as any bond he'd ever witnessed. He said Griffin and Tessa were already madly in love when they bonded. The bond gave them a mental connection that you and I already share, but it didn't force them to love each other. It was the best kind of bond, one done out of love instead of obligation or as a means to end suffering. That is what I am asking you for, Lovely. I want the best kind of bond. I want you to bond to me out of love. Just as you would marry me if I were human and blood bonds didn't exist for us. Can you give me that gift? Will you be my mate as well as my bride?"

Dani smiled through the tears of joy. "I would give you anything to make you happy and keep you with me, Chase, anything." She was so relieved to understand his point of view. She knew for sure he didn't care how the bonding turned out. She wouldn't question him again.

Dani left their home that evening to go stay with Mason and a very pregnant Debbie because it was bad luck for the groom to see the bride before the ceremony on the day of the wedding. Of course that was a human superstition, but Chase was humoring all of her customs. Danielle couldn't wait to stand beside him at the altar and truly become his bride.

It was to be an evening ceremony. The celebration afterward would be held outside under a huge sheer tent. The weather would be perfect, with no clouds in sight. His Lovely wanted a candlelight reception, so the stars could be seen through the sheer tent. He wanted everything to be perfect, so he spent most of the day overseeing the last-minute setup, making sure every detail was met to her specifications. It was clearly love when a guy willingly spent an afternoon discussing floral centerpieces and seating charts.

Finally, the time had come. Chase walked to the front of the chapel to await his Lovely's arrival. The music started, and the doors at the rear of the chapel closed. Chase noticed an envelope addressed to him on the step below him. Thinking it might have been from Soleil, he quickly bent to pick it up.

It wasn't from his bride, and the contents made his blood run cold. It was from Darren:

Chase,

She is my mate. If I can't have her, no one will. Our old friend was very interested to know Danielle was changed and that she retained her human gifts. Without all that pesky human blood to block him, I don't imagine it will take him long to catch up with her. She should be a tasty treat when he drains her for real this time. You should watch your back, because I am.

Darren, your bride's true mate

Chase tried to pull himself together. Rage at the threat spread through him. Darren would have to be dealt with permanently. It wouldn't be the first time Chase had taken a life to defend the female he loved more than anyone or anything. He took a few deep breaths, attempting to recapture the warm glow of joy and anticipation.

The doors in the rear of the chapel opened to admit Soleil, and that was all it took to wash away his anger. He would deal with the threat later. It was a time for celebration.

His Lovely was breathtaking in a white Grecian gown. Her mahogany, white, and red hair spilled all around her. She looked at him with such love and adoration.

He reflected those raw emotions right back to her. His one true mate would share his bed and his blood that night. They would be one. He would cherish her love and protect her to her last breath.

She entered the chapel and started the slow walk down the long aisle between them. Chase held himself steady, watching her move toward him with love shining in her beautiful eyes. Then he could wait no longer. He walked down the aisle and met her halfway. She laughed and wrapped her arms around his neck, kissing him passionately. Like they were the only two people in the room, they vowed their lives to each other, pouring all of their love into their private connection and sealing it with a kiss.

Chase lost himself in Danielle and her sweetness for a moment. Someone loudly cleared his throat and reminded Chase of his surroundings. Chase lifted his head and looked around at the sea of smiling faces. Their guests began to applaud the eager show of affection between them. Danielle blushed and took Chase's hand. Together they walked down the aisle toward the altar to exchange blood and say the sacred vows. Hand in hand, they would walk forever.

About the Author

Cat Miller was born and raised in Baltimore, Maryland. An avid reader and fan of all genres of romance, from historical to contemporary to paranormal, Cat began writing her first novel on a dare from her eldest daughter. She's never looked back. When Cat is not reading, writing, or indulging her addiction to café mochas, she is a certified medical coder. The mother of two daughters and a stepson, Cat lives in Maryland with her husband and their dog. She loves hearing from fans; please visit her online at www.catmillerbooks.com. *Unbound* is the first novel in the Forbidden Bond series.